MUD FLOWER BLOOMING

A TALE OF TRANSCENDENT LOVE

Praise for *MUD FLOWER BLOOMING:* A TALE OF TRANSCENDENT LOVE

"The complexity of this novel should not escape the eye of the reader. The lover of romantic novels will find romance aplenty here, as the heroine explores more than one stirring relationship with men in her life. Yet there is more. Parent-child relationships and strong friendships also count importantly in her life and—in both their delightful and conflictual dimensions—must be integrated with the romantic component. Finally, the novel affords us something of the social and historical variety of its several geographic settings. A rich 'read' indeed."

MARY ANNE SIDERITS, Ph.D
Clinical Psychologist

******

"This book sparked an awakening within me. J.Martin-Thomas masterfully draws the reader into a place of authenticity, unveiled, in experiencing the kaleidoscopic journey of the heroine in the story. In a very direct fashion the reader is given an invitation to explore love in many forms. Loving relationships matter. This book lifts the bar for what is possible in a faith-focused vibrant life. This is a memorable read."

DANNA RHINEHART
Semi-retired Disability & Crisis
Navigator

******

"Mud Flower Blooming represents a labor of love for J. Martin-Thomas, one which lay dormant in her mind and heart long before it was so eloquently transferred to the pages of this beautiful work of art. So many life lessons are gleaned as she traverses from her native Key West, Florida to Wisconsin, to South Dakota, and all of her stops in between. The well-crafted stories and subsequent lessons learned should prove to be very informative, inspirational, and enjoyable to all who are fortunate enough to read this wonderful work."

TYRONE CARTER, Ph.D
Retired Clinical Psychologist

✶✶✶✶✶✶

"I love this book. I am not usually much of a reader, but I could not put this book down. I didn't know a book could have such an impact on you. J. Martin-Thomas captures your mind, body and spirit as she creates a story that takes you on twists and turns through hard times and joyful victories. The characters become your friends, especially the old ladies who are so wise and comforting. Difficult issues like colorism, grief, and violence are set beside the fruits of forgiveness, faith and love. It is all so real! This book offered me a different way to see my life's journey, and for that I am deeply grateful."

BRENETTE SMALL
Grateful Reader

✶✶✶✶✶✶

"J. Martin-Thomas has crafted a love story that focuses on the fate of a Key West 'conch', a woman whose life comes full circle as she lives out her destiny. The prospect of one's senior years revealing seeds sown in youth comes to life in this woman's eventful saga and has us all looking at our story and its greater meaning and purpose."

JEANNE SCHROEDER, Ph.D
Clinical Psychologist

✶✶✶✶✶✶

"There are so many teachable moments in this book. Life lessons leap from the pages as you laugh heartily, cuss quietly, and tearfully navigate through the challenges and victories. The characters are so welcoming. The relationships are so engaging. The unwavering faith is so inspiring. The story speaks to love on many levels and puts a delightful spin on aging. This is an inspirational read."

TYLER MARIE BROWN
Motivational Speaker

✶✶✶✶✶✶

"Mud Flower Blooming is a spellbinding novel that covers all of the bases. It is a romantic, spiritual, thought provoking piece of work. It gives a very adventurous but realistic perspective of middle age life and beyond. As a 26 year old I call this book a refreshing read."

DANIELLE JACOBS
High School Teacher

******

"The author's messages of 'life's changing journey' open to the reader on each page. You must recognize these messages, fit them into the tapestry of your life, and glow in the beauty of the picture."

JUDY WAGNER, RN
Breast Care Advocate

******

"Love plain and simple, yet complex and multidimensional, is the message that J. Martin-Thomas delivers in Mud Flower Blooming. She allows us to experience each character's uniqueness with vivid imagery. We are inspired and excited that love never dies but is transformative no matter the age. The reader is left wanting to know more about each character's journey. The resilient heroine in this story is undeniably one of the most engaging characters ever penned in literary fiction. A memorable read indeed."

PTOSHA DAVIS
Public Relations Consultant

******

"This book is a spiritual journey on the bumpy roads of life, with uncertainties, disappointments, and triumphs. Reasons and explanations for events are often not immediately understandable, but ultimately there is a reason 'why things happen' and seem to work out for the best. This story is portrayed in the backdrop of various localities, including the colorful culture of the 'conchs' in Key West, Florida. This is a wonderful read with inspirational messages."

RICHARD O. WAGNER, MD
Breast Care Advocate

******

"*Mud Flower Blooming radiates with deep-seated lucidness and grace, offering life-changing perspectives on love, civility, and ethics in relationships, particularly among relatives, lovers, and friends. Cross-generational relationships are presented as vital to each character's narrative, showing the healing power of connections across the life-cycle. Martin-Thomas adeptly shepherds the reader over fertile terrain bearing challenges and triumphs, insightfully showering the journey with wisdom, faith and hope. I am excited about the potential trajectory of this book: it is truly inspirational.*"

YAHMINAH MCINTOSH
Author, Poet, Speaker

✶✶✶✶✶✶

"*I am a native of Key West, Florida and I am thrilled with this book. It is a compelling faith-driven story that will inspire you and make you smile. The story reveals colorful features of our island city. The characters are wonderfully complex and the cross-generational relationships, in particular, yield extraordinary positive regard filled with wisdom and humor. In this book aging is an adventure!*"

URSULA WELTERS ELLIOTT
A Key West "Conch"

✶✶✶✶✶✶✶

"*Martin-Thomas has created a humanitarian masterpiece of the multi-faceted realities of love among relatives and friends. It would engender engaging discussions in many college classroom settings, especially in the humanities.*"

SHAWNEE M. DANIELS-SYKES, Ph.D
Professor of Theology and Ethics
Mount Mary University, Milwaukee, WI

✶✶✶✶✶✶

"*This book stimulated my appetite for learning on multiple levels. Not only does Martin-Thomas introduce dining scenes comprised of graphically inviting food choices (many of which I am longing to taste for the first time), she craftily spins a complex but compelling tale embodying a substantive look at an array of life issues, including aging and forgiveness. Essentially, she positions the reader on an expedition from*

South Florida to South Dakota seemingly designed to unearth hearty morsels bearing character-building experiences and impressive spiritual, cultural, and historic manifestations: all memorable encounters. I desire more. I want to know more about Chief Crazy Horse, Harriet Tubman, Theophilus Thompson, Margaret Lawrence, Vusamazulu Credo Mutwa, John Horse, Black Indians, 'drug lords', Santeria, conch salad, Capoeira, Sapelo, mud cloth and much more. This is not a mere novel: it is an invitation to stretch!"

MARVIN PITTS-MUBASA
Semi-retired " Baby Boomer"

******

MUD FLOWER BLOOMING

A TALE OF TRANSCENDENT LOVE

by

J. Martin-Thomas

ISBN 978-0-578-59325-8

Published by
JMTC Publishing LLC
3900 W Brown Deer Rd
167 Suite A
Milwaukee, WI 53209-1220

Book cover design by *C.A. Martin II*

*This Book Is Dedicated
In Loving Memory
To*

MY FATHER, Oscar Leo Mc Intosh Sr. (1917–1975)

*

MY MOTHER, Julia Welters Mc Intosh (1916–2005)

*

MY HUSBAND, Edward Leroy Thomas (1937–1998)

*

MY BROTHER, Oscar Leo Mc Intosh Jr. (1941–2014)

*

MY COUSIN/BROTHER, Adrian Martin Welters (1951–2007)

*

***

*****

****

Author's Note

MUD FLOWER BLOOMING is a work of fiction inspired by a number of real-life moments. In truth, it seems that I have carried the seeds for a book like this within me from the time I was a little girl. It seems that these fertile seeds found nurturance in the climate of my life's journey, spawning fruitfully through my passion for storytelling. I have always cherished storytelling. I thoroughly enjoy peeking behind circumstances, looking for the rest of the story, or creatively conjuring up possibilities for what the rest of the story and the story behind the story could or should be. I love to entertain all sorts of intriguing scenarios, allowing my imagination to run wild, completely savoring the uncharted course. As such, the inventive path to this book has been truly satisfying. I urge you to embark upon what I consider an engaging experience by reading the entire book, including the Acknowledgments section, which offers history and insights of import. And by reading the Prologue, which sets the tone for the fervor, magic and mystery of the book.

Welcome to MUD FLOWER BLOOMING: A TALE OF TRANSCENDENT LOVE.

J. Martin-Thomas

Acknowledgments

I am truly grateful for loving parents who set me at the feet of wise elders, many of whom had been mentors to one or both of them in their youth.

I am grateful for the deep faith in God instilled in me by the elders, who did not flinch in hard times but seemed to intentionally praise God in my presence no matter the circumstances, always teaching me to soar above difficult experiences.

I am grateful that these elders were true griots who were positioned early in my life to share so much history with me. They passed on much of what they learned about unusual people in uncommon situations. They were consummate storytellers and encircled me in their gifts.

I am grateful that the elders were equipped to cherish diversity as they drew from a tourist-driven, military/artisan climate (at the time) in the seaport culture of Key West, Florida. There, one could encounter a rustic Australian seaman alongside a classy Canadian sculptress eating conch fritters with a half-dressed shiny Black sponge diver of Bahamian descent. All is well.

I am grateful that these elders, mostly senior Black women, had taught school, sorted shrimp on the docks, took in laundry, cleaned houses and kept children in diverse households, and traveled a bit. All while learning and ultimately passing along nuggets from their life experiences to me. So many of their nuggets inspired moments in *MUD FLOWER BLOOMING.*

I am particularly grateful for this special nugget from the elders: as a native of Key West, I am a Key West "Conch" forever. They would laugh about our symbolic kinship with the actual conch, the large edible sea snail found in the waters off the shores of South Florida and often in delectable island dishes like conch fritters and conch salad. Their stories about the conch still make me laugh.

I am delighted to acknowledge that the elders would certainly clap their hands and switch their hips in praise of the book about Black Key West written in recent times by Norma Jean Sawyer and La Verne Wells-Bowie. I am certain the elders would smile gratefully. I applaud this effort. I am grateful for this book that shows aspects of Key West also glimpsed in *MUD FLOWER BLOOMING.*

I gratefully acknowledge my family, friends, and colleagues who patiently listened to me go on and on about the dreams I began having in the 1990s about Chief Crazy Horse, dreams that ultimately inspired parts of the story and a few of the dreams portrayed in *MUD FLOWER BLOOMING.* People were very loving in extending support to me in my search for meaning of the dreams. They were supportive in various ways:

In 1995 my friend and colleague Dr. Rhoda Miller delighted me with my first book about Chief Crazy Horse, by Mari Sandoz. The following year she brought artifacts from a trip to South Dakota. She visited the Chief Crazy Horse Monument for the second time and encouraged me to go there. Thank you, Rhoda.

My friend Elaine Harris gave me a book about Chief Crazy Horse, by Mike Sajna. A few years later my world traveling friend and I journeyed to South Dakota to the Chief Crazy Horse Monument. It was my first trip there. Thank you, Elaine.

My friend Kwabena jjemba Falson surprised me with a book about Chief Crazy Horse, by Martin S. Goldman. A year later he traveled to South Dakota to visit the Warrior Chief's Monument. That year he gifted me again with a book, this one about Black

Seminoles, by Kenneth Porter. Thank you, Kwabena.

Of course, I have bought many books over the years about Chief Crazy Horse and traveled to South Dakota again in 2015 to visit the monument for the second time. This trip I shared with my friend Danna Rhinehart, who has graciously read every draft of *MUD FLOWER BLOOMING* I have put before her. Thank you, Danna.

Like Danna, my cousin Ursula Welters Elliott has been willing to digest every draft of *MUD FLOWER BLOOMING* I have sent her. Over the years she has graced me with bracelets and earrings bearing lotus flowers, which symbolically represent the mud flower theme of this book. Each gift is steeped in her prayers. Thank you, Ursula.

Mirroring the graciousness and support of Danna and Ursula, my daughter, Yahminah Mc Intosh has read every draft of *MUD FLOWER BLOOMING* set before her. Her keen eye for detail and insightful questions often pushed for creative clarity. She co-directed the self-publishing process, which required great patience and focus. Thank you, Yahminah.

My friend and Colleague Dr. Mary Anne Siderits has read a number of drafts of *MUD FLOWER BLOOMING* and has been most generous in giving her time to discuss changes in the book. Like my cousin Ursula, she kept an eye out for a beautiful lotus flower and found a pendant representing the mud flower theme of the book. Thank you, Mary Anne.

I am pleased that I approached the editing process by allowing many people to read various drafts of the manuscript of *MUD FLOWER BLOOMING* and render their thoughts. I experienced a spectrum of comments, some of which set me down for a few days. I have learned that I can take a punch, and for that I am grateful. Therefore, many thanks to those whose comments contributed to the editing process in some way, especially Gail Flowers, who did the initial formatting of the book, and Ptosha Davis, who after reading the first draft began to speculate about marketing strategies. Thank you, Gail and Ptosha.

Thumbs up for Pat Olson! I am deeply grateful for her painstaking assistance in editing. She is patient. She is kind. She is a consummate professional. Her gentle prodding about various changes in the manuscript still makes me smile. I appreciate her. Thank you, Pat.

I offer warm regards to all who wrote endorsements for *MUD FLOWER BLOOMING*. I love that they found the book substantive. Gratefully, I lift their names:

Tyler Marie Brown; Tyrone Carter, Ph. D.; Ptosha Davis; Ursula Welters Elliott; Danielle Jacobs; Yahminah McIntosh; Marvin Pitts-Mubasa; Danna Rhinehart; Jeanne Schroeder, Ph.D.; Mary Anne Siderits, Ph.D.; Brennette Small; Shawnee Daniels- Sykes, Ph.D.; Judy Wagner, RN.; Richard Wagner, MD.

I offer praise to my son, C.A. Martin II, for designing the cover of this book. He is so talented. His creativity brought things together easily for us. And praise to my daughter T. Martin, who is fastidious in her efforts to keep us on budget with the publication of *MUD FLOWER BLOOMING*. Thank you, C.A. Martin II and Tee.

Hugs to my son-in-law, James, and my grandsons Isaiah and Micaiah for nudging me past computer glitches.

I humbly acknowledge my Milwaukee community of elders who over the years have showered me with candor, wisdom, support, prayers, kindness, and love. In gratitude, I lift their names:

Christine Bass; Joan Boehm; Elizabeth Boyd; Gen Bruenhoffer; Sr. J. Delores Brunner; Susie Harrington; Sr. Sylvia Hecht; Sr.Joselma; Marilyn Miller, Ph.D.; Sr. Marjorie Nolan; Harold Rose, Ph.D.; Henderson & Diane Sanders; Thomas Stampfl, Ph.D.; Billie Thomas; Mitty Truly; Rudolph Walker; Moses & Emma Williams.

And to my St. Martin de Porres church family, especially our monthly prayer group, I thank you for your prayerful support.

Finally, as a semi-retired clinical psychologist showing many years of service, I acknowledge that I continue to be in awe of and humbled by the healing potential of loving relationships. In gratitude, I offer *MUD FLOWER BLOOMING: A TALE OF TRANSCENDENT LOVE.*

J. Martin-Thomas

Table of Contents

PART III

PART IV

Key West

It was at dusk on an ordinary day gone awry that little Jewelle *encountered predictions about her life's journey. That Saturday in January 1952 turned out to be curiously uncommon, a day to be remembered. But, as the predictions foreshadowed, many disconcerting circumstances in little Jewelle's trek from girlhood to womanhood would push these fertile memories beneath time-governed barriers. There they would lurk until beckoned by common and extraordinary occurrences to seep through voices of those sent to call her to remember. She would be reminded to accept the wondrous nature of her unconventional mission.*

"Spell it again," the old ladies chirped in unison, jovially calling upon little Jewelle to demonstrate a solid grasp of what they had been working on in their usual Saturday morning session. "F-O-R-G-I-V-E," little Jewelle rendered with poised deliberation. She smiled brightly, basking in the jubilant approval given to her by the gray-haired, bespectacled, diverse cadre of Key West seniors. Little Jewelle's maternal grandmother — whom everyone called Mamacita — and four of her lifelong friends were little Jewelle's Saturday babysitters. Every Saturday morning they taught her to spell, define a new word, and use it in a sentence. They took pride in her accomplishments; she made them feel useful!

Little Jewelle enjoyed her Saturday morning sessions; she especially liked being at Mamacita's house away from her much older, bullying, light-skinned siblings. She knew the old ladies loved her even though she was chocolate like dark cocoa. She knew that didn't matter to them. They loved her anyway and prided themselves on teaching her things. "And what does **FORGIVE** *mean?" one of the five old ladies asked with fervor, pointing her finger in little Jewelle's direction. "It means to be excused if I am sorry for something I did wrong," little Jewelle responded in a sing-song fashion. "Now use it in a sentence," another of the old ladies directed. "You can forgive me if I am sorry, and I can forgive you if you are sorry, and I can even forgive myself if I am sorry for doing something wrong," little Jewelle said confidently. Her response came without delay. Then she paused for a moment and added with a big smile, "God forgives us because God loves us all the time."*

While the old ladies recognized that little Jewelle's portrayal of the word was governed mostly by rote memory and in line with her little-girl awareness of the world, they hoped her life experiences would richly expand and deepen her understanding of the word, placing it within a more evolved context. But that day the old ladies looked at each other with pride, not attending to the grammar or depth in little Jewelle's sentences, but marveling over the essence and potential therein. They had taught her well, they thought. They laughed and clapped — a few even stood up and shook their hips — celebrating little Jewelle's agile mind and the group's good work at sowing seeds right there in Mamacita's kitchen.

As if on cue, the timeworn greenish-gray JULIETTE radio on the kitchen table — where the group usually sipped tea and milk — sent forth a tune that all the old ladies loved. Mamacita turned up the volume on the radio. Majestically they all left their seats and began to dance and sing. They sang passionately along with the fellow crooning on the radio, showing pride for specific points in the song that heralded Poinciana trees, delectable conch dishes, and soothing sea breezes. As they sang their hips swayed rhythmically to the calypso-like beat, their vigor belying limitations due to old-age ailments of any kind. "Damn, I love that boy's singing," Mamacita shouted as she grabbed little Jewelle's hand and twirled her around in the middle of the other dancing old ladies. Each one then took a turn spinning little Jewelle with vigor. At 77 years old Mamacita was glad to be alive and vibrantly present in little Jewelle's life. It was a mighty good thing, she thought, as she danced and sang, smiling lovingly at her soon-to-be five-year-old granddaughter, who was savoring every bit of the joy and love encircling her. It was a festive interlude, certainly at odds with what was to come later that day.

*The moment the cherished song tapered off and a report about another calamity occurring in Haiti sailed through the air from the radio, the old ladies shook their heads in dismay. A few conversed about the ongoing suffering in Haiti, offering mumbled "Lord, have mercy" statements with their eyes closed. But soon they became detached from the radio. They seated themselves around the kitchen table with tactful precision, each claiming her usual spot. Quietly little Jewelle found her place. She climbed upon the chair where two sturdy burnt-orange pillows lifted her just enough to rest her elbows atop the table; she was almost eye-to-eye with the old ladies. She waited eagerly to be given the rest of her lesson for the day. True to form, the old ladies engaged in their usual banter as they sipped tea and milk from colorful cups, but before long they returned in earnest to the word of the day. **"FORGIVE,"** they said grandly, each one talking at length about what it had meant in her life to forgive and to be forgiven. As little Jewelle listened she learned that the old ladies believed that forgiving oneself and forgiving others was what God expected us to do. She heard them say as well that to forgive was a way to set yourself free, and you could forgive people even when they were not sorry for what they had done. As she listened she was puzzled, but she didn't say a word.*

*Before the Saturday session ended the old ladies did their usual review with little Jewelle, carrying her through bits and pieces of what they had taught her over the past year. They asked her to stand before them as they talked briefly about a number of subjects, ranging from the slaves given respite in Key West during the 1800s to the courageous runaway slaves who they believed lived among Indians in the Everglades. They reminded little Jewelle that the Seminole word for the Everglades was **PAHAYOKEE**, and without hesitation she spelled it correctly for them. As they breezed from subject to subject* *the old ladies continued to praise their student. She in turn flashed her million-dollar smile and promised to continue working hard to remember all of her Saturday morning lessons. She believed learning new things was the key to their hearts.*

When it came time to pray (the usual way the old ladies began and ended their Saturday sessions), little Jewelle climbed upon her burnt-orange pillows again and joined hands with Mamacita and another of her teachers, who were positioned on each side of her. Hands held tightly and beginning with Mamacita each old lady gave a prayer. The prayers went from person to person as each one squeezed to the right. The prayers were fervent and diverse, reflecting the various religious denominations represented around the table. Prayers for Haiti echoed orderly, each old lady commenting on Haiti's suffering. As always little Jewelle was the last to pray. With eyes closed and head bowed she mirrored the old ladies and prayed for Haiti, too. Then she thanked God for her grandmother, her father, and all of her Saturday babysitters. And silently she offered her usual prayer that her mother and siblings would began to love her even though she was chocolate like dark cocoa.

Following the prayer there were the usual hugs and kisses before the old ladies headed to their respective homes, all living within walking distance. By then it was lunch time, and through their expedient partnership in pulling together leftovers of a number of staple Key West dishes, Mamacita and little Jewelle enjoyed a delicious lunch. They had conch salad, Cuban bread coated with butter, avocado pear, and fried plantains, all of which was washed down by more tea and milk. Pleased with their lunch and comfortably full, they quickly did the necessary chores. Then they moved from the kitchen to the front room where they snuggled on the overly stuffed couch, ultimately napping for quite a while. This was their special time together.

It was nearly evening when the day began to take on a different hue. Mamacita and little Jewelle were sitting on the porch relaxing and considering what to have for dinner. They had decided that after sundown they would water Mamacita's flourishing garden. Her garden was considered exceptional among Key West Conchs, and tourists couldn't believe it remained so vibrant even in the month of

January. Mamacita concluded that she was forever talking to tourists about her flowers because she lived so close to two major Key West tourist attractions, the lighthouse across the street and Hemingway's house up the street. And of course, she mused, her house was situated on US Highway 1 at the corner of Truman Avenue and Whitehead Street, a noted dividing point that tourists often became confused about. She reflected that most Key West Conchs, especially the Black ones, believed tourists were pre-warned about going farther south past that intersection, unless it was their intent to sightsee in "Black town." Mamacita chuckled wryly as she thought about her house being a landmark for such a line of racial demarcation. Then suddenly out of the corner of her eye something caught her attention, and she was shaken from her reverie. Quickly she pulled off her glasses and wiped them briskly. She couldn't believe what she was seeing.

"My God," Mamacita said under her breath when she recognized the woman from Stomp Lane with a huge yellowish-brown and white cat at her heels heading towards her gate. The woman from Stomp Lane gave a command to the cat, and it sat obediently as she worked to unlatch Mamacita's gate. Little Jewelle jumped out of her chair as her grandmother made the sign of the cross in the air and stood up with urgency to greet the odd-looking woman and her overgrown cat as they bounded up to the porch. A strange kind of energy filled the air along with the scent of eucalyptus. Mamacita's thoughts raced, and many unnerving questions hovered on the tip of her tongue. She knew the woman from Stomp Lane, and she knew that she seldom left her house. Her uninvited visitor was considered the city's most prominent soothsayer, sought out by many, though she almost never left her house. But there she was, standing on Mamacita's front porch holding a Bible in her right hand and a walking stick in her left hand, her oversized cat poised at her ankles.

Little Jewelle had never seen the woman from Stomp Lane before and found her physical features a bit unnerving. She was a very dark-skinned, petite, wiry woman with a rather large head, gray unruly hair, piercing eyes, and bushy gray eyebrows. She wore red lipstick, large gold earrings, and rings with a variety of stones on all of her fingers. She had on combat boots under a brightly-colored long skirt, a maroon low-cut blouse, gold and silver necklaces around her neck — one with a large crucifix attached — and a leather pouch hanging across her chest. "Mamacita, do you remember me?" the woman from Stomp Lane asked. Her voice was high-pitched and had a definite ring of authority. Curiously, she was speaking to Mamacita but was staring at little Jewelle with those piercing eyes that made little Jewelle cringe. "I know who you are," Mamacita responded in a mellow tone that belied the mounting tension she was feeling. "How can I help you?" Mamacita went on, putting her hand out in a greeting. The woman from Stomp Lane shook Mamacita's hand but continued to train her eyes upon little Jewelle.

"I am here to help your granddaughter," the uninvited visitor said, now pointing in little Jewelle's direction. "Her father's mother, Mama Dee, is on the other side, you know," she went on. "I was told she crossed over the year this child was born." The uninvited visitor took a deep breath and continued, "She came to me in a dream last evening and asked me to come here to give you a message and to read your granddaughter's shells. Your granddaughter must hear the words now for she will live them in years to come." Again the woman from Stomp Lane spoke with authority. She did so as she motioned for them to go into the house, offering her Bible to Mamacita. "Thank you, but I'll get my own," Mamacita said as she pointed the way to the kitchen. She had known and liked little Jewelle's paternal grandmother. She had attended her funeral years before, and now she was clearly on edge to hear the message from her. As she waited, her heart beat rapidly and her stomach churned. She began to sweat profusely by the time she put her hands on her own Bible. She could not imagine what urgent message Mama Dee had for her.

After the woman from Stomp Lane seated herself at the table and removed her leather pouch, she turned her gaze upon Mamacita and spoke slowly. "You will cross over soon, dear," she said in a chilling voice, allowing her eyes to rest upon Mamacita for quite some time. Then she went on: "I don't know exactly when, but it will be unexpected, and your granddaughter will miss you terribly. Before you leave, you must teach her that love is in her bones. Read to her Jeremiah 31:3 every time you see her." With that message given, the woman from Stomp Lane turned her attention to little Jewelle. Mamacita was riveted by the uninvited visitor's words. It was as if a shower of ice-cold water were being doused upon her; she was drowning, and she had no words. All she could do was pull her Bible to her heart, and in doing so the birth certificates of her children and grandchildren fell to the floor. In that moment she felt weak and lost; she wondered who would become the keeper of the family's birth records when she crossed over, a thought she had not considered before that moment. She scurried to pick up the papers, imploring little Jewelle to help her. But little Jewelle had become engrossed in the uninvited visitor's casting of cowrie shells drawn from her leather pouch.

The woman from Stomp Lane peered for a while at the configuration of shells resting on the table. While humming, she took a little book from her pouch and silently read a few passages. She put her hand on little Jewelle's forehead and in the songful form of a prophetic cantor relayed the first message from the shells: "You will bear much suffering in a cold place far away /and yet/ The angels and ancestors and spirit guides sitting at the feet of the Great I Am will lift you, and joy will find you /and yet/ You will walk on your pain /and yet/ Your secrets will hold you captive till you speak your story /and yet/ You must speak your story /and yet/ In the cold place miracles will find you /and yet/ Conundrums will hover about you /and yet/ You have been here many times before /and yet/ In this lifetime you will be hurt by many /and yet/ You will heal many / and yet/ So much of this day will be shadowed by clouds /and yet/ Memories will be in your bones, seeping through from time to time." She stopped to breathe heavily. Her monstrous cat jumped on the table and eyed her intensely for a moment. Then with one screeching sound, it returned to the floor and sat near her right foot. Little Jewelle was entranced by the experience. The message was far beyond her soon-to-be five-year-old mind, but she felt it in her heart.

When the woman from Stomp Lane cast the shells the second time, Mamacita stood close to little Jewelle, holding her tightly for protection and for her own support. She was shaking inside as her eyes leaked tears of fear and sorrow, and she prayed a fervent prayer.

While she wanted to discount this visit and all of the messages therein, deep within herself she knew she could not. She knew she had to weather this storm and to walk with her granddaughter through the fallout of the forbidding messages. Her heart pounded thunderously as she watched the uninvited visitor reach for little Jewelle again.

Looking directly into little Jewelle's eyes, the woman from Stomp Lane chanted softly: "You have knowing eyes /and yet/ You are the image of your father's mother /and yet/ You are blessed to see beyond darkness /and yet/ You walk in this world and that world all at once /and yet/ Your dreams will speak to you /and yet/ Your mission will be hidden for years." Sitting as still as a statue, little Jewelle was silently engrossed in the process, but Mamacita wept and whimpered as she pulled her granddaughter away from the uninvited visitor. On the final casting of the shells the woman from Stomp Lane stood up and sat down three times as she blew over the shells. She placed her hand over little Jewelle's heart and chanted loudly: "You are loved by your grandmothers, and your heart is a kind heart /and yet/ You have a healing kindness, and you are loving /and yet/ You will search hungrily for love /and yet/ Late in life from the mire you will bloom like the mud flower /and yet/ Your late-life spirit guide the warrior chief has taken his assignment /and yet/ In gratitude for your healing kindness to one of his own he will guide you." She stopped abruptly, and with a flick of her hands the woman from Stomp Lane deftly gathered her shells. Her reading was done, the messages delivered. She waved off questions, and as swiftly as she had come, she left Mamacita's house, her obedient cat at her heels.

That night Mamacita did as she was told. She sat little Jewelle before her and read Jeremiah 31:3 repeatedly, her countenance showing the passion and utter urgency she felt. She sobbed as she read the words professing God's abiding love. Little Jewelle cried along with her grandmother, but she was not certain why their tears were falling so freely. Finally, when sleep was about to overtake them, little Jewelle asked her grandmother, "What does crossing over mean?" Exhausted, Mamacita promised they would discuss it in the morning before she took little Jewelle home. Sadly, that never happened: Mamacita died in her sleep during the night.

Sleeping soundly beside her grandmother, little Jewelle was not disturbed at all when Mamacita crossed over. It was the morning sun that brought many jarring challenges that plagued her dreams and pushed tears from her eyes unceasingly for weeks. She felt all alone. Grief enveloped her like quicksand sucking her into an abyss. She floundered helplessly until an unseen force pulled her from it. It was the night before her fifth birthday in March 1952 that a striking dream re-charted her course. In the dream she saw Mamacita and another old lady. Highlighted by the morning sun, the old ladies stood side by side, rendering a beautiful picture of contrasting hues. Mamacita was honey-brown like a sugar cookie, and the other woman — who called herself Mama Dee — appeared chocolate like dark cocoa. In the dream little Jewelle's grandmothers gave her a box, but before she opened it an unseen force pulled from her heart remnants of grief and placed them under her feet inside her pink house slippers. She would walk on her pain, she was told. When she opened the gift from her grandmothers, a beautiful butterfly took flight, but in a blink of an eye it landed on her forehead. She could see beyond the shadows. Swiftly her grandmothers kissed her cheeks, placing tiny silver earrings in her ears; she could hear even the quietest sounds. With joy, little Jewelle and her grandmothers danced together in the sunlight. The dream was transformative! On her birthday little Jewelle asked her father to buy her a pair of pink house slippers, and lovingly he granted her wish that day and on every birthday up to her thirteenth year.

In the year of little Jewelle's thirteenth birthday her mother became weary of trying to meet the challenges of parenting her very-dark-skinned seventh child. Against Jewelle's father's wishes, she sent her to a Catholic boarding school far away from Key West. There, Jewelle saw snow for the first time and found it curiously inviting.

PART I

"...you are loving /and yet/ In this lifetime you will be hurt by many.... You will search hungrily for love / and yet/ Your dreams will speak to you and joy will find you...."

CHAPTER 1

Milwaukee

I *can't accept it,* I thought. My maudlin reaction was so unlike me, but when I heard the ABC morning newscaster describe the devastation caused by an earthquake in Haiti, I cried spontaneously. Through my tears, I gazed at my naked image glaring in the brass-rimmed full-length mirror in my bedroom, wondering where the years had gone. I examined my reflection, noting that in about a month I would grudgingly turn 63 years old. Although my dark-brown complexion kept my face essentially wrinkle-free and the gray in my hair was regularly colored away, my body revealed seeping signs of aging and lack of exercise. *Nature running its uncompromising course,* I thought. While pushing my melon-like breasts into a newly-acquired custom-made bra that brought a youthful lift to my post-menopausal figure, I caught the gist of the carefully enumerated list of things needed in Haiti. "Lord, have mercy!" I heard myself say when the newsman underscored the need for clean drinking water. Pondering sorrowful thoughts, I continued to dress for work, intermittently attending to the news rolling on in the background. Curiously, the report of Mother Nature's attack on that already-impoverished country felt like a personal assault to me. It was as if Haiti and I had suffered in common, and while I wouldn't let myself cry for my own troubles — aging and so much more — I seemed to be tearfully bemoaning her plight.

For a while, melancholy skewed my vision. In my mind, it appeared as if Haiti and I were incessantly destined for immersion in some catastrophe or general malaise. This prospect held my usual stoicism at bay, fueling another round of tears that flooded my cheeks as I slid into my favorite red sweater, leaving wet tracks on it. Ultimately, I changed from the tear-dampened sweater to a freshly ironed burgundy button-down blouse, noting that my dark mood was slowing me down. By the time I was ready to apply makeup, I had managed with great effort to quell my tears but was still in a rather somber place. On the right side of reason, I acknowledged, I was feeling sorry for myself and should not trivialize the plight of Haiti by comparing my life challenges with the suffering there. "I am really wallowing this morning," I said out loud, coaxing my thick curly afro into place. With effort and through vigorous self-talk, I accepted that I needed to dry my tears, "buck up," and roll with the punches of life. Usually, my early-morning prayer ritual would give me a boost, but it was a struggle today to move past the deep sense of fatalism, stemming from so many disappointments. "It is 2010, and shortly, Jewelle, you will be 63 years old. Get over it," I said to the image in the mirror as I took one last look at myself before bounding down the stairs and moving with vigorous agility despite the years. *I am far more fit than my image shows,* I thought, and ventured a slight smile as I raced to gather my winter garb.

Donning boots and all of the necessary winter gear to ward off the frigid Wisconsin weather took more time than I had allotted. There was no time for breakfast. Shaking off a wave of angst, I grabbed a banana while breezing through my kitchen, almost tripping on the welcome mat as I raced through the back door and out to the garage. My journey into melancholia had taken too much time. I was running behind schedule. Hurriedly I threw my briefcase into the trunk of the car and jumped behind the wheel, thinking I needed to eat a substantial breakfast and put a vigorous exercise regimen in place if I expected to keep my diabetes under control and ward off nature's love affair with gravity. "Tomorrow," I told myself resolutely, and with that mental commitment to a healthier lifestyle, I turned my thoughts to the rigors of the day before me. In my mind I repeated my usual mantra, *I surrender all,* many times as I backed out of my garage and turned onto the street. I was hopeful my mantra of surrendering all to The Creator would ultimately lift my spirits and "magically" part the clouds hovering over me.

I was deep in thought when without warning my elderly neighbor, Mrs. Barnes, walked in front of my car. I slammed on the breaks, cussing under my breath. Seemingly unruffled by her risky behavior, she tapped on my window, trying to share something about a trip to Las Vegas. She was animated and seemed eager to spill all of her plans, but I barely waved or smiled in her direction. I didn't mean to be rude, but I had too much going on to entertain her chattiness this morning. I wondered about her willingness to stand out in the cold to talk, but that was her way. She always wanted to give me an update on the various adventures in her life. As I drove away, I reflected on her probable loneliness since her husband died last year. I thought about it and decided that if my day went well, I would give her a call in the evening to discuss her forthcoming trip. That would give her time to share, but I didn't have the time or inclination to engage in chit-chat now. I was intent on heading to The Family Resource Center, my workplace, known to most as just The Center, and I didn't need any distractions. In truth, being pleasant this morning was at odds with the clouds hovering over me.

Moving through the fast-paced morning traffic, I reminded myself to stay focused as I heard a reporter on National Public Radio say something about Haiti. "Enough," I said out loud as I quickly changed the station to smooth jazz, feeling a need to hear soothing sounds in preparation for the challenges of my work day. Through a deep sigh, I made a conscious decision to drive with deft purposefulness, while trying to beat the proverbial clock: I didn't want to be late. At that moment I realized I was speeding. I muttered a prayer hoping to eek by the nearly hidden patrol car on my right. Easing past the well-known speed trap without incident, it occurred to me that navigating my way through the demanding daily tasks at The Center was often similar to my time-laden ride to work today. I know despite what is going on in my life, I must be nimble and focused in managing the sensitive and potentially dangerous situations surfacing in the domestic violence cases we serve at The Center. I found myself hoping that my journey into melancholia this morning would not leave any distracting residuals. I repeated my mantra, "I surrender all."

I pulled into the parking lot at The Center with a few minutes to spare before my first group. In that time, I put a forced smile on my face, separated my troubles from those of Haiti, and decided to call my friend Cullen, the psychiatrist. I believed a talk with my friend would help put things into perspective for me. I felt a need to share things I had not said out loud to anyone, not even to Eva, my world-traveling best friend. Cullen, of course, was my best male friend. He and Eva were neck and neck in how I valued them. Both were very close to my heart. Upon entering The Center, my "hellos" to the support staff were weak, but I managed a smile and acknowledged everyone. It was great to finally get to my office and quietly shut the door. I noticed the huge wall clock in the hall said I had four minutes before my first anger management group; deftly I made the call to Cullen. Just as I thought, his voicemail kicked in, and I left him a hurried message. I knew he would call back at his first opportunity. He would convey a combination of curiosity and concern while efficiently tweaking his calendar to set something up with me shortly.

The first anger management group went well, and by the time the second group of the day convened, I felt almost at the top of my game. I was in full facilitator mode, handling myself well in difficult situations with angry men, most of which were court-ordered due to domestic violence episodes in which they had been the perpetrators. That stoic thing that happens inside of me surfaced, and I was appropriately focused, showing no evidence from my morning bout of Haiti-driven melancholia. It was a little after two in the afternoon when I received a call from Cullen. It just turned out that I was waiting for a client who was late for his court-ordered session. I had time to talk. It was good hearing Cullen's voice, and I told him so. In his warm and gracious way, he asked about my health and about all of my children and their children. He then invited me to La Crosse for the coming weekend. I smiled at his invitation, pleased that he and his wife were both eager to spend time with me. Cullen and I decided that I would take the train to La Crosse (a college town in Western Wisconsin located by the Mississippi River) on Saturday and stay at their place two days, returning to Milwaukee on Monday evening. That worked for me. I imagined our talking well into the night over the weekend, and I knew his African-born wife, Gahti, would see to it that their live-in housekeeper would have something very special for us to eat, most likely delectable African dishes.

As we firmed up our plans, I actually felt my mood lift exponentially, and I began to get excited about finally being able to get the past four months off my chest. I found myself humming on my way to the ladies' room after a late lunch. As I flossed my bottom teeth and painstakingly cleaned my upper dentures (a result of an accident more than 30 years ago), I looked directly at my five-foot-four-inch image in the mirror and thought that now I really didn't look my age, particularly with my clothes on. I told myself, "You look pretty good, girl."

It didn't take much effort to arrange to have Monday of the following week off since I seldom took time away from The Center. Things worked out great for a train connection to La Crosse. As I boarded the train Saturday morning, I smiled, thinking that I had made a good decision. I just didn't feel like driving on the winter roads. There wasn't much snow, but there were many icy spots. While I enjoy highway driving, negotiating Wisconsin's roads in the winter can be challenging.

As I made myself comfortable for the three-hour trip, my mind began to formulate ways I could get into my concerns with Cullen. There was so much to tell him. *It would be great*, I thought, anticipating the connection with my friend and his wife. Overall I felt great heading to La Crosse, but for a moment my mind slipped to Haiti's troubles, and a bout of sadness washed over me again. Quickly, I uttered a fervent prayer for Haiti, asking for a nurturing wind to blow over her shores and bring her all that she needed for healing to take place. Then, I closed my eyes and dozed off. My spirit was purposefully hopeful, though I reminded myself not to say anything to Cullen about the recurrent dream — that was off-limits even for him.

After a restful hour or so, my mind went to my children. They had been suspicious when I told them I was going to visit Cullen. I think they were not quite sure whether to believe me, since I recently included a man by the name of Kojo in my life. Of course, they knew nothing of the scathing disappointments with Kojo. They were still reeling over the thought that at nearly 63 years of age their mother could have romantic interests and, more surprisingly, someone could be romantically interested in her. "Are you sure we will get you if we call you at Cullen's house?" two of my daughters asked with hands on their hips and eyes flashing. I laughed but decided not to answer their impertinent question, thinking I'd let them stay out of "grown folks' business." Sometimes my daughters Kaimen and Lorri could be intrusive to a fault, both bearing such strong personalities. Thinking about them, I decided that all of my children were unusual characters.

Momentarily, in kaleidoscopic fashion, the faces of my children flashed through my mind, reflecting the character of each. I smiled, thinking it was odd that God had given me two sets of mixed-gender twins, born seven years apart, and one daughter born in the middle. The older twins, Aimen and Kaimen, are an adventurous hermit and a diva warrior, respectively, and the younger set, Korri and Lorri, are a gentle guardian and a restless gadfly, respectively, while the middle child, Thea, shows herself to be a peace-loving humanitarian.

With the lulling motion of the train fostering a near trance-like excursion into the issues within my family, I considered that Thea was probably my most complex child. She seemed to struggle with her place in the family. "I am different than they are," she would say, pointing out that both sets of twins were born on a Monday in the morning and she was born on a Sunday afternoon (she had taken the time to search that information out). Curiously, she has the lightest complexion of all my children, bearing the coloring of her father's people, my mother and my siblings, while both sets of twins are of a darker hue, like me. And she is shapely, but plump, unlike her svelte sisters, who work out diligently to remain definitively toned. At times, it appears she looks for things to add to her roster of differences, which is interesting in light of the fact she is the only one of my children who has chosen to couple with a Caucasian. Not that it matters to me, but it has put her in a category of her own.

Through my excursion into family personas, I realized it is hard to think of my children without triggering memories of Emory, their stepfather. All of my children loved Emory, immensely. His illness and death have been difficult for each of them. Considering the years since Emory's death, I realize the void left by him has been filled in some way by all of my children, each taking up a particular space in my heart and life. I believe I have kept them too close. I have often wondered if I have been trying to make up for both the divorce from their father, Claude, and the death of their stepfather by holding on so tightly and giving in to them so often. I chided myself for coddling them despite my better judgment. "I will behave differently," I said to myself, realizing the train ride was taking me to places within myself I had not intended to go.

I shook my head, trying to force myself to shift away from anything that could continue to dampen my mood. I turned my thoughts to my six grandchildren (four born out of wedlock and two post marriage), the lights of my life. While it took prayer and effort for me to accept how some of them had come into being, I have forgiven all of my daughters and myself for their major indiscretions. All three of my girls became pregnant out of wedlock: Kaimen once, Thea once, and Lorri twice. I am over that now, but I am still working on the difficult circumstances of having a five-year-old granddaughter, Ajoy, Lorri's girl, sired by a former drug lord, the infamous Squire Black. My granddaughter's father has spent time in prison more than once and is still noted to test the law, although he now owns and operates a thriving legitimate tow-truck business. I can feel anger surge within me as I note that he is a philanderer and refuses to pay child support in the traditional way, relying only on his discretion as to when he chooses to give Lorri money for their daughter.

Stirred by anger, my mind reeled on to other nerve-racking matters. Thea's partner popped up. Whereas Lorri's former drug lord triggers rage, the father of my only mulatto grandchild evokes other disturbing concerns. Norbert Kosciuszko Raczek is Thea's live-in companion and the father of her only child, Francis. Of German and Polish descent, he brings a host of challenges to our family. While he is responsible and has been asking Thea to marry him for years, she continues to turn him down, contending that many people in his family are closet racists. She does not allow their son to spend time with them unless she is present, and that is often a source of raucous conflict. I am still not certain how she reconciles their common-law relationship with her rather strict religious views about cohabitation. She is a puzzle!

The lulling motion of the train and time to think about things in depth seemed to open the door for reflection upon many troublesome family matters I seldom give consideration. I realized it had been a long time since I took an honest look at my family and assessed how we relate to one another, especially since Emory passed away. My mind slid over to my daughters Kaimen and Lorri again and the battles they have from time to time. These brawls always seem to happen at my house and are so volatile that they have culminated in actual physical altercations. Remembering their fights, especially the venomous things they say to each other, I made a mental note to speak with them about how they treat each other. Instantly, I became exhausted at the prospect of having such a conversation.

When the train pulled into La Crosse, I was surprised to find tears on my cheeks. The roller-coaster-like excursion into life in my family had touched a nerve. I wanted more than anything for my children to connect and be loving to one another, and that did not appear to be the state of affairs at times. Through this unexpected assessment of my family, it seemed as if somehow I had dropped the ball as a mother, and that made me sad. In a flash, my mind shifted to Haiti again, and for a moment I felt melancholy reach for me. "Stop that!" I heard myself say as I gathered my things, preparing to exit the train. It was good to finally be in La Crosse!

CHAPTER 2

Welcome to La Crosse

Stepping off the train, I smiled when I spotted Cullen. He looked wonderful! My 65-year-old friend, in his towering six-foot-four-inch frame, postured like a welcoming lighthouse in stormy waters. His smile appeared to leap out ahead of him, showering warmth in the space between us. Gratefully I moved towards his open arms. I thought about how comforting it is to have a friend like him. Cullen interrupted my thoughts with a big hug and a solid kiss on the cheek, noting that it had been a while since we spent any quality time together. Holding on to him, anticipation welled up within me. There was so much to say, and I knew Cullen would listen intently without judgment. As I walked with him to his car I savored his calm demeanor, which has become an ongoing state for him since his marriage to Gahti. I smiled thinking about their relationship.

As we drove along, listening to Miles Davis, Cullen brought me up to date on what had been going on with him and Gahti. I could hear the contentment in his voice. He talked a lot about a forthcoming trip to Africa, Gahti's home in Tanzania. They would spend about six weeks there providing pro bono medical services out in the "bush." He seemed excited, revealing a much deeper sense of philanthropy than I had remembered. I was sure this awakened-level of global consciousness was born of his relationship with Gahti. While he chatted about the particulars of their trip my mind slipped to the past, calling up so many remarkable things about my friend. I remembered his bitter divorce from his first wife and how he had struggled with the death of his eldest son. Specifically, I remembered the day he was told that his son was decapitated in a direct collision with a semi on a highway near the Chicago/Indiana border. His son had been going the wrong way; suspicion of suicide was never really cleared up. Sitting beside my friend, I marveled at his resilience. *He continues to prosper despite the suffering he has endured,* I thought. I squeezed my friend's hand remembering the heart problems and surgeries that seemed to level him immediately following his son's death. I had been afraid that sorrow would destroy my friend back then, but he survived and in the midst of all the suffering Gahti came into his life. Cullen smiled as I squeezed his hand again. He didn't question it, he just smiled.

When we pulled into the garage of their spacious home, Gahti came out to meet us. Her coal-black skin always seemed to shine just a bit, and her delightful graying braids appeared to smile along with her very white teeth. Nearly five years younger than Cullen, she had soulful dancing eyes, and whenever she was in Cullen's presence, her eyes sparkled brilliantly. As they embraced, the sharp contrast in their skin tones spoke loudly of the generations of miscegenation in this country. Cullen is "high yella," as many folks in the South would say. He has kinky reddish-brown hair, most of which is rapidly graying, and — yes — he has freckles. A "high yella" Black man from Oklahoma, tall and muscular, he towered over Gahti's petite frame. The picture of them together made me smile as I thought about their miracle meeting. Whenever they told their story people would just shake their heads in amazement. As the story goes, Gahti was a Catholic nun working as a pediatric oncologist. She was in the cardiac unit visiting the parent of one her young patients when she met Cullen a few days after his surgery. Their spark was ignited and seven years later after she followed the protocol that took her beyond her vows as a nun, she and Cullen were married. They moved to La Crosse where Gahti took a post in Pediatrics at a noted oncology center and Cullen went into private practice. *WOW! A powerful story,* I thought, reaching for Gahti.

She hugged me warmly, and the clip of her accent was melodious as she went into detail about what their housekeeper had prepared for supper.

With thoughtful precision, Gahti gave us the itinerary for the day. She would eat with us but had to leave right away to return to the oncology center for evening consultations and rounds. Her radiant smile said our gathering was special. I felt so warm and safe in their beautiful home encircled by African artifacts set among bold modern-art pieces. In his free time, Cullen painted. He had become fairly well known for his artwork, much of which he declared was inspired by energy gleaned from his patients' stories. While that was his thought about his artwork, I knew better. I knew that his own story was as much a source of the sublimated emotions gracing the walls of his dwelling and the dwellings of those who were lucky enough to secure some of his artwork throughout the years, including me.

After a delicious spice-filled dinner of peanut soup, shredded beef, rice, plantains, avocado salad, and sweet potato pie, Gahti left for the oncology center. Pena, their South African housekeeper, shooed Cullen and me off to his den, which also functioned as his "in-home office." I offered to help clear the table, but Pena was adamant and I didn't put up much of a fight. I was full and ready to relax with my friend. On our way to the den I explained to Cullen that I needed to say out loud the details of the past four months. "I need to hear myself tell the story of the past four months and I need you to listen mostly as my friend," I directed haltingly, hoping I wasn't being unreasonable. Through a smile, Cullen responded, "I know you need a friend right now Jewelle. I will do my best to listen mostly as your friend, but if the psychiatrist in me shows up, please believe I want only the best for you." I smiled thinking, *my friend certainly knows how to put me at ease!*

The den was warmly inviting. It was a colorful haven of assorted exotic artifacts. This included many beautiful charcoal renderings of elephants mounted on the walls like a legion of regal trunk-bearing mammals. They appeared to parade before the huge modern art painting in striking blues and greens that hung boldly above the fireplace almost to the ceiling. The artwork was spectacular, especially the breathtaking piece that Cullen created when Gahti accepted his proposal of marriage. He called it *Living for Real!* It is a stunning work of abstract art and certainly reveals so much of who Cullen is now, the soulful person he has become since Gahti entered his life.

I sat in the huge burgundy leather chair immediately in front of the fireplace, but far enough away that I could just about savor the entire room in one glance. I covered myself with a very inviting multicolored afghan and took in all the room had to offer. Cullen took his place behind his noble-looking desk, put his feet up, and leaned back in a chair that matched mine in color and fabric but was more majestic in shape. His relaxed posture gave me permission to begin or to take my time. There was an air of comfort filtering through the space between us. Soft melodious sounds flowed from a stereo system somewhere above the gently smoldering logs in the fireplace, creating comfort and warmth everywhere in the room. I smiled as I sank deep into my chair. I had so much to say, but at that moment I was not sure where to begin. Searching within myself for direction, I sat for a while, reflecting upon the touching prayer Gahti had offered before our meal. She had called upon the Creator to bless all words that would be uttered among us, and she thanked the Creator for nourishment coming through wise and kind hearts. Her words had welcomed God to our gathering. She welcomed the ancestors as well, and her quiet confidence in her invocations remained with me. Silently, with eyes closed, I said a prayer.

Finally, I decided to begin my story with the rather pregnant event that seemed to lay the groundwork for the roller coaster ride I have been on for the past four months. "Cullen, I think I told you that I was asked to serve on the committee to develop a retirement event to honor Robert Henning. You know him as the community activist who has been the force behind so many transformative ventures in the African-American community. And, he serves on many boards, including the board of our Center for years. I was asked to be the one to introduce him at the event because our paths had crossed in many ventures over the years, and that was truly an honor for me. I spent countless hours working to perfect my brief introduction, and was told I did a spectacular job.

"The entire event turned out to be an exciting historical reunion, a forceful statement about the love and talent within Milwaukee, particularly the African-American community. Many gifted people were there freely sharing their talents. More than 500 people attended, many of whom had long histories with Henning. It was a wonderful tribute. The energy in the room was electric!

Among the many talented performers was an outstanding Afro/Latin-jazz ensemble led by a very accomplished conga/jimbee drummer whom the mistress of ceremony called Olokun. He was massive with arms honed like powerful oak trees that exuded raw strength. His gray-strewn locks hanging below his waist danced about powerfully as he drummed magically. Without a doubt the Afro/Latin-jazz ensemble stole the show. It was amazing to learn that all of the musicians, with the exception of Olokun, are ordinary Black and Latino retired men who perform for the joy of it.

"While it was clear Olokun was the force behind the group, the tall, wiry man called Kojo emitted a singular presence. Oddly, from the moment I laid eyes on him I felt tremor-like sensations throughout my body. He was a honey-brown, bespectacled guy with Don King-like fly-away hair who played the alto sax mostly, though he changed up from time to time to include a tenor sax and a flute. He was something to behold. The way he handled each of his instruments with such passion gave you pause, and he seldom opened his eyes as he played. Behind his horn-rimmed glasses, it was as though he was enthralled in an ocean of melodies that transported him places far beyond earth, and the audience responded to his mystical fervor. We loved every minute of the ecstasy he offered. He was fabulous! His rendition of a mellow crowed-pleasing favorite, stole the show. It was utterly sublime, making you just want to holler. People called out his name again and again as he stroked his sax. I, too, joined the crowd in hollering, 'Go, Kojo, Go!' Although I was seeing and hearing him for the first time, something about him seemed familiar. Something felt

15

familiar. I dismissed the odd sensation that came over me — kind of like déjà vu, telling myself it was all about the stirring energy in the room. But at the time, I had no idea of how the tall, wiry man called Kojo with the Don King fly-away hair would affect my life."

With that much of my story laid out before Cullen, I looked directly at him trying to assess how he was processing what I had said so far. And, true to form, my friend offered only a slight smile, motioning with his hand for me to go on.

Taking heed to Cullen's gesture, I thoughtfully prepared to return to my story, again making a point to stay away from the recurrent dream. I carefully began my story again. "I was riding high for some days following the event but soon fell back into my routine of long hours of work and very little 'play,' which was how I had been living for a number of years. Then one Sunday, I elected to go to Mass at the church I attended when the kids were young — back in my full-fledged Catholic days before my marriage to Emory, a divorced man. As a divorcée myself, my second marriage simply added insult to injury in the eyes of the Catholic Church, rendering me disenfranchised. But in the years following Emory's death — which essentially changed my status — I was acceptable, and feeling a need to connect with that particular church community again.

"It was a beautiful service that morning, and I was feeling particularly Spirit-filled, so much so that I wanted to do something special after church but didn't know quite what. My friend Eva, the world traveler, was not scheduled to get back from Japan until the following Tuesday, and she possibly would have been the person I called. But I decided to call my friend Flora, the fastidious homicide detective, to see if we could have lunch and 'hang out' for a while. It had been a while since she and I spent quality time together, and I knew that Flora was not into attending church at this time in her life. *She is sure to be home,* I thought. With eagerness I pulled out the rather expensive cell phone my children bought me for Christmas, again noting that it was too complicated for me — much too much technology for my taste, but a good thing nonetheless.

"The phone rang only once, and Flora's voice seemed tired, but she agreed to have lunch with me. In her usual direct manner, she explained we could have lunch right away, but before we actually 'hung out' — which really meant going to a movie or some play she desired to see — we needed to go by a friend's house so she could have her ears cleaned. I didn't question the meaning behind her statement because I knew Flora was into all sorts of alternative health care strategies. In fact, she and Eva both have a penchant for that sort of thing, which was all they have in common outside of their friendship with me.

"When I found out that Flora's friend, the person who would clean her ears through ear-candling, was the conga/jimbee player from the Afro/Latin-jazz ensemble, I was excited. I would not mind going with her to see him. I had heard how interesting he was to talk to. He had traveled all over the world and was well versed in spiritual practices from around the world, which piqued my interest. I signed off from Flora and headed directly to her house with an invigorating sense of anticipation. Actually, at that juncture, I didn't have an inkling of the ultimate pivotal nature of that day and the impact it would have on me.

"When I pulled in front of Flora's place, I took note of her well-kept lawn and precisely trimmed hedges, which spoke volumes about my friend's meticulousness. For years, I have marveled at Flora's penchant for precision. She is so given to exactness that her petite, well-toned physical frame was always neatly clad, and her closely cropped afro reflected her attentiveness to detail. As I watched her agile trek to my car, I noted that everything about her seemed to be in place, projecting her finicky nature. I couldn't imagine a guy putting up with Flora's proclivities. It made sense to me that at nearly 63 years of age (we were born the same year, six months apart), she'd never been close to marriage and didn't seem to care much about her single-woman status.

"She had recently been promoted again and her newly-attained status made her even more formidable in the relationship game. I doubted she could find someone to appreciate her personality coupled with her professional accomplishments. Despite the fact that she could have retired years ago, she tenaciously held on to her job, vowing that she would keep it till the age of 66. If there was a vulnerability to Flora, I knew it was her unabashed love of Chinese food, which could be paled only by her avid interest in African and African-American art and history. She studied continuously, often pedantically given to imparting volumes of information to her friends whether we were open to hearing it or not.

"I chose to please her by going to a place where there was an all-you-can-eat buffet with many of the special treats people like Flora long for from Chinese restaurants. I was particularly interested in the plum wine we ordered. It was delicious and hit the spot for me more than any of the dishes Flora found so delectable. I probably had more wine than I should have because by the time we left and headed for the drummer's house, I was feeling pretty good. Even Flora, who is most often rather stolid in her presentation, was slightly gleeful, and that was truly something to see; she actually had a glass of wine, too. Our ride to the drummer's house was filled with laughter, revealing a much more relaxed side of Flora than I had seen for a while. I found myself thinking about this softer side to Flora, one that could perhaps attract a confident, adventurous fella.

"When we pulled in front of the drummer's house, I was impressed by the well-manicured lawn and hedges surrounding his home. It was almost like looking at Flora's lawn all over again. Upon ringing the gong-sounding doorbell, George, aka Olokun, the drummer, as Flora called him, welcomed us with a warm smile. His frame appeared mountainous as he ushered us into his very spacious and colorfully decorated home. His living room was like a museum, showing artifacts from around the world, including huge masks from New Guinea and South Africa. He showed us around, punctuating each artifact with a story laced with humor and youthful gusto until his wife entered the room and his tone changed. He became almost staid in his manner. The shift in his demeanor was quite striking.

"I had not met his wife, Shayla, before that day. When she entered the room, her height commanded attention. I was taken aback. I guessed that she had to be at least six feet three because she was slightly taller than her husband, and he was certainly well over six feet tall. Her shoulder- length locks revealed graying threads here and there, making me wonder about her age, since her face was so youthful. She moved with grace, sort of like a gazelle, but there was a no-nonsense air about her, too. Upon our introduction, I learned she was Canadian of Jamaican ancestry and she and Flora had been friends for years. So when she greeted us warmly, I smiled, thinking how blessed I was to have such a diverse group of friends who could connect me with people from all walks of life. Before long, George asked us to call him by his other name, Olokun, and he offered us a liqueur he said he attained in some city in Central America. I knew Flora wouldn't taste it because she seldom went beyond wine in her adventures with alcohol, but I told Olokun to pour it up, and he, his wife, and I toasted to the blessings of the universe. It was a wonderful toast, shedding more light on the spirituality in the life of our host and his wife.

"I watched Olokun work with Flora and the ear candling procedure as Shayla, a pharmacist, talked at length about some trials and tribulations with a sick relative and the perils of the health care system in this country. She was invigorating to listen to. It wasn't too long before Olokun and Flora completed their work with the ear candling and Shayla was off to see about her sick relative, leaving Olokun to set the tone for the rest of our time in their home. And he didn't miss a beat. As soon as Shayla closed the door behind her, he became the jovial kid-like character he had been before she had joined us that afternoon. It was clear that he had a number of per- sonas, and the one he was into at that moment must be prohibited by his wife. At least that was my take on the situation. I found him to be quite a character.

"Olokun and Flora talked at length about African art and dance, something Flora traveled to Chicago regularly to enjoy. I listened intently as she and Olokun discussed many things I had not even considered before that afternoon. I found myself marveling at how much I was learning from their conversation. But I had no idea of what was to come. Out of left- field Olokun jarred me with his next move. I couldn't tell if it was a question or a proclamation of

19

some kind when he referred to my husband's demise. I struggled for a moment trying to make sense out of his sudden shift in conversation, but ultimately nodded my head in agreement that my husband had made his transition, noting that it would soon be 12 years. Truthfully, I began to feel a little strange about his inquiry. He seemed to have an agenda of some kind and I had no idea of where he was heading.

"Olokun got a strange look on his face and began to talk about the alto sax player from the Afro/Latin-jazz ensemble. Both Flora and I smiled as we reminisced about how wonderful the music had been at the Henning event, and the sax player had been spectacular. In a flash memories of the strange sensations I experienced that evening came to me and I shuddered a bit. Olokun went on and on about how the sax player was still grieving for his wife who had made her transition nearly six years ago and I found myself being a little suspicious of his motives. As he talked about his friend with such compassion, I noticed he kept looking at me, and I asked him why. But, he overlooked my question and talked more about the sax player. Then he asked another jarring question about my being from Florida. I answered him with a resounding 'Yes,' indicating precisely that I was born and reared in Key West, Florida. Olokun smiled and immediately proceeded to say that the sax player, Kojo, talked about Key West all the time. I was shocked because I thought I knew all of the other people of color living in Milwaukee who had relocated from Key West. Besides me, there were only two African Americans that I knew about, and Kojo was not among them. Olokun laughed loudly, seeming pleased to have gotten a spark out of me. He went on to explain that Kojo had been in the army and was stationed in Key West for a number of months in the mid-sixties before he was sent to Vietnam. Key West was where he met his wife, who had been on vacation there with her family at the time. He had planned to return there but had not made it back yet.

"I sat, mesmerized, by his account of the sax player's history in my hometown. According to Olokun, Kojo talked often about a group of Black elders in Key West who were consummate chess players. Interestingly, Kojo, who hailed from Lexington, Kentucky, had not known what to expect in the Florida Keys and had been more than pleasantly surprised to find a community of avid Black chess players there. He found that both military personnel and tourists were welcome to join in chess games that went around the clock on weekends at the noted Conch Palace on Thomas Street, located in the heart of the area mostly populated by African Americans at that time. I was amazed at the precise nature of Olokun's report of Kojo's experiences. I knew from my own history that chess games went on around the clock at the Conch Palace.I knew that in the garden of the Conch Palace there were tropical fruit trees — sapodillas, tamarinds, sugar apples, and Spanish limes, to name only a few — hovering in places so inviting that the chess players enjoyed much more than chess and conch fritters (the main dish offered at the Conch Palace). It was eerie hearing Olokun convey such an accurate picture of a historic place in my hometown.

"Entranced by Olokun"s report, I remembered that it is said that the patriarch and originator of the Conch Palace, old man Palacious, a product of a Cuban father and a Bahamian mother, had been a fisherman/sponger and a seasoned chess player. People laughed about the fact that he told everyone that he had named his eldest son after the famous African American chess player of the 19th century, Theophilus Thompson, who is said to have written a book on chess. Old man Palacious was a devout initiate of Santeria, which people wondered about and he made no bones about the spiritual beings that protected his scrumptious garden at the Conch Palace. I remembered he had a pond in his garden that was off limits to most people. But, as children, my cousins and I ventured to the clandestine place more than once to see the pond filled with vibrant white and pink flowers. The water in the pond was always muddy, but the flowers there were pure and beautiful. People said old man Palacious grew spiritual flowers. Some people called them Mud Flowers. That memory stirred me as I spotted a picture of a lotus flower in the hallway of Olokun's home, a white one just like those I had seen as a child in old man Palacious' pond. A chill ran through me, but I didn't say anything about my memories or the painting.

"Reflecting on all of those memories made me smile and I was intrigued with all that Olokun had to say about Kojo's story. I certainly had been in Key West at the time this Kojo person was there, and I wondered if I had run into him. I had many friends in the military at that time, and my cousin Vy, short for Viola, and I were equal opportunity daters: we included all branches of the military. While Vy, in all of her petite diva grandeur at the time, was partial to men in the air force, I had a thing for navy men, especially navy frogmen. Kojo was an army man, but that didn't count him out. I wondered if our paths had crossed. Even if they hadn't, I was piped up with knowing that he had been in my hometown among my people. According to Olokun, Kojo had been stationed in Key West for about eight months before he was sent to Vietnam.

"Smiling broadly, Olokun handed me Kojo's email address as he went on a bit more with Kojo's story. I accepted the email address thinking that Olokun was really quite a character. While I didn't know what to make of Olokun's behavior, I knew I was excited about connecting with someone who had been to my neck of the woods. I looked forward to talking with Kojo. *It would be interesting*, I thought, *very interesting*. I had no idea then of the rollercoaster ride ahead of me.

"Days later when I talked with Flora about the details of that afternoon, she, too, had found it odd that Olokun was so invested in passing the email address on, but she was used to Olokun's antics and encouraged me not to make too much of his actions. Interestingly, she surprised me by talking more about Kojo. She told me that she connected with him a number of times over the years and thought he was a noble man, very involved in the community. I was surprised to hear the positive way she spoke about him, because, with the exception of Olokun and a few other very Afrocentric brothers, Flora really seemed to believe that we as a people were experiencing a drought in the flow of healthy Black men and should see them as endangered. She would often say, 'We have lost a generation of Black men to the street.' I thought she was probably jaded by all she encountered over the years as a cop."

Once again I stopped and looked at Cullen, wondering what

he was thinking. As I waited for him to say something, I found myself smiling at my own thoughts about how much my cousin Vy's physical appearance had changed over the years. While she is still very attractive, her demure, petite frame of years ago had shifted from a size six to a voluptuous size 12-14 today, right up there with me. We both have become hefty women, but the change has been much more of a stretch for Vy than for me; my buxom bosom and hips, in particular, had been around for a very long time.

CHAPTER 3

Connecting in La Crosse

By now I had gotten up from the leather seat and was walking around the room. Seemingly moved by my own words and caught up in the fervor of my story, Cullen seemed to be deep in thought and listening with every part of himself. He was clearly engaged. With a sense of mission, I closed my eyes, breathed deeply, and went back to my story. "Within a few days I sent a formal email to Kojo using his birth name, Fred Richards, which I had secured from Flora. I actually addressed him as Mr. Richards. I told him about my visit with Olokun and the conversation we had about his tour of duty in Key West during the sixties. I also told him how much I enjoyed his very fine playing in the Afro/Latin-jazz ensemble at the Henning celebration. I then told him that my place of origin was Key West and that my father's people hailed from the Bahamas. I sent the email and then with routine fastidiousness facilitated two anger management groups. When I returned to my computer four hours later, there were two email messages from Fred Richards, aka Kojo. He was excited to know that I was from Key West, noting that he had been there in the sixties and had met his wife there. He asked that I not call him Mr. Richards, suggesting I consider calling him Fred or by his African name, Kojo, which he explained means Monday child. In his second email, he pointed out that he has always felt strongly connected to Key West. He wanted to return there for an extended visit but did not know anyone who could make useful connections for inexpensive but safe lodging. Then he said the thing that really got my attention. He pointed out that his financial advisor, whom he had met at Florida Agricultural and Mechanical University — commonly known as FAMU — was from the Bahamas and could perhaps be a relative of mine.

"What really struck me was his mention of FAMU. Although I had not made it to graduation, I considered it my undergraduate alma mater. Curiously, judging from his email address, which I assumed had parts of his birthdate, if he had gone to FAMU, we would have been there about the same time. Intrigued by my mental detective work, I sent him an email to that effect, clearly noting when I left FAMU at the end of my junior year. I sent a few other particulars about my father's family, including my maiden name. I sent all of this with a degree of eagerness. I thought it would really be something if we were at FAMU at the same time so many years ago and were just making a connection for the first time now. I searched my memory for his name during my days at FAMU but could not come up with a connection. As I sent the email, I couldn't remember his face or how tall he was. All I could call up was the phenomenal sax playing, his shaggy fly-away Don King gray hair, and his giant smile. Two days later I was riveted by his email. He had been at FAMU when I was there. He asked that I give him a call as soon as I could, which I did that evening." I left my story again for a moment to look Cullen in the eyes to see how he was reacting to the sheer oddness of what I had shared thus far. But my friend was his usual warm but unshakable self in true poker-face form. So I returned to my story unruffled.

"I tell you, Cullen, when I heard his voice, it was as if I had heard it before, a long time ago. And his laugh was so familiar that I began thinking we had met before and I had forgotten. But as we talked for a while, it became obvious that either we had not met before or we both were showing faulty memories. I guess I was affected by the familiarity of him. It was weird. His laugh seemed to trigger memories, but I just couldn't put my finger on what the memories were about. We talked for about forty minutes, and in the conversation we discovered that we had many other experiences in common. He laughed jubilantly when we made that discovery. I didn't laugh, but a chill went through me, and I had found myself thinking about Miss Ella, the old woman who had promised that my next husband would find me. It was all beginning to be a bit eerie, the connections that were unfolding. As we talked, I promised that I would connect him to people in Key West who could probably provide lodging there at a reasonable rate. We then scheduled a meeting for the following Monday afternoon at Bay Shore Mall, a place I often walked late in the evening. It was comfortably familiar to me. We would have a bit of wine and just talk. I couldn't believe what I was feeling. I felt giddy. I had to laugh at myself as I thought of Miss Ella again. I wondered if what she had helped me put in place years before could be coming to fruition.

"When I hung up the phone that night, I couldn't explain what I felt inside. In a foggy state, I couldn't find my diabetes medicine. I had been about to take the Metformin when Kojo returned my call, and after the call, I couldn't find it. In truth, I didn't find it until two days later, and I had a good laugh about that. In my openness, I shared this with Kojo when we met, and he graciously said, 'I won't tell anyone about that.' We both laughed, and it was interesting, the level of kinship that just seemed to well up between us. My comfort level had me concerned. I couldn't believe how comfortable I began to feel at our first meeting. We talked about four and a half hours nonstop and drank quite a bit of wine. I had brought the name of a person in Key West who was open to having him rent one of her units for whatever period he needed for his holiday. She is a friend, and I knew she would be fair. She and I talked about it, and she asked why I didn't let him stay at the house owned by my family, which was governed essentially by my brother. My reasoning was based on the understanding that Kojo wanted privacy. Although there was room in our family home, where my brother and his wife lived, I knew he would not have much privacy there despite their willingness to be hospitable.

"Along with the name and number of my friend in Key West, I gave Kojo a piece of cake from a dinner I had attended. I felt quite comfortable giving him the little gift bag with these items in it. I would do this for any friend. In receiving the gift bag, he seemed surprised but comfortable with it. He graciously paid for all of the wine we imbibed in that afternoon. We laughed a lot, and in more somber moments we talked about him and his deceased wife. He called her his queen, making it clear that he missed her terribly. Listening attentively, I realized I was six years ahead of him in the grieving process. Kojo seemed to be still connected to his wife and had not yet given himself permission to move on.

"We talked about spirituality at length, a topic that had always intrigued me. For some reason — I am not sure why — I had brought the magazine *Shaman's Drum* to share with him, and we talked a great deal about his interest in the supernatural, which a family elder had introduced to him. As we talked, it became clear that we connected deeply on this topic, sharing similar beliefs. He was versed in spiritual practices from the continent of Africa and expressed an interest in learning more about practices in other parts of the world. I shared my interest in Native American spiritual rituals, noting that I was interested in the shamanic practices of Ecuador and other places. When we finally wound down our conversation, we decided to meet again to discuss all of the things we had not gotten to share about our time at FAMU. With mutual anticipation, it seemed, we scheduled a time to meet the following Monday afternoon, but at Mayfair Mall, where I would be getting my monthly pedicure. As we walked to the parking structure together, he noticed that I didn't wait for him to open doors for me. He commented on that, and I willingly accepted the probable conclusions that could be drawn from his observation — I was independent to a fault. I put it in context by noting that I would work on that, and we both laughed, seemingly aware that it would take me some time to settle into letting someone handle me with a sense of chivalry. It was a lovely afternoon."

I found myself smiling at the memory as I looked to Cullen once again for some form of reaction. In response to my pause in the story, Cullen smiled slightly, waving his hand, urging me to go on. I complied, "My drive home was filled with many thoughts, mostly about the strange connection I felt. At times, while with him, I had the sensation of being in the presence of some significant figure from my past. There was such a strong connection that his laughter triggered elusive memories. And there were instances when I could almost hear a chant of some kind. It was uncanny how strong the sensation of kinship was. That, coupled with a hint of past intimacy, kept my mind racing as I listened to the CD a friend had given me for Christmas a year ago. The sister on the CD was melodiously calling for someone to watch over her. I found myself mouthing the words along with the song and thought, *Yes, that's what I want.* I didn't need anyone to take care of me, but I did want someone to be there with whom I could share my thoughts and ask their opinion about things. *Yes, that would be nice*, I thought, as I put my car in the garage. It would be wonderful if this connection turned into a special thing between us. I thought about Miss Ella again, and I smiled. I wouldn't know quite how to act if someone came into my life now. In fact, Kojo and I had laughed about my forwardness and simultaneous awkwardness. While in the mall, I reached for the bill, opened my own door, and even walked ahead of him as we were leaving. I had admitted I was out of practice being in a man's company, at least from the perspective of non-business or collegial situations.

"I told only one person about our first meeting. That was Flora, and she was eager to hear about our discussion. Though Eva was back from her trip to Japan, I wasn't ready to share this with her just yet, but I wasn't sure why. I guess it had something to do with the fact that I knew Flora thought Kojo was special. And you never know what you might get for an opinion from my dear friend Eva. That night, Flora and I talked for hours. She said she heard laughter in my voice, and I knew what she meant because I could hear it myself. I could feel it, the grandeur of possibilities, something I had dismissed as ever being part of my future. I kept thinking about Miss Ella and kept smiling.

"I could barely wait until Monday. We were scheduled to meet at 3:00 p.m. in Mayfair Mall, which was substantially different than Bay Shore Mall, even its location on the far west side of the city. Because I would connect with him following my monthly pedicure, we scheduled our second meeting at Mayfair. The setup there was not as accommodating as at Bay Shore. The only places to get a glass of wine were two restaurants that were rather isolated from the general area of where I would have my pedicure. Throughout the time the Asian woman worked on my feet, my thoughts raced. I wondered whether Kojo and I would talk as long this time as before and what other connections we would stumble upon. By the time the pedicure was done, I nearly raced to the agreed upon meeting place. By 3:15 p.m. I began to worry, so I called him only to discover he had gone back to Bay Shore Mall, where we had met the first time and was there waiting for me. For a moment I was disappointed and had an eerie sense of forebodingness like a dark cloud rising, a sure promise of distinct disillusionment and discord. I tried to shake off the dark feelings and let him know I would come to where he was waiting rather than give up on our time together. As I drove across town, the strange chant I heard the first time we met began again, but this time it was louder in my head and I could make out some of the words. It was a different language, one that I had heard before in dreams and visions."

Departing from my story again, I looked directly at Cullen after I said these things. I wondered how he was receiving this part of my story. I scrutinized his countenance carefully and concluded he was certainly very engaged. I turned away from my friend and went back to my story. "By the time I reached Bay Shore Mall, I was lightheaded and felt strange. I didn't see Kojo when I first stepped out of the elevator. But, soon he moved towards me, and for some reason he seemed dark, as though draped in some kind of cloudy mist. He said something to me, but I couldn't make it out. Before I could stop myself, I blurted out everything about the chant and the words I heard on my ride from one mall to the other.

"Kojo looked at me strangely as we took our seats in the dining room/bar. The feeling of ease we had the first afternoon we met was not there this time. Actually, there was a sense of discord between us, and still we talked and drank our wine. We had a different waitress this day, a young model-like person with fair skin, long black hair, a gap in her teeth, and exceptionally elegant hands. I couldn't quite put my finger on it, but there was something about the way she and Kojo exchanged glances that made me uncomfortable. My thoughts raced as he and I continued our conversation. Pangs of jealousy gripped me. I was really uneasy and oddly, without forethought, I found myself talking almost frantically, pulling topics out of the blue. With a sense of urgency I began telling him about my deep connection to the historic figure Chief Crazy Horse that began in 1995. *Don't know why I am doing this,* I thought. But, with almost pressured speech, I laid out the whole story about Chief Crazy Horse, highlighting the part about my deceased husband. I told Kojo about how in October 1995, three days after my husband Emory returned from The Million Man March in Washington, he insisted on taking a road trip alone to Savannah, Georgia to meet with a healer. He had met the healer's grandsons at the Million Man March. In keeping with a spirit of brotherhood, the two young men had graciously held him up a couple of times when he experienced bouts of dizziness, symptoms of a mysterious disorder at the time. He told them about the recent diagnosis of prostate cancer and they in turn encouraged him to come to Savannah to meet with their grandmother, the healer, who had been helping people for years. They said he would have to come soon, because she was about to visit relatives in Bermuda and would be out of the country for a number of months.

"While I never doubted the veracity of Emory's story about the healer, I was overwrought by the prospect of his road trip. But, there was no stopping Emory when his mind was made up. Clearly, in pursuit of a nontraditional strategy to address his prostate cancer, he was like a man possessed. He left for Savannah, driving alone and I was terrified for him. Not only were the bouts of dizziness a concern, but he was traveling to a place he knew nothing about (the healer was really in a small town outside of Savannah), to meet with people he knew very little about and he insisted on doing it alone. I didn't understand that and I felt utterly helpless. For hours after he left, I entered into deep prayer for my infirmed husband. Through soulful tears I begged God to encircle him in Divine protection, imploring, 'Send a legion of protectors to shield him.'

"Cloaked in earnest supplication I threw myself before God. I prayed throughout the night and following day, ultimately experiencing a triumphant dream that would change my life. In my dream, I was walking behind a Native American warrior leader mounted on a massive horse. Distant voices called him Chief Crazy Horse. He appeared strong and clear in his mission. I could see him vividly and even smell the dust kicked up by his legion of warriors as he commanded them to the four winds. The warriors hovered over and around my husband as he climbed a mountain. They chanted as they hovered around him protectively. It was a sight to behold. I could hardly breathe as I took note of all that was going on around me in the dream. Before long a sense of victory engulfed me in the dream and stilled me in the morning as I embraced my day with wonder, certain that my husband was safe. It was amazing that the name Chief Crazy Horse kept reverberating through my thoughts for days. Up to the point of the dream, I knew very little about Chief Crazy Horse, nothing more than what we read in the history books about Custer's last stand. But after my encounter with the dream, I began to read everything I could find about the warrior chief, and in a way he became a constant companion.

"When my husband returned home, safe and fulfilled, I gratefully shared the details of the dream with him. While he seemed uncertain of what to make of it, he did not discount my near obsession with studying Chief Crazy Horse's life or besmirch my rapidly budding connection to the warrior chief. I was certain that my prayers had somehow tapped into the collective unconscious and fostered a bridge across time, manifesting true kinship. I was grateful to the Creator for answering my prayers. I didn't question why the warrior chief was sent as opposed to some other protector/ guide. I just bowed in gratitude.

"Amazingly, as I was sharing all of this, Kojo didn't react at all. He just listened, unruffled. When I finally sat in silence, I felt misunderstood, odd, and exhausted. Offering very few words after my emotional soliloquy, we prepared to leave the mall, and I noticed how Kojo touched the waitress on our way out. I was jealous! It was a seductive kind of exchange between them, and I wondered about it. Observing how he touched her, it occurred to me that though we discussed many deep things, he never touched me. He seemed careful not to touch me. Realizing this, I asked him if I could touch his hands, and he put them before me. I touched them, noticing their strength and how cold his fingertips were. I wondered if he had a serious problem with circulation. There were no answers! Everything about our time together this day seemed strange.

"In the elevator on our way to the parking structure, I was light-headed, both from struggling to stay in this realm and from embarrassment. I did not know how to explain the rather odd turn of events. Kojo appeared to be comfortable with spiritual things, but the occurrences of this afternoon seemed to be straight out of a weird place, even to me. As we walked towards our cars, he gave me the magazine that had been sitting on the table in front of him. It was quite a gesture. He seemed to be trying to comfort me in some way. I took the magazine and am sure I mumbled something, but my mind was set on getting away from him. I felt embarrassed! So much had transpired, and I was weak with it all!

"On the drive home, my mind raced, but ultimately went to memories of one of my deceased spiritual mentors, Homer, who had taught me so many things over the years. I wished he and his wife Minnie were still alive and available to me; they had been great friends, a part of my Midwest family of choice. They understood the spiritual experiences I shared with them from time-to-time. I remembered the day, he and his wife had urged me to accept the dream about the warrior chief as a sign of answered prayer. Homer was adamant in pointing out that he believed our 'help' comes in many forms and the warrior leader was an answer to my prayer. Homer believed that there probably was another connection, but I may not ever come to know it. In his view, my best response to the dream was to be grateful and to know that the warrior chief as I experienced him would be with me for as long as I needed him. According to Homer, we must be grateful for our 'help' and be so without questioning, because our 'help' comes from the Creator Source. I smiled as I remembered the lessons from Homer and his wife.

"When I got home, I could barely get through my nightly prayer ritual before I fell into a deep sleep and encountered an inviting dream. In the dream world, I was walking with Kojo in a green mist, and we were laughing heartily. We were warm and friendly. Upon awakening in the morning, I went directly to my computer. As I adjusted my glasses, I smiled because there was an email from Kojo sent at about 4:00 a.m. He wrote that he couldn't sleep and began to clean out a closet. In so doing, he opened a clothing bin, and a book on Chief Crazy Horse tumbled out. He didn't remember buying the book, but it was brand new and there in his house. James Marshall III wrote the book. Reading his email, I began to laugh. It tickled me that he had come upon a book he had no idea he bought, and it was one of the books I had read about Chief Crazy Horse. All of this happened within hours after I had shared so much about my encounter with the warrior chief. I immediately sent an email telling him about the book and how I keep that particular book in the bookcase at the head of my bed along with many other books on Chief Crazy Horse. It was quite a morning! I was certain the universe was speaking to us. This was another rather uncanny connection, but I wasn't sure what it meant. I simply prayed about it and thought of Miss Ella and Homer."

Again, I stepped away from my story to assess Cullen's expression. I wondered what my friend was thinking. In that moment I wished I hadn't been so adamant in asking him to just listen. On the one hand I wanted to hear myself say all of this out loud without interruptions, but I still found myself wondering what Cullen was thinking. *I confuse myself,* I thought, shaking my head trying to push myself past this moment of uncertainty.

CHAPTER 4

Still Connecting in La Crosse

M oving forward with the story,
    "I thought about the uncanny connections all day. That evening I called Flora with the news about the Chief Crazy Horse book. She was amazed that so many extraordinary connections were coming through, and her cop-driven mind worked diligently to find a rational reason that particular book was in Kojo's home, packed away in a clothing bin to be discovered on the morning following my frantic-like discourse about my connection to the warrior chief. She just couldn't figure it out rationally. So she set that particular conundrum aside for the moment, immersing herself in other aspects of my report. We talked at length about many of the details of my meeting with Kojo, but I didn't tell her about the chanting or my concerns about the young waitress. I was still trying to make sense out of all of that for myself and didn't need Flora's ultra-rational mind interfering with my reflection process. In truth, I was concerned and ashamed about my reaction to the thought of the 'high yella' young waitress being with Kojo. That very thought made my head hurt, though I believed up to that point I had gotten beyond my feelings of resentment of light-skinned African-American women.

"Over the years, I experienced so many hurts in that area that I hoped I had reached a point of forgiveness, but this situation was triggering feelings I hadn't acknowledged in years. As Flora and I hashed and rehashed various points about relationship possibilities with Kojo, my mind flitted from one thought about the troublesome skin color issue to another. I couldn't shake my feelings and was annoyed with myself about their juvenile quality. At my age, I had hoped to be well beyond such minutia. When I hung up from Flora, I sat for a while trying to sort through my feelings about the waitress, finally concluding that I was not only upset about her skin color but was equally put off by her youthfulness, which was elegantly ensconced in her slender well-proportioned frame high-lighted by long, flowing hair. There was no way I could compete with her youthful vigor, and that pissed me off. Once I concluded that it was not just the color of her skin that raised my ire, I felt a little less adolescent. I believed that many women in my age group had to contend with the perils of youthful women captivating the attention of senior men. That realization saddened me, but I mused that I was in good company with many female baby boomers.

"As I mulled the plight of seasoned, single Black women, I checked my email and was pleasantly surprised to find another email from Kojo sent while I was on the phone with Flora. I tried to stop myself from smiling, but I couldn't. I was so excited to hear from him! In his email, he talked more about the book by Marshall, stating again his surprise at having it in his possession and how it had presented itself to him. He was unclear why the book had been in a clothing bin but was even more puzzled as to where it had come from in the first place; he didn't remember buying it. Interestingly, however, after a number of hours of careful reflection, he speculated that he had probably bought the book a year or so ago after he heard an invigorating lecture on the merging of the Lakota Sioux and Seminole Indian religious cultures. The book, he surmised, had probably been secured as a step in the direction of learning more about the spiritual practices of the Lakota Sioux. Of particular interest to him were Seminole spiritual traditions. To say I was totally engaged with his fertile knowledge base would be an understatement: I was nearly entranced. *In his own way, he is a teacher*, I thought. I was impressed. Further into his email, he noted that he would be going out of town for a while but would check in with me when he returned. He ended his message by encouraging me to use my African name, Afua, which means Friday's female child with the energy of fertility all around her. We had talked about that in our last meeting when he asked my birthdate. I smiled at the thought of being called Afua, thinking that to begin using my African name would make me more connected to him.

"In response to his email, I let him know I would consider using the name Afua. I thanked him for the gift of the name and the wonderfully informative sharing about the merging of the Lakota and Seminole spiritual traditions. I then stepped boldly and asked that he consider adding the name Cowaya to the array of names he used in salutations, asking that he consider calling himself Cowaya (my push for a mutual naming moment). In doing that, I explained, he would claim the energy of a lauded Black Seminole leader, a runaway slave, also known as Gopher John and John Horse, who had been a valued advisor to Seminole Chief Osceola. As I wrote the email, I was amazed how adept my memory could be. It had been years since I thought about the stories of Gopher John and other nuggets from the elders in my childhood.

"Responding to my email, Kojo noted that he was aware of Gopher John but had not known the extent of the aliases he carried. In gratitude for his new name, he sent a slide show which was beautiful, highlighted by the melodious tunes of saxophonist Dave Koz. It was fabulous. And he added Cowaya to the array of names at the end of his email. I was delighted. In its simple beauty, the slide show was touching to the point of evoking tears. After I had savored it a number of times, allowing myself to get lost in the music, I sent an email to him acknowledging that I was deeply moved by his tender gesture. In addition, I told him to have a safe trip and that I would be open to connecting with him when he returned. In return, he sent an email that said only, 'Awesome, Afua!!'

"I smiled as I pulled myself away from the computer, nursing my feelings as I tried to make sense of the raw emotions I was experiencing. Pushing myself to think about my response to the slide show and Kojo in general, I realized I hadn't felt so connected to a man since my husband, Emory. For a while, I kept myself from the computer. But before the night passed, I returned to the slide show. I sat at the computer playing the gift from Kojo again and again. The flowers in the show were exquisite and the quotes piercingly poignant. I read and reread his statement about the merging of the Lakota and Seminole religious traditions, marveling at how easy it had been to share with him and learn from him. The more I thought about him, the more I felt there was something familiar about him. I thought about Ms. Ella and hoped she was watching over me.

"In the following ten days, I was immersed in my work. Two very challenging domestic violence cases that had the public in an uproar and drew upon my special expertise, particularly my debriefing skills, kept me on my toes. There was so much pressure to perform optimally that I was preoccupied with my work from the moment I hit the floor in the morning to the time I crawled between the sheets at night. The fact that I didn't hear from Kojo via either telephone or email (he knew not to text me) crossed my mind, but I certainly didn't wonder too deeply about the reasons behind that. I was pretty certain he would get in touch with me when he returned to the city. There were moments when I was in the shower or driving to The Center that I would allow myself to feel all warm and hopeful about Kojo, while at other times I would challenge myself about the connection I felt to him. I would talk to myself out loud, admonishing myself for feeling so connected to a man I knew so little about.

"In those moments, I would do a litany of the connections: 'Yes, we both attended FAMU. And yes, we both moved to Wisconsin, and yes, he has a book in his home on Chief Crazy Horse, and yes, the book had just dropped into his hands the very morning after I told him about my connection to the warrior chief, and yes, it is my favorite book about the warrior chief that I keep close to me, and yes, he has a passion for learning just as I have.' I said 'Yes' to all of these things out loud to myself, but then I had to raise the question, 'Does any of this mean anything other than a host of coincidences?' No matter how much I chastised myself about my eagerness to believe there was something special going on, I couldn't shake the feeling that there was some sort of cosmic connection that had a meaning beyond this realm. I thought of Miss Ella and Homer, wishing I had someone to guide me. I wished they were still alive.

"Towards the end of the ten days I shared my thoughts with Eva, who had finally settled in from her fourth trip to Japan. I chose Eva to share my thoughts about the unusual connections with Kojo because she understood cosmic connections and the world of the unusual. She had been under the tutelage of various shamans from all over the world, and she read unceasingly on the topic. It was interesting that, unlike Flora, she didn't allow the grooming implicit in the preparation for her profession as an attorney to temper her spiritual interests or to predispose her to search narrowly for only rational answers to life's puzzles. She was an open-minded, stead-fast, God-believing retired attorney who chanted and prayed daily, though she had issues with organized religion.

"Once I heard all about Eva's adventures in Japan, including the varieties of sushi she'd tried, we talked for a couple of hours about the events in my life over the previous few weeks, and she was taken aback by the connections Kojo and I shared. She was intrigued by it all but insisted that I relax in my process. At 73, Eva could get a bit philosophical about the twists and turns in relationships. I'd seen her do it with other friends. At times I wanted to pinch her, particularly when she would say something like what she had just said to me, 'Relax in your process.' Deep inside me I shouted, *Stop that Eva. What the hell does that mean anyway?* I thought that but didn't say it. I wanted her full attention, and I didn't want to debate. She could go 'lawyer' on you in a moment, particularly when she felt cornered. I held my breath as she laughed after I told her how uncomfortable it was for me to feel so connected to Kojo. She laughed even louder when I finally said I was ambivalent about what I hoped would happen between us. I knew she wasn't making light of my discomfort. I knew her well. We had been friends for years, and I knew she didn't intentionally put people down. But in her unique way, she was trying to encourage me to be more upbeat about what was unfolding: 'These are your lessons, Jewelle. Embrace them. Just know it is all in divine order.' There were times

I could barely contain myself with my friend. I wanted to yell at her about her spiritual insights and the quips she imparted.

"In the face of my irritation, Eva chuckled again, unshaken in her stride, and quietly asked, 'Did you say the drummer from the Henning event gave you the saxophone player's email? And did you say the drummer calls himself Olokun?' I sighed a yes into the phone, wondering where she was going with my answer. Then Eva went into teacher mode. She explained that Olokun was the name of a Santeria Orisha whom some called the Mysterious One. She reminded me that as a child in Cuba she had been immersed in Santeria because it was the secret leanings of her mother's family, though they had been openly devout Catholics. There she learned all about the Orishas according to their Santeria beliefs but had in later years also studied with a Yoruba priest here in the states as well as in Brazil. 'How the Orishas are viewed varies a bit from place to place,' she said, making special note that her own view of Olokun was that of a welcoming wealth of mysteries. Others perceived Olokun as a more foreboding energy.

"As she shared more and more about Santeria, I began to remember things from my childhood in Key West and thought of old man Palacious and the flowers in his secret pond. As it had been with Kojo, I was grateful for Eva's vast knowledge base, despite the fact that through her pedantic endeavor, she cautioned me about the veracity of the drummer's agenda. While she didn't think he was a man given to creating harmful scenarios, she wanted me to know that if he embraced the energy of Olokun, things may not be what they appear to be on the surface. The deeper story would likely reveal the truth. She directed, ' Look for the mysteries beneath the sea'. By the time she was done with all she believed she needed to tell me, I was exhausted. I am not sure why. Though I respect her spiritual depth and vast knowledge base, at times I wished she could just be a good girlfriend and not a wisdom-driven guru. When I hung up from her that night, I called you, Cullen."

At that point I stepped away from the story to make an inquiry of Cullen, "I don't know if you remember that I just needed to hear your voice that night I called you. I needed to be anchored by your loving, unflappable presence. I intentionally did not share anything about my situation. In fact, I didn't say anything at all about Kojo. We just talked for a few minutes about family, yours and mine, and that was it. I just needed to hear your voice that night to set me straight." Looking directly at him, I asked, "Do you remember that call, Cullen?"

Cullen nodded his head but said nothing. He shifted in his seat, motioning with his hand for me to go on with my story. I was always amazed at his ability to listen in such a focused way. I am a good listener, but Cullen seems to listen with his entire being. He appears to soak up every word and store it in a memory bank that has an incisive sorting system, which effectively identifies patterns and proclivities, setting the data aside for future analysis. As I prepped myself to get back to my story I found myself standing closer to the fireplace, actually leaning against the mantle. While the fireplace was very welcoming, I found myself getting too warm. So I decided to sit down again. But this time I moved to the leather couch; it was far enough away from the fireplace that I wouldn't feel the heat so strongly. I wondered if this issue of heat were some kind of metaphor, depicting where I was going in my story. Cullen cleared his throat for the second time, urging me to get back to my story. Without further thought to the metaphor, I jumped back inside my story.

"Exactly ten days after receiving the beautiful slide show, I received an email from Kojo about getting together soon. He wanted me to send a few dates to schedule lunch. I was so pleased to hear from him that I couldn't stop smiling. In his email, he talked a lot about his trip to New York. He attended the wedding of the son of a friend, a young man he was proud of because he'd acted as a mentor and surrogate father after the young man's father had passed away. Kojo was pleased to see that his influence made a difference in his protégé's life; he is now a trauma surgeon at a hospital in upstate New York, where his new wife has a thriving dental practice. Kojo shared many of the details of the wedding and reception, clearly showing that it was a high-end affair. He had pictures which revealed the elaborate nature of the event. For the first time, I realized that I had not considered what it would be like to be included in Kojo's circle. Aside from his music and avid pursuit of knowledge, he had a life and friends that I knew very little about, and from what I was seeing with the opulence of the wedding, this part of him was at odds with who I am. *I must not be so judgmental,* I thought.

"In the midst of chiding myself, I came upon the zinger at the end of his email. While his most recent email accompanying the slide show had been closed out with an array of his names, including my gift, Cowaya, this one was pointedly assigned the salutation 'your brother and friend,' and Cowaya was not included among his array of names. Now, of course, it may seem as if I was making too much of his salutation, but I had a feeling about it. Something in me screamed, *This man has gotten involved with someone,* I thought about it for a moment and decided that they were on the trip together and now he was redefining our connection by assigning it to the brother/friend category. In my mind, I told him to go to hell, but in my email back to him I addressed him as Kojo, Cowaya, my brother and friend. For a moment, I was annoyed by seeing the shift in our budding relationship, but I soon convinced myself that I had no reason to be annoyed because we were just getting to know each other. I forced myself to smile as I sent four possible times we could schedule lunch. I sent the email and waited."

Haltingly laying out this part of my story for Cullen, I realized this was a part of the experience that touched me deeply. In keeping with the mounting feelings within me, I stood once again as if I needed to give height to my words, making them more powerful in some way. I studied Cullen carefully, and his demeanor still conveyed the depth of his attentiveness; he seemed totally engaged. I took in a deep breath as I went forward with the story.

"In our other times together, Kojo always arrived at the site of our gathering before I did, but this time I waited for more than ten minutes or so before he came around the corner near the theater with a glowing smile on his face. 'You look like a lost lamb,' he said, and I didn't know how to take that. It was as if he were dancing in my head, reading my mind, and while it was interesting, it was also rather unnerving. When we entered the bar/restaurant, our table of the last two meetings was taken, and we both reacted to that with territorial comments. It is odd how people can claim territory. Certainly, we in no way owned anything in that place, but we put 'dibs' on that table way at the back of the place — out of the way, secluded, and very comfortable. Grudgingly, we chose another spot almost in the center of the room. There were many patrons there this day, and the young waitress was nowhere in sight. This time a busty Caucasian waitress breezed over to us and in a rather haphazard manner took our order. As always, I ordered Riesling, and Kojo had some red wine. His pattern was to shift back and forth between Merlot and shots of Tequila. Today was a Merlot day for him.

"We immediately lapsed into bringing each other up to date on what had been going on in our lives since we last met. He talked briefly about his trip out East but spent more time talking about other things. As he told me about his daily preparations for his trip to Key West, which was to occur in a matter of weeks, he showed a level of excitement that I hadn't seen in him before. He professed gratitude for the referral I had given him, noting that he had connected with the people in Key West I referred him to and was pleased with the offer they made. He was excited and grateful! As he talked, I noticed something seemed different about him. I couldn't put my finger on it, but there was an air of mellowness that had not been there before. I found myself wondering about it and then decided that my thought of a few nights before about his connecting sexually on his trip with someone was probably what was going on. *Well, he is a man*, I thought, as the waitress brought our drinks. I told myself he was entitled to be sexual with someone else; I was just getting to know him.

"With ease, Kojo turned his attention to the uncanny situation of the book about Chief Crazy Horse he had found in his closet. He had brought his copy for me to see, and we both commented on the sheer eeriness of the matter. He had not read the book yet but would do so on his trip to Key West. He had a number of books set aside to devour while in the Keys. Among them was a book about the history of runaway slaves in the Everglades, from which he expected to learn more about communities of runaway slaves and their involvement with Native American communities throughout the south.

"Once again I was impressed by his appetite for learning. I enjoyed hearing him discuss his diverse interests, and before long we went head first into sharing positions on various topics from the will of God to the likelihood of past life experiences. I loved every minute of the discussion, particularly when he talked about elders in his family of origin and their spiritual gifts. He made a point of noting that some family elders shared many spiritual things with him throughout his life that he did not speak about often, and it was freeing for him to be able to discuss them with me. I liked that he felt that way!

"Before too long, the people who had annexed our favorite table left the bar, and on cue we claimed our usual spot. We both laughed as we set ourselves up comfortably at 'our' table for the rest of our time together. And without missing a beat, we resumed our chatter. He acknowledged that from the time he was a child, he was told on more than one occasion that he had a special gift and should not run from it, but he still struggled with it. As I savored every word, I was not sure if he found the possibility of bearing a spiritual gift an asset or a liability. While he seemed to love the elders in his family, his feelings about their spiritual proclivities were less clear. Nonetheless, he was very open to talking with me about such things as translocation, clairvoyance, extrasensory perception, shamanism, and the like.

"Time flew by, and when we turned our attention to our years at FAMU, it seemed to stop. Feeling very comfortable, I shared that I didn't have much of a social life at FAMU, that I had dated only one guy and his name was Kenneth Rayburn. When I said Ken's name, Kojo put his hand over his heart and sighed deeply. 'NO,' he said emphatically, 'You have got to be kidding.' He shifted in his chair as if something I said made him uncomfortable. I responded with emphasis that Ken and I had dated just about my entire time at FAMU and he followed me here to Milwaukee after he graduated.

He never told me how he found me. For a moment or so, we were both silent, and then Kojo said that Ken had been his best friend. I almost fell off my chair. I couldn't believe what I was hearing! Here was another connection, one that I would have never considered. I couldn't believe that Kojo and I had never met.

"As we reminisced about Ken, it was clear that we were talking about the same person who was so very close to both of us. *I can't believe Ken never talked about me,* I thought as we immersed ourselves in memories. We laughed about Ken's green army jacket that he wore year-round and both shook our heads in deep dismay when we addressed Ken's serious addiction to drugs. He was such a brilliant man, but his love for heroin was legend. I remembered when I finally realized that drugs came first with Ken, though I loved him deeply, I knew I had to get away from him. Silently, I remembered that I escaped from him by marrying Claude, my first husband, whom I met on Christmas break during my junior year. We got married the following June and moved to Milwaukee: I had found a way to break away from Ken. I didn't tell Kojo that Claude had been my way out from Ken.

"Kojo and I became misty-eyed when he described the last years of Ken's life. With sadness in his voice, he shared that Ken died about ten years ago. I was not aware of that. It was strange that I was finding out about Ken's death while sitting here with his professed best friend in whom I was rapidly developing an interest. *It is all too odd,* I thought, *and has to have some underlying meaning.* Ken and I loved each other at one time, but his love of drugs came between us. Kojo passed a napkin across the table for me to handle my tears. I was not ashamed of the tears and didn't stop myself from going further into the story about Ken."

At that point I stepped outside of my story again for just a moment, quickly reminding myself to stay away from the recurrent dream. Looking in Cullen's direction, I said, "Actually, Cullen, I don't think I ever told even you all the details about Ken, did I?" I looked to my friend, but he just shrugged and motioned for me to go on with my story. I plunked myself down on the couch and returned to my story, experiencing a genuine sense of anticipation.

"Well," I continued, "Kojo listened to my story about Ken with great interest. He leaned back in his chair and watched me intently as I spoke. His eyes held me so engagingly that I felt as if I were being held by him. I told him about the day in the early 1970s when a friend and I were walking down Wisconsin Avenue and I heard the name 'Shug' called out loudly. I stopped dead in my tracks because not only did the name have meaning for me, the voice was familiar. When I turned around, I was caught up in a dream. There was Ken in a little red MG sports car, the one he said he would buy one day when he finished his degree in pharmacy. There he was with those alarmingly striking light brown eyes that danced in the sun. He stopped his car almost in the middle of Wisconsin Avenue and raced to me. My friend Mickey didn't know what was happening because I was a married woman. Mickey just stared in shock as Ken came to me and threw his arms around me, saying over and over again, 'Look at you, Shug!'

"I did not tell Kojo that the day of the uncanny meeting on Wisconsin Avenue really put me in a quandary, one that I had to work through in deep prayer because I had not really gotten over Ken and he could feel it in the way I returned his embrace. Something inside of me came alive as he held me there on Wisconsin Avenue, and I had to work that out. But I didn't work it out right away, and for a few months Ken and I resumed our relationship. I am not proud of that, but it was wonderful until I discovered the tracks on his arms: he was using drugs again. That day, I became physically ill with all that I had been doing. He hadn't lied to me about the drugs. I just hadn't asked. Perhaps I didn't want to know. The tracks brought it all gushing back to me: the reason I left FAMU at the end of my junior year and the reason I quickly responded to Claude's advances during Christmas break. Once again I knew I had to get away from Ken and I did. I am fairly certain that Claude never found out about my indiscretion, but it remains with me.

"Gradually recovering from the shock of both of us being connected to Ken, Kojo shared many stories of fun times with his friend, but our conversation didn't end with Ken. We talked for about six hours that day, and Kojo shared quite a bit about his relationship with his wife. They were married for nearly 35 years. I listened to him express his grief. Along with stories about him and his wife, he spoke quite a bit about his grandfathers on both sides, who worked in the coal mines of West Virginia. He shared that he has two brothers, both younger and both still in Kentucky. It is obvious that the loves of his life are his twin daughters, both successful, single career women. Once again we marveled at another connection; the twin connect. In this case, the only difference was that his daughters are identical twins. As he spoke about them, I could see the pride on his face. They, too, had graduated from FAMU in business and landed good jobs, one in the Milwaukee area and the other near Madison.

"As the evening began to wind down, there was a warm quality to the energy that flowed between us. Kojo appeared more comfortable than he had been, remarking that he'd never sat and talked for six hours with anyone. I smiled at that because the time just seemed to melt away. It was an easy afternoon/evening, very easy. When we parted, there was a feeling of kinship in the air that made me smile. I think I might have even smiled in my sleep that night because the next morning as I read an email from Kojo, I found myself laughing out loud. He was thanking me for an 'awesome' evening and again noted that he had not ever talked with anyone for six hours. This time his salutation included Cowaya among his array of names. I smiled when I saw that, feeling vindicated in some way.

"Later that day, he called, and I was delighted to hear from him. We recounted some of our conversation about Ken, and there was a distinct tenderness to him that exuded a familiar spirit. Again, his laugh was infectious and triggered memories from deep inside of me. I told him that I awoke with laughter in my spirit, and he said that he slept all night for the first time in years. We both laughed, noting that we would get together again soon. I didn't think about his trip to New York or the strange salutation upon his return that had troubled me so. I relished the memory of a special afternoon and evening, believing that there had to be something very cosmic afoot."

Once again, I eyed Cullen, trying to sense what he was thinking, but still all I got from him was his deep commitment to the process of listening intently, nothing more. I checked my story, thinking how difficult it had been to side step the recurrent dream, but I had done it and was pleased with myself.

CHAPTER 5

Pushing Forward in La Crosse

I stopped and breathed deeply, immersed in the mystery of Cullen's thoughts, but didn't query him. I pushed myself forward without more than another deep sigh with the hope that he would make some comment soon.

"When I hung up the phone from Kojo, a quick glance out of the window revealed the beginning effects of the promised mid-November snow. For me, there was always something special about rain and snow. I understood my enchantment with rain — coming from Key West, Florida, the sound of rain on a tin roof was magical to me. Not only does it remind me of home. It seems to lull me a bit deeper into the safety that surely stems from childhood memories: being read to and then later reading to myself on rainy days about fantasy-like charismatic figures making dreams come true. The snow part was more of a mystery to me. But from the first time I had experienced the mini morsels of fluffy white crystals falling from crisp Virginia skies so many years ago, my heart seemed to hop with glee. My first experience with snow had come during my stint in boarding school. That particular experience was etched in my memory, giving me so much pleasure each time I revisited it. But today, I felt wonderfully encircled by what the weather was doing, which interestingly led to the same kind of feelings of safety that were a part of my love affair with rain. Some people think it odd that a Key West Conch like me could be so enamored of the wonders of Wisconsin winters.

"Resting on my bed that day, engaged by the falling snow, I went into an altered state of consciousness. I don't know if it was a deep fantasy or a dream, but it was wonderfully vivid. For the first time since my husband's death, I found myself in the throes of a torrid fantasy-like sexual encounter with someone other than my sweet husband, Emory. It was Kojo who was with me. His deep, resonant laugh stimulated me beyond belief, and we were naked and entwined. Before that day, all of my sexual fantasies had been about my deceased husband, and, to be honest, in recent years those fantasies had become few and far between. Even the sexual dreams had just about stopped, and I was beginning to think that I had commanded my libido to disappear, by way of my rational self. My life truly became my family and my work. I had shut myself down, I thought. Interestingly, I thought about my friend Tina, who spent most of her adult life trying to find 'Mr. Right,' had been praying for God to take the 'spirit' of sex out of her body and mind. She was saying this prayer for quite a while but was once again involved with a much younger man and being very sexual. When I shared with her on more than one occasion that I virtually had no interest in sex, she would just roll her eyes and say, 'I don't know what God is doing. Maybe He has His wires crossed, giving you what I am praying for.' We'd laugh, and I would always chide her about making God a man. Each time I had an opportunity to do so, I would suggest that God could be viewed as a beautiful, strong woman, a loving mother, who was just as capable of looking after us as a bespectacled, bearded male God. That conversation would spark a heated discussion about the actual gender of God, which would send Tina into a tizzy, taking us far away from a conversation on sex.

"That afternoon as I rested on my bed, enthralled in the passion of a fantasized Kojo's firm embrace, I found myself smiling and excited about what the actual real-life possibilities could ultimately be. In this altered state, Kojo came behind me and cupped my breasts in his hands. My nipples responded to him, and the firmness of him made me breathe rapidly and yearn for more. His slight, bristly beard tickled the back of my neck as his hands wandered in places that had not been touched by another in years. His breath was hot, and he called me Afua, my African name. I couldn't believe that ecstasy like this was still available to a woman my age. As my body and mind exploded that afternoon, I told my rational self to go to hell! The reality of this would be worth any risks, I found myself saying out loud, almost as if I had a need to hear myself acknowledge my willingness to accept whatever consequences there could be for such a steamy afternoon."

It was interesting that I had become so engrossed in the report of my memories that I almost forgot I was still in Cullen's office and he was listening to all of this. I quickly turned to look at him, and the practiced psychiatrist had a poker face, showing nothing. I felt a little embarrassed about the details of what I had just shared with my friend. But I hesitated for only a moment and then returned to my story, thinking there was so much more to share if I wanted Cullen to help me through my disappointment.

"For days after that torrid afternoon, I experienced something akin to an elongated afterglow. Even my children commented on how exuberant my spirit had become, and I literally sang in the shower. I didn't hear from Kojo for more than a week, and it was really difficult not to contact him, but my fantasies kept me filled. On some level, I felt as if we really had been together sexually and he was now distancing himself from me. That was my thought until he showed up in my dreams the night before I received his email. The dream was almost a replica of the snowy afternoon, but the difference was that I had become much more forward, leveling passion upon him with such fervor that he moaned my name again and again and I smiled at his joy. In the dream, we were equally forceful in our lovemaking, pushing limits and investing all in the pleasure of the other. There was an utter selflessness to our passion in the dream, and I loved every minute of it.

"When I read his email revealing his plans for Thanksgiving, my heart plummeted. He would be leaving the city again for a week or so but hoped we would get together when he returned.

He mentioned the book by Marshall again, noting that he had come upon another book about the Lakota, one he would share with me when we connected again. I could feel my rational-self surfacing, and I forcefully tried to set her aside as I worked on my response. I tried to convey an air of coolness when I really wanted to say, 'Man, can't you feel me? We have been together in another realm, and it has been breathtakingly wonderful!' I wanted to tell him so many things, but my rational-self won; she had years of practice and was powerful enough to override the intense force of my sex-filled fantasies and dreams. Instead of revealing myself to him, I wished him well, confirming that we would talk when he returned. It was good that I had a couple of important consulting contracts to fulfill that required focus and painstaking research over the next week. Throwing myself into work always helped. I have often marveled at my ability to do that: to take myself away from things by becoming so focused that almost nothing else exists but family and work. Now, it came in handy, and I handled my situation adeptly, moving through the Thanksgiving holiday with a sense of grace.

"A few days after Thanksgiving, I received a call from a fellow by the name of Randy who was an angry young man at one time and a challenge to handle in my anger management group. It had been years since I saw him. He was the type of batterer who punched walls, broke lamps, and jaws all because someone else made him do it. He had been woefully immature and difficult to work with at one time. As I remembered it, our time together was court ordered for more than one set of anger management interventions over a period of about two years, but he ultimately learned to self-regulate and turn his life around. In his phone call, he told me that he would be graduating from college in December with a political science degree. He was no longer acting out violently and was grateful that he didn't have a felony on his record. He wanted to share his good news with me. He and his fiancée, the mother of his recently born son, were inviting me to dinner to celebrate his achievements. I agreed to have dinner with them but stumbled over my words when he asked if I would like to bring a guest, noting that he was aware that my husband had died. *Wow,* I thought, reflecting upon the years since Emory's death. *It has been just that long since I have seen Randy.*

"Immediately, the thought of Kojo popped in my mind, and I could hardly wait for his return to ask him to be my guest. When his email came, it was again warm and friendly, but he once again signed, 'your brother and friend.' This time he included Cowaya in the array of names at the end of his email. He wanted me to give him a few dates so that we could set a time to get together. The small thing about how he closed off his email almost sent me into a rage. I had so many mixed feelings about that. How could he be my brother when in the dream state and the fantasy/spirit realm we were lovers, passionate lovers? It was at moments like this that I wanted to scream at him, 'Don't you feel me?' But of course, I didn't scream or cuss. I sent a very polite reply with a number of dates, noting that it would be good to see him. I also told him about the dinner invitation and wondered if he would like to be my guest. His 'Yes' about being my guest made me smile, and the dinner was quickly arranged for the first Saturday in December, about ten days before he planned to travel south for the winter.

"My schedule was extremely busy at The Center, forcing me to recognize that the consulting I had added to my schedule, while lucrative, was too time-consuming, so much so that I was considering cutting back on some contracts. I was very busy, and yet I still had dreams that sent me into the stratosphere. And as I drove back and forth to work, my mind filled with questions about how I was handling this thing with Kojo. A number of times I thought about calling you, Cullen. Once, while talking with you, I almost told you about my quandary, but at that time I didn't want your sharp clinical acumen messing with my stuff. Rather than share this with you, I talked more about my consulting contracts and the challenges therein. You know that in and of itself can fill volumes. I often wondered if you suspected that something of this nature was going on with me. Did you?" I turned to Cullen again, and he nodded but said nothing, motioning for me to continue with my story. Again, I took a deep sigh and returned to my story, wondering what my friend was thinking.

"In many ways during the days leading up to Kojo's departure, I stopped sharing with Flora and Eva. I had not said one word about my steamy fantasies and dreams. For some reason, though they were my good friends, I did not allow myself to talk about that kind of thing with them. As for my friend Tina, who is still praying for God to heal her of her sexual proclivities, I thought about telling her some of it just to let her know that I am still alive in that area. But I decided to keep it all to myself, that is until I spoke with my cousin, Vy, in Key West. We have so much history together, from childhood on, that I could say just about anything to her and not feel judged. Over the years, we shared private things with each other from time to time. That is what made me comfortable in sharing the sexual fantasies with her, and our laughter took us back to our hot and fast days when she wholeheartedly embraced men in the air force and I held fast to navy men, particularly navy frogmen.

"As we discussed these things, she was captivated by the dates involved throughout this entire encounter with Kojo. It seems that the day I had heard about him from Olokun, the drummer, for the first time was the actual day her mother died. Her mother, my aunt Mavis, had been a character. When I told Vy Kojo's birthdate, she just gasped and said a string of cuss words that surely marked her as her mother's child. 'That's Mama's birthday,' she said. 'What kind of shit is this?' I was stunned again by the odd connections. Vy summed it up perfectly when she closed off our phone conversation with an old Key West saying, 'What a time! What a time!' This essentially means that life can be shockingly exciting and we should accept it as such.

"I was pretty excited about the dinner date and planned to wear a special outfit. It had been years since I went shopping with a man in mind, but I did just that in preparation for the date. That is why I could hardly take the disappointment when Randy called to say that we needed to reschedule because his fiancée and their son had swine flu, which was raging throughout the country at the time. I didn't know I could be so selfish. I was saddened to recognize that initially I thought only about my disappointment and nothing about the potentially fatal flu Randy's family had contracted. I am sure Kojo heard the disappointment in my voice when I called him with the news because he immediately said we could do something else. With that wonderful laughter in his voice, he said we could go dancing, look at music DVDs at his place, or perhaps do both. It was interesting how he was trying to pick up my spirits. I felt silly for a moment, behaving so immaturely. I felt let down, and it showed in ways I would have preferred to hide. I told him I would think about it and call him in the morning. I made a dish to take to Randy's place and bought wine for the meal as well. But now I was considering a way to share those things with Kojo. When I finally made up my mind, my decision was based on the venue that provided the most privacy. I wanted to be with him in a place where we could truly touch, not have sex yet, but closeness. I was okay with my dreams and fantasies, hoping that at an appropriate time, when we knew each other much better, the passion would reveal itself in powerful, real-life manifestations.

"I decided to go to his place to view music videos and would bring the dish and wine I had set aside for the original dinner. Kojo was fine with that, immediately taking charge by deciding he would pick me up that night. Further, he decided that we could plan on a dancing date before he left the city for his southern vacation. I was elated. It was freezing the night he picked me up. I felt like a school girl when he rang the doorbell for me. I was almost giddy as we walked to his car. The ride to his place was short, and his spirited laughter permeated the air. He was in great form, making jokes and offering comments of anticipatory delight about the seafood dish I prepared. When we arrived at his place, one of his daughters was there. She and her sons were cordial but not in the least bit warm. Kojo introduced me as a classmate from FAMU. I embraced his daughter warmly and gave a friendly smile to her sons. She, in turn, said in a rather cool tone, 'FAMU, well, that's a start.' I took note of her icy countenance, thinking she loves her dad and is not up for some woman coming into his life anytime soon. I was okay with that because I just wanted to get to know him better, not to muscle in on his life. I had a full life of my own, I surmised.

"Kojo's Victorian home was comfortable, handsomely furnished, and well kept. He lived alone but said he cherished having his family around him often. His grandsons were working on a project in his study and would be doing that as we watched the music videos in his music room. Yes, he had a music room with all sorts of high-tech equipment. Apparently Kojo had taken the attic of his spacious Victorian house and turned it into a spectacular music room. He gutted a wall to create a loft-like structure with high ceilings brandishing rustic rafters. African art and shelves of DVDs lined two walls from floor to ceiling, and a portable, seemingly custom made ladder rested near the DVD section of the east wall, readily perched to provide access to DVDs near the ceiling. A huge wide-screen television stood boldly in the center of the room facing the stairway, and lined up with the television was a cream-colored leather couch with four African mud cloth pillows plumped on it.

"I noticed that on the west wall, beneath the two highly placed windows, were three saxophones on elaborate racks positioned next to a keyboard and two large conga drums. Walking into the attic music room was like stepping into another world, one governed by music of all kinds. The acoustics were phenomenal, enhancing the quality of the expensive audio system. From the music room, you could look down into a spacious room that majestically evidenced a California king-size bed draped in an African mud cloth comforter, shouldering an array of pillows of a variety of shapes, sizes, and colors. At the windows, mud cloth valences brimmed off-white mini blinds, giving the room a masculine hue, and yet the elaborate off-white throw rugs brought a regal softness to the space. This room, too, showed a number of forms of African art, including masks, wall hangings, and giant wooden sculptures. I was certain it was the master bedroom and thought it was a space suited for a king. As I was processing all of this, Kojo handed me a huge flashlight and told me to explore his library of DVDs and select a couple to enjoy for the evening.

"With the delight of a child on Christmas morning and with painstaking precision, I made my choices (George Benson, Marvin Gaye, and Dave Koz). Kojo smiled when he saw them, and with seasoned adeptness placed down a tray with the food and wine I had brought to share along with bread pudding he learned to make over the Thanksgiving holiday. He did a good job of laying out the food and drink, showing adeptness for entertaining that had style.

"The DVD by George Benson was fantastic. Before long, I was caught up in the music and rapidly becoming mellow from the company and the wine. It was great sharing that experience with Kojo. It was clear he loved music because as George Benson played, his fervor was being mirrored in pantomime by Kojo. He had taken one of his saxophones from its rack and with smooth agility assumed a playing stance, casting pure vibes with Benson's musical genius. For a moment, I thought he would actually play, but he didn't. He just basked sublimely in pantomime, seemingly savoring each note. His energy was infectious. The climate in the music room was warm and rich, and I wanted to touch him. I wanted to hold him and to hear his heart beat. I think we moved on to Dave Koz when I asked him to dance. I shocked myself. It was a slow tune; I don't remember what. But he held me close, and we moved slowly to the music. His body, though lean, felt strong, connecting with me in a way that made my head spin.

"It had been years since I was held that way, and it felt so good. So I began to pat him on the back in sync with the beat of the music, seemingly sparking within both of us a clear, deep connection: his body was responding to mine! There we were doing a slow dance, patting each other comfortably as if this were a re-enactment of many years of closeness. Savoring the moment, I aggressively nestled into him, instantly recognizing the beginning of an erection. But in that moment, he pushed me away from him, saying in a staccato-like fashion, 'I can't be like Tiger Woods.' This was the year of the Tiger Woods fiasco, and everyone was talking about it. And here it was creeping into my glorious slow dance. For a moment, I was blown away by where I thought he could be heading. But I was really leveled by his candor when he told me point-blank that he had gotten involved with someone else before he met me and felt a need to honor that connection. For a moment, I felt as if I were having an out of body experience. Wind was blowing through my head, and I thought I heard a chant. I shook my head and thought: *What does he mean before he met me?* Question upon question raced through my mind and I concluded he was not being completely honest: there were pieces missing to the puzzle.

"I can't believe my ultimate reaction. Out of nowhere, my cool, rational-self showed up, and Kojo and I sat on the couch, side by side like buddies, and talked. We talked dispassionately about his newly found companion. Yet the conversation going on inside my head was heated and at times profane. He explained that his new companion is substantially younger than he, and he was surprised at her interest. But he was going for it, although he didn't know what his time away would do to their budding affair. My mind raced a mile a minute as we talked about his relationship. I realized that my suspicions about his trips having a sexual component were on target, and, thus, the salutations of 'Your brother Kojo' after each time away reflected his sexual encounters. Behind my cool demeanor lurked a rage that could have ignited a vast forest fire. I asked questions about his new companion's birthdate. He told me the month and day, but not the year. From the information he gave, I concluded that her birth sign was Leo. I asked whether she knew me, and he said, 'No, but she knows about you.' My quiet fury escalated as I intentionally turned my attention to Marvin Gaye's melodious fervor, which filled the room. Amazingly, Marvin Gaye's songful questions were on point. In order to save my sanity, I put my hand out and said, 'Let's dance.' I shocked myself again. He accommodated me and encouraged me to learn to step Chicago style. As I moved to the music, my mind was far away. I realized that this man wanted my friendship or something. I didn't know what at that point. My mind immediately went to the weekend Kojo had decided that we would go dancing. As we danced, I asked in a rather nonchalant fashion, 'Are we still going dancing on Friday night?' He answered, 'Yes, absolutely we will go dancing. That date is not negotiable.' That answer left me wondering, *What the hell is this?* But I said nothing."

Cullen coughed but said nothing. I focused intently on my friend's face, trying to get a reading of his thoughts. Before long, I returned to my story, chiding myself about being impatient while my friend tried to help me with this process of self-exploration. *I need to be patient*, I said in my head, and then turned back to my story.

"When we left his place that night, I was operating on automatic pilot. My outward demeanor was calm and personable, but inside I was a mixture of many things, including seething anger, which was directed mostly at myself. I can remember thinking no seasoned woman in her right mind would try to compete with young stuff, particularly when a man's appetite is in that direction. I've never intentionally competed for a man in my life. I never had to, I thought. It seemed immature and not ladylike to battle over a man, I told myself, and besides, I was too old for that sort of thing anyway. My mind was in the midst of mental gymnastics that had the adrenaline in my body surging to such an extent that the cold, blustery air did nothing to the heat being generated by my thoughts. When we arrived at the door of my home, Kojo gave me a big hug and then a kiss on my cheek. He said, 'Good night, sister' and watched me go in the door. I don't remember if I said anything to him in return. All I know is that I went straight to the bottle of brandy in the kitchen that had been in the cabinet for quite some time and poured a hefty drink over ice. I sat at the kitchen table and went over my evening.

"I can recall banging on the table when the memory of our exchange about the new young woman surfaced. Her youthful countenance, in my mind, was clearly overshadowing my presence in his life. I had mistakenly allowed Kojo to know that I was attracted to him. I was rather bold in my actions; but as I sat at my kitchen table, I didn't feel bold. In truth, I was ashamed of myself. Curiously, he professed his interest in the younger woman, but while we were slow dancing, his body said something else. Okay, so he didn't want to be like Tiger Woods! As I went over and over our discussion of the younger woman, I cussed out loud, recognizing that my affinity for analysis could be a pain in the ass. I reiterated words of consolation to myself, noting again that one thing I knew for sure was that there was no way in hell a seasoned woman like

59

me could compete with young stuff, particularly when a man's appetite is in that direction. I had seen Kojo lick his lips when he told me about the young woman. That was certainly not a good sign. On that note, I took a long swig from my drink of brandy and poured another.

"As I nursed my injured ego, I thought of calling either Eva or Flora or maybe both, but I ultimately decided that this would be one of those things that I would tell only to Jesus. I climbed the stairs to my bedroom, prepared for bed and deep prayer. For years, I had been fervent about my prayer rituals (in the morning and at night), and tonight I would go into crisis prayer mode. I would add a Novena to my nighttime prayer ritual."

I immediately looked at Cullen and explained, "What that means is that for nine consecutive days I would add a series of prayers to my regular prayer regimen, which would include the rosary, a very Catholic thing." With that explanation given, I moved back to my story. "As I pulled out prayer books, making my selections, I began to experience a sense of comfort. Over and over I called out to God for guidance and care, and by the time I climbed between the sheets, I was weary, but comforted. Interestingly, the next morning did not bring memories of any dreams. I rested well, and my morning prayers lifted me. I told myself repeatedly that God and I would work this out, and with that thought, I approached my work day. As I have said before, my work has seemed to save me over and over again. *Work and prayer have been coping strategies that carried me through so many things and will carry me through this,* I thought. But as I drove home from The Center that evening, I asked myself, 'What is this?' I wasn't sure. I'd opened myself up to feeling again. I'd allowed myself to feel things I hadn't let myself experience in years, and to what avail? I was uncertain of how to assess it, this risk I had taken. Mulling it in depth, I realized that although feelings of rejection didn't resonate well with me, the risk taken was not a bad thing. I consoled myself, searching for the pivotal thing to satisfy the longing within me. Once in the comfort of my home, I made my routine check of the caller ID on my telephone in the kitchen, and my heart skipped a beat when I saw there was a call from Kojo. I checked the time of the call and realized it had come at midday. I wondered why he didn't call my office and then speculated that he really didn't know my schedule. He would not have known where to reach me. I immediately pulled out my cell phone, and, yes, there was a voicemail message from him there, too. He was thanking me for a wonderful evening and hoped that I was well.

"Against my better judgment, I smiled. It was automatic, so natural. As I dialed Kojo's number, I held my breath. I wasn't sure what would happen next. His voice was booming. He called me Afua and noted that he tried to reach me earlier that day — a point I surely knew since I was giving him a return call. I chuckled at his discomfort but listened intently. He thanked me again for a wonderful evening, commenting on the food, wine, and conversation. I thanked him as well for the engaging music and conversation but said nothing about my inner turmoil. He wanted to confirm the time of our Friday outing, and with that taken care of, he wished me a pleasant evening. After I hung up the phone, I just sat for a while, feeling as if I had stepped off a very tall building and were hovering in mid-air, not certain if I would fly or fall.

"By Thursday, the day before the night of dancing, Flora called, just checking in. I knew she wanted an update on Kojo. With great tact, I let her know that we were going dancing on Friday but that he was involved with someone else, a younger woman, and he indicated it was serious. I'd never really heard Flora cuss before. I knew she was not someone to play with — a real serious sister when it came to men — but I had never heard her say a cuss word. But that night, Flora cussed, immediately begged my pardon, and then went on to ask, 'What's wrong with these brothers?' I found her indignation amusing. She was annoyed with Kojo and mentioned a deep level of disappointment in him. She had seen him as a real noble brother, in her mind representative of those deep Afrocentric brothers that she marched with in the sixties. After she stepped out of character by ranting for a while, I tried to explain that Kojo's interest in the younger woman did not necessarily mean he wasn't a noble brother or a good person. Like most men, he would probably opt for the younger, more vital woman at the stage of his development, I said pedantically. I wanted to slap myself as I pointed out vigorously that he seemed to be just stepping beyond his grief and it is easy to understand his choice at this time. Flora actually cussed again and told me in no uncertain terms that I needed to stop the social worker crap. 'The man is acting like an adolescent, and I am disappointed in him,' she said. Well, with that, I let my argument fall. There was no fight in me for that cause, though I believed what I was saying to her. When we finally said good night, I was amazed at what I learned about Flora. She told me that she had high hopes that something special would come out of my connection with Kojo. She hoped that we could restore for her a belief in Black male/female relationships. That was some real heavy stuff Flora was dishing out. I wasn't aware of how important this connection was for her. It was an interesting turn of events. As I did my nightly prayer ritual, I prayed for Flora and wondered what Eva might say about all of this."

CHAPTER 6

A Brief Pause in La Crosse

I stopped to take a breath and noticed Cullen checking his watch, an indication that perhaps we had been deeply in the throes of my story far beyond the allotted time. I said this out loud, and Cullen noted with a yawn that it was well beyond two in the morning. We had been immersed in my story for a number of hours. As the two of us agreed to pick up where we left off whenever we got up that day, I couldn't resist questioning Cullen about what he thought so far. Of course, my friend was his true self in these matters. He would not be rushed, and he let me know that quite clearly. "Relax, Jewelle," he said with a wave of his hand. "We'll tackle this thing again in the morning or whenever we find our way from the cloudiness of sleep sometime today. Sleep well, Jewelle," he said as he wandered off towards the other end of the house where he and Gahti shared a room. I watched him walk away. I had so many feelings going on inside of me. I was curious, ashamed, sad, eager, and a host of other things that I couldn't quite put my finger on. I certainly wanted my friend to help me wade through this thing with Kojo, but at the same time it felt as if I were breaking some kind of covenant, spilling all of this out in the open. I kept so much inside that I even considered the thought of betrayal as I went over in my mind what I had said so far. *Betrayal*, I thought. *Whom would I be betraying?* That question left me stumped as I found my way to one of the invitingly comfortable guest rooms.

I did a cursory form of my nightly rituals before I fell into a very deep sleep.

Interestingly, I did dream, and in the dream Kojo was pointing his finger at me in a very accusatory manner. He was mouthing something that I couldn't make out. It was all jumbled, almost as if he were speaking another language. In the dream, I felt very disconnected from Kojo, but I kept reaching for him. My hands were held out to him, beckoning him to me; yet he kept pointing at me in that accusatory way and speaking in words I couldn't understand. The dream was very disturbing, and I believe I pulled myself out of my slumber to be away from the unseemly disconnection. It felt awful! It made me feel so sad. When I sat up in the bed, it was as if I had come back from a very distant place. I was breathing heavily and felt tears on my cheeks. I got out of bed and sat by the window for a while, hoping that my dream would not keep me from returning to sleep. It began to snow again, and true to form, I became captivated by the white morsels falling from the heavens. As I watched the silent blanket of whiteness cover the walkway, I found myself praying out loud, "Gracious God! Gracious God! Give me strength and the wisdom to do your bidding." Before too long, I found my way back under the blankets and quilts. Soon I drifted to sleep, but this time to a very restful place.

It was almost 11:00 a.m. when Cullen knocked on my door, inviting me to brunch. "Jewelle, are you there?" he called playfully. Upon opening my eyes, I immediately took in the delightful aroma of very pungent coffee brewing. It smelled wonderful, welcoming. I didn't take long to do my morning rituals, including my prayers, because the wonderful smells from the kitchen were calling to me. Pena had made a beautiful table again with lively colored plates and napkins and flowers. In the dead of winter, Pena produced a table reminiscent of a bountiful spring or summer day. The food was colorful, too. Sweet potato biscuits rested aside inviting slices of avocado pear and crisp turkey bacon set beside exquisite omelets with asparagus and onions. Huge coffee mugs in a variety of colors graced the table. We each had a different color mug. Mine was green, Cullen's was blue, and Gahti's was yellow. Our juice glasses held a brilliantly inviting sparkle all of their own. We were using crystal juice glasses this morning. There were grapefruit juice, cranberry juice, and orange juice canisters on the table. The flowers in the center of the table seemed to blend in some way with everything near them. It was a beautiful sight to behold. The ambiance was warm and festive, belying the frigid scene outside. It was still snowing, and everything outside was just plain white. Gahti gave us the weather report, positing that it seemed we were experiencing one of Wisconsin's sneak snowstorms. For a moment, I wondered about the train and whether I would be stuck in La Crosse for an extra day, but that thought didn't bother me for long. I knew things would work out. It would have to be an uncommonly massive snowstorm to stop the trains from running. I smiled as I thought how great it was that I wouldn't have to worry about struggling with snow and ice on the highway. Contiguous to my thoughts, it was as if Gahti read my mind because she chimed in her ideas on the matter. "Oh, girl, aren't you glad you had the presence of mind to take the train?" she asked with an engaging smile. She had a way of lighting up a room with her energy. It was easy to see why Cullen fell for her. She has such an engaging spirit.

Our prayer over brunch mirrored the deep spiritual grandeur of the prayer we shared over dinner the night before. Cullen never prayed out loud; he just assented to Gahti's moving words of praise. With hands held tightly, we welcomed God's blessings for the day. As we prayed, I noticed that Pena stood very still with bowed head and her hands held palms up as if she were behaviorally welcoming the blessings she was certain would find their way to all of us. When the prayer was over, we all seemed to sigh in unison and dove into the scrumptious food. Gahti had so much to say about her ventures at the hospital the night before. She talked about the resilience of her patients and their families. I noticed Cullen's eyes as he looked at her. I could see the love. It was gratifying to see love exude from him. That practiced poker face of the psychiatrist did not have a place at this table.

Laughter and banter filled our time together during brunch. I felt so welcome in this place, grateful to have a friend like Cullen, and of course appreciated Gahti's understanding of our friendship. As she shooed us back into Cullen's study, she offered words of wisdom that ultimately turned out to be prophetic. She said, "You two are certainly learning quite a bit about each other this visit. I am sure this time together will be like climbing a huge mountain of near-endless mysteries. Enjoy!" She then prepared to rest a bit and return to the hospital. Pena's husband, Benny, would drive her. That was the plan after he shoveled the driveway. Pena and Benny lived on premises and handled most things for Cullen and Gahti. They are a great couple, deeply indebted to Cullen and Gahti for so much. I thought about their story and knew in my heart that God would bless this household for all of the kindness they have bestowed upon others. It had been through Cullen's connections and Gahti's prayerful urging that Pena and Benny were given an opportunity to remain in this country and ultimately work toward attaining citizenship. Pena was Mexican, though she had been raised in South Africa by an American missionary family, and Benny was from Cameroon, Africa. They were outwardly an unlikely looking couple, she massive and he very slender in stature, but their love seemed to jump out at you whenever they were together, and they were devoted to Cullen and Gahti. Over the years, Pena learned to prepare all of Gahti's favorite African dishes, and the two women seemed to dote on each other, creating a family-like bond that everyone experienced when in their presence.

Once Cullen and I found our places in the den, we recreated the ambiance of the evening before by revving up the fire in the fireplace and turning on the smooth jazz again. The brightness outside spilled into the room as Cullen opened the drapes to the massive window near his desk. The white world of snow and ice outside seemed to speak with certainty about the real world, which was starkly different from the world we were about to conjure up through my story inside the warm and colorful climate of my friend's in home office. I began again by asking Cullen what he thought so far. In response he smiled warmly and urged me to go on with my story. That is exactly what he did, but for the first time I noticed he had a small notepad before him with notes written on it.

For a moment, my mind seemed to lock as I peered at the notepad. I didn't recall seeing it the night before. I turned it over and over in my mind and was certain my friend had not taken notes last night. *That's the psychiatrist showing up,* I thought. Rather than question my friend again, I just settled in my mind that he had jotted some things down either after we left his study the night before or this morning before brunch. Perhaps he had specific questions for me that would show up throughout our time together today. With that thought, I immediately began to talk about the night of dancing.

I reflected, "I remembered the evening was bitterly cold; the temperature hovered at zero, and the wind chill factor placed the temperature at about 17 below zero. It was cold, very cold, unusually so for the month of December. I was surprised to learn that Kojo was eager to take on the challenge of the frigid weather. In fact, during the day, he called to remind me to dress warmly. His statement was friendly and nurturing. I smiled as I promised that I would dress warmly for our evening of dancing.

"Interestingly, as I made myself ready for my night out on the town, my 10-year-old grandson, Anthony, followed me from room to room asking question upon question about my night out. He was staying the night at my house while his younger sister, Ajoy, would be with her father because their mother, my daughter Lorri, had to work late. My son, Korri, would look after him at my house until I returned. Anthony's inquisitiveness was enough to wear a person out, but the nature of his questions that night truly worked my nerves. For example, when he asked me if Kojo liked me as a girlfriend, I wanted to scream at my grandson. But I didn't. I simply said, 'Kojo is my friend, and that's that'. But I am sure my voice conveyed my irritation.

"When the doorbell rang, my grandson raced to the door and had it opened before I could get there. He had invited Kojo in before I could object. There was no stopping Anthony when he set his mind to having questions answered. He introduced himself to Kojo, and they had a fine conversation about weather conditions, which was not just a platitude for my grandson. The weather and all of its mysteries were Anthony's favorite things to talk about. He actually studied the weather, attesting that he would be a meteorologist when he grew up. As I put on my coat, hat, and gloves, I had to chuckle at the ease with which Kojo conversed with my grandson. They were quite comfortable musing about the course of the frigid bout of weather we were experiencing. I could see Kojo was pleasantly surprised to find that Anthony was so versant in such matters of weather conditions around the world. I found myself wishing that the image of the two of them together could be prophetic about a family bond developing — Kojo bonding with his grandson-to-be. As that thought flew through my mind, I wanted to slap myself. I felt silly and vowed to put myself on notice again about this thing. *This is just a friendship*, I said to my heart, *nothing more than that!"*

I stopped for a long breath, looked in Cullen's direction and, without missing a beat, went on with my story. "We went dancing at a place I had heard of but had not visited before that night. It was a Caribbean club on the near east side of the city. The club was called Papa's. The aroma of Caribbean food was most inviting, and after a few minutes of taking it in, I began to ask questions about the delightful prospects attached to the smells coming from the kitchen. I was disappointed to learn that goat was their main attraction because I don't eat goat but soon quieted down when I learned that there was a fresh batch of oxtail soup just waiting to be ordered. Before long, Kojo and I sat, savoring the dishes before us. He had the curried goat, and I delved into the oxtail soup with white rice and a side order of plantains. It was wonderful. We enjoyed our food as we watched other couples dance to the calypso melodies interspersed with a bit of pop and reggae. As the evening progressed we danced a few times, but mostly we drank and talked. That night was a tequila night for him and a brandy night for me.

"Memorably, he seemed very relaxed with me that night, relaxed in the way he had been the day we spent six hours talking and discovered our respective relationships with Ken (our mutual friend from FAMU). I found myself wondering if he felt comfortable now that he had told me about the young woman. His laugh came easily, and he even touched my hands a number of times as we talked.

Once again, he talked a lot about his deceased wife and their life together. He talked about her with such tenderness. It was clear that he loved her deeply, and I respected that. I empathized with him. He shared a lot about the fun times he and his wife experienced. They had traveled throughout the world, and it was obvious he still had a lot of pain simmering within about her death. It was the way he asked the question 'Why her and not me?' that made me realize that he'd been locked up for many years in his grief and still had many steps to take before he could let himself move beyond it. I felt so close to him as he expressed his grief. I wanted to hold him and comfort him, but I just listened.

"The evening was comfortable, and time flew by. It was well after 1:00 a.m. when we decided to head home, both of us feeling no pain. For a moment, I felt hopeful again about our connection, and then his cell phone rang. I could tell he was a bit uncomfortable as he looked at the number. I looked away, certain that my eyes would make the cell phone explode if I set my gaze upon it. I was enraged by this intrusion and wanted to yell that loudly. But, of course, the rational me came out of nowhere, and even though she was a bit hazed by the brandy, she set me straight. I remained outwardly calm and unruffled but seething to the bone.

"At my front door, Kojo again gave me a big hug and a generous kiss on the cheek. I forced a smile and a deeply felt 'Thank you.' As I turned to walk in the door, he said, 'I will call you when I get on the road next week.' He was reminding me that his arrangements in Key West had worked out and he would be driving to his family in Lexington, Kentucky for the Christmas holidays and then on to Key West by New Year's. His reminder really did jar my memory. I brought him a gold-plated butterfly, one from my collection that had at one time hung on a chain around my neck. I gave it to him right then for good luck, and he smiled. I thanked him again for a lovely evening and went into the house and to the kitchen to have one more brandy before I went to do my nightly rituals. To my surprise, my grandson came running down the stairs. He'd been waiting up for me and tagged along as I gathered myself in preparation for my nighttime rituals. I thanked my son for keeping an eye on Anthony, but he seemed concerned about my taking another drink. 'You are going to have another one?' he asked, heading out the back door. I didn't respond, but I did think about his question.

"In many ways, I was fit to be tied. On the one hand, it was clear that Kojo enjoyed talking with me. He said many times that he liked my mind and that I made him think. He made a point of saying that he talked to me about things he didn't share with other people. In those instances, I knew he was being genuine and that he felt a connection, too, but that was the end of it. He was connected to my mind, it seemed, and would hold on to the friendship for that reason. *Damn*, I thought, *this is not how I wanted things to be*. My grandson wanted to snuggle next to me that night, insisting he missed me so much that he needed to make up for lost time. I didn't mind a bit. It felt good to be needed by someone, and I was not bothered by his incessant chatter about all the new information he learned about weather systems. After my prayer rituals and the prayers we said together, I let him talk me to sleep. We dozed almost in unison and ultimately rested well.

"The following morning, I didn't expect the phone call from Kojo that pulled me out of my deep slumber. When I heard his voice, my eyes flew open, and I sat straight up in bed. He was calling, he said, to say 'Thank you' for a lovely evening and to check on how I was doing after so much brandy. Of course, he said all of this with that forever-engaging laugh that stirred my heart so much. I sighed deeply as I wondered about our 'friendship.' I don't think I said much because I was rather enthralled with the possibilities again. He was acting the way I would expect my man to act after a pleasant evening. It really felt good. Once I signed off from our conversation, I headed directly to the bathroom and then to the computer. I chuckled, realizing that I had completed the conversation with him without having to interrupt it by racing to the bathroom for my early morning release. That was a near miracle because since menopause had raised its challenging head, my early morning bathroom visits were like clockwork upon opening my eyes. This morning was something different. The thought of that coupled with the unexpected phone call made me smile. My smile broadened when I saw the email from him. In it, he thanked me again for a wonderful evening and promised again to be in touch next week when he got on the highway. My whole body seemed to be smiling when my grandson woke up and asked for breakfast.

"I was certain Kojo did not count on the snowstorm that hit Milwaukee the day he planned to leave the city. Almost 14 inches of snow covered us. The schools were closed, and everything seemed to have come to a stop. Many people in the school system were upset about having to shut the schools down so close to the holiday break, but it had to be done, and in a way things were very festive. Christmas was in the air, and the snow made it seem real. By midday, I wondered if Kojo had ventured on his way south, and I called him to see. As always, he was very gracious when he answered his phone. He was near Gary, Indiana, having left home about six hours before, a rather slow start, but he was pleased just the same. The roads were getting better as he moved south. He made a point of letting me know that he had the butterfly I had given him hanging on the visor of his car. He thanked me again for the gift and noted that he would keep it in a special place. We talked for a few more minutes, his Bluetooth serving its purpose. I can't remember what we talked about. All I can remember is that I felt warm inside and very hopeful. I prayed for his safety and hoped for all good things possible. Once again I was feeling things that I never thought I would feel again after my husband's death. For a moment, I forgot all about the younger woman and basked in the possibilities again. I did not let the rational part of myself surface. She had no place that day or in many of the days that followed. I was caught up again."

Hearing myself say these words, I looked in Cullen's direction, and he was true to form, virtually expressionless; but at this point, my own words pissed me off. So much had happened since the wonder of those moments of the snowstorm and the engaging telephone conversations. I felt foolish, even a bit ashamed of myself. I wondered if I had been desperate. I wondered if I had misread his behavior, if he had been manipulative and conniving, or if he was caught in his own dilemma in the midst of his recovery from grief.

My mind raced for a minute, and then I told myself that my friend would help me understand. He would put a frame around this thing and help me find a healthy perspective. He would ultimately be brutally blunt — that was his way. He would be on point, and I'd be ready to heal and to grow past this thing. He would help me make sense out of all of the uncanny connections across the years. I breathed deeply and pushed myself onward with the story. *I have to get this all out*, I thought. I needed to hear myself say it all, even the feelings I had not let be said out loud. *I need to hear it and I need Cullen to hear it*, I thought. It was time to put it all out there and be vulnerable to someone else's scrutiny. Yet, I would not talk about the recurrent dream that had plagued me over the years. Right at the moment, a mournful Billie Holiday song flowed through the air from Cullen's sound system, and I felt tears roll down my cheeks. My eyes flooded as Billie Holiday sang the blues. My friend handed me some tissue, but his expression did not change. I sobbed and cussed and prayed all at once. I hoped God understood this odd lamentation. I knew my friend would help me put all of this pain in perspective. I just knew, as Eva had opined early on, there was a lesson for me in all of this. There had to be!

CHAPTER 7

A Breakthrough in La Crosse

I stumbled through my tears and returned to the story. "The week between the holidays seemed to move quickly. Kojo called Christmas morning to extend his greetings and to chat for a while, but I didn't hear from him again until December 29th when he was traveling to Miami to visit a friend, stopping briefly before he headed to Key West for the New Year's Eve celebration there. I had encouraged him to get to Key West in time for New Year's Eve, noting that it would be a time he would not forget. New Year's Eve in Key West, as I remembered it, even from childhood, was a jubilant time with dancing in the street and a lot of merrymaking. People came from far and wide to be in the Mallory Square area of Key West on New Year's Eve. Embracing my recommendation heartily, Kojo expected to arrive in Key West on the evening of December 30th, giving himself time to get comfortable in his new dwelling before the big, festive night. With anticipation, we talked at length the evening of the 29th. On a whim, I decided to call him early on the 30th only to find that he couldn't wait to get on the road and was already heading to Key West hours ahead of schedule.

"We talked long-windedly as he glided over bridge after bridge, his Bluetooth phone continuing to make our conversation legal. He shared the grandeur of his view as he embraced the beauty of the Upper Keys. He saw miniature deer and began to encounter quite a bit of traffic moving towards Key West, and we mused that it was a parade of folks coming in to celebrate New Year's Eve. It was great carrying on such a conversation with him. I felt so connected to him, which he seemed to experience as well because at one point he just came out and said, 'You know you are special to me, Afua.' When he called me by my African name, I just melted inside. This level of contact felt so right, and I was having trouble remembering that he had told me he was involved with someone else. I began to believe that this was not just a friendship thing.

"When Kojo was about 12 miles from Key West, we hung up. I had errands to run. With hesitancy, I signed off from him, yet with a song in my heart. I had told a few relatives in Key West about his visit and asked that they show him a level of hospitality appropriately due one of my friends. Of course, people had questions, but I insisted that he was just a friend, holding on to the hope that one day I would be able to tweak that just a bit to call him something more than that. Of course, my cousin Vy knew the whole story and would be keeping an eye out for all things of interest.

"Kojo and I talked briefly during the day of New Year's Eve. I called to let him know that just as I had attended midnight Mass on Christmas Eve at the Catholic church where all of my children had been baptized, tonight I would attend the Watch Night service at the Baptist church near my home; I didn't know of any Catholic churches in the area that observed Watch Night. Kojo had many questions, and I explained that I found it freeing to be able to participate in the traditional rituals of many religious denominations. I loved midnight Mass, mainly because it reminded me of my childhood coupled with the years my own children were young. Back then, we attended midnight Mass as a family. Over the years, I learned the history behind Watch Night and loved Watch Night service for its historic significance to Black people — the services in Black churches on that night commemorated the night the slaves waited for slavery to end. It was a special time of testimonials of challenges overcome and reasons for hope to which I had been introduced in my adulthood. Both services touched me deeply on a spiritual level. I let him know that I would not be home until well after midnight just in case he would call. At that point,

I was feeling very connected to him again, and no one could have convinced me that there were not good possibilities to the future of our relationship. I didn't know then what was unfolding.

"I lifted my hands in praise during the Watch Night service. I sang and cried along with others in the congregation. I was in a sea of praising Black people, and it was a spiritual time in that church. The presence of God filled me. The minister preached from Isaiah, calling for people to let go of the past and to embrace the new. 'Behold. God is doing a new thing. Can't you see it?' he asked over and over again. As he worked that text, his words seemed to penetrate my soul. I prayed for the strength to embrace whatever new thing God was doing within me. At the end of the service, I was greeted by many people I knew. It was great being caught up in a sea of well-wishers. I felt so blessed. The air was very brisk when I left the church. There was a song in my heart which I hummed as I gingerly handled my car, taking special pains to glide safely over the icy roads. 'Thank you, God,' I sang loudly as I pulled into my garage. I was glad to be alive.

"I bypassed the phone in the kitchen, thinking I would take off my clothes and get comfortable for bed. But when I made it up the stairs to my bedroom, I immediately checked my caller ID to see if Kojo had called. I intentionally did not have voicemail at home. I had a thing about having to handle messages at home. I had too much to address in my work situation and did not need another venue to manage. Thus, no voicemail, but caller ID. There wasn't a call from him noted on the house phone, and I don't know what made me check my cell phone because he seldom called me on it. But I checked it anyway. To my delight, there was a message from him. He was singing to me, 'Happy New Year to you. Happy New Year to you.' I think my face must have lit up like the Christmas tree downstairs in my living room. I was so touched by his sensitivity and affection. I was smitten, and there wasn't a thing I could do about it. For some reason I didn't call him back. I just savored his phone call.

"In the late afternoon on New Year's Day, Kojo and I talked for quite a while. He had so much to tell me about his adventures on

New Year's Eve, and of course I wanted to hear about every minute of his fun. I was feeling closer and closer to him. He talked about the food, the dancing, and the laughter. He met people from all over, including Wisconsin: a White couple vacationing in the Upper Keys. They, of course, had heard about the jubilant times to be had in Key West on New Year's Eve and drove down for the fun. Along with a gay couple from New Jersey, they and Kojo joined the Junkanoo parade that danced all over the city, including in Bahama Village where most of Key West's Black population lived. Kojo danced past the house he was renting and got a big kick out of seeing many of his new neighbors standing on their porches and at their windows moving with the music. He was surprised to see how many Whites are now living in the area of Bahama Village as well. We talked about issues of gentrification and a host of other sociopolitical issues related to the plight of Black people in Key West, and I think we both felt good about our time together on the phone. I know I did. I felt as if there were a good reason to look hopefully towards the New Year.

"I didn't hear from Kojo for a few days and didn't think much about it. I had some work to do around the house before I returned to The Center and kept myself busy with that. This part of the New Year was always full of planning. I set my appointment book up for the year, scheduling significant events and the regular anger management groups as well. I was very hopeful about the New Year when I got the call from Kojo that Thursday evening. He had so much to say about his adventures and the people he was meeting, including a couple of my cousins, who invited him to dinner. He hadn't heard from my cousin Vy yet but expected to call her about a few tourist things he had in mind. We talked about so many things, and then he said the thing that made my stomach turn. He called me by my African name, Afua, and said in a nonchalant way, 'I will be driving up to Ft Lauderdale on Friday. I will return the following day.' For a moment, my heart stopped because I knew what quick turnaround trips to Ft. Lauderdale meant. Usually, people could get cheaper flights into Ft. Lauderdale than into Key West, and folks would just drive the four hours or so up the road to pick up their visitors, saving quite a bit of money. I didn't ask the question. I just had the overwhelming feeling that the woman he had spoken about was flying in to be with him. For a moment I thought my head would explode, but I said nothing about his trip. I let him talk about other things, though I was certainly less involved in what he had to say than usual. Before long we hung up. I detected a bit of distance in his voice and was annoyed.

"For the rest of the day I was upset about our conversation, but I kept telling myself a number of discordant things. In truth, I was arguing with myself. On the one hand, I kept saying, 'You don't know that he is going up to Ft. Lauderdale to meet her,' and on the other hand I sternly chastised myself about being concerned at all: 'You know this man is involved with another woman, a younger one at that. Stop your foolishness and leave this thing alone.' I went back and forth all day. It was Thursday, and he would be going to Ft. Lauderdale on Friday. I don't remember exactly what I was doing when the thought hit me that I knew who the younger woman was. I don't know why I hadn't considered it before, but in a flash the image of the beautiful, stately bartender from the club at Bay Shore Mall came to mind. *She is younger,* I thought, *probably in her early to mid-forties.* I would not think she had made 50 yet, but I didn't know.

"I allowed the memory of one of the times we had sat for hours nursing our wine and in deep conversation. Kojo went to the bar often that evening and in one instance had been very playful with her. I remember thinking that he was stepping over a line, but she didn't appear to mind, and of course he and I, at that point, were just getting to know each other. As I reflected, I wondered why this memory popped in my head, and as I turned it over in my mind, I came up with a way to find out if the waitress/bartender was the younger woman in his life. He told me her birth month and day, but not the year. She was a Leo, August 10th. I decided that I would go to the club and engage her in conversation. I would somehow find out her birthdate, and then I would know for sure whom this man was venturing out of his grief to be with. I thought deeply about my plan and realized that I had no idea about her work schedule.

I thought back to the evenings we had sat for hours talking in the club, and she was there on only a few of those evenings. I racked my brain to remember the days and finally settled on Thursday and Friday.

"I was beside myself with excitement because, as I reflected further, I would need to go there immediately. It was Thursday, after all. Friday night could be too late if she would be going down to the Keys. I quickly checked the clock, changed my clothes, put some money in my purse along with my credit cards, and just about raced out of the house. I couldn't believe what I was about to do. As I drove to the mall, I wondered if she would remember me. I intentionally wrapped my head in a colorful scarf, African style, which I hoped would alter my persona a bit; I had never worn a head-wrap in that place with Kojo. The moment I entered the club, I saw her. She was at her regular post behind the bar and was engaged in banter with the other bartender, a young White girl. There weren't many people in the club; a few couples seemed to be enjoying a meal, and there was one guy at the bar who appeared to have had quite a bit to drink because he was singing along with a Whitney Houston song. I made my way to the bar and sat directly in front of the woman in question. I smiled broadly and said, 'Riesling, please.' She smiled in return but barely glanced my way. She moved with a sense of confidence and seemed very sure of herself. I looked her over from head to toe. She was tall, slender, and very fair-skinned with long, flowing hair. The only physical flaw I noted was in her smile. She had a slight gap in the front of her mouth. I suppose some people might think of it as cute, but I saw it as a flaw and wondered why she hadn't had it fixed. Everything else about her seemed fashionable. It seemed odd to me that she hadn't taken the time to have her teeth fixed.

"When she presented me with my wine, she smiled again but didn't have anything to say. So I started the conversation. I asked about the bowling alley adjacent to the club, and she gave me a lot of information about that, including her feelings about the under-age young people who came to bowl and then tried to get drinks from the bar. We talked about young people and how things have changed over the years. She didn't seem to recognize me. I asked how long she had been working there, and she said a little more than a year. This was her second job. During the day, she worked for a major law firm as an executive assistant. She'd been working at the firm for nearly 20 years and loved her work. Interestingly, she became very talkative, explaining that she had gotten into bartending and waitressing on a whim, which turned out to be fairly lucrative. She was working the second job to put money aside for traveling. She loved to travel, genuinely planning to take exotic vacations to places such as Dubai. I couldn't believe this sister; she surely had expensive taste.

"Over two glasses of Riesling, I learned that she was divorced with two adult children, a daughter at Hampton University and a son in the army, currently somewhere in the middle east. I remarked that she must have been a young mother, hoping she would spill her age, but she didn't. She did say that she married young and had been divorced for many years, volunteering with a wink that she was looking for a man of means who could help fulfill her dreams of travel and the good life. When she said that I laughed, and she did, too. I returned her wink, thinking at that point that she was a piece of work, for sure. She went on to divulge that she didn't think very highly of men. She didn't trust them because she had had her fill of promises that turned out to be nothing. As we talked, she became brash in her presentation. She appeared to have deep-seated negative feelings towards men. With that thought in mind I took the leap and asked, 'So you're not seeing anyone right now?' She laughed and responded, 'Yeah, sort of,' but she didn't go further because two customers came to the bar and she sauntered towards them to do her job.

"I sat and watched her interact with the two men who were new patrons. She was flirtatious and very engaging in her manner. Perhaps it was a way to get tips and sell drinks, but I chose to see her at that moment as a floozy. One of the guys was a very dark-skinned brother, and he seemed to fall off the bar stool each time she came near him. He just grinned and looked at her like she was better than light bread. I wanted to throw up. I tried to figure out how I would raise the question of the birthdate, and before too long I decided to do it as I paid for my drinks. I motioned for her to join me and asked for my bill while saying, 'You operate like a Leo. I bet you were born under the sign of Leo and you are probably an August Leo rather than one born in July 'cause you got style.' Well, that did it. She laughed out loud, saying, 'What did you say your name is?' I hadn't expected that, but I responded with a sense of ease that I really didn't feel at the moment: 'People call me Shug.' I pulled that name from my past. It had served me well at one time in my life, and I believed it was fitting for this occasion. She put out her hand and said, 'Shug, I am Charice, and you just hit a bullseye. I am a Leo, and I was born on August 10th. How did you know that?' she asked, eyeing me curiously.

"She was full of laughter as she took center stage now behind the bar, calling attention to herself, heralding the fact that I had just guessed her birth sign and nearly guessed her birthdate. She strutted just a bit, swinging her hips rather evocatively, really putting on quite a show for the patrons who were interested already. The two guys with whom she had been carrying on yelled down the bar to me, 'Can you do us? What is my sign?' The dark-skinned brother chimed, 'I want to know if this fine sister and I are compatible,' while reaching across the bar to kiss her on her cheek. I wanted to spit on all of them. I was disgusted with this episode. I got what I came for, and I was seething inside. I ignored the man's question, paid the bill in cash (realizing that my credit card would blow Shug's cover), and threw a tip on the bar in Charice's direction before exiting. As I walked through the mall to the parking lot, I cussed under my breath while thinking Kojo deserved whatever this bitch had in store for him. That was not a proud moment for me.

"Once in the parking lot, I called Eva. I had to tell somebody about this experience and chose Eva, my very light-skinned friend with whom I tried to work on the feelings I had been harboring for years. Perhaps because of her unusual world consciousness, Eva was willing to talk things through with me. Throughout the years, she helped me with this issue of light-skinned versus dark-skinned entitlement. We'd never really gotten into the age issue at all, seeing that she is 10 years my senior, but I felt confident that she would be open to exploring this experience with me. We settled into a close friendship, though she could pass for a Caucasian if she were so inclined to do so. In fact, she was a mulatto, hailing from a light-skinned African-American father and a Caucasian-like Cuban mother. I had seen pictures of Eva in her young years, and she had long, flowing black hair just like the waitress. Now 73, she wore a close-cropped haircut, and her hair was entirely white. I knew my friend would be there for me, whatever that meant. After I dialed her number, I stilled myself trying to prepare for what would probably come out of her mouth. When she answered, I actually had second thoughts about having made the call. Of course, in her very annoying way, she had a host of 'What if's' that just made the situation worse. 'What if this is just a coincidence?' she asked. 'What if she tells Kojo you quizzed her?' She had question after question, but I didn't care about any of that. I just could not believe that Kojo actually hooked up with someone he met while he was with me. Or had it happened that way?

"I thought he told me that he met her before we met. I was so mad I could hardly drive home. I promised Eva that I would not jump to conclusions, but deep down inside I knew Charice was the one. I would come back to the mall on Friday to be sure she was not at work, and then I would be sure that she was the one flying to Ft. Lauderdale to be with Kojo. *Damn!* This was truly too much for the blood pressure! Here it was again, me losing to a light-skinned woman, and this time she was a double whammy. Not only is she a vanilla flavor; she's also young. And I knew better than to try to compete with young stuff, especially when the man's appetite is in that direction. As I drove home, I came up with a number of ways to cross-validate my findings of the evening. Before long, I was absolutely certain that I would know who was down in Key West with Kojo. I would know without having to ask him. I would know, and he wouldn't know that I knew. My thoughts made me feel silly. What in the hell was I doing?

"I didn't call Kojo that night. But I heard from him early Friday morning. He called to say he had been thinking about me and that he wanted to touch base before he left for his trip. I was gracious but weighed his words carefully. I was pretty sure he was calling me to be certain I heard from him, hoping that I would not call after he connected with his woman. Well, if we were just friends, why wouldn't he just tell me that this woman was coming to town? I thought about this a bit more and decided that he really didn't know how to handle this situation. He was playing it by ear.

"That Friday evening I couldn't wait. I went to the mall and directly to the club: Charice was not there. I spoke with the young White female bartender. She told me her name was Niki, and she was very friendly. She greeted me warmly, remarking about the uncanny way I had come up with Charice's birth sign. She remembered me. She had been there the night before but mostly in the background. I laughed with her, assuring her that it was just a wild guess. I was rather forceful in my presentation, hoping she would accept that there was nothing special about the way I came up with Charice's particulars. When I was finally able to move her past the birth sign tangent, she told me that Charice had gone to Florida and would be away for 10 days. I laughed with her about how lucky Charice appeared to be, but I really wanted to throw glasses at the mirrors, and perhaps even a few chairs would help me vent. I ordered a glass of Riesling just out of courtesy and left as soon as I gulped it down. As I left, I thought I should have had a shot or two of brandy. I called Eva to report my latest news, and finally she accepted that perhaps I was on to something. This time, though, she had a different kind of thing going on. It was about the lesson in this for me. She said, 'Pull back, Jewelle, and find your lesson in this. It is all about lessons. You know that.'

"I hung up on Eva at that point because I was tired of lessons and wanted to think about where I had put Bird Lady's phone number. I was about to go to plan B, and to do that I would need to connect with Bird Lady, whom I hadn't talked to for quite a while. Bird Lady was an elderly woman from Canada who had been coming to Key West for more than 25 five years to paint all kinds of birds, including roosters. She and my mother were fast friends, even up to my mother's death. Bird Lady was the name

Key West folks had given her because people came from all walks of life to buy her very colorful paintings of birds. She had given me a large painting of a magnificent rooster for my wedding, and we talked from time to time, usually when she would call me. Her winter home was located directly across the street from the place Kojo would be renting. Her son lived in the house year round, she was a very happy snowbird. She would be there now and would certainly answer any questions I would have about the people across the street. I had to find her number."

I was caught up in the energy of my story. Emotion stirred within me. For a moment I stopped, took a long breath, glanced at Cullen, and then returned to the pathos oozing under the words, revealing what I wanted Cullen to assess. I poured the details out for Cullen: "Frantically I tore my house up looking for Bird Lady's number. A large part of the problem was I had been calling her Bird Lady for so long that I had forgotten her actual last name. I knew her first name was Gladys, but that was all I remembered. Finally, I gave in and called my sister-in-law down in Key West, and she was able to help me with the last name: it was Chopin. She and my brother were friendly with Bird Lady and her son for quite a while but didn't have her number. I didn't want to call my brother's home about this because I was trying to keep him out of this part of my life. Emory had been his good friend, and after his death, my brother seemed to think I should just be satisfied being a mother and grandmother. I finally put my hand on Bird Lady's number. I was unable to get it through directory assistance because it was unlisted. After much searching, I found it in a most unlikely place, on the appraisal that accompanied the painting she gave me as a wedding gift. As I jotted the information into my current address book, I thought about my children and their prized telephones. They seemed to keep everything in their phones. Well, I was certain I would never get that comfortable with technology. I could not imagine keeping so many important things in my telephone.

"I felt pleased with myself once I found the number, a sense of mastery. I had been a fine detective over the past few days and would be on top of things to the end. Kojo would not know what hit him. For a moment, a cold chill came over me as I processed a rather foreboding thought. *What if Gladys Chopin, the Bird Lady, had passed away? Wow,* I thought, *that would be a catastrophe,* but somehow I would muster the courage to draw her son into my little cloak-and-dagger thing. He was always up for a few dollars. My only fear would be that he'd likely try to see if Kojo would be willing to pay more to keep information from me. Bird Lady's son was a character. I found myself praying that Bird Lady was still alive, well, and in Key West. I was so ashamed of myself for all of my self-involved thoughts, but I just kept going with my cloak-and-dagger plans.

"I didn't hear from Kojo on Saturday or Sunday. By Sunday evening, I called Bird Lady, and in a perky voice she actually answered the phone. We talked for quite a while about her work and newsworthy items in Key West before I moved on to the real deal. She laughed when I asked her a few questions about the visitor across the street. She already had met him and shown him some of her paintings. Her son, of course, secured some information for her, namely that the man across the street was a friend of mine. Bird Lady laughed as she said the thing that put the icing on the cake for me. 'I was hoping for you, girly,' she said, 'but I see he's got a woman, a young model-looking woman. I saw her for the first time yesterday.' I took a deep breath and let my mind settle on knowing what was going on. I felt a sense of power right at that moment, and I let that feeling override everything else. As I signed off from Bird Lady, I mentioned that I might call again. Her words were so profound. 'You call as often as you need to, girly. Your mom is right here in spirit, and she's looking out for you, too.' She seemed so certain about what she was saying, as if deep down she knew what my hopes were for Kojo. I chuckled as I hung up the phone. Kojo didn't know what he was up against. I had eyes everywhere. For some reason, that gave me enough peace to sleep very well that night.

"For nine more days, Kojo didn't call, and I didn't call him. During this time, I experienced just about every emotion possible, but I went to work and handled my business day in and day out. I made one more call to Bird Lady, and she had a lot to report. She told me that Kojo and his woman had bought a bunch of fish and shrimp from one of the well-known Key West fishermen. And she told me that she had seen his woman sitting on the porch in a bikini a couple of times. She finished her report by noting that Kojo was very friendly, spending a number of mornings talking with her at her front gate and quizzing her about various tourists' ventures. She had grown to like him, but his woman was not friendly at all. I think I got the final report from Bird Lady on the evening of the ninth day. I was full of information and all of the thoughts attendant to her report by the time Kojo did call. I had not heard from him for too long and was seething but worked very hard to remain cool. Curiously, he had not contacted my cousin Vy, but she had heard about his guest.

"In truth, an odd element in his voice the night he called sounded like guilt or something akin to it. He had quite a bit to say about his trip up to Ft. Lauderdale and his friend in Miami. I was the one who could not contain myself. A few minutes into the conversation, I simply blurted out, 'If we are just friends, why haven't you told me you had a guest?' There was a long silence at first, but he fell into the conversation skillfully. He didn't miss a beat, seeming to overlook the tone of my voice. He told me he had a guest and that they had tried many of Key West's famous dishes, including souse made by Ms. Bertha. He talked on and on about the various things he and his guest had done. At one point, his chatter had a nervous quality to it, but all in all, he did a fine job of sharing, just as if he were talking with his good friend. I wanted to yell cuss words in his ear but didn't. I simply said her name, Charice, and there was silence again. I knew that had taken him by surprise, and I was pleased. I went on to say, 'You could have told me that you were dating the bartender/waitress from the mall. I see you like your women as you do your alcohol, truly diverse.' With that, I said, 'Goodnight' and hung up. I was on the verge of tears, but defiantly, I wouldn't let myself cry.

"When the phone rang almost immediately after I hung it up, I knew it was him, and I hesitated but picked it up anyway. His voice sounded concerned. I could hear it. It seemed genuine, and I listened as he reminded me that we were friends and that he told me that he was involved with someone. He went on to say that he cherished our friendship and hoped that I understood where he was coming from and could continue to be his friend. He talked more and more about something special we would do together as friends, something very important, but he wasn't quite sure yet what. He had been told by the ancestors that our friendship was no accident, but we are to be just friends at this time. As he talked, my tears finally began to flow, and I just listened. I don't think he knew I was crying, but I am not sure. I was so sad inside but couldn't hang up. I felt so connected to him and knew he felt connected to me. I didn't understand it, but I listened to him as he talked to me about our pure friendship being directed by some kind of destiny. As I listened to him, I was having another conversation in my head with God. *Why just a friend, God*? I asked. *When is it my time to have someone love me again?* I thought about Ms. Ella and disappointment engulfed me."

I hadn't realized as I was sharing this part of the story that I was sobbing. I must have been crying for a while because the front of my blouse was wet and my nose had begun to run. Owning the wealth of emotion this part of the story evoked seemed to send me into some kind of momentary hysteria because I began to sob and lament in a way that seemed foreign to me. *Who is this person?* I thought. With the swiftness of a cat, Cullen moved from behind his desk to my side, seizing what appeared to be a fertile clinical moment, seemingly drawn by my uncommonly expressive emotional state. He began to say in a nearly-inaudible chant, "Express your feelings. Release your feelings, Jewelle. See yourself on the screen as if you are in a movie. Better still, who would you have play you in this movie? Who?", my friend whispered in my ear as he held my shoulders, and curiously I remembered at that moment that in medical school he had done a rotation with a protégé of the father of psychodrama. I tried to remember his mentor's name, but could not. I did remember that over the years the crafty Dr. Cullen had fashioned his own brand of psychodrama therapy techniques and the psychiatrist in him was very present in that moment.

Before I knew it, I closed my eyes and screamed, "Loretta Devine, Loretta Devine!"

"Then see her as you playing this role now. Be her, let her be you, and give her the words," Cullen commanded. Magically, I could see Loretta Devine sobbing jarringly. She was wearing a wrinkled black dress and seemed angry and sad and afraid all at once. She fell to her knees and began to scream repeatedly. I could hear the screams, and I could hear her ask "Why?" over and over again as places in my body began to come alive with feelings. She called out to God, and I could hear parts of my life come out of Loretta Devine's mouth. She called my pain by name as her body writhed in the throes of each emotional trauma: the drunken battles of my first marriage, the sting of academia's pungent racism, the duplicitousness and sexism in the professional world, the smell of my deceased husband's declining toileting ability, death and pain again and again. I saw my children, and they did not appreciate me! I could see Loretta grab at her heart, and my hands found their way to my chest, too. I could barely breathe, and then I heard it: that guttural, raw, primitive, animal-like sound. It was a screech, a howl, a primal call to God. I heard it, and Loretta rolled over on her side, struggling to stay away from that awful place that fed long-ago horrible memories and the recurrent dream.

I knew the sound had come from me, from a place so distant and yet deep within me, a place so intimate with my soul. Soon, the faces of every man I ever cared about danced before me, and Loretta called them by name as she cried. When Kojo's face appeared, I closed my eyes, but Loretta saw him and called his name. The soliloquy went on and on with childhood haunts and pains I had forgotten, and yet they paraded themselves and were called by name. Still, the thunderous purge slipped past elusive, shame-filled hidden places. There were doors that still would not open, but I could feel the presence of their secrets and sank deeper into my tears.

I don't know how long Loretta commanded her post or how I came to be so wet. I never knew tears could soak you through and through, but when I came to myself, I knew my tears and sweat had partnered in hydrating my soul. I was wet and limp, and both Cullen and Gahti were with me on the floor of Cullen's in home office. Gahti had tears, and Cullen seemed exceptionally poised. They had wrapped me in afghans and had a steaming cup of tea waiting for me. Gahti was the first to speak. "Allow yourself to rest in God's grace and receive many miracles," she said. Cullen just smiled. Finally, he said, "Jewelle, my friend, this has been a long time coming. You can finally receive now and move to a different level." In deep thought, he said, "There is more to get at, but for now many blocked feelings and emotions are out of the way." I was too weak to ask questions. I took the cup of steaming tea from Gahti and sipped quietly. Though I was soaked, I felt lighter somehow. I kept thinking about Loretta Devine and soon felt a smile come over me. With a lifted spirit, I fell into a deep sleep.

I don't know what was in the tea concoction Gahti made, but it certainly was a powerful potion in concert with my super cathartic release. I slept deeply and had the most intriguing dream. In the dream, Kojo led me into a dense forest. He held my hand tightly until we reached the deepest part of the woods, where the lushness of the trees and vines almost hid the starlit sky. It was quiet and dark, and before long Kojo disappeared. I was alone and afraid. I turned around in a circle, calling for him. In the dream, I could feel my tears, and with a sudden, almost startling movement, I was magically lifted upon the back of a fast-moving horse by a Native American bareback rider. I had seen him before! He had lightning bolts across his face and only one feather in his headband. I could smell his sweat and feel his muscle-ridden, clammy body. He was chanting a word over and over again as we moved swiftly through the forest. I hugged him tightly as I rested my head between his damp shoulders. We surged like the wind. I looked up and could see the stars and the moon as we moved at a pace that seemed to defy reality. The rippling muscles of his back were welcoming, the closeness of him fulfilling. "Who are you?" I asked again and again. He did not answer, but somehow, deep inside, I knew. We rode and rode as he chanted for miles and miles. Finally, light broke through the trees, and we raced over barren terrain, which soon led to the side of a mountain that finally morphed into a huge, chiseled figure.

Once I was able to focus clearly, I realized where I was. The warrior helped me dismount and in a flash was gone. He did not ride away; he just vanished. In awe of the majesty of the figure looming above me, I bowed and breathed a breath of amazement. I heard the word "Come" booming from the majestic figure of Chief Crazy Horse, which is being honed out of the side of a mountain. I knew I was in South Dakota standing before Chief Crazy Horse's mountain. I felt invigorated, very much alive. In my dream, he was calling me.

The afternoon sun shook me from my reverie. I had fallen asleep on the lush carpet in Cullen's study, and he and Gahti elected to let me rest there. As I sat up and assessed my circumstances, my dream was fresh in my thoughts. It was so vivid, so real. I could feel myself smiling as I played and replayed the word "Come" that boomed from the mountainous majestic figure. I thought more and more about the warrior chief who I believe had brought me to himself. I had seen him before years ago. As in this dream, he had shown up, back then as an answer to a prayer. I must have been deep in thought when Gahti beckoned me to brunch. "You were sleeping so well," she said, smiling broadly. "We decided to just let you rest here. It is good you are awake now. Come eat with us." In return, I said something about the potent tea concoction, and we both laughed as I headed to the washroom to get cleaned up for brunch. While viewing myself in the mirror, it came to me that I had not done my usual prayer ritual the night before or this morning. I had been exhausted the night before and only uttered a single prayer for guidance before sleep had usurped my power. Thinking about my prayer rituals, I decided I would double up on my prayers tonight, and with that resolute promise, I turned my thoughts to the smells coming from the kitchen. They were engaging me, and I was hungry.

After Gahti blessed the table, Cullen pulled out a part of the Milwaukee Daily newspaper which he had delivered to his home and handed it to me. I almost choked on my coffee when I saw the large picture of Chief Crazy Horse's Monument. The *Milwaukee Paper* was doing a story on the development of the structure that had been in process for more than 60 years. I took a deep breath and allowed emotionally laden words to spill from me, words that described my dream of the night before. Gahti clapped her hands joyfully, stating, "There you have it. It is confirmation. There is a deep message in your dream for you Jewelle. I believe dreams have a prospective value. Perhaps you are to go to South Dakota," she chimed. Calmly Cullen shared his thoughts, "Interesting, very interesting. Certainly there appears to be synchronicity in this situation," he posited. As they mused on and on, I sat quietly. I was almost immobilized by the pregnant nature of this experience. I knew that this was more than coincidence, and the thought of what it could mean left me awe struck. The intrigue and the possibilities were overwhelming. Gradually we gave our full attention to the delicious food before us. After we enjoyed another fabulous brunch, Cullen and I returned to the study. This time his step was quick, and he seemed eager to share his thoughts. Gahti gave me a warm hug while urgently reminding me, "Allow yourself to be at peace in God's Grace and receive many miracles."

Cullen had his notepad open on his desk when he motioned for me to sit in the chair near him. The look on his face was pleasant. He did not appear to be the bearer of bad news, so I let myself relax. "Well, Jewelle," he began, seemingly pleased with himself for what he was about to say. "My friend" he went on, "Over the years you and I have relied upon each other for guidance and I think we have served each other well. So, this weekend, we draw once again upon our bond in friendship to provide what is needed to seed the healing process. I am hopeful about what happened here. I offer my thoughts with hope in mind." Cullen took a deep breath and went on. "I must say Jewelle, that While you may feel this guy Kojo has not given you what you wanted, he has, in my opinion, surely opened the door for you to deal with your feelings in a healthier way and to perhaps seek and receive love from a man again. Actually, in a curious way, your dream speaks of this, particularly the part about being taken into the forest. I think this

Kojo fellow realizes he is not yet ready for the kind of woman you are. You are a wife-type, Jewelle, and from what I can gather, he is still in love with his deceased wife. From what you have told me about him, it seems that he is a noble sort of fellow who has not yet learned that over a lifetime a man can love more than one woman deeply and with honor."

Cullen switched his position in his chair and then went on, "I suspect that he has yet to accept that one love does not have to diminish the other love in any way. I wonder if he is still in awe of the way his wife loved him and perhaps still feels unworthy of her love. Sometimes that happens, you know, and people spend the rest of their lives paying homage to their deceased spouse because they are still trying to get it right, their worthiness of such love. Also, you must realize, Jewelle, that your husband died close to 12 years ago. You have had almost double the time to grieve and move on with your life than Kojo has. And it is important to take into consideration you were the lover of his best friend. Certainly, that could be a hurdle for him, making you off limits for many reasons. Remember as well, Jewelle, it has been your habit to shut yourself off. Your celibate and rather abstemious lifestyle since Emory's death, particularly in recent years, is not fruitful. It has been your choice, I believe, for many reasons, but I am not certain that your reasons have been healthy. Though you have grieved for your husband, you have most often behaved as if your marriage to him prohibited new romantic relationships, setting near-un-attainable standards. You have denied yourself opportunities to learn and to grow, my friend, particularly when you have made a mistake or chosen wrongly. Your solution has been to isolate yourself. Truthfully, my friend, I think you have been afraid and I wonder if you are punishing yourself for something. But, that's for another visit."

As Cullen shared his thoughts, his words stung me, but I listened to my friend because I knew he had reflected carefully on our time together and had filtered what I shared through the lens of a friend and psychiatrist. And, I was certain that he and Gahti loved me. Seemingly, with great care he pushed on,, "Jewelle, you have kept a lot of feelings locked away, and Kojo tapped into them for some reason. I don't know why. Perhaps all of the coincidences with the two of you going to the same college and having the same man, Ken, as a friend may have some special meaning. I am at a loss for what it could be. All of those things are rather uncanny when you think about them, but surely they may have come together for you. They make this connection with Kojo seem of extraordinary significance for you. More importantly, I think you are at a point in your life where you realize you are running out of time. You know that we are in our 60s now, and it is time to be real about the things we say we want. We must not let our apprehensions and foibles get in the way of our joy. My friend, let Kojo be. He is not yet at a place where he can be with a second wife. All of his honor and love are still with his wife, and he knows that. It is likely that the young woman in his life now is an adventure ; she quells his appetite for the moment. Interestingly, keeping a distance from you at this time may be his way of being your friend, though he seems to be ambivalent about many things. Take it for what it is, and decide if you can be his friend without wanting or expecting more. That is your call, Jewelle. Go on with your life. You are on your way, but I will encourage you to continue peeling away those things that burden you. There is more to address, but not now. Embrace your future with vigor, my friend!"

I looked deeply into Cullen's eyes as he touched my hand gently, denoting he was done. I can't say that I liked all of what he shared, but I sincerely appreciated it. All I could do at that point was give my friend a hug and thank him for listening. We made small talk for quite a while before I got myself ready to head to the train station. I would be leaving at 5:00 p.m., arriving in Milwaukee at about 8:30 p.m. That would be a good time to get settled and ready for the rest of the work week. I knew I would have so much to think about on the way home. I was actually eager to get on with my thoughts. Cullen's words were so fertile, and, of course, the dream and newspaper article would stand out. Gahti's resolute statement, "Allow yourself to rest in God's grace and receive miracles" had a special place within my thoughts as well. I saw my time with

Cullen and Gahti as an invitation to attain another level of being. I was so grateful!

While I gathered myself for the train ride home, my mind curiously went back to a visit I had with an old Bahamian woman, a seer, who came to Milwaukee from time to time to visit her daughter and service her clients; she had quite a following in Milwaukee. People called her "Monkey Jo" and exalted her spiritual insights, especially about romantic relationships. Secretly, I had gone to her for a reading early in the new year, during the time Kojo's young woman was visiting him in Key West. I was searching. I needed to know what was going on with Kojo. The old woman threw her cowrie shells, ultimately telling me that Kojo and I were inextricably tied together. She said with confidence that Kojo and I had been married in a past life, sometime during slavery, and Kojo had sacrificed his life to save me and our two sons. She was certain we were connected in at least one lifetime from the past, and that is why Kojo's laugh seemed so familiar to me. She was certain Kojo had been tortured before his death but refused to give up information about where his wife and sons were hiding. Monkey Jo was certain that Kojo held remnants of that memory on an unconscious level, mostly triggered in my presence, which served as an obstacle to our reconnection in this lifetime. "What a memory," Monkey Jo had exclaimed, sadness resonating in her voice. But then she said the strangest thing, "No obstacle is insurmountable for God." She did not explain herself, and I did not push for more. That is how my reading had gone that day. I left Monkey Jo with many questions running through my mind but, on a deep level, felt something familiar about the story the old Bahamian woman told. I never said a word, even to Eva, about it. I wondered what Cullen would say about my experience with Monkey Jo. I am not sure why I hadn't mentioned it to either of my good friends, but like the recurrent dream, that, too, I kept within me.

PART II

"...angels, ancestors, and spirit guides sitting at the feet of the Great I AM will lift you.... Your late-life spirit guide the warrior chief has taken his assignment.... In gratitude for your kindness to one of his own he will guide you /and yet/ In the cold place miracles will find you."

CHAPTER 8

Miss Ella and Calling Ell Joi Di Crazy Horse

The ride home from La Crosse gave me ample time to reflect deeply on many things. So many loose ends came together for me. Memories from years gone by danced in my mind with the constant patter of the train, taking me to so many places I had pushed aside, revealing new meaning to things that at the time of their occurrence seemed frivolous. Awareness enveloped me, and it felt good. As I reflected, I marveled again at how an old woman, Miss Ella, in a nursing home, had taught me so many things years ago. She laid the groundwork for me to learn to connect the seemingly random dots in life. Her wisdom was plentiful, and her gentle hand was still guiding me. I could feel it. I smiled at that thought. The dream of Chief Crazy Horse and the newspaper article about his monument seemed like a sign urging me to return to the wisdom of Miss Ella.

As the train rolled on, I remembered that I started visiting Miss Ella about seven years after Emory's death. My visits to one nursing home or another on a monthly basis had become a significant part of how I chose to express my deep relationship with the Creator. It became a form of church for me. Being present in the lives of people, who in many cases had no one to be close to, became a ministry for me. When I met Miss Ella, she had stood out among the various people I visited. She was an unusual woman in so many ways. To look at her, one would never guess the breadth and depth of the experiences life had given her. This coal-black-skinned, petite, cat-like old woman was a walking encyclopedia who could knowledgeably expound on all types of money matters, general information, philosophy, and spiritual wisdom at the drop of a hat. The sheer number of places she had lived was impressive and often laid out by her as a calling card, a sort of advertisement to draw people into fertile and captivating discussions.

Upon my second visit with Miss Ella, we both knew we were to be kindred spirits because it was then that I discovered her deep respect for Harriet Tubman, the person in history I embraced as my mentor in absentia. Miss Ella read many books about Harriet, probably as many as I, if not more. We dove unabashedly into the nuts and bolts of Harriet's life along with many of the moral/ethical questions sometimes raised about her brazen eccentricities. In one story about Harriet's bold behavior (one that I had not known about), Miss Ella recalled that an author brought up concerns about her having taken a relative's young child without the mother's permission, and the mother never saw the child again. I learned from Miss Ella that Harriet made a split-second decision and didn't have time to equivocate with the child's mother about taking the child to freedom. Because at any time a slave master could decide to separate a mother and child by way of auction, Harriet believed making her choice to carry the child with her to freedom, though away from its mother, was a better decision. While Miss Ella and I hadn't disagreed totally on this matter, I had much more difficulty with Harriet's decision than Miss Ella. In fact, Miss Ella believed that for Harriet to leave the child playing in the yard in a context of the abhorrent rigors of slavery when she could almost guarantee the child's freedom would be a crime. Miss Ella argued that Harriet could not have left the child given her passionate beliefs about freedom. While I understood Miss Ella's point of view, the mother in me had a hard time reconciling Miss Ella's position. At that point, I was unaware that Miss Ella was a mother, too. I suppose my position could be perceived as a selfish one, my desire to raise the child in slavery rather than let her go to freedom without me. Of course, the added wrinkle of the mother not knowing what had happened to her child made Miss Ella's argument even more difficult for me to accept. Nonetheless, our vigorous discussion that day captivated both of us. Clearly our bond was sealed that afternoon.

As I reflected, the lulling motion of the train called up images of Miss Ella sharing her fundamental view of how she took life on. I closed my eyes and I could hear her explaining that she had been "raised" to be a nanny/housekeeper by her grandmother and mother in the employ of the Kemps, a wealthy Caucasian family living in Maine. She said she never met her father, but was told that he was a gardener, a seasonal worker, from somewhere in the Caribbean. As a child she had many questions about him, but was told by her grandmother to think less about him and more about her mother who was present in her life. Complying with her grandmother's dictum, by the time she was an adolescent she didn't think about her father at all. She grew to be focused and intentional in her quests. Her mother and grandmother set the path for her, but unlike them, she became exceptionally literate, mostly self-taught. She was an avid reader, spoke four languages in addition to English, and was exceptional at handling money, which was a boon for her in her later years.

According to Miss Ella, her intellect and verbal adeptness won the favor of Dr. Theodore Kemp, the head of household at the time she assumed her role as nanny/housekeeper. His wife, Doris, was a timid, sickly woman who had little to say other than to address matters regarding their three precocious children from time to time. This left much in the efficient hands of Miss Ella. Dr. Kemp was a noted forensic anthropologist who fashioned himself a progressive liberal, particularly in matters regarding his "colored help". He often drew Miss Ella into demonstrating her intellectual prowess and broad knowledge base for amusement. He would show her off to his friends and instructed his three children to share with Miss Ella whatever they were learning in school. He credited her achievements to his own progressive liberalism.

I remembered she shared that Dr. Kemp became internationally known by the time she moved into the top position of nanny/housekeeper over her ailing mother. Her grandmother passed away the year before. With her mother comfortably provided for, she managed the house with such efficiency that she was given uncommon leverage, including access to all kinds of documents about a vast array of topics, which she readily absorbed. She loved to learn and liked the attention Dr. Kemp gave her, though she despised some of his ways. Unlike her rather timid mother, she reveled in unmitigated cheekiness, seemingly groomed by her grandmother.

Most often she saw herself as the woman of the house, particularly when she would sit with Dr. Kemp at dinner, deeply engaged in discussions about world affairs. When the conversations began, Mrs. Kemp would retire to her room, leaving them to talk for hours. Miss Ella was clear on the role she played in the good doctor's life. He had shaped her to be something of a companion, at least an engaging conversationalist, who by her very status in his house would defer to him. She knew he had sexual relationships with women other than his wife, but he had never approached her in that way. She was grateful for that because had he fancied more from her than good conversation, she was certain there would have been a showdown. He would likely have discharged her from her job and left her wanting while having to care for an ill and aging mother.

I remembered how animated Miss Ella was when she shared that through Dr. Kemp's work they traveled extensively, spending varying periods of time in India, Canada, Cuba, Ecuador, Mexico, France, and many states within the U.S., ultimately ending in Wisconsin, where Dr. Kemp took his final post. She actually beamed when she shared that she had thrown herself into learning all she could about the people and culture of the various places. And, in doing so, she learned much about herself, particularly her ability to adapt. As a result of her worldwide experiences, she concluded that the blackness of her skin had no real bearing on the swiftness of her mind. Her ongoing thought was that you either like dark chocolate or you don't. She knew she was an exceptionally dark skinned woman with strong Negroid features and it would take someone who appreciated all of that to choose her as a life-partner.

I smiled as I recalled Miss Ella chuckling as she shared what had happened when they were in France. She connected with a man from Nigeria who wanted her to leave her secure employment with the Kemps, marry him, and stay in France. Although she cared for him, she rejected his offer even while aware that she was pregnant with his child. Her rejection of his proposal did not turn out well, closing the door on any future communication between them. She and the Kemp family left France. Dr. Kemp had taken a post in Mexico, and that is where her son was born. Her beautiful jet-black son became a part of the Kemp household. Even Mrs. Kemp doted on the baby, at times getting beyond her ailments to rock him or build blocks with him on the living room floor.

I remembered how proud she was the day she shared that after the birth of her son she became intentionally proficient in handling her finances, showing adeptness at investing almost her entire salary since she didn't have many expenses. It was clear she was proud of what she had accomplished. She said that such freedom with her finances could not have occurred with her son's father. Years later when her son was diagnosed with the debilitating disorder of schizophrenia, she provided the best psychiatric care for him. Her wise investments and frugality made this possible. Miss Ella was clear about the decision she made to stay in the Kemp household as a single woman, and she encouraged me to be clear about the things I want in my life.

Basking in the memories of Miss Ella, I surrendered to the soothing motion of the train and found myself in a dream-like state. It was as if I were seated before a movie screen that portrayed specific segments of the final months of Miss Ella's life. I could hear her voice and curiously I recalled in minute detail so much of what she said in those final days. The reverie began with the memory of a very important afternoon, a time that would forever stand out in my life. Memories flowed in vivid detail. I was there again. I was there with Miss Ella, captivated by the intensity in the sequence of events. It was a few months before Miss Ella made her transition that she told me she had a gift for me and needed to give it to me that very day. With a sense of urgency, we found a comfortable place near a table which she said we would need later, along with her Scrabble game. I was puzzled, but I did exactly what she asked. Once we sat down, she began telling me about her grandmother, noting that I needed to hear the story behind the special gift. Her grandmother, known as Nan, was a very religious woman who had been deeply involved in her Pentecostal church in rural Tennessee when she signed on in 1901 with Dr. Kemp's father to be his housekeeper and nanny to his children. Old man Kemp, as Nan called him, had been a character. He had won the right to offer Nan a job in a poker game. Significantly, on the very day he offered Nan the job, she had been praying for a big change in her life. A recent widow at the time, she was overwhelmed by the demands of life. Miss Ella shared that she remembered clearly that her grandmother told her she had prayed distinctly to have a job that would take her and her daughter from poverty. She had prayed to go north, far away from Tennessee. She believed her presence in the Kemp home in Maine was the answer to her prayer. Miss Ella believed, as did her grandmother, that you must ask specifically for what you want: you must call it by name! Miss Ella said she had been doing that all of her life, and she wanted to share that with me.

With the story of her grandmother out of the way, Miss Ella stated emphatically again that we have to be specific in asking God for what we want. "We must call it by name, and sometimes the answer will be yes, and sometimes the answer will be no," she advised. "We must be clear on what we are asking for." She made the point that she wanted me to have the gift of calling things into being. She said she appreciated my visits and wanted to give me this gift before she made her transition, which she felt was not too far away. She had asked to live to the age of 93, the age we believed Harriet Tubman attained before her death, and she was getting near that time. Her gift was to teach me to call my next husband or male companion into being. She made a point of saying, "although I never married, I have enjoyed the company of exciting and accomplished men when I have chosen to do so."

Her gift was a surprise! She knew I hadn't asked for or implied that I wanted another husband or male companion, although we discussed at length the challenges I encountered with the men in my life. "A woman your age, Jewelle, still has a lot of life in her. You deserve to keep company with a sturdy, good man," she said with her hands on her hips. "Well, you must be certain of what you want dear," she advised through a smile. "You must give him a name based on what you desire him to be and begin calling him by that name. The name should have meaning for you! You must have a keen sense of the essence of the man you want in your life Jewelle and call him by that name." She spoke passionately while locking me in a motherly-like embrace. That afternoon, caught up in her fervor and aiming to please my dear friend, I agreed to allow her to direct me in the venture of calling my next male companion or husband into being.

Immediately, Miss Ella began to pray for me, thanking God for sending me to her. She praised God for my diligence, asking God to keep me hardy and willing to rise above all adversity. One part of her prayer puzzled me: "God, let her rise from the mud like the lotus flower, embracing the light." She directed me to take deep breaths and to focus on the abundance of God. As I did that, I began to pray that my friend Miss Ella would live a longer life. I was not ready for her to leave me. While I continued to pray quietly, Miss Ella opened her Scrabble game and asked that I close my eyes and choose as many tiles as I would need in forming the first name of my next male companion or husband. She encouraged me to allow the Holy Spirit to direct my hands. I closed my eyes and prayed that I would be directed to do what would be best for me. My hands seemed to have a mind of their own leading me to randomly pull eight tiles from the box, leaving them face down on the table. With urgency I opened my eyes to look at Miss Ella, who was deep in prayer with her eyes closed and head bowed in reverence of the moment.

Soon, in a very soft voice, she instructed me to position the tiles in the way I wanted them. "Let the Spirit move your hands," she said firmly. I did what she told me to do, and to this day I am not sure why I set the tiles up three, three, and then two. I couldn't imagine a name spelled in that way. But when I was finally directed to turn the tiles face up, I was amazed at what I found. Before me, the 3 x 3 x 2 subset configuration turned out to be "ELL JOI DI." "Interesting," Miss Ella said as she repositioned her glasses, "now visualize a person who symbolizes the essence of your man to be and call out his name confidently." I did so and stated without hesitation, "Crazy Horse." The name jumped out of my mouth. I had been doing quite a bit of reading about the Lakota warrior chief since the dream I had about him years previous, before Emory's death. I continued to view him as one of God's angels in my life. All of my reading showed him to be a very spiritual man, a humble mystic who suffered much in his life. *If I am to have another husband or male companion,* I thought, *I want him to be blessed with the spiritual energy of the great warrior Chief Crazy Horse.*

Once his name left my lips, Miss Ella grabbed a piece of paper and wrote down what was revealed in the tiles, capitalizing the first letter of each of the subsets followed by the name Crazy Horse. She turned the paper around so that I could see the name clearly, and then she read it over and over again. I couldn't believe the feeling I got as I heard her read the name. Something in my spirit quickened. It seemed familiar to me. It felt right! That was the beginning of my calling Ell Joi Di Crazy Horse to my life. Miss Ella gave thanks in prayer while holding me tightly. She asked that God bless me "real good," and then she began to give praise in a way I had never seen before. For a moment, I worried something would happen to her, as she expended so much energy the way she was jumping around. But there was a place within me that knew she would be alright. I sat with my eyes closed, settling into deep prayer. Although there was no music, there was a rhythm in the room that permeated the air. It was as if we were in sync with some cosmic beat that transcended time and space. In my left ear, I heard drums and a chant. I turned quickly to see where it was coming from but soon realized I had partially stepped into another realm. With that awareness, I closed my eyes in prayer, but not before I said "Ell Joi Di Crazy Horse" out loud and felt a chill run through my entire body.

When Miss Ella quieted down, she was physically spent but smiling in a way that let me know she was in a good place. "I am pleased with my God. I am truly pleased," she said, panting a bit but not appearing to be experiencing any discomfort. With her eyes trained upon me she said, "Jewelle, you have been led to call to you Ell Joi Di Crazy Horse, The Joy of Crazy Horse. What a lovely thing that is!" I smiled realizing that she was giving me clarity on the name I would call my next male companion or husband. Feeling exuberant, I chose in that fertile moment to ask about the lotus flower, and Miss Ella explained that it was an unusual flower in that it bloomed in muddy water. Some people call it the mud flower. It closed at night and flowered in the light of day. She went on to say that many people see the flower as representing self-awareness and enlightenment. I asked her to explain her specific prayer about the lotus flower, and the only thing she offered was, "God showers us with grace, but we must give ourselves permission to rise through the mud of life." I looked at the old woman, thinking that she was something else. And I remembered the flowers in the secret part of Mr. Palacious's garden in Key West. Another memory lurked there, but I couldn't grasp it.

Almost six weeks following her 93rd birthday, a few months after we brought the name Ell Joi Di Crazy Horse into existence, Miss Ella passed away in her sleep. Losing her was difficult for me! I wept quietly for days before I was able to shift from grief to gratitude. I was grateful for all she shared with me and I knew she was ready to make her transition. It was her time! As she wished, her body was given to science and ultimately cremated, with her ashes given to her son and a few friends, including me. There was a simple ceremony in the chapel of the nursing home. Her son attended, along with his court-assigned guardian. Interestingly, he elected to sit next to me rather than in the seat provided for him at the front of the chapel. I smiled when he put out his hand, acknowledging that he was familiar with me. In turn, I hugged him, telling myself that I would visit him regularly at the elite group compound where his mother's well-invested money was keeping him. His excellent care was a testament to her patient brilliance and her faith in asking specifically for what she wanted. As I sat through the service, I thanked God again for having placed Miss Ella in my life.

A sudden shift in the motion of the train shook me from my dream-like state as we pulled into the Milwaukee station. There was clarity about so many things. I realized that when Kojo showed up in my life, given all of the uncanny connections and unusual circumstances, I was certain he was the answer to my call. Disappointment engulfed me until this visit to La Crosse, the talk with Cullen, the dream, the newspaper article about The Chief Crazy Horse monument, and Gahti's prayer all poured life into Miss Ella's hopes for me again.

Energized, I called out to Ell Joi Di Crazy Horse as I stepped off the train, collected my bag, and walked to the car waiting for me. I smiled as I thought about Miss Ella and wished that I could tell her in person about my dream and the decision I had made. I would go to Rapid City, South Dakota, to Chief Crazy Horse's mountain, and I would do it soon. I thought Miss Ella would laugh, but then I told myself, *She IS laughing. She is here with me in spirit.* I mouthed a "Thank you" to her as my daughter Kaimen drove me home.

CHAPTER 9

Miracle in Rapid City

I called Eva that night and told her about the wonderful dream and the invocation Gahti had given. Eva was intrigued by the dream and jumped at the opportunity to go with me to South Dakota. We talked a lot about the mode of transportation. Normally when she and I would go on trips, I would drive. We would either take my car or rent one, and sometimes we would go on the train. Immediately we thought about the train since it was still winter and we did not want to take the risk of driving in bad weather. It was an exciting thought. We would go as soon as I could clear my schedule without too much conflict. I needed to do this soon. We decided that we would set our departure for the first week in March.

A flurry of telephone calls and online research filled the next week. Both Eva and I discovered that the Crazy Horse Monument attraction and gift shop would be open in early March and we could tour and shop there. We lined up a personal tour guide service that was a little expensive but certainly quite accommodating. We could explore both Mount Rushmore and Crazy Horse Mountain, along with other tourist attractions. We were excited. The downside was that there was not a train going to Rapid City, South Dakota, where we needed to be. Before too long, one of us came up with the idea of trying a bus trip since it was so very cheap and we both were eligible for the senior rates. Once we learned the bus rate, we both were pleased with it and set our time for our trip to South

Dakota. It would take 17 hours, a long ride for sure, but we looked at it as an inviting adventure. I was pleased that Eva understood my issue with flying. I just didn't like it. I did not text and almost never climbed upon an airplane.

Over the ensuing weeks, we told everyone about our trip. Eva's daughter, her only child, was very skeptical about the trip. While she was accustomed to her mother's traveling just about all over the world, she seemed to have a bit of a problem with her taking the Greyhound and another bus line to Rapid City, South Dakota. My children just looked at the trip as another weird adventure their mother was embarking upon. They couldn't quite understand why we were opting to take the trip to South Dakota in winter but were certain the timing had something to do with some spiritual thing that they didn't want to know about. When I finally heard from Kojo, he was still down South. He was excited about my trip — I could hear it in his voice. He cheered me on, pointing out a host of intriguing possibilities. I didn't mention anything about the dream or say anything about my time in La Crosse with Cullen. Our conversation was warm and friendly, with his asking that I call his name out at Chief Crazy Horse Mountain. I promised I would, assuring him that as soon as I called his name out I would call him, so that he could experience the mountain with me. He seemed pleased and signed off with that engaging laugh. For a moment, I felt the yearning for him return, and then it left as it had come, quickly.

I called my cousin Vy in Florida to tell her about the trip and let her know some of what Cullen had shared with me. Of course, being the prayer warrior she is, she said she would continue to pray for me and cheered me on about my adventure. Flora was less enthusiastic about the trip. She was still stuck on why things couldn't work out with Kojo. I tried to explain some of what Cullen shared with me, but Flora didn't have a kind place in her heart for any kind of therapy talk. She was back on her soapbox about brothers needing to shape up, so I just left her there.

When the first week of March came, Eva and I were like children ready to embark on an engaging adventure. She had her usual snacks of fruits and nuts, which she graciously shared with me. We decided that we would handle the bus trip the way we handled our train trips, spending very little money on food. We never bought anything on the train and would dine well at major train stations, but within a budget. Eva was very frugal, and her wisdom spilled over onto me. So our bus trip mirrored our train escapades. As we made our way across the Midwest we ate very little, and all we did eat was very healthy. That was another area of Eva's expertise. She knew a lot about nutrition and was more than willing to pass what she knew on to others.

Interestingly, the bus was full when we left Milwaukee. The bus route had originated in Chicago, as the Chicago to Minneapolis run. We would have to change in Minneapolis to another bus line that would take us directly into Rapid City. For the first part of the trip, Eva and I did not find seats together. We had to take the only available seats. She sat next to a rather unhealthy-looking young woman who was not dressed in proper winter clothing. I, on the other hand, sat next to a rather odd-acting young African-American man who had a terrible cough. After I had offered him a Halls cough drop, he kept asking for more. While I continued to honor his requests, I was pleased when he exited the bus in Tomah, Wisconsin. I wondered what he was doing in Tomah since this part of the state had so few African Americans, and then I thought about the veterans' hospital there and decided that he was either a patient on a pass or someone who worked there. The bus had thinned out appreciably by the time we reached Minneapolis, and when it was time to change to a different bus line, Eva and I had first pick of the seats. We sat together after we both scurried to the restrooms in the station. Neither of us wanted to bother with the restroom on the bus. In our minds, those bathrooms were for an absolute emergency only. From Minneapolis on, we talked just a little and then fell asleep. We were scheduled to arrive in Rapid City at 5:30 a.m., and we were looking forward to a day of rest in a very comfortable Comfort Suites motel. That was our staple place to be. If we couldn't book a Comfort Suites, we would take a Comfort Inn. That was just how it was with us on our road trips.

We pulled into the Rapid City station about seven minutes ahead of schedule. Both Eva and I were surprised to see that there wasn't any more snow in Rapid City than there was in Milwaukee. As we left the bus, we noticed that the temperature was about the same as it had been back home. We were expecting to see some cabs waiting, but there weren't any. We were the only people de-boarding at that point, and the station seemed desolate. We both went to the restroom and then talked to the one clerk at the ticket counter. He assured us that a cab would come soon; the bus had arrived early. As we went to the seating section, I saw a man who looked as if he could be Native American waving to us. Eva, in her usual playful way, said, "Your boyfriend is calling you." I, in turn, laughed and said, "Don't try to give me your man." We both laughed, but little did we know what would happen next.

Soon, the man who I concluded was certainly a Native American — because of his skin tone and long braids — walked directly over to me. He was very slender, and his skin looked like parched leather. He had a backpack hanging from his left shoulder, and he smelled of tobacco. The smell was pungent but not offensive. He stood directly in front of me and began to speak, looking directly into my eyes. He said: "Sister, I've been looking for my sister. All over I've been looking for my sister." He pointed his finger at me and went on, "You want to know who you are. I say to you, you are a healer. It is not your choice; you live, you love, you heal. It is your mission. You will have four husbands before you leave to join the thunders. You had two husbands. One has joined the thunders. You are here to be claimed by the third one, who was by your side when you were young. And you have crossed paths with the fourth one in many lifetimes. You were kissed by the grandmothers. You have grandmother energy. Men bring boulders for you to carry and come to you for healing. It is your mission." With that said, he turned and walked away. I was stunned!

Eva looked at me expressionless and said, "There you go, Jewelle! You heard the man. You've got work to do." I wanted to choke her right there for her whimsy. For a moment, I wondered how she could make light of something so profound, and then I remembered who Eva was. She had sat with shamans in distant lands and had witnessed all sorts of unusual things. This particular incident was like a pimple on an elephant's ass to her. I think it was the cab driver who jarred me back to reality because I was speechless for a time. As I watched the bearer of the news walk farther down the street, I prayed a silent prayer. I told myself that I was going to rest in God's hands because I didn't know what would happen next. I just needed to surrender all to the Great I Am. I guess I must have been caught up in my prayer because Eva was yelling at me to pay the cab driver. I didn't remember getting into the cab. Eva and I had a method of checks and balances that we adhered to on our trips. My responsibility was the transportation, and hers was the lodging. We go back and forth with the food and other things. We keep a running record of everything we spend and even things out at the end of our trips. I must have been totally distracted because by the time I got my wallet out, Eva had paid the cab driver and had hopped from the cab. We were at the Comfort Suites.

Once comfortably situated in our room, Eva and I didn't talk much. The accommodations were very pleasant; the color scheme of the room was comforting and festive. Eva opted to go to the pool before partaking of the continental breakfast and settling in to rest while I, on the other hand, decided to soak in the bathtub with bubbles and scented oil. It was lovely. I was not hungry: there were too many things to think about. As my body relaxed in the steaming hot water, my mind replayed our encounter with the Native American at the bus station. Each time I went over his words, I couldn't shake the feeling that the whole episode seemed scripted by some unknown movie director/writer team preparing a blockbuster film. Things had fallen into place, each of us playing a role seemingly preordained. It was a puzzle to me. The meeting with the Native American self-ordained prophet was engaging, baffling, and to some extent disquieting.

How did the man know that I'd had two husbands? In my mind, that was too much for just a wild guess, and he seemed so confident in his forecast. And what did he mean that I had come here to be claimed by my third husband, who had been at my side when I was young? To my knowledge, I knew no one in South Dakota; this was my first time here. And what did he mean I would have four husbands before I would join the thunders and that I had crossed paths with the fourth one in many past lifetimes? That part of his forecast took me back to the seer, Monkey Jo, and all she had to say about my relationship with Kojo in a past lifetime. As I thought about the idea of reincarnation a bit more, I realized that it was not at odds with my spiritual beliefs at all. In fact, it made sense to me that the soul energy did not die and would return to the earth plane again and again to glorify God. That part of the man's forecast/ reading didn't disturb me one bit, but the idea that I would bury or lose another husband did trouble me deeply. If there would be four, I would have to marry a third and then somehow lose him. The thought of that was disconcerting. I had been divorced and widowed, both very painful experiences in my life, and I didn't want to repeat either one.

The thunders he talked about intrigued me. I remembered reading something about them in one of my books about Chief Crazy Horse. I recalled that the thunders were like ancestors or spirits existing in another realm. I wasn't sure, but it seemed the man was saying I would marry four times before I made my transition. As I soaked and thought, I tried to come to terms with what was happening in my life. I reminded myself that I had surrendered my life to the Creator. I would come to rest in God's grace and receive miracles as Gahti invited me to do. Surrendering would not be easy for me but could ultimately carry me to a more evolved place. While drying myself off, I remembered that tomorrow, March third, would be my birthday. I looked at my naked self in the mirror and thought that despite a bit of wear and tear, I looked pretty good to be turning 63. This, of course, was a far cry from my assessment of a month or so ago. I winked at my image in the mirror feeling pretty satisfied with myself. And in a flash, I reminded myself to say a prayer for Haiti.

After calling my children to let them know we had arrived safely and then methodically doing my prayer rituals, I finally snuggled between the lush covers and fell quickly into a deep sleep. As had occurred at Cullen's place, a vivid dream presented itself. In the dream, I was once again with the Native American from the bus station, and he had his hand on my forehead. I could smell tobacco and soon heard drumming. Instantly, the Native American from the bus station changed shape, the drumming escalated, and the figure before me was a smiling man dressed in colorful African ceremonial garb. He looked like my father! He handed me a feather, and as I reached for it, he changed and became two beautiful old women of markedly different hues. They seemed familiar to me, but before I could place them they morphed into a honey brown woman with wings. She held the feather out to me. The drumming stirred me, and I began to dance, my feet moving and hips swaying back and forth in ways that spoke of a level of agility that belied my age. The woman before me seemed familiar. She smiled and beckoned me to reach again for the feather. I could smell roses as I reached towards her, bent on grasping the feather with my right hand. Magically, in a mist of vibrant rose-scented droplets, I was lifted and then let go as if tumbling off the side of a cliff. I heard drums and chanting as I landed on the back of a massive bird.

I could hear myself call out the word PAHAYOKEE as I grabbed the feathers of the enormous bird. I had heard that word somewhere before but couldn't recall where. Soon I realized I was on the back of an eagle, soaring majestically and free. I could see the Native American, the African, the two beautiful old women and the honey-colored woman with wings smiling and waving at me. In my dream, I was amazed at the power and strength of the bird. I was also amazed at my own comfort level. I actually felt covered in safety. The immense flapping wings heralded power and grace. I held the feather in my mouth, trying to remember specifically when I claimed it as mine. I could not recall, but I wrapped my arms around the eagle's neck, thinking the word PAHAYOKEE must have meaning in my journey. It was so familiar. Astonishingly, the eagle and I soared into the beckoning light. It was as if we were being drawn into the moon. But it was daytime, and the moon appeared more vibrant than the sun. I was in awe of it all.

I woke from the dream smiling but didn't say a word about it to Eva, who was diligently dealing with her email on her laptop computer. She greeted me cheerfully. I just smiled in her direction and said nothing. I needed to savor my dream for a while. It was almost 7:00 p.m. when I jumped out of bed to make my bathroom run. Apparently I'd slept the day away. On the other hand, Eva had been up for a while and visited the pool again. She bought soup and juice for us to share from the hotel canteen, expecting not to leave the hotel until morning. I was pleased that she had done that, but I wasn't sure just soup and juice would stave off the appetite I had developed. As I heated up my soup, Eva talked at length about the interesting people she met at breakfast and during both times in the pool. She was especially impressed with the hotel staff. In her estimation, they were exceptionally gracious and found humor in most situations. Then she said the thing that really captured my attention: "I don't know what you were dreaming about, but you yelled out that word PAHAYOKEE a couple of times. And you were smiling in your sleep, too." She said all of this without looking in my direction, but I knew she was interested in hearing what I had to say. Eager to hear her thoughts, I told her about the dream. Eying me carefully, she set her computer aside and quipped, "There you go again, riding on birds and hanging out with people you don't know. I don't know what I am going to do with you, Jewelle." Although she was joshing me, I knew she was captivated by what I had just shared, and I was certain that before the night was over she would have more to say about it.

True to form, after her nighttime shower, Eva said, "Girl, I don't know what's coming, but Spirit has something big for you. Riding birds and all into the light is quite impressive. I am going to pray that you don't fall off that bird." Then she pulled out her prayer books and began her nightly prayer ritual. I laughed to myself, but I knew there was no need for more words on this dream thing tonight. Eva had thought about it and surmised that Spirit was working. I knew she said things only when she felt pretty confident that what she was saying was on point. And, as usual, she laced her words with a bit of dry humor. After watching a few episodes of *Fresh Prince of Bel-Air,* I turned off the television and fell asleep again. My venture into deep sleep this time did not give me a memory of a dream, but I rested well. I felt so comfortable that when Eva insisted that I had better get up or miss the free continental breakfast, I had to make myself push back the covers and make my bathroom run. Once fully awake, I embraced the thought that today, March 3, 2010, heralded my 63rd birthday.

Eva offered her happy birthday wish to me cheerfully as we dashed down the hall to the site of the continental breakfast. We both hoped that the maid service would come early just in case we wanted to nap or just rest after our early morning walk. Yes, we had decided we would spend this day getting to know something about the neighborhood surrounding the Comfort Suites and perhaps do a little shopping if there were stores close by. Eva was into hiking and walking for health purposes, and I enjoyed walking, too, but not as much as she did. It didn't matter to us that it was cold outside. After cheerily taking birthday calls from my Milwaukee clan, Eva and I bundled up and headed out into the South Dakota weather, noting how similar it was to our weather back home. The hotel staff told us that we were experiencing a good side of South Dakota weather. Had we been there a week or so before, we would have been singing a different tune. It had been exceptionally frigid, with some days below zero. Eva and I both laughed when we heard that because we knew we would not be taking our early morning stroll in subzero temperatures.

The area around the Comfort Suites appeared to be a well-kept part of the city. The hotel was located on an incline that dropped sharply down to a busy intersection. There were a number of restaurants and shops in walking distance. As we walked down the incline, making a point of stepping over patches of ice, I saw the culprit right before Eva put her foot down. I tried to get the words out, to tell her to look out for the patch of ice that would bring her tumbling down. Not only did she fall, but she rolled a bit, and we both heard something snap when she hit the ground. The fall occurred near the intersection, and there was a man in a gray truck stopped at the red light on our side of the street. He pulled the vehicle over and hopped out. To my amazement the man looked Black, but the long braids hanging below his shoulders made me think again about that.

The Good Samaritan's booming voice raised the question a couple of times, "Are you hurt, lady?" as he leaned down to see about Eva. I bent over to help, but he quickly hoisted Eva over his right shoulder as if she were a sack of sand, and he did it effortlessly as if he had been doing that sort of thing all of his life. There was something rather stilted about his movements. Curiously, it seemed as though his left arm and hand were frozen or something because he did just about everything with his right hand and arm. Then I saw the patch over his left eye. I was processing all of this when he asked in a friendly voice, "Are you at the hotel over there?" He was pointing to the Comfort Suites, and Eva and I said "Yes" in unison. "I'll take you there. Get in the truck," he said with a degree of authority. Now, this was an unusual thing for me to do, hopping into a truck with a strange man. But for Eva it seemed just fine. She had been on safaris in Africa, on fast-moving trains in Japan and China, in homemade rafts on creeks in India, in carts and makeshift coaches in South America, and in cabs throughout Europe. Hopping into a truck in Rapid City, South Dakota with a black-skinned Native-American-looking man we did not know did not appear to be an issue for her.

He placed Eva on the backseat of the truck. She seemed to be in pain but did not complain. Hesitantly I got in the front seat and found myself asking his name. I just needed to know something about him, I thought. "Rawlston, P. G. Rawlston. And you?" he said with a smile, looking at me closely. In truth, he was actually gazing at me as if trying to remember me from somewhere. In turn, I pointed to Eva, "This is my friend, Eva, and I am Jewelle." When I said my name, he dropped his keys but regrouped quickly and got the truck moving up the hill to the Comfort Suites. It was a short ride but felt long because I could feel him watching me out of his good eye. It was kind of creepy. He appeared to be a nice enough fellow and was certainly fine looking with distinct Negroid features, all set within deep-brown skin encircled by long silken black hair with tinges of gray. He removed his hat for a moment, and I got a good look at him. He looked a lot like the Creole guy in the movie *Eve's Bayou*, but this man, P. G. Rawlston, was taller and thicker in stature than the man in the film.

As he lifted Eva from the truck and carefully carried her into the Comfort Suites, it was clear to me that he was favoring his left side. Something was wrong. His left arm was stiff. Although his left hand was encased in a glove, it didn't appear to move flexibly. I wondered what impediment his winter attire kept hidden. Clearly, he was a strong and agile man. He moved like an athlete seasoned by the years. I guessed him to be in his late forties or early fifties. Once inside the Comfort Suites, Eva became an instant celebrity, especially when the staff learned for sure that her fall had not occurred on their company's property. I took note of their concern and marveled at how litigiousness permeated the culture. Folks fussed over Eva. They had her leg propped up and made her a steaming cup of tea.

Eva was basking in the attention as she thanked our Good Samaritan many times. He, on the other hand, seemed intrigued by something I had said. He asked a third time, "What is your name again?" I think I may have blushed as I told him my name for the third time and he, in turn, asked, "How do you spell your name, and where are you from?" I thought that was odd but immediately spelled my name and told him that Eva and I both live in Wisconsin and were in Rapid City mainly to visit the Chief Crazy Horse monument attraction. When he heard that, I saw him shake his head as if he were trying to clear something away. Then he asked, "Were you born in Wisconsin?" Such inquiry seemed strange to me, but I answered, "No, Eva is originally from New York, and I am from Florida." When the Good Samaritan heard my response, he seemed to grow a few inches. He stood erect, raised himself to his full stature, and smiled broadly. It seemed as if he were waking up and stretching, welcoming a new day. Before long P. G. Rawlston, our Good Samaritan, patted Eva on her shoulder, shook my hand, and said good day to all. I noticed he looked back a number of times as he walked to his truck, and each time he shook his head as if in disbelief. The women behind the desk were curious about our Good Samaritan, making light of Eva's falling on the ice just in time to be rescued by a prince of a man. One woman just came out with it. "He sure is a fine drink of water," she chimed. "I am thinking about going out there and tripping on the ice, too. Maybe there's another one out there for me." We all laughed, but I had a funny feeling in my stomach that I couldn't identify.

When we got to our room, Eva admitted she was in quite a bit of pain and we probably needed to go to an emergency center to see what damage the fall had done. Eva was known for having a high tolerance for pain, so her insistence about going to see about her injury let me know that she may have much more damage done to her ankle/leg than we at first thought. We had both heard something crack when she hit the ground. We called a cab and went to the nearest emergency center. The Comfort Suites staff called ahead, and when we arrived at the emergency site, the staff there was well informed about our mishap and very accommodating. Again, Eva and I both commented on the graciousness of the people and the cheekiness of the women, in particular.

The women we had met thus far were all Caucasian, assertive and full of fun. They found humor in just about everything and were uncommonly verbal about their likes and dislikes from their men. Eva and I just kept looking at each other when one of the ladies at the emergency center said a couple of risqué things about her man on the heels of how she liked drinking corn whiskey and gambling at the casino. The conversation was free-flowing and comfortable. When the results of the x-ray came back and Eva was told that she had fractured her ankle in at least three places, we took it in stride, asking for advice about what to do next. Should we give up on our tourist venture scheduled for the next day, or could we manage it somehow? We were directed to the orthopedic and spinal injury center. The nurse who had the most stories to tell made all of the arrangements, noting that we would be expected, confirming that the pertinent information had been sent by computer. We just needed to take the x-ray with us.

It was interesting that in this mishap of Eva's falling on the ice, we were encountering so many jovial and gracious people who all gave me cheerful greetings once Eva spilled the beans about my birthday. The next cab driver treated Eva as if she were a fragile piece of glass, making her comfortable and managing her wheelchair when we arrived at the orthopedic and spinal injury center. As we waited to be seen by a specialist, Eva and I talked a bit more about P. G. Rawlston, our Good Samaritan. There are times Eva can be exceptional in her observations. She may not appear to be aware of what is going on, but she is most often on point. Her assessment let me know she had been very invested in observing the behavior of our Good Samaritan. She said in an off-the-cuff manner, "It seems to me that our Good Samaritan thinks he knows you from somewhere. I heard his line of questioning and saw how he looked at you." In response, I told Eva that the pain pills she took at the emergency center must be messing with her mind. I said this despite the fact that I had a feeling about Mr. Rawlston but just couldn't put my finger on it. Eva mentioned that she saw him favoring his left side and wondered if it had something to do with what was going on with his left eye. He was wearing a patch, and she believed the patch and the way he moved his body were all connected in some way. Out of sheer fun, I challenged her about her reasons for looking at P. G. Rawlston so closely. "You were really into him, weren't you, Eva?" I asked, with laughter spilling forth in the midst of the question. "Yes!" she quipped emphatically. "Any man who can hoist my butt up on his shoulder with just one hand has got to be special," she said, and we both laughed. P. G. Rawlston had been spectacular in his chivalry. I wondered if we would see our Good Samaritan again.

It was near evening when we finally left the orthopedic and spinal injury center. Eva underwent many tests and learned that — because she fractured her ankle in three places — she might need surgery at some point but could carry on with her tourist adventure if she took special care of herself. We both laughed as they wrapped her leg and put it in a boot. She was issued crutches, which Eva complained about as she struggled to use them effectively. We were advised that once we made it back to Wisconsin, the decision about surgery and other protocol-related issues would be made. Eva was advised to call if the pain became unbearable. She received a prescription for pain medicine but on our way back to the hotel decided not to get it filled. She didn't like to take medicine and had a number of pain pills still left over from the emergency center. She believed she would be just fine. I was too hungry to argue with Eva.

On our way to the Comfort Suites we had the cab stop several times for me to secure a hefty box of chicken wings, some potato salad, biscuits, apples, oranges, and a couple of bottles of wine. I even bought two cupcakes to celebrate my birthday. After we made certain that one of us had packed a corkscrew, we decided we would head back to the hotel. There was no way for us to have known what would greet us there. There was no way for me to know that my life would never be the same again after that evening. Neither of us had even an inkling of what was to come.

As we disembarked from the cab — Eva with her crutches and booted foot and me with the bags of goodies — we were stunned to see two beautiful bouquets of flowers waiting for us. The two new women behind the desk acted all hyped about the flowers, who had brought them, and the story behind Eva's mishap. It seemed that the story had been told again and again among the Comfort Suites staff throughout the day. People were buzzing about the handsome Good Samaritan who saved the day. Once we made it to our room, Eva settled on the couch with her foot elevated to read her card first. The card read, "Glad to be of service to you. Sorry you fell. Hope Rapid City docs are looking after you well. Patrick G. Rawlston." We both chuckled, enjoying his playful attempt at poetry, and now we both knew his first name. I am not sure why I took so long to open the card that came with my flowers. There was a part of me that was eager to see the message, and then there was a part of me that had a sense of hesitancy. I just didn't know what he would say. Eva pushed me. "What are you waiting for, Jewelle?" she asked impatiently. I responded by tearing open the envelope and looking at the card. I don't remember what happened next, but somehow I barely made it across the room to my bed. I sat on the bed saying in amazement, "It can't be, it can't be. It just can't be." "It can't be what?" Eva asked, intrigued by my response. It took me a while to collect my thoughts. I looked at the card again. It read, "Jewelle, I knew I would see you again one day, and here it is. Please call me." Under the phone number listed were the words Je m'appelle Eagle Feather, and then he had signed it Patrick.

This was beyond coincidence. I began to cry as I explained to Eva that Patrick appeared to be someone I had known many, many years before, about 45 years. Eva perked up and in her smart aleck tone said, "The man in the bus station said you would be claimed by someone who had been by your side when you were young. Maybe this is the one." I sat quietly for a long time and then began to tell Eva about the little boy I once knew who has apparently turned into the man who acted as our Good Samaritan. As I talked, I felt weak. It was as if something well out of my control were steering the course of my experiences, like a roller coaster ride but in slow motion. As I told Eva the story, I kept wondering if this were some kind of cruel joke. How could it be that the robust handsome man that attended us so graciously could have developed from a plump little boy, the grandson of the head cook at the all-girls boarding school I attended in Virginia so many years ago? I just could not believe it. But I knew I had never told a soul about Je m'appelle Eagle Feather. While thinking about this, my most recent dream came looming into my consciousness, and all I could say was, "Oh, my God."

Eva and I talked for hours. Though we had shared many things over the years, I had never gone into great detail about my years in boarding school, perhaps because while those years were great for me academically, I did not fit in well with many of the girls there. In summary, I believed I had three strikes against me. I was dark-skinned, from the Deep South, and poor by comparison. As I talked about the school, so many memories I had pushed away came through. My cousin Vy also attended the school, but she stayed connected with many of her classmates while I did not. Vy was a year behind me. Although she was also born in Key West, the proverbial Deep South, she spent many summers in New York with her mother's relatives and of course she was not dark-skinned like me, I thought. I didn't begrudge her that, but I often thought about how different our memories were about the time we spent in boarding school. Although Vy and I are cousins, our stations in life were very different at that time. Her mother, Aunt Mavis, was a crafty and industrious woman. She was assertive and driven, managing her money like a Wall Street financier. She was a strikingly beautiful barber by profession, born in the North and very capable of handling herself in business. People still talk about when she first came to Key West and opened her shop. Folks there had never encountered a Black female barber up close, and her assertive manner gave everyone pause. But she built a thriving clientele comprised of Key West Conchs and military personnel alike, often playing jazz in her shop and offering treats. In truth, her shop at one time was the place to be for fun and news-driven conversations.

On the other hand, Vy's father, Uncle Venton, one of my mother's brothers, had been a rather staid military man, a chief in the navy near retirement age when he met Vy's mother while they were both vacationing in Cape Cod. They knew each other only a short time before they tied the knot and Vy's mother packed up and moved to Key West. Uncle Venton had another family comprised of an ex-wife and three grown sons in Tampa, Florida. They had moved there after the divorce to be near his ex-wife's family. He was in his fifties when Vy was born and passed away when she was still a child. So my cousin Vy was not poor. Her father left a rather hefty insurance policy for her which, coupled with her mother's business sense, put them in a socio-economic category well above where my immediate family was back then. And Vy had only one brother from her mom, whereas I had six older siblings.

Most of what I was thinking about I hadn't thought of in years. It was a part of my life that seemed distant from me, and yet here it was opening itself up right before my eyes. I explained to Eva that the school I attended was a Catholic boarding school located next to the James River in Powhatan, Virginia, about forty miles outside of Richmond. It had been rather famous at one time for educating Black girls and was founded near the end of slavery. The school's historic value, coupled with segregation, made it a premier place for middle- and upper-class Black Catholics to send their children at one time. Of course, there were a few of us who were from the lower socio-economic ranks who made it in there and managed to make it through. My mother, a devout Catholic, was committed to the idea that I must have a solid Catholic education through high school, which was not possible in Key West at the time. Back then, the Catholic school for Black students went only through the 8th grade; public school was the only high school option. Overriding my father's concerns, my mother insisted that unlike my siblings, I should not attend a public high school. I am not sure why she insisted that I be sent away to an expensive boarding school! But, she pontificated for years about the sacrifices made to give me a Catholic education through high school.

I had just turned 13 when I went to boarding school, and the plump little boy in the kitchen was about eight, I think. The nuns prided themselves on teaching us all to be industrious. You couldn't be lazy and do well at this school regardless of how much money your parents had. Everyone had to work and work hard. I was assigned to kitchen duty after morning and evening meals. That is how I met little Patrick. He was about to turn twelve when I graduated, and the nuns were talking with his grandmother about finding him another place to be after school because he was getting to be close in age to the incoming freshmen girls and they didn't want any trouble. Even at nearly twelve, he was still rather pudgy, his grandmother constantly stuffing him with cakes and pies and all of the things she was so good at making.

Mrs. Johnson was Patrick's father's mother. As I remember it, he came to live with his father's family when his parents were killed in a car accident. He didn't have any siblings. His grandmother often talked about Patrick's father, her firstborn. He was the son she prayed for in her first marriage, which ended abruptly when her first husband drowned while on a fishing trip. She clung to her son then and was devastated when as a man he too died suddenly in an accident. While sharing all of this with Eva, it occurred to me that I had never known Patrick's surname; his grandmother,

Mrs. Johnson, carried her second husband's last name. It seems that Patrick has his father's name; from Mrs. Johnson's first husband. The accident occurred when Patrick was about five. He had been in the car but was not badly hurt.

I pulled more of the story from my memory and recalled that Patrick visited his mother's people from time to time, but Mrs. Johnson was not open in allowing him to connect with his mother's ways. His mother had been Native American and did not embrace Christianity. That infuriated Mrs. Johnson and her husband. Their family essentially embraced a very strict Pentecostal faith. It was interesting to hear Mrs. Johnson talk about the Catholics, particularly when she was out of earshot of the nuns. Though she had worked for the school for years, constantly professing a love of her job, she never really believed that the nuns would go to heaven. On more than one occasion, I heard that conversation in the kitchen.

During my entire four years at the school, I had opted to work in the kitchen and developed quite a friendship with both Mrs. Johnson and Patrick. The nuns often commented on how nicely I mentored the little boy, often helping him with his homework or even teaching him things I was learning in my classes. Actually, many of the girls spent time playing games with Patrick or teaching him one thing or the other. He had become special to just about everyone, but he and I had an uncommon connection, one that allowed us to laugh easily and to be comfortable in each other's presence, even when silent. On the Saturdays when I would volunteer for phone duty rather than go to some concert put on by students from area colleges, Patrick would sit with me and talk, as his grandmother prepared for our Sunday dinner the next day. Sometimes I would help him with his homework, or we would play board games until his grandmother called for him.

Pushing myself to call to mind things I had not thought about in years, I remembered that it was on one of those Saturday afternoons that I taught him a few new French words I was learning in class. On that day he told me the name he had given himself to embrace his Native American culture and heritage and we both said it using the French I was teaching him. "Je m'appelle Eagle Feather," we said many times as if in a chant. We both knew his grandmother would not be pleased with him calling himself by any name akin to his mother's heritage. Whenever we could get away with it, I would ask, "Comment tu t'appelles?" And he would respond, "Je m'appelle Eagle Feather." It had become our secret.

It was clear that Eva was engrossed in the story because she did not ask one question as I went on unearthing detail upon detail. I almost lost track of time when she finally said, "Aren't you going to call him? You'd better do it before it gets too late." She smiled and picked up her computer. I knew she had questions, but for some reason she just kept them to herself. For a moment, I debated with myself about the best time to call Patrick. *Perhaps I should wait until morning when I would be fresh*, I thought. But then I gave into a sense of curiosity tinged with apprehension and excitement, and I dialed his number.

CHAPTER 10

Exploration in Rapid City

When I dialed the number from the card, I held my breath. My mind raced, and my heart pounded. I wasn't sure whether I was more concerned about what I would say to Patrick or what Patrick would say to me. The phone rang only once, and I heard his booming voice. "Hello, Rawlston here," he bellowed. Then he must have looked at the caller ID because his voice softened and he asked, "Jewelle, Jewelle, is it really you?" There was notable joy lacing his words. He seemed eager, excited, and exuberant. I had to take a deep breath before I could speak. I actually felt unsettled. Things just didn't seem real. When I finally found my voice, I heard myself laughing and saying out loud what I was hearing in my head. "This can't be real. It just can't be true. You are all grown up and so far away from Virginia. What are you doing here, Patrick?" I asked, trying to make sense out of things. His laughter, in response, was warm and engaging. It was very comforting to me. "This is my mother's home," he said, "the land of my mother's people. I came here to my grandmother's burial. Her ceremony was a few days ago." He went on to explain he had driven out to South Dakota because he brought his youngest son to the service. Some of his children and other family members flew out to the burial services, but his youngest son has special needs and is afraid to fly.

I wondered what he meant by special needs but didn't ask. I just listened to him go on and on about how he never forgot me. He even told me that I'd grown into a stunning woman. When he said that, I laughed and pointed out to him that it had been years since I thought of myself as stunning but appreciated his graciousness. In truth, I felt all warm inside as I processed his words, remembering what Cullen told me about now being open because of exploring my feelings towards Kojo. I smiled, thinking that perhaps Cullen was right. Something happened to me, and maybe Kojo was some type of catalyst for positive change in my life after all. With laughter in my voice, I returned the compliment by letting Patrick know he had come a long way from the pudgy preadolescent boy I left after my graduation so many years ago. He was now quite a hunk in 2010. We both laughed, and he immediately suggested we get together. He intended to leave for Virginia the following day but would postpone his departure until we had a chance to meet and talk. "I will not let you get away from me again," he said with fervor. I wondered what he meant but didn't ask. As we went back and forth about possible times, he continued to say my name over and over again. It was obvious the little-boy crush he openly attested to had found a resting place within his heart, leading him to make it unabashedly clear that it was still vigorously there. Before signing off, we made a definite date for the evening of the following day. We would meet around 8:00 p.m. after I had time to get cleaned up from my day of adventure with the personal tour guide Eva and I hired.

Based on our agreement with the tour guide, Eva and I expected to be picked up at the hotel at 9:00 a.m. and to return around 7:00 p.m. after having experienced Mount Rushmore, the Chief Crazy Horse Monument, and a host of other tourist delights. Obviously, I would need to push Eva around in a wheelchair from time to time, but that was not a problem. We learned that both the Chief Crazy Horse Monument and Mount Rushmore furnished wheelchairs at no cost. We were pleased to hear that. I just needed to have the energy to get my friend around comfortably and have energy for a special evening. Patrick let me know that he could hardly contain himself until we had time to catch up. He was clear that he had so many questions, particularly when he found out that I was a widow. While it was apparent he was intrigued by the little information I shared with him, he hadn't said anything about his marital status or the reason for the eye patch. I found that curious but felt sure we would ultimately get into all of those details the next evening. I had no idea then of the trauma and drama woven in his story.

When I signed off from Patrick, I noticed Eva was smiling. With authority she posited, "It is amazing. You seem to have already rekindled an old friendship, and the tone of your voice says it is a comfortable friendship, too. Isn't Spirit good? You are having a hell of a birthday, girl!" I smiled and nodded, realizing how truly out of the ordinary the day turned out to be, and of course Eva was enjoying my process. Patrick's joy had affected me. It seemed to reach through the phone and encircle me. There was an easiness about him that was disarming, stirring something within me I couldn't yet name but embraced. His laugh was deep but whimsical. A couple of times during our conversation, I imagined the plump boy of years ago, and the deep laugh just didn't fit with that image. I had trouble reconciling the image from the past with the man in the present. Little Patrick had grown into a gorgeous man. I smiled about that as I wondered what kind of man he really was.

While preparing for bed, I found myself looking forward to spending time with Patrick. In a way it was difficult to accept all that was actually happening. So many years had passed, but here we were about to rekindle an old connection. "Wow," was all I could say. There was so much to catch up on, so much to consider, so much to say. My thoughts covered a lot of territory. I explored a host of what-if scenarios, including the statement by the Native American in the bus station. I laughed at the thought of that but curiously did not rule it out. Miss Ella came to mind and I thought again about Gahti and her invitation to come rest in God's grace and receive miracles. I would have to call her soon and tell her about this miracle. I had to agree with Eva, this birthday was one to be remembered. Sleep was a long time coming that night, but when it found me I dreamed of blue skies and warm breezes. In the dream, I saw Miss Ella and she was smiling. It was such a soothing dream!

Our private tour guide turned out to be a female, a senior like us and as cheeky as the other women we met in Rapid City. She explained she normally did the tours in the summer but her husband had gone ice fishing and left her to carry out the task of getting us around. She asked us to call her Beverly, which was the middle name emboldened on her tour guide badge—-she liked that name best. Without hesitation she gave us a number of particulars about herself that let us know she was quite a character. A mother of six and a grandmother of 16, she was a hunter, a gambler and an accomplished violinist who gave music lessons only in the winter. All of this on top of being a tour guide. She asked many questions, especially about Eva's accident, and when we told her about our Good Samaritan she had some choice things to say that let us know this grandmother was as feisty as the day was long. Her humor and cheekiness set the tone for our adventure.

The ride to Mount Rushmore was beautiful, and Mount Rushmore itself was breathtaking. There weren't many tourists around but still more than we expected this time of the year, and people were very friendly. As I pushed Eva in the wheelchair, we marveled at the scenery. We took pictures and asked people to snap a few photos of us. Beverly stayed with the van. She would be waiting for us by the gate in one hour; that was the agreement. We experienced a video presentation giving historic information about Mount Rushmore that lasted about twenty minutes. I was struck by the absence of Black people. There was not one Black person in the video depicting the history. While there was a degree of patriotism revealed in the video and I experienced twinges of it as I watched history unfolding, I was still miffed by the fact that I didn't see any Black people in the video, not even one Black worker. I kept saying to myself, "How could that be?" Eva and I talked about this and both felt kind of sad. Perhaps that is why when we got to the bookstore, I bought so many coloring books that had President Obama and the First Lady in them along with a book about Black pioneers. I jumped for joy to see that we as a people were included somewhere in all the grandeur of Mount Rushmore. Interestingly, throughout our time at Mount Rushmore my mind flitted to various thoughts about Patrick. I entertained all sorts of possibilities.

Our ride from Mount Rushmore to the Chief Crazy Horse monument was festive. Beverly told stories about her escapades carrying tourists around. We laughed a lot. She was a fabulous storyteller and could make things come alive for you almost as if you were watching a movie. The closer we moved towards the monument the more eager I became. Excitement welled up within me and when I caught a glimpse of the massive structure towering majestically above us, I was awestruck. It was compelling in its majesty and might. Although not yet complete, the monument in all of its prominence and intricate detail evoked true reverence within me.

When we pulled into the vast parking lot in front of the huge gift shop aside the Chief Crazy Horse monument, I remembered I promised Kojo that I would call his name out near the monument and say a prayer for him there. In reviewing my promise, I realized I had not given him much thought in the past day or two, and that was different. I smiled about that and wondered what it meant, if anything and immediately my mind went to Patrick. Once out of the van, Beverly cleared with us how our time would be spent at the monument. She advised us to avoid the tour that would carry us directly to the monument, because Eva would not be able to walk the stairs and there was no wheelchair access. According to her, we would be able to have a grand view of the monument from the huge deck on the other side of the gift shop, which was wheelchair ready. We told her that we expected to stay at the monument for a couple of hours. In turn, she advised us that she would take a break and rest in the van.

Leaving Eva near the van with Beverly, I swiftly proceeded to find the place to secure the much-needed wheelchair. My mind raced as I entered the uncommonly large gift shop. I couldn't believe my eyes as I walked through the outer rooms. There were walls covered in artwork depicting Native Americans in various contexts and poses and beautiful ceremonial attire. I became enthralled, lost in the moment. Soon, a very brown man, remarkably similar to the man in the bus station, came over to me and with an engaging smile offered his help. He directed me to the place where I secured the wheelchair. I was filled with excitement, eager to get on with my mission. Once I settled Eva comfortably in the wheel chair, I found myself reflecting on the dream I had while in La Crosse and the word "come" from the dream danced within my mind. *I am here,* I thought, reveling in anticipation.

As soon as I pushed Eva through the doors of the gift shop, a young male guide showed us around while reporting various significant historical facts and pointing out choice items to consider buying as keepsakes from the trip. There was so much to see, and I was totally impressed with how the Chief Crazy Horse monument is supported and maintained. Donations and the sale of items in the gift shop subsidized everything! After about 10 minutes, we were directed to the theater where we experienced a video on the development and maintenance of the Chief Crazy Horse monument. It was an engaging informational video. It was a compelling story, and I found myself wiping tears from my eyes as the development of the likeness of Chief Crazy Horse evolved over time. I could not help but notice again, however, that in all of the work invested in honing the mountain sculpture, there was not even one Black person in the video—— at least I did not see one. Coming to terms with that was not easy for me. We asked the tour guide about the absence of Black people in the video and he explained that there were not many Blacks in the area. Despite my eagerness to learn and my excitement in being in the presence of the Monument, my mind went to Patrick from time-to-time. Among many questions, I wondered what he knew about the warrior Chief.

After much thought and a cup of strawberry Jello secured from the cafeteria, I rolled Eva out on the huge wooden deck from which we had an exceptionally clear view of the Chief Crazy Horse monument. The sculpture was awe inspiring. As I gazed upon the model-prototype and the gigantic likeness of my kindred spirit, I called my name out and then the names of the people whom I had promised to celebrate in Chief Crazy Horse's presence. Then, with arms raised above my head in a gesture of praise and gratitude to the Creator, I mouthed the words "I am here." Eva and I took many pictures of each other against the backdrop of the monument and we had the tour guide take a few pictures of us together. Before long, as promised, I tried to dial Kojo's number, but we were too high up in the mountains to get any kind of reception on the cell phone.

I bought lots of souvenirs from the gift shop, including hats with Chief Crazy Horse's name on them and books and a delightful pair of silver and jade earrings. As I picked up each item, I convinced myself that I was supporting the monument project and not just overspending. That rationalization worked, and I bought mementos for my children and grandchildren along with Kojo and a few others like Cullen and Gahti. Eva maintained her frugal stance. While she bought a few things, her bags were nowhere near the volume and girth of mine. I still marvel at the way she can conserve a dollar. We both bought loads of postcards, which we vowed to get mailed before we left Rapid City. When I paid for the last group of items, I wondered if I should get something for Patrick. Just as that thought crossed my mind, I saw a butterfly clip bookmark that was quite elegant. There were two; one had a yellow cast to it, and the other seemed almost aqua. I decided to get both of them. *I will keep one and give the other to Patrick, a gift from a friend*, I thought. It would be something to remind us of our time together. I smiled as the woman put the butterfly bookmarks in the bag and asked myself, *Woman, what are you doing?*

By the time Eva and I made it back to the van, Beverly was in deep conversation with a few of the Native Americans from the gift shop. They commented on all the bags we carried, noting that we must have enjoyed ourselves. With laughter and well wishes we climbed into the van, promising that we would return, perhaps in the summer when there were many festive activities scheduled, including a light show on the mountain. The tour guide had told us about that and it did seem inviting.

As Beverly maneuvered the vehicle down the mountain, I tried reaching Kojo again but did not get a connection for quite a while. When I did connect, I reached his voicemail. I left a jubilant message, noting that I had called his name out on the mountain. I must have sounded like a kid babbling because Eva began to mimic me, making fun of my childlike joy. We laughed, and Beverly chimed in, too, noting that she enjoyed our friendship. Before too long, we were headed back up into the mountains again, this time to have dinner at a casino. Beverly continued in her role as guide by telling us about other tourist attractions in the city. The one that seemed very intriguing was the opium tunnels, where it is thought Chinese mine workers used to go to smoke opium many, many years ago. We considered stopping there after dinner but decided against it because there were no wheelchairs available for Eva and it would be too much of a hike for her on crutches. With a hint of humor, both Eva and I lifted the idea again that we would return in the summer to partake of the opium tunnels and other attractions.

After dinner, I played the slots for about 30 minutes while Eva and Beverly just relaxed. I won about $50.00 before we decided to move on. While Beverly entertained us with more stories, we weaved in and out of mountain territory and finally stopped in front of a quaint little shop with colorful flags majestically hanging from the windows. Beverly told us it was a prize-winning candy shop run by a pair of French Canadian sisters. "They have the best chocolate in the world in there," she said as she quickly stepped out of the van. I went with her, leaving Eva behind but not before learning her heart's desire in chocolate. In fact, I questioned Eva a number of times to be sure I was certain of her wishes. She was very clear. She just wanted a couple of pieces of dark chocolate, nothing more than that. Upon entering the beautifully decorated little shop, I was struck by the delectable aromas. The climate in the shop was heavenly.

The two older women waiting on customers seemed to have stepped out of a fairytale. They spoke with heavy French accents and in a couple of instances spoke French with a few customers. I marveled at this uniquely European-like place high up in the mountains of South Dakota. It was as if I were in a fantasy of some kind. I gasped when I got a clear view of the broad variety of chocolate laid out on beautiful trays. It was very fine, so much to choose from. Beverly went directly to her chocolate-covered cherries as I found the dark chocolate for Eva and picked up as much white chocolate as I could carry for myself. *This place is a chocolate lover's dream,* I thought. I may have even smacked my lips as I paid for my stash. I could hardly wait to dig my teeth into the delights in my bag. Caught up in the moment, I forgot about my diabetes. I even bought candy to take back home, and I picked up two catalogs that told all about the award-winning candy shop. What a treat! Something truly novel to behold in the land of Chief Crazy Horse. I wondered if Patrick knew about this place.

Beverly laughed as she gingerly turned the van back on the highway and headed down the mountain again. I handed Eva her dark chocolate, and all three of us engaged in childlike joy, savoring our respective delectable choices. Before long, Eva dozed off, leaving me the recipient of Beverly's entertainment. Although a bit drowsy myself, I asked questions about this or that, but generally I just listened, with my mind drifting to my prospective evening with Patrick. I couldn't believe what was happening, and I was both anxious and curious about how the evening would go. Pushing myself to stay awake, my mind went back to Cullen and Gahti. I decided I would give them a call in the morning to tell them about my adventures in Chief Crazy Horse's country, and I would have quite a bit to say about my encounter with Patrick.

It was about 6:45 p.m. when Beverly pulled into the driveway of the Comfort Suites. Eva woke up immediately, and we signed off with Beverly, noting we had a terrific time and would recommend her service to others. We gave her a hefty tip for which she was most grateful. She helped us tote our stuff inside as we engaged in banter all the way. Saying goodbye to her was rather like signing off from a friend, and we were sure we would pass her name on to others.

The women at the front desk were interested in our day-long adventure, and Eva took it upon herself to give them a blow-by-blow account of our time with Beverly. We even shared our candy with them.

When we opened the door to our room, I noticed a card on the floor addressed to me. I smiled, knowing instantly that Patrick put it there. Eva sat watching me as I devoured what the card presented. It was a humorous card that had a dog chasing a butterfly on the front. Inside, written in well-scripted cursive, was, "Happy Birthday, and do you still like butterflies? I'll pick you up at 8:00 p.m. I am so happy I found you yesterday on your birthday, Jewelle! Yes, I remember your birthday is 03/03, similar in double digits to mine, which is 11/11." He signed the card "Je m'appelle Eagle Feather." I was speechless. He remembered my birthday from all those years ago and that I liked butterflies. A tear rolled down my cheek. It came out of nowhere. The card and the message were so tender; I was touched by Patrick's thoughtfulness. Instantly, I racked my brain trying to remember when I'd gotten into butterflies, but I couldn't. I remembered in boarding school I had a chain with a cross and a butterfly on it and had worn it for years. But I had been into butterflies for years before that, I thought. Reflecting deeply, I touched my neck to find the relatively new silver chain with two butterflies and a crucifix. I smiled as I passed the card to Eva, thinking I was glad Patrick had jogged my memory about his birthdate, which I had forgotten.

I had to decide what I would wear. I did not bring anything dressy, but Patrick hadn't said what we would be doing. I thought about calling him to be clear about our evening but decided against it and ultimately chose to let the evening be a surprise. Eva laughed out loud when she read the card, and I felt great about her approval of what was transpiring with Patrick. Our ten-year age difference seemed to give her that mentoring quality from time to time. And now it seemed that she was thinking I was heading in the right direction. She saw my tear-stained cheeks, and I didn't mind.

CHAPTER 11

Experiencing Patrick in Rapid City

Once I had my bath, I noticed that Eva was deeply involved in eating pieces of my white chocolate candy. We argued about that as I got dressed and ended up laughing at her boldness. She just decided to do what she wanted to do with my candy. She could be cheeky when she wanted to be. In our little argument, she pointed out that my white chocolate was the only candy she would be getting tonight, but I had the possibility of stumbling upon a batch of really scrumptious candy if I played my cards right. I couldn't believe my ears or my eyes because Eva winked at me as if she were giving me permission to be a hussy. That was out of the norm for her and for me, but the thought was very engaging. I finally decided to wear a white sweater with my jeans, brown boots, and a white fleece cap. I was told often that the cap set off my dark skin. Of course, I put on all of my silver jewelry, including the lovely earrings I bought at the Chief Crazy Horse gift shop. As I sprayed on my usual scent, I glanced in the mirror and had to admit that I did look good for my age. My 63 years did not show on me, and tonight I felt good about that. Since my weekend at Cullen's, there had been a change in me that people were noticing.

One woman told me a few days before the trip to South Dakota that if she didn't know better she would guess that I was either pregnant or in love. She was pretty confident that I was not pregnant but less sure about the in-love piece. She asked me that question outright, and all I could do was laugh. I told her I would be the first one to shout my joy to everyone if I would ever be in love again. But tonight I could see the glow in me. I wasn't sure why it was there, but I was pleased to bear witness to it. The room phone rang as I was gazing at myself in the mirror. Eva picked up the phone and nodded in my direction. He was in the lobby! My heart raced, and I stumbled a bit as I grabbed my coat, purse, and gloves and rushed for the door. I gave Eva a long look, and she just smiled. The women at the front desk were all smiling when they saw me. They spoke in muffled tones, but I knew they were talking about Patrick and me. Lord, when I saw him, my heart stopped. He looked marvelous, absolutely marvelous.

It was pleasing to me that we were essentially color coordinated. He had on a white wool cap that fit tightly across his forehead, with a braid hanging down his back. His brown suede coat had a white fleece lining that showed at the collar, and he had on a beige sweater and jeans over a pair of wild snakeskin boots. As I moved towards him, he opened his arms and with a scrumptious smile gave me the biggest hug. I almost lost my balance and my breath as I caught a solid whiff of him. He smelled wonderful, like hickory and vanilla and something else I just couldn't put my finger on. He said my name over and over again, "Jewelle! Jewelle! Jewelle!" He said my name with such gusto that I found myself laughing gleefully. I remembered to put the bookmark I bought for him in my purse. My mind went to it as he directed me out to his truck. It was then that I noticed the Virginia plates and that his truck was a 4x4 of some kind. The frosty winter night called to us, and I felt all aglow inside.

As we drove through the streets of Rapid City, I felt as if I were in a fairytale and Patrick was a long-lost prince taking me to a higher place, and I was not afraid at all. There was a blues CD playing. I smiled at the lyrics of the down-home blues. The man was singing about being in a dangerous kind of mood. Patrick looked at me and laughed, pointing to the CD player. "Who is that?" I asked, stirred by the engaging words and the clarity of the voice. "Keb Mo," Patrick offered. "That is the great Keb Mo. No one can sing the blues like that man," he posited with true pride in his voice. I had never heard of the brother, but something told me I would know a lot about him before too long. I looked at Patrick out of the corner of my eye and just smiled. We rode for a while before we began to talk. It was as if we both couldn't believe what was happening.

Patrick was the one to break the silence. "So you are a widow, right, Jewelle?" he asked while reaching over to touch my hand. Though his hand was gloved, I could still sense warmth, and my breath caught in my throat as I answered, trying to remember if I had mentioned that the night before. "Yes, I have been a widow for nearly 12 years. How about you?" I shot right back at him, realizing that I was holding my breath for his answer. "Divorced for many years," he said, and I believe I detected a bit of sadness in his voice. I went on to ask how long he was married and was surprised to learn that he had been married more than 30 years and had nine children(eight with his wife and one outside child) and seven grandchildren. We were deep in conversation by the time we pulled in front of a downtown, seemingly upscale steakhouse. Interestingly, I found myself waiting for him to open doors. I was being a lady! Patrick was agile, and although he favored his left side, he moved with elegance and a smooth sense of strength. At that moment, I felt alive and very special. I chuckled under my breath, just because.

Once we removed our coats, Patrick gave his name to the hostess in a booming voice, and we were ushered to a table bearing silver and gold balloons and a dozen red roses in what appeared to be a special, more private section of the restaurant. The hostess made it known that she had been forewarned about my birthday, warmly wishing me a joy-filled evening and a long life. It was clear Patrick had been busy, and when he revealed a beautifully wrapped gift, I felt lightheaded. He was meticulous in planning the moment. There were so many surprises, and everything was so elegant. He saw to it that I was comfortably seated. He kissed me on the cheek and whispered "Happy Birthday" in my ear while encouraging me to open my gift right away. It was then that I remembered how he was about gifts years ago. He loved giving and receiving presents and would almost always preempt the gift-opening process by telling what was inside the box. I chuckled, thinking that at least now he was not doing that but still wanted me to know what was inside the box right away. My heart pounded as I removed the silver and gold paper and set the silver bow to the side. My eyes watered a bit when I saw the beautiful butterfly on a very delicate silver chain. The stones in the wings of the butterfly sparkled vibrantly, and I thought to myself that this had to be a very expensive item, which made me wonder about Patrick's economic status. He insisted on placing his gift around my neck; a kindred spirit to the butterflies and crucifix already hanging there. My mind raced, but I just smiled and gushed words of appreciation. Remembering the book mark from the gift shop, I handed it to him and he thanked me with a kiss on the cheek. Patrick beamed, and for a moment I could clearly remember the pre-pubescent boy I left in Virginia many years ago. It was a touching moment for sure.

Everything about the restaurant was mellow and invitingly romantic. Not too far from our table on the other side of a delightfully colorful silk-screened transparent partition was a Native American woman playing jazz on the piano and scatting out an Ella Fitzgerald song. I couldn't believe all of the quaint experiences I was having in Rapid City. Savoring every delectable aspect of my surroundings, I smiled at Patrick, noting to him that while this was not his favorite down-home blues place in Virginia, he made an excellent choice for the evening. In turn, he told me I needed to come to Virginia so that he could really wine and dine me deep in soulful Southern blues. In all that we had done to get comfortable and ready to order dinner, I noticed how much he favored his left side. I suppose I must have been staring quizzically when he caught me watching him and quickly began an explanation that captivated me. "I was burned in a house fire, Jewelle," he said without emotion. "They say I am lucky to be alive, and I guess I am. People still don't know how I made it out with the one toddler." He seemed to choke on his words then, and before the waiter brought our dinner, he told me the source of his pain. I learned that after the navy, he became a firefighter in Richmond and worked his way up to lieutenant when his near-fatal experience occurred.

He had not been on duty the night of the lethal fire. He was leaving the gym where he worked out three times each week when he heard screams coming from a rooming house nearby. The woman said her babies were inside the burning building and she was running back inside to save them. On impulse, against his better judgment, he went into the building. He brought out one child but could not find the other. He went in again to find the second toddler, but the floor had given way, and he was not able to find the other child, almost losing his life in the process. As we talked about the fire, I heard deep sadness in his voice. I could hear his suffering as he made note again of his regret about not finding the other child. Though so many people saw him as a hero, he didn't see himself that way and for years had punished himself and others for his failure.

He told me he'd spent nearly six months in the hospital initially and to date has undergone 17 surgeries. He was scheduled for another one soon to hopefully gain more mobility in his left arm and hand. He showed me his hand, and it was markedly disfigured but not grotesque. He told me that for years he hated himself and drank to cover up his pain. Because of his extensive injuries, he could not return to his career as a firefighter; he was deemed disabled, and that broke his heart. Because he wasn't on duty at the time he sustained his injuries, there had been problems securing compensation from the fire department, but ultimately things worked in his favor. He pointed out that he wallowed in self-pity for quite a while and acted out in many ways. In all that had happened, his wife left him and had since married someone else. He did not blame her for leaving because he had become a monster in his pained state. In sharing the story about the divorce, he didn't appear bitter. In fact, he noted that he understood his wife had tried to support him in his suffering after the fire, but he was so caught up in pain that he pushed her away, admitting that he was hostile and verbally abusive towards her and his children. In addition, he had been unfaithful. He acknowledged that she made the right choice to save herself.

Listening to Patrick, I realized how fickle life could be. *We never know where the twists and turns of life will carry us,* I thought.

Though our food was tasty, we barely touched it. We were much too involved in savoring every morsel of each other's life. I hung on to every word Patrick shared, and he seemed to be immersed in my life story as well. Patrick was open about having gone into treatment for his alcohol abuse and the residuals of post-traumatic stress disorder (PTSD) and believed he was a much better man for having gone through all of those

experiences. In his treatment, he discovered a deep need to reconnect with his mother's people in a meaningful way and had journeyed back and forth to South Dakota a number of times each year for the past six years. Through all of his trials and tribulations, his father's brother Paul, the one everyone thought was gay, stuck by him and supported him. Even when he had been hostile and "falling-down drunk," his uncle would look for him in bars, drive him to his home, and take care of him for days on end.

It was his uncle Paul who had been his emotional support when he was in treatment for his alcohol abuse. His children were mixed in their support, vacillating between their loyalty to him and to their mother. His sons from his marriage seemed to have been hit the worst by his abuse. He noted that so much happened after the fire. It appeared every dark issue suppressed before the fire rose to the top afterward. Of his four sons with his wife, one went to prison for a drug deal gone bad; one was killed in the Middle East; and one is a career soldier and still overseas somewhere on a third tour of duty. The youngest from his marriage is now living with his mother and her new husband while attending College. He plans to be a psychologist.

His daughters are another story. Of his four daughters, all are career women. One owns a day spa in Richmond along with her dermatology practice; another is a podiatrist in New York; another is an officer in the navy (everyone thinks she is gay) now living in Japan; and the youngest is a pediatric ICU nurse in Richmond. All of his grandchildren are the progeny of his sons, most out of wedlock. His daughters have not yet begun to give him grandchildren, though two have been married for a number of years. He laughed about his very assertive and career-minded girls, noting that the two unmarried ones, the podiatrist and the navy officer, would probably never marry. Interestingly, his girls were all born before his sons. He shocked me when he went on to tell me about his nine-year-old son, Paul(named for his uncle), the one with special needs.

This child was an offspring he sired during his wild drinking days after the fire. Though married at the time, he connected with a woman who was a free spirit and who used drugs heavily. Once she told him about the pregnancy, he begged her not to abort the baby. They made a deal, one that he didn't regret. The information about his new son came on the heels of his eldest son's death overseas, and he felt he was being given a gift. His wife, of course, did not see it that way. The pregnancy and the deal were more than she could take, and it was a deal breaker for her. She filed for divorce the year after his son was born. The divorce had been a long time coming, with his wife vacillating a number of times before she finally threw in the towel. During the first year after his son, Paul's birth, Patrick gave his son's mother quite a bit of money, and she gave up her rights to the child. It was obvious Paul had special needs (later diagnosed as autism). She did not want a special-needs child in the first place and jumped at the opportunity to take Patrick's money offer and run. He smiled as he claimed his single-parent status, noting he had brought his son to be with his mother's people — a couple of cousins — while he went in for his next series of surgeries and extended recovery process.

Engulfed in his story, the social worker in me came alive, and I questioned him about the timing of the surgery and how it seemed to disrupt his son's school schedule. He explained this round of surgeries was rare and deemed experimental, performed only by a few doctors in the world. And the surgeon scheduled to do his surgery would be leaving the country for a position in Spain in a matter of a few months and would not return to the U.S. for quite a while. This governed the timing of the surgery. His son would spend the rest of the school year and the summer in Rapid City with relatives with whom he had been around quite regularly during his short life. Patrick would have an opportunity to heal and to have the level of follow-up care he would need via additional surgical procedures, if necessary, and months of painstaking physical therapy. From years of surgeries and physical therapy, he knew he would not be at his best in caring for his son. He explained that he thought of hiring a nanny for his boy for after the surgery but decided he would rather let his family support him and benefit financially for their graciousness. As I listened intently, his thoughtfulness struck me. It was refreshing to hear such honesty about past transgressions and his struggle to put his life back together. "I am a better man now, Jewelle," he said. "The fire has honed me into a much better man, and I am grateful for that." It was a touching statement. I found myself reaching across the table to stroke his left hand, his burned one. He smiled as he said my name again. In truth, at his touch, I struggled to breathe. Something was happening within me. If Cullen was right about Kojo's opening the door for the feelings I was experiencing, then I had a huge "thank you" for Kojo.

We talked freely, and before we knew it, the restaurant had cleared out, the singer had stopped crooning, and our waitress gently nudged us to pay the bill. Patrick was stirred from his deep excursion into his past and handed the woman a credit card as he spoke with urgency in his voice. "I am not ready to let you go, Jewelle. Can we keep the evening going for a while?" In a flash, Eva's statement about candy crossed my mind, and I wondered what I would do if he wanted to take me back to his place (wherever that was). I wasn't sure: I might just say yes ! I smiled at my thoughts and told him I was with him and he could decide about the evening. In turn, he laughed heartily while promising he would show me the country under the light of the moon. He went on to say that after our moonlight ride we could go to one of the casinos up in the mountains for a while. I smiled to myself, thinking about the luck I had in the casino earlier in the day. His plan sounded good to me, instantly making my heart race as we made our way out to his truck. Though I did not have much wine, I felt light and girlish. He asked if I was sleepy, and I quickly chimed a melodious "no" that could be set to music in some love song. I allowed myself the luxury of relaxing as our evening unfolded.

When we were comfortable again in his truck, he reached in a case on the backseat and pulled out another set of CDs. As he inserted one, he asked, "Have you heard of the Uppity Blues Women?" Of course I hadn't, and he went on to tell me that he saw them with his uncle Paul at a club back in Richmond years ago. To his surprise and his uncle's delight, he enjoyed their witty lyrics. He thought I would find them amusing. And as we rode in the moonlight, I found myself laughing freely at the lyrics of the Uppity Blues Women. They seemed to sing out loud the thoughts of many women past fifty, including thoughts of younger men and life's challenges in general. One song about wild women grabbed me, and I found myself singing along. The words were set to a catchy tune. Patrick hit the replay button repeatedly, allowing me to savor the witty lyrics. He joined in gleefully as the moon beamed down on us. It was as if heaven were smiling on our time together.

Before too long, we pulled in front of a large ranch-style house with a rambling fence gracing its perimeter. A few cars were parked in the huge driveway, and to the left of the house was another building that appeared to be a barn. We parked in front of the house, and Patrick began to tell me about his grandfather's legacy. This grand place was where his son was living now with his cousins and where Patrick himself bunked whenever he came to Rapid City. This was his grandfather's legacy to them all and had been owned by his grandmother until her recent death. She was cared for here in this house by her granddaughters and grandsons. All of her children made their transitions before she did, many due to various types of accidents, including Patrick's mother who was killed in a car accident. From what he shared, there had been so much trauma among his mother's siblings; great suffering within the family, which solidified the family bond. We sat for about an hour in front of the house. All seemed quiet, and though there were a few lights on inside the house, Patrick was certain that most of the folks inside were asleep. He made a point of letting me know that if it were up to him, I would meet his entire South Dakota family at another time. He said this with certainty, and hearing the confidence in his voice made me smile. As we sat in the night, he told me that his grandfather had worked on the Crazy Horse Mountain site for many years, as had some of his uncles and cousins. One cousin was still among the construction crew at the mountain site, but his other cousins were now in the professional arena. The one living at the house was a dentist with a thriving practice. His wife was a stay-at-home mom who did part-time medical billing from her home. They would be looking after his autistic son. He explained that while his son showed high-level functioning, he was given to bouts of emotional explosiveness that required special attention.

His cousin's wife had worked with autistic children when she was in college. That was another reason Patrick chose to bring his son to be with them while he recovered from the forthcoming series of surgeries. Again, I listened intently, and I allowed him to hold and caress my hand as he talked. As time passed, he deftly shifted his attention from one of my hands to the other, gently massaging each finger on each hand as he talked. It was a moving experience. I never had anyone touch me that way before. It was as if he were conversing with each finger, carrying on a second nonverbal conversation that was sensual and sure. As he talked, his resonant voice filling the truck and his gentle touch reaching to the depths of me, there were moments I thought I would not be able to breathe. It was not exactly a sexual experience I was having at first, but it still took my breath away. Once, I found myself muttering something about how welcoming his touch was, and he stopped, looked at me, and ultimately smiled. He explained that touch had become so important to him after the fire, particularly after the excruciating hours of physical therapy coupled with the soothing healing massages he experienced throughout his recovery. He grew to value touch in a way he never considered before and now felt more connected when he was touching as he talked.

With that said, I found a kind of permission to respond to his hand massage with an eager mirroring of his gentle movements, and he moaned softly as I massaged both his right hand and his seriously scarred left hand. I surprised myself, taking liberties with his hands. I wondered what had come over me; I just kept on going.

146

It was a magnificent thing happening in that 4x4 truck. The cold night air did not bother us at all. Once again, Patrick uttered my name, and I detected ecstasy in his voice. For a moment, I wondered if I had lost my mind and stepped over into some kind of kinky abyss. The stoic Jewelle peeked her head out and threatened to put reason into the mix, but I shut her down and allowed myself to savor every moment of the pleasure. It was as if we were making love right there and it wasn't about sex. I can't explain it.

My mind went to a book I once read about the art of Tantric sex, and before I knew it, I said that out loud. It came out in the form of a question to Patrick. "Are you familiar with Tantric sex?" I asked with my eyes closed and my breath raspy. I was shocked at my boldness! "Yes," he said strongly, breathing deeply. "I have been practicing Tantric yoga for years as part of my healing regimen." He went on detailing his experiences with yoga as he leaned over and pecked me slightly on the lips. In response, I asked boldly, "Is that what is going on here with us?" "Perhaps," he said, breathing deeply and placing my right hand to his lips, seemingly not tentative at all about what was happening. "Whatever this is," he said, "isn't it great?" And with that, he took three of my fingers into his mouth, and I thought I would sprout wings and fly. We were behaving like cheeky adolescents, and I couldn't believe I was such a willing participant.

I think we both forgot where we were for a moment and didn't see the man heading to the truck. The rap on the window on Patrick's side startled both of us. Patrick chuckled when he saw the intruder. "This is my cousin James, the dentist," he said, touching my hand affectionately. James was a tall man in a heavy top coat over pajamas. There was laughter in his cousin's words as he welcomed us inside. But what really got me was his cousin's knowledge of me. He spoke to me as if he knew me. "So you are the great Jewelle," he said confidently. "My cousin has been smiling at his fate. You have brought joy back to his life," he went on. I was embarrassed to be caught in the midst of whatever was going on between us, but Patrick just laughed and chided his cousin about being nosey. Their friendly banter spoke volumes about their relationship. It was clear that they were close and respected each other. Patrick and I learned that James saw the light of the truck when we pulled up. He watched for a while, thinking we would come inside the house. When we didn't, he decided to come out, introduce himself, and poke a bit of fun at his cousin, who was seemingly re-experiencing a gust of adolescent fervor. His wife and all the children were asleep, but we could come into the warm house and get comfortable.

With lots of laughter and joking, Patrick thanked his cousin but pointed out we were going to one of the casinos up in the mountains to round out the evening. Patrick made that decision confidently and conveyed it with such diplomacy that I let my embarrassment ease. Patrick promised his cousin that he and his wife would ultimately have an opportunity to spend time with me. I smiled and didn't utter a word. I recognized at that moment for sure that Patrick had plans, and while I didn't quite know what they were, I knew they were going to be okay with me. For a moment, a memory of the plump 12-year-old boy I left behind in Virginia so many years ago flew through my mind, and I chuckled thinking how incongruous that image was with the strong and confident hugely handsome man sitting next to me. I pushed the memory aside and basked in the power of the moment.

We filled our ride to the casino with conversation. This time Patrick pulled out another Keb Mo CD and the brother's soulful presentation was enthralling. His earthy mellowness encircled us as we talked on and on about our evening thus far. We laughed about his cousin's intervention, admitting that James stepped upon a very special moment. Throughout the ride, Patrick kept his hand on me in some way. I was surprised at how well he was able to manage the truck with his infirmed hand. When we left the truck for the warmth of the casino, he pulled me to him as we walked in. I must say it felt good to be enveloped in his arms. He wanted me right there beside him, and I enjoyed knowing that!

The climate of the casino was still festive at this late hour. A group of Asian tourists milled around having a grand old time. Deftly, Patrick ordered two huge mugs of hot herbal tea, graciously noting that I could have a shot of spirits in mine if I chose to do so. He made a point of indicating he was at a place in his recovery process where he could be in the presence of others who imbibed and not be affected by it. I smiled, indicating that the herbal tea would be just fine. We sat across from each other in a booth, and I could look directly at him now in the bright casino lights. A pure frontal view of him revealed a very handsome man with exquisitely even white teeth (a great set of dentures perhaps, I mused) and of course the eye patch. He saw me staring and immediately answered many of the questions I had churning in my head. "My left eye remains closed at all times except when I apply the medicine that is mostly to moisturize the area or I am using an optic prosthesis," he told me. "No, I will not be able to see out of that eye ever again, but I am learning not to think of that as so much of a loss. My right eye is very strong, and I do regular exercises to strengthen it." He further explained he had a number of prosthetic eyes. But his son had gotten a hold of the one he had with him and misplaced it. That is why he was wearing the patch until he returned to Virginia.

He talked more about the fire and the surgery he would be having soon. As he talked, he encased my legs in his under the table, grinning sheepishly. He knew he was being forward but elected to do just that while enjoying my response. If this had been the first date with anyone else, I would not have allowed such intrusiveness. But Patrick, cheeky though he was, seemed like a long-lost friend returning home. I convinced myself of this as I smiled back at him and he winked at me, giving his good eye a moment of exercise, he said. He talked about the many surgeries and challenging bouts of physical therapy he'd endured over the years. Some of it made me cringe. I could not imagine the pain he went through to get himself in shape again. Doctors told him that if not for his overall fitness and body building before the fire, he would probably not have made it.

He talked at length about his spiritual life as well. For years before the fire he essentially kept a distance from God, rejecting in part the punitive God of his father's mother, the woman I had known back in boarding school as Mrs. Johnson. But deep down inside, he always felt a connection of some kind with a loving and nurturing higher force, which, since the fire, had become the Great Spirit of his mother's people and the equally powerful and loving spiritual practices of his paternal grandfather's people down on Sapelo Island,where slaves and their descendants embraced spiritual beliefs native to their African heritage. In addition, he admitted to reading about the faith walks of many powerful people like Presidents Obama and Carter, along with Black Elk and Dr. Margaret Lawrence. When he mentioned Dr.Margaret Lawrence, one of the first Black female psychiatrists in the U.S., I questioned him about his interest in her spiritual walk because she was a particular favorite of mine. I was surprised he was familiar with her work. In response to my query, he said that during one of his long hospital stays, an African-American nurse gave him the book *Balm in Gilead: Journey of a Healer*, which was Dr. Lawrence's biography, written by her daughter, Sarah Lightfoot. The nurse had been taken with her life for several reasons but was particularly intrigued by a connection to Richmond, Virginia in her story. In turn, Patrick was deeply moved by a quote from the book that urged individuals to explore their history and lineage.

As Patrick recited the quote, it was apparent he was passionate about what it had led him to become. He explained the quote reawakened within him a yearning to know more about himself, especially his mother's people and his paternal grandfather's people down on Sapelo Island. It was then that he pushed forward in making connections with his Rapid City relatives in earnest and went on a spiritual quest. He believes he was seeking his TRUE identity and ultimate connection with the Creator, the Great Spirit. What he learned gave him pause. Some of it could not be proven by hard facts, but oral history tied his maternal grandfather's lineage to Chief Crazy Horse himself. The story continues to be passed on in his family, which turned out to be his grandparents' primary legacy. They had been adamant that their clan was made up of descendants of the great warrior chief through the outside child born to Black Buffalo Woman.

Stories passed down through oral history note that Chief Crazy Horse and Black Buffalo Woman loved each other deeply, though she was married to someone else. She and Chief Crazy Horse ultimately had an intimate relationship from which a girl child was conceived, according to many storytellers. It is said that this child had curly light hair just like that of Chief Crazy Horse, but she was claimed by Black Buffalo Woman's husband, No Water. As Patrick told the story that had been passed down in his family, I got chills. It was an extraordinary thing happening in this moment. I couldn't believe what I was hearing. I had read many accounts of Chief Crazy Horse's life, but as I could recall at that moment, only the book by Goldman mentioned the curly light-haired girl born to Black Buffalo Woman after she returned to her husband's house from the relationship with Chief Crazy Horse. I pondered this information and felt almost faint — it was beginning to be too much for me to digest. I closed my eyes and prayed as Patrick talked. I heard him, but I was lost in the questions racing around in my head. Could I be sitting with an actual descendant of the great Warrior Chief?

I thought I was merely imagining this, but Patrick answered, "Yes, Jewelle, it could be. We can't be certain, but it could be true. The possibility has made me giddy on more than one occasion. I am grateful to my grandmother for keeping my grandfather's legacy alive. She was truly a spirit walker." Patrick and I held on to each other. I think I reached for him. I thought about the Native American in the bus station and was amazed at his prophecy. There were so many connections, too many to just be happenstance. I don't know how long we sat in silence but remember thinking, *God, this is too much for the blood pressure, so I am going to give it to you.* Once again, I breathed deeply, trying to surrender all to the Creator.

What shook us from that moment was my need to go to the bathroom. I purposefully didn't take my diuretic for the sake of keeping the evening smooth and without too many bathroom runs. But at that moment, the urge hit me with such fervor that I found myself almost racing to the ladies' room. Patrick took leave as well as if my bathroom run had broken some kind of spell, and he, too, had to contend with mundane things again. Interestingly, he had only one bathroom visit during our entire time together, certainly suggesting that he was free of any prostate problems. I smiled as I thought about that. Good news, I thought, and, yes, I was being a bit naughty. When I returned to the table, there were fresh mugs of tea, some fry bread, butter, and honey. I smiled at Patrick, and we just sat quietly for a while, savoring our treats. And then Patrick began to eye me carefully, intentionally making his thoughts known. Softly he offered, "Jewelle, you have beautiful skin, piercingly engaging eyes, a precious smile, and I love your hair. You are a stunning woman." He reached across the table to cradle my hand. I was sure I was blushing under the glowing energy of his words. But true to form, I made a comment about needing to slim down a bit, to which Patrick responded without hesitation, "Not for me, Jewelle. I like you the way you are. You are a pleasing armful, and I like that!" My heart pounded as he gave me another wink of his right eye. He seemed so confident and genuine in what he was saying, and it appeared that through his words he was staking claim because under the table he was again encasing my legs within his while boldly giving me a crooked grin and a wink. "Exercising my good eye again," he said, bringing additional ease to our exchange. I could hardly breathe. His touch at that point became intoxicating.

For a while we sat quietly, but ultimately he began talking about his next surgery again. His manner was upbeat as he clearly seemed excited about the adventure to come. He explained that the surgery would be something almost out of a science fiction movie; he would have a prosthetic hand attached after the remnants of his burned hand would be in part surgically restructured. His prosthetic hand would be a variation on the "Luke" arm/hand made popular by the movie *Stars Wars* via Luke Skywalker. If all went well, Patrick would have a significant level of fine-motor mobility in the hand to the extent that he could possibly tie his shoes and perform other fairly intricate duties with his left hand. His thoughts would govern much of the mobility.

He jovially admitted he didn't understand all of the intricate details behind how the hand would work but said he would attend a class when he returned home. He noted that the surgery was done first in China some years ago and became a feature of a few physicians devoted to healing U.S. veterans, hoping to provide them with a new lease on life. It was still, however, considered an experimental procedure for the general population. As a result, his disability Medicare insurance, coupled with a supplemental insurance plan, would not handle the cost of the surgery. The cost was prohibitive for most, but despite all of the bureaucratic rancor, he would be able to handle the debt of the surgery himself because upon his uncle Paul's death, he had become a fairly wealthy man. Leaning forward and squeezing my hand, he shared that his uncle's life insurance policies alone yielded a little over a million dollars, and his estate beyond that had been substantial. He and his son Paul were the only beneficiaries.

There were other blessings as well; his uncle's financial planner became his advisor, which brought him a number of good investment opportunities that defied the downturn of the recent unstable economy. Patrick talked freely about his assets and I looked at him intently trying desperately to keep my mouth from falling open. The sums of money he was tossing around were off the chain, and I could not help but think that here was the once-little Patrick laying claim to such a fortune. For a moment, I felt rather small in light of all he had amassed because I, on the other hand, was still tied to my rather meager income by comparison, hoping that my Social Security years would afford me a level of comfort that my hard work over the years warranted. But I wasn't sure. Many of the investments in my humble portfolio went south with the downturn in the economy, and I was hoping for a major turnabout over the next year or two before I would seriously consider retirement.

Eying me carefully as he shared, he must have noticed something in my countenance that made him shift the focus to me. Uncannily, he seemed to read my thoughts again and pointed out in his rather boyish way that he was grateful for how he had been blessed despite the many losses he experienced in his life. He went on to say that without a doubt he would really see it as a befitting blessing to be able to share his good fortune with a good woman at this stage of his life. Again, I just breathed and thought this whole scenario must be a dream. Any minute I would wake up and find myself in the room with Eva and we would laugh hysterically about all of this. But it wasn't a dream. I was sitting in a casino in the mountains of South Dakota with a robustly handsome man whom I had known as a mere boy. And the crush he showed many years ago was still present and seemingly blooming into something more. Additionally, this man who could be the descendant of my revered Chief Crazy Horse had his legs wrapped around mine and I was nearly faint with excitement.

Everything about him relayed he wanted me and his wants were a serious matter to him. I could not believe I sat comfortably entwined within his long strong legs as if we had been intimates for many years. I could not believe that in the short time we were together at this stage of our development, I was feeling a closeness to him through which I felt safe. I couldn't believe that if he wanted me to sleep with him, I might just do it: not because I am a hussy but because there was a level of connection I was beginning to experience that I had not known in years, if ever, and it felt so good, so very right. On top of all of that, his financially secure status in life was more than I could ever hope for, coming from someone who seemed so willing to share. I breathed deeply again and uttered my rendition of Gahti's words, "I rest in the will of the all-knowing God, and I expect miracles."

Patrick saw me mouth the words and asked me to say whatever I was saying out loud. I did, and I was shocked when he repeated the words again and again. He then leaned across the table and kissed me squarely on the lips; this time it was not a peck. He began saying my name again and pointed out that he believed our meeting was no accident. For him, it was an answer to many years of prayer. He prayed for a good woman and believed I was the answer to his prayers. In that moment, tears spilled down my cheeks as he squeezed me with his legs and said my name again. It was another special moment for us. He seemed to draw upon the intimacy of the moment to move forward with an agenda that sparkled in his eyes. He said, "Jewelle, I've been thinking that you and Eva can turn your plane tickets in or keep them for another trip, and I can drive you back to Milwaukee. I am going that way, and it will give us more time together. I know this sounds selfish, but I don't want to let you go. Please say yes, Jewelle. Do you have to be back right away?" He said all of that without taking a breath, and it reminded me of Patrick the boy I once knew. In turn, I explained Eva and I came out on the bus, just for pure adventure. So shifting to a car might be better for Eva given her ankle situation, but I would need to talk with her about the change, knowing full well that she would jump at the opportunity. Patrick just about jumped out of his seat. "So you say yes, Jewelle." He bellowed, "We can travel together and the trip will give us more time, so much more time." We both laughed. It was in the midst of that joyful moment that my cell phone went off. I was stunned, thinking it had to be Eva calling me at this hour. And then I looked at my cell phone, only to be shocked to find that it was 6:00 a.m. Mountain Time. It was morning, but nothing in the casino gave the time away.

The voice on the phone rattled me. It was Kojo. My mind raced, trying to make sense of the time of the call. Well, he is in Florida, I thought, and that would make it 8:00 a.m. there. His jovial voice jumped through the phone, and Patrick whispered, "If that is your man, tell him I am here now and that's that!" I chuckled at his cheekiness but felt warm inside. I realized I had never spoken with Kojo while in the presence of another man, and it was uncomfortable. I considered that this must be how Kojo felt when I called him and he would be with his young woman. All of this churned through my mind as I managed to get out a "hello".

Kojo immediately apologized for missing the phone call to him the day before, and he had many questions about the Crazy Horse monument. As I carefully shared some things with him, Patrick squeezed my legs tightly under the table and said out loud what he whispered before. Kojo heard the voice and asked, "Jewelle, are you at breakfast? I hear people in the background." I laughed, noting I was with a friend. Well, there must have been something in how I said the word friend because Kojo became very quiet and there was an uncomfortable lull in the conversation. "Call me later," he said as he signed off rather abruptly, and I loved every minute of his uncertainty. There was something in his voice that made me know he knew something was up. I loved it! I said I would call him later and turned my attention completely to Patrick, who had many questions about the phone call. I laughed at his questions but did not answer any of them before I turned the tables on him.

With seasoned finesse, I queried, "Now tell me, how many women are there in your life, Patrick?" He laughed at that but responded immediately, indicating that there was no one center stage but me. He went on to note that he had a number of friends back in Virginia but nothing serious and certainly nothing that could stand in the way of our becoming as close as we chose to be. With that said, he looked at me squarely and told me he did not intend to let me leave his life again. I shared a bit of information about Kojo but nothing too deep, and I watched him intently as I did so. As I went on with my story, he smiled and winked at me. At the end of my report, I leaned across the table and kissed him on the cheek. In response, he came around to my side of the table and held me close, kissing my cheeks and face and finally landing a very seductive kiss on my lips. My heart sang, and I didn't care if there were people watching us. I felt as if we were in a movie as compelling as *Love Story* or *Lady Sings the Blues*, and I was caught up in the script for sure. Patrick held me and I soaked in the smell of him. It engulfed me. I savored every whiff of him, thinking this had to be a piece of heaven. I could hardly wait to tell Eva every detail. This moment was surely better than my white chocolate candy.

CHAPTER 12

A New Plan

When we climbed into the truck, morning was well established. It was a clear day, and the snowy roads glistened in the sunlight. As we moved over the highway, Patrick returned to the earthy sounds of Keb Mo's blues. Again tantalizing words spilled from the CD player, and I had to laugh at the timeliness of that particular piece. We were about 15 minutes into our ride to the Comfort Suites when my cell phone rang, and to my surprise it was Kojo again. His opening question stunned me. "You got friends out in South Dakota, Jewelle?" he asked. The tone of his voice was different than I had ever heard before. I was amused by it. Kojo seemed worried about something, I thought. I responded with a resounding "Yes!" and noted with a chuckle in my voice that it was a very long story, but I would tell him all about it when I returned home and would have time to discuss it. Again there was a long silence, but I eventually filled the gap by talking more about the visit to the Chief Crazy Horse monument the day before, giving details painstakingly to fill the time.

Patrick behaved himself, although he kept kissing my cheek from time to time and never lost his smile. Kojo talked about a number of chess matches he had had within the past few days. He won them all and was feeling quite full of himself about that. He would be leaving for Milwaukee soon, thinking he would spend a few days with friends in Nashville before he headed home. He heard about a place in Nashville that made spectacular cupcakes of all flavors and wondered what flavor would please me. I looked directly at Patrick before I answered his question and told Kojo to surprise me. With that said, I signed off from Kojo, hoping he would not call again before Patrick dropped me off. In my mind, all I could think about was Kojo's tone of voice. It was not like him to seem worried about anything. He prided himself on keeping a positive attitude, and worry didn't fit that. But this morning he tumbled off Mount Olympus. Without taking his eyes off the road, Patrick said with great confidence, "The brother will have to get used to it. It is over for him. I am in the picture now, and I am not going anywhere." I smiled at Patrick and turned the volume on the CD player up. Keb Mo was singing about life being beautiful. I laughed feeling pretty pleased in the moment. *I guess it is true,* I thought. *Life is beautiful.*

Before long, I learned that Patrick had a knack for taking charge, and I thought we would sure have our moments when we would bump heads, but I just let him roll on. He set the plans for our trip to Milwaukee despite the fact that I hadn't cleared it with Eva yet. I quickly pointed out his forwardness, warning him I was not accustomed to being handled. With a chuckle, he said, "I know I'm being pushy, Jewelle, but I am so excited, so hopeful about all of this. This plan has to work." He would spend the rest of the day sleeping, hoping that Eva and I would do the same. Then the following day he would bring us out to meet his family in the morning, perhaps have breakfast with them, and then take off on our trip in the afternoon. He didn't mind night driving, and we could stop along the way as often as we needed to. As he went on and on, he sounded like a kid planning a party or something. I laughed as he put in place the details of our jaunt back to Milwaukee, and then out of the blue he asked, "What's your ultimate fantasy for a romantic time, Jewelle?" I couldn't believe his question. It came out of nowhere. But I thought for a moment and began to play with the idea of sharing with him something I had never really said out loud before that moment. "Well," I began smiling sheepishly, "I love rain, and I would love to slow dance on a rainy day with my special man. He would have his shirt unbuttoned, and we would hold each other lovingly, gliding to the music as if we were one. He would whisper sweet things to me, and I would be able to hear his heart beat, allowing the scent of him to engulf me. I would kiss his chest and gently call his name over and over again. We would savor each other, holding on to each other for dear life. In that moment, I would feel I could crawl inside of him and be safe. I would imagine curling up inside of him comfortably next to his heart, and I would fall asleep."

When I finished my statement, Patrick said, "Wow, you are deep, Jewelle." I surprised myself. I had thought about the slow dance part many times before but had never really allowed myself to go beyond that point in the fantasy. All the talk about wanting to feel safe just materialized as I delved into the fantasy, and my words struck a clear chord in my heart. More than sex or romance, I wanted true intimacy, which to me meant experiencing a level of vulnerability that I had not known for a long time. I questioned him about his fantasy, but he asked that I allow him to savor my fantasy for a while. He would eventually share his, but he just wanted to turn mine over and over in his mind.

I teased him about his reluctance to be as open with me as I had been with him, but he insisted that he just needed to reflect on my fantasy a bit more to get inside my desire to feel safe. I let him off the hook and sat quietly just listening to Keb Mo do his thing. We drove on in silence, and I was surprised at how far we had traveled from the motel after our experience at dinner and with his cousin the night before. I was just about to say that when Patrick broke the silence. He said, "Jewelle, my greatest wish — and I suppose it is a fantasy — is to have the woman I love fall asleep with her head on my chest. And throughout the night she and I would remain lovingly entwined, holding on to each other and even whispering endearing things to each other throughout the night. I would throw my leg over her leg, pinning her down close to me, showing that we belong to each other." He went on to say again that there was something about touch that mattered so much to him, and touch in sleep throughout the night was the ultimate for him. At this point in his life, he believed he needed that level of comfort and intimacy. I could hear his sincerity in each word. He spoke from a deep place within himself, and I could not stop myself from touching him gently as if my hands were saying yes, yes, yes. In my mind, all I could say was *Lord, have mercy. This is so very wonderful!* Once again my eyes welled with tears, and I was at a loss for words.

When we arrived at the hotel, Patrick and I agreed I would speak with Eva right away and give him a call immediately. He walked with me past the curious eyes of the clerk behind the desk, who smiled a great "good morning" in our direction. We laughed, knowing we would be the topic of conversation for the rest of the day among the hotel staff. When we got to my room door, Patrick scooped me up in his arms and kissed me solidly on the lips while uttering my name repeatedly. He took my breath away. As he walked down the hall, I heard Eva hopping on her crutches from the direction of the dining room; she never missed the continental breakfast, and I was certain the hotel clerk let her know we had arrived. She passed Patrick as he turned the corner, and I could hear them greeting each other. I chuckled to myself, knowing it would be a while before I would get to sleep. Eva and I had so much to talk about. First, I would run Patrick's plan for our return home past her, and then I would fill her in on many of the fabulous details, including the phone calls from Kojo. I knew she would love hearing it all. I felt like a teenager, full of wonderful energy, and I was grateful to the Creator for how things were going.

Once Eva and I were in the room and discussed Patrick's plan, I called to let him know she agreed to it. She thought it was great for many reasons, including the more comfortable riding situation for her injured ankle. When I gave Patrick the news, he just laughed and said, "I miss you already, Jewelle. So you know I won't let you get away from me ever again." I grabbed my chest as I hung up the phone, and Eva laughed at me. She and I talked for a good two hours, there was a lot of laughter and even a few tears. I kept saying that I could not believe what was happening. But Eva in her wisdom cautioned me about my disbelief, noting that it was far more important to give praise to the Creator for all things great and small. "Go on and bask in this," she encouraged. "Let yourself sit on the mountaintop for once, Jewelle, and give true praise."

Everything that had happened had so overwhelmed me that I could barely contain myself. I was in the midst of sheer joy and didn't know what to do with myself. I even found myself singing in the shower. I marveled at the steamy water rushing over me and allowed myself to cry with joy. Everything seemed magical, and I wondered for just a moment when the joy would end. As I dried myself off, I shook that piercing thought out of my head and went back to the powerfully engaging thoughts of Patrick.

Reviewing my time with him at the casino, I could feel his strong legs engulfing mine under the table and I smiled, recalling his cheekiness. There were so many endearing things he had said and done. I marveled about how handsome he had become, and I just about fell over myself thinking about how we connected again. With a critical eye, I examined my naked image in the mirror and wished there were fewer wrinkles and sags. I was in reasonably good shape for a rather plump senior citizen, but I longed for the tight buttocks and slim waist, along with the bountiful bouncing breasts, that had once looked back at me from my mirror years ago. Patrick had called me a pleasing armful and I hoped he meant that. I laughed at my own cheekiness as I put on my nightgown, thinking that I was acting like an old, foolish woman.

After a brief chat with Eva, she decided to go back to the lobby area to read and work on her laptop. She wasn't sleepy, she reported, because she was not gallivanting all night with younger men. We both laughed at her pithiness, and I resigned myself to deep slumber but not before I deliberately shut off my cell phone. I couldn't imagine Kojo's calling again, but he just might, and I really didn't want to deal with that. And, after due consideration, I told myself I would call my children later. Grateful for all that was unfolding in my life, I went through my prayer ritual and snuggled under the covers. My thoughts were all about Patrick and how good his legs felt encircling mine. I am sure I must have fallen asleep with a smile on my face.

I slept for hours but didn't remember having a dream. All I remembered of my deep slumber was that it felt so good, so rich and true. I eased out of bed around 8:30 that evening. Eva was busily working with her email and seemed content to do so. Ready to take off in the morning, she had packed most of her things, a task I had not yet gotten to. She reminded me that we had food in the fridge, luckily we didn't have to go out for dinner. In the midst of putting together my evening meal, I thought about Patrick and decided to stop and check my cell phone. When I heard Patrick's voice, I just smiled. He had called twice, once to wish me sweet dreams and the other time to let us know he could pick us up around 10:00 a.m. the next day. He suggested that we wait to have breakfast with his cousins. It was clear that he had been busy putting a multileveled plan in place. He asked that we give him a call, if his plan did not work for us. I smiled, thinking that the once little Patrick seemed to be pretty comfortable managing people and handling situations.

I gave Eva a chance to think about his message to see if things seemed comfortable to her. She didn't have a problem with Patrick's plan except that she would have the continental breakfast before we left the hotel. She would be open to having some tea and juice and perhaps a little something else when we met with his family for breakfast. I called Patrick with the news, and we chatted for a while. I told him that we didn't have to have breakfast with his family because we didn't want to create work for his cousin and his wife. Patrick insisted that everything was already arranged, and there wouldn't be any extra work for anyone. With that settled, he told me again that he was so happy to have found me and was not going to let me go. I laughed and simply said okay. I had no idea how that would work or what it would mean, but I meant what I said; it was okay.

I was diligent in calling my children. I spoke with each of the Milwaukee clan on their individual cell phones. My eldest daughter and her family were spending the weekend at my house, which meant there would be tension if Lorri came over. I was given the details of each person's endeavors, including Thea's venture. I learned that Lorri was out socializing, and Ajoy, her five-year-old daughter, was spending the weekend with her father, the infamous Squire Black. Lorri's son, Anthony, was at my house with his cousins. Thea and her son, Francis, along with his father, Norbert, were still in New Mexico at an urban farming institute, but would be leaving for Africa in the morning. Korri was nestled comfortably in the Mother-in Law Cottage adjacent to my home. As for Aimen, no one had heard from him recently, but the upper Florida Keys have been his usual hermitage. I chuckled when I hung up the phone and reviewed the detailed update on the whereabouts of my progeny.

I hummed as I packed my things, methodically preparing for our morning exit. As I worked quietly, Eva asked if we should plan to offer Patrick money for gas. I hadn't thought about that, but I said we could do just that, feeling pretty certain he would not be expecting it and might even be offended by the offer. But we decided we would make the offer. I did quite a bit of reading in my meditation books before I felt ready to embrace sleep. Eva retired for the night without hesitation, noting that she would have the continental breakfast early and then find out about the weather for our trip.

When I dropped into slumber, I was not prepared for the nightmare I would have. It seemed to come out of nowhere and to hang on. I felt blindsided by the weird quality of the dream experience. In the nightmare, I was deep inside a giant horn of plenty, similar to what you see on dining room tables at Thanksgiving time. I was inside this cornucopia, and it was dark, but I could see a man on a horse at the mouth of the horn. For some reason I could see inside and outside of the horn all at once. Standing outside was the Warrior Chief with the lightning bolt across his face, the Warrior Chief from former dreams. He was beckoning to me, but for some reason I was caught deep in the crook of the horn, standing in readiness with both feet apart. I had on a beautiful cream-colored tea-length dress, like a wedding dress, and I wore combat boots that appeared to go up to my knees. Over my left shoulder hung a machine gun. Across my chest was a leather pouch. And there were white flowers in my hair. I was crying and trying to get to the mouth of the horn of plenty when a big yellowish-brown and white cat jumped on the back of my neck and began to bite and claw me. Keb Mo was singing (I couldn't make out the song), and in a flash, an odd-looking woman with piercing eyes and bushy gray eyebrows began jumping up and down in front of me shouting, "Shake it off, mud flower, shake it off!" I had seen her somewhere before, but I couldn't remember where. Curiously, beside the odd-looking woman was the baby from the recurrent dream I never talk about. The baby, in the army-green jacket and sailor cap, was looking at me mournfully with those beautiful light eyes. I felt a churning in my chest and thought I would choke.

All of this went on as the Warrior Chief kept beckoning to me with a feather in his hand to come to him. I struggled to get to him but could not move. It was awful! I felt trapped, and the cat was digging deeper and deeper into my neck. I felt the pain from the wounds inflicted, but no blood seeped from them. Instead, feathers oozed out of me, and there was a heavy scent of eucalyptus and the poignant scent of tobacco, like that emanating from the Native American in the bus station, but I didn't see him. I felt so helpless. I must have been screaming because when I opened my eyes, Eva was standing over me calling my name. I was drenched in sweat and had to run to the bathroom.

Taking a good look at myself in the mirror, I saw there were marks of fatigue under my eyes as if I were worn out. I put a cold cloth on my face and told Eva, who was standing wide-eyed in the door of the bathroom, that I was alright. I decided to jump in the shower to ground myself. I was baffled by the nightmare and needed to wash it away. I had no idea of what it was foreshadowing, and I didn't want to think about what it could mean. It was eerie and just plain weird. When I got out of the shower, Eva was back at the bathroom door again. She asked me to tell her about the dream, and I did, detail by detail. After I had shared the entire dream, she laughed and called me a weird woman, but I could hear concern under her words. "Just pray about it, Jewelle," she said as she climbed between her covers again. Before she dozed off, she reminded me: "What Spirit has for you is for you. No need to worry." This was certainly among the times that I just wanted to beat Eva. I needed more than her usual pithy remarks, but I did follow her instructions. I prayed and prayed, but it was a while before I returned to sleep. And this time I didn't have a dream to report.

Eva shook me vigorously while calling my name when she returned from the continental breakfast. "I let you sleep a little longer, Jewelle," she said as she went about her morning prayer routine. She made jokes about my weird dreams, seemingly making an effort to lift my spirits because she knew I was troubled by the most recent dream. "You shouldn't eat too much and hang out with younger men," she quipped, noting that the source of my nightmare probably had to do with my being too fast for my own good. Her jokes helped, and before long we were laughing about the most unusual things that had happened to us on this trip. We even found ourselves chuckling about her fall and the attendant broken ankle. With each incident recalled, we found something funny to laugh about, and soon any foreboding residuals from the dream were lost in the sheer joy of knowing that I would be seeing Patrick.

When Patrick picked us up, I was excited about the day before us. He looked absolutely fabulous in the morning sunlight. His long braid hung majestically down his back, and the winter-white knit cap that framed his face looked great against his deep bronze skin. He was a picture of walking promise, and I am sure my smile gave off my delight. With bold vigor, he threw his arms around me, giving Eva reason to laugh at the familiar way we connected with each other, her attendant comments in line with her humorous nature.

It was a beautiful, brisk morning that gave promise of a fine day for traveling. Patrick forecast our itinerary as he saw it, ticking things off like a captain of a mighty ship. Eva and I laughed at the precision of his words and together chimed a hearty, "Yes, sir." We all laughed as we left for his cousin's home to have a meal and meet some of Patrick's family and friends, including many friends and business colleagues of his cousin James. Patrick explained that this was the weekend for a regular monthly gathering at which there would be good food, conversation, and lots of laughter coming from a very diverse group. He seemed excited to share this experience with us before we got on the highway. And as we listened to his glowing description of the prospective communion among friends, Eva and I asked probing questions that allowed us to get pretty clear on what to expect. We did all of this as George Benson, in his mellowness, provided a welcoming context to our conversation. Again, I smiled at Patrick's thoughtfulness. Somewhere in our time together the night before, I mentioned to him that I loved George Benson, and true to his eager desire to please, he provided that which I found most engaging. His attentiveness warmed my heart. Smiling inside, before we reached his cousin's place, I remembered to thank him for his graciousness, and he just squeezed my hand in response.

With anticipation, we pulled onto his cousin's property. There were many cars parked in front of both the house and what I believed to be the barn. Patrick gently directed us to the barn-like structure, carefully leading Eva into the place as she rested on his right arm for balance. I teased her a bit under my breath, and she responded by giving me a wink. But we were both blown away by what awaited us when we made our way into the place we thought to be a barn. Actually, we found ourselves standing in a very large hall-like structure resembling a library because the walls were lined with shelves weighted down with books. And there were four huge, round tables with eight or nine chairs hovering at their perimeter, each bearing a number of books. There were conference tables against the walls with all sorts of pastries and fruit along with many types of juice, coffee, tea, and bottled water. Against the wall at the back of the room were tables presenting meats, pastries and salads. It was a feast.

People were milling around, laughing and talking comfortably. Children ran about, and two infants rested sublimely in a playpen-like structure. The climate of the room was invigoratingly warm. It seemed as though everyone was smiling, and when folks saw Patrick, they raced towards us and hovered around. Introductions seemed to go on and on, but I was most impressed by Patrick's cousin's rather touching way of introducing me to his wife, Jasenia. "This is Patrick's Jewelle," he said, beaming. Jasenia, in turn, grabbed me, noting that she was sorry she missed me the night before. We both laughed at the subtle innuendo running through her statement. It was clear her husband shared the details of his first meeting with me. While I was a bit embarrassed, I felt special and enjoyed the other introductions and attendant discussions as people marveled over the sheer uncanny way Patrick and I connected again after so many years. I was surprised to learn how the story had gotten around. Interestingly, it was referred to as the miracle in Rapid City.

It seemed everyone in the room knew Patrick and I had known each other more than four decades ago and that this meeting was special. A few of the other women were very bold in their inquiries about the romantic and spiritual nature of our reconnection. They seemed to enjoy talking about our miracle meeting. It was interesting to note that ethnicity didn't matter on that point. The women in the room, regardless of age, race or ethnicity, were all confident there was some kind of soulmate thing going on. Without a doubt, the diversity in the room was amazing. Looking around, you would think you landed in a major metropolitan area like Montreal, New York, D.C., or Miami. I thought to myself that no one would believe we were in Rapid City, South Dakota. Besides Native Americans and Latino men and women, there were Asians and a range of individuals of Black African descent.

The African-American waiter from the restaurant the night before was very talkative, sharing that he was originally from Louisiana but had lived in Rapid City since the early 1970s. He married a Sioux woman, and they had five children. There were at least three Hispanic couples there, perhaps four, but I couldn't be sure about the male half of one of the couples. When I asked Patrick about him, he admitted he was not sure about him, either. But he was certain his wife was Mexican because she was related to Jasenia, James' wife, who was Mexican-American. An African physician from the orthopedic and spine center where Eva and I had spent so many hours a few days before was very amiable and in deep conversation with Eva about some part of Africa she had visited on one of her many trips.

I speculated there was at least one gay couple for sure and another one I thought could be the second gay dyad. I didn't ask Patrick about that because I didn't want him to think I was prejudiced in any way, because I am not. But I truly marveled at the cosmopolitan diversity of the group. As I moved around the room, piling food on my plate and examining books on the large tables, I was surprised to note the breadth and depth of the reading material. It seemed the group was a very liberal-minded body of individuals. I smiled to myself as I moved from table to table assessing the contents of each. As I mused, deeply engrossed in my venture, Patrick came up behind me and kissed me on the back of the neck. I am sure my knees bent and shook a bit, but I maintained a sense of composure as I basked in the sheer warmth of such an intimate move. It said he was claiming me in full view of all who would be interested in knowing. This thought was eclipsed when Patrick presented a rather thin but absolutely gorgeous little boy to me.

The boy clung to him for dear life, and I knew immediately that this was Paul, his special-needs son. Patrick leaned down and lifted his son up to greet me. I kissed the boy on his cheek, but he quickly turned his head away from me and in a sing-song way began saying "Papa" repeatedly as if he were his own echo. In the most gentle way, Patrick soothed his son by rocking him back and forth and saying softly, "Look at me, Paul. It's okay. This is Jewelle. She's our friend." He was so compassionate with his boy, conveying so much tenderness. My heart went out to them as they embraced, and the boy, once let down from his father's arms, still clung to him. I smiled knowing just how much Patrick cherished his son. It was an endearing encounter which Eva must have seen from a distance because later she mentioned how devoted to his son Patrick appeared to be. She, too, was moved by what she had witnessed.

The few hours we spent with this motley group were outstanding. The conversation was great, and the warmth just engulfed us. Eva and I learned this was a study group comprised of family, friends, and colleagues of both James and his wife. They had been meeting monthly for nearly seven years, and it seemed their meetings turned out to be a time of respite and rejuvenation. People in the group connected with others of the same ilk around the world via email, blogs, and Facebook. Technology was their mainstay. We learned that for many, including Patrick, this was a support group of sorts, one in which pertinent research covering a range of topics was shared with others throughout the world. I noticed books about female balding, breast cancer, erectile dysfunction and a host of other topics people seldom discussed candidly in a group setting. I marveled at the apparent progressive nature of the study group — there appeared to be uncommon openness.

Amazingly, we learned that the group engaged in communal prayer, as well, though members represented many religious denominations and practices, including those indigenous to Africa, the Caribbean, and South America. The prayer circle was extraordinary! Eva was quite conversant with many of the spiritual practices presented and basked in her ability to share in depth during the communal prayer. But, what really blew me away just before we were about to make our exit was when an elderly East Indian woman came up to us insisting that she knew Eva. "Ma'am, I think I know you," she said as she reached her hand out to Eva. And Eva in her usual calm way indicated, "Well, we are all of one spirit, so I suppose we do know each other." To which the woman replied smiling broadly, "Yes, and I dare say nearly forty years ago we were in Peru together on a venture. I am certain it was you." At that, Eva gasped, and her usual nonchalant demeanor gave way to pure shock. She had been in Peru at that time, and there was no way for the woman to know that unless she had been there, too. Eva and the woman reminisced for a while, sharing why they both were in Rapid City. It was an amazing set of circumstances for Eva and the East Indian woman, connecting first in Peru and now in Rapid City. I could hardly wait to hear Eva's take on her experience. Clearly, there were many miracles in Rapid city, South Dakota.

After spending additional precious moments with his son, Patrick ushered us out to his truck, promising a festive and comfortable ride to Milwaukee. When we pulled onto the highway it became clear to me that there was no way to be certain of what would happen next; there had been so many unforeseen occurrences!

Instantly, I prayed a silent prayer, remembering what Eva posited early in the morning when I struggled through my nightmare. She said, "What Spirit has for you is for you." Although she annoyed me with her sense of certainty, I now leaned heavily on her words. Closing my eyes, I challenged myself to be okay with wherever our journey would take us. At that point I had no idea of what was about to unfold.

PART III

"... you will bear much suffering in a cold place far away /and yet/ You will walk on your pain.... You have knowing eyes. You are blessed to see beyond the darkness /and yet/ Your mission will be hidden for years...."

CHAPTER 13

Shock on the Road from Rapid City

During the first hour of our trip we recapped in great detail many aspects of our time with the group. Patrick put some melodious instrumental music by a harpist in the CD player, and we talked about the various encounters we had. Even Eva admitted to amazement about her exchange with the East Indian woman, which led to a very engaging report of her visit to Peru. Both Patrick and I were surprised to learn how many years she had been traveling throughout the world. We listened to the account of her time in Peru, and then Chile and other countries in South America, with great interest. Patrick, in his true cheeky way, just put it out there that he found it very refreshing to know that a Black woman had decided she wanted to see the world, had done so with vigor, and planned to continue for as long as she could. He laughed heartily when Eva called me a chicken, noting I didn't like to fly. Though I would fly when necessary, my dislike of it kept me from traveling to other countries with her, which annoyed her. Her comments interjected humor once again, and we laughed and chatted vigorously for hours. With his flair for presumptuous optimism, Patrick promised Eva he would be the person to get me to fly over the Atlantic and thereby open my mind to world travel. In turn, I just laughed, not believing a word of it.

As time flew by, Patrick and Eva learned they had visited some of the same places, particularly in Africa and Japan. And they had been to Sapelo, one of the Gullah islands off the coast of the Carolinas and Georgia; Eva recently traveled there with friends. It had been one of those times I could not get away to travel with her. She and Patrick traded stories about the people on Sapelo Island. It was heartwarming listening to them chatter as if they, too, had some hidden connection that transcended time.

At times, it was difficult for me to imagine the plump little boy of so many years ago holding his own in such sophisticated conversations. Eva could get really deep at times, drawing upon all of her reading and encounters with numerous shaman-like people from various countries. She was even in the audience when Vusamazulu Credo Mutwa gave his notable talk in Japan many years ago. Eva was privy to his work long before most Americans had even known about him. She was unique that way. So when she brought the great Mutwa's name up and Patrick chimed in without missing a beat, he stunned me with the breadth and depth of his knowledge.

While the two of them talked freely about various experiences, I relived the morning Eva slipped on the ice in Rapid City and Patrick came to the rescue. I am sure my smile was illuminated as I thought about the unbelievable nature of the whole encounter and how exciting it would be trying to explain it to my friends. This was the thought churning in my mind when my cell phone brought me back to the present. Immediately recognizing the number, I laughed out loud because it was as if my thoughts had conjured up one of my most inquisitive friends, Jodi. I had become certain that Jodi made it her life's mission to find another husband for me. If that wasn't her quest, she certainly made it seem that way.

Most often when we talked, she would preface our conversation with "Are you dating yet?" Everyone knew how important my love life was to Jodi. She was pretty disappointed in Kojo and sent all kinds of negative energy his way, but she finally settled down in her vengeance when I explained Cullen's assessment of the situation to her. During that conversation, she hung on to every word. She was particularly drawn in by Gahti's optimism, along with Cullen's notion that Kojo's role in my life had been to trigger something in me to prepare me for my next "true love." After that conversation,

Jodi had called Gahti to discuss what they could do as my friends to keep the momentum going that had started during my last visit to La Crosse. She and Gahti were longtime friends, having worked together in the Milwaukee Children's Oncology Center long before Gahti and Cullen moved to La Crosse.

Now a retired pediatric nurse, Jodi spent many years caring for children, usually in the ICU. Her husband, Russell, was a renowned composer and concert pianist who had the polar opposite of Jodi's bubbly, open personality. Though he was friendly enough, he stayed in the background in most social situations while Jodi talked and forecast the lives of anyone who would share their birthdate and give her their undivided attention. Along with the many talents and skills she shared with others, Jodi was an accomplished astrologist/palmist. In fact, she gave seminars on astrology and health at one of the local colleges and was rapidly becoming noticed nationally for her diagnostic ability using alternative techniques.

When I said hello into the phone, Jodi chirped a hello back and immediately lapsed into an update of their recent trip to Bermuda, where she and Russell had a timeshare. I listened intently to my friend, taken in by Jodi's description of a baby shower she attended while in Bermuda. I asked a few questions but essentially listened as, with great vigor, she described one experience after the other. I was doing more listening than talking when out of the blue Jodi said, "Something is different with you, Jewelle. What's going on?" *There it is again,* I thought, *that thing that Jodi has in scouting things out.* All of our friends laugh about it all the time, but she could sense differences in various communication factors, such as tone quality, even your breathing patterns, it seemed.

On more than one occasion she stopped people in their tracks with her adept ability to pinpoint changes. Perhaps this gift was the cornerstone of her uncanny capacity for rendering medical diagnoses. Jodi picked up on something. I was more than willing to let her in on the fabulous turn of events since she hadn't opened our conversation with her usual question, "Are you dating yet?" I laughed, looked at Patrick, and went into my Rapid City miracle story. As I talked into the phone, Patrick leaned over and kissed me on the cheek again, and I heard Eva chuckle. On the other end of the phone, Jodi squealed with joy: "Oh, my God! Oh, my God!" And before I knew it, she put Russell on the phone for me to tell him the whole story. Jodi did this often when she wanted to include her rather reclusive but patient husband in the very exciting features of her life. Usually Russell would listen and make a polite comment. But this time, after I had given him an encapsulated version of the story about Patrick, he said, "Damn, that is unbelievable, Jewelle. I am happy for you."

I could hear Jodi laughing in the background, and then she came back on the phone. She pushed me to give her a detailed physical description of Patrick. I laughed as I described him but did not talk about his having been burned. I told her he had a patch over his left eye due to an accident. I knew she would pull the details out of me eventually. In all of this, Patrick, of course, had to add his assessment of the situation and chimed in by noting he found me and was not about to let me go. Jodi heard him and just howled with delight. She then wanted to know who else knew the story. Clearly, she wanted to be the privileged one to know first and to share the story with all of our friends.

I explained that I hadn't spoken with anyone else in our circle of friends about all that was happening except Eva, and of course Jodi immediately wished me well and politely signed off. I knew she would be calling Gahti and Cullen and I would hear from them soon. I took a deep breath as I smiled at Patrick. He took that as a cue to kiss me on the cheek again, and of course Eva had something smart to say about that. She apologized for being a third wheel but thought it was probably good we had a chaperone or we might not ever get to Milwaukee. We all laughed, but in that moment I felt as if I could just stop right there on the highway, hold Patrick close to me, and stay like that forever. It was weird how I felt so close to him in spirit. His touch made me all warm inside. The rational Jewelle who showed up so often and had kept me in check over the years was nowhere to be found, though the dream of the cornucopia still triggered a tinge of apprehension whenever my mind would go there. But in that moment, I pushed it away and basked in the fun of considering what could be. Again, I heard myself say in my thoughts, *This is too good to be true. How could this be? Is it possible for this to actually be happening at all, or am I having some odd spiritual experience from which I will learn all kinds of lessons?*

I was wallowing around in those questions when my cell phone rang again, and this time it was Cullen. His voice was full of laughter as he said, "Well, well, Jewelle, leave it to you to test the limits of life. I hear you have a gift from the universe you want to talk about." Cullen's laughter made me feel good. Like Jodi and Russell, he wants me to be happy. I thoroughly enjoyed sharing the story with him and didn't mind letting Patrick see and hear the joy that swept over me as I gave detail after detail about the miracle in Rapid City. Cullen posited that he couldn't wait to share this news with Gahti, who was at the hospital. Jodi was pretty good with the details, he said, but it was great hearing the story firsthand from me. Before Cullen signed off, he encouraged me to enjoy life. "I know Gahti will call you when she gets in, and I am sure she will have all sorts of wonderful things to say," he said, his tone conveying the smile that was surely on his face at that moment. I felt tears in my eyes and a knot in my throat. I told Cullen I loved him and hung up the phone. I didn't have to explain my relationship with Cullen. Patrick just seemed to know.

I had barely taken a breath when the phone rang again. This time it was my cousin Vy down in Key West. *This is another Jodi alert*, I thought. Jodi had become Vy's prayer partner years ago when she and Russell spent a few weeks at their timeshare in Key West. Of course, I connected them, and their friendship had grown over the years to the point that Jodi and Vy had made me one of their special prayer projects. Both women were certain I needed another mate. Jodi opted for a husband, and Vy encouraged a companion with benefits, similar to her situation. Vy had met a Cuban fellow who owns a number of shrimp boats. They have been dating for about two years but not interested in marriage. Both have been married twice before and have grown children. Neither wants to think about anything other than what they have right at the moment.

I was not surprised to learn that Jodi had called Vy, and I was not surprised to hear Vy's scream when she made certain this was the same Patrick from our boarding school days. She, too, had spent time with him back then but was not nearly as close to him as I was. In truth, I don't think any of the other girls connected with Patrick the way I did. With the unfolding events in mind, I can only think that God knew what was to be. As I spoke with my cousin about Patrick, I smiled and put the phone close to his ear — so we both could hear — telling him that Vy had also attended the school. He laughed and without missing a beat brought up an incident that made both her and me laugh. Patrick remembered when Vy and I got into trouble for having unsanctioned food in the locker room. Vy's mother had come to visit, and we brought back all kinds of cookies and canned meats that had not been inspected by Sister Anna Marie, known to all of us as "the sergeant." How Patrick knew about this long-ago incident we couldn't figure out, but we all laughed. Then Vy said she thought Patrick's grandmother was mean and a little bit off. She even brought up that his grandmother hadn't liked Catholics, though she worked for a Catholic organization. Vy remembered some of the things we heard her say about Catholics not going to heaven.

I repeated some of Vy's conversation for Patrick to ensure he heard it. He laughed about the rather narrow views of his grandmother, noting she meant well but was hard to deal with at times. He then filled us in on how he learned about the infamous food incident. According to Patrick, it seemed everyone had known about the incident and why Vy and I received demerits. His grandmother, in particular, had talked about it as an indication of how the nuns were losing control of the students. She was shocked I had broken so many rules and had considered keeping her beloved grandson away from me during my kitchen duties. That is why he remembered the details so well, because he had promised to get all A's in school that whole year if she didn't keep him away from me. And he had done just that to prove I would not be a bad influence on him. He studied hard and had done extra schoolwork to be certain he could keep his connection with me during my kitchen duty and other free moments. His report was touching.

As I listened to Patrick's rendition of his valiant commitment to preserve our connection years ago, I couldn't believe how much I overlooked what had been going on with Patrick. He seemed proud of what he did to preserve our friendship back then. His grandmother had probably been a crafty woman who deliberately used that experience to get Patrick to spruce up his grades. I think she knew how important our friendship was to him and would not have wanted that to stop. I also think she knew I was not a trouble-maker and probably laughed about the food incident, particularly in light of how she felt about the nuns not going to heaven and all. Vy thought Patrick's story was sweet, a testament to his capacity to care with diligence. His grandmother's antics intrigued her, and she seemed to conclude as I did about Patrick and his forward surge in grades.

The conversation with Vy was wonderful. Patrick seemed com-fortable reminiscing with us, bringing up things Vy and I had dismissed or forgotten. I was flabbergasted when he talked about my graduation and how he cried that whole day, anticipating my leaving and never seeing him again. I had no idea what that was like for my pre-pubescent plump friend. I guess I was too excited about graduation, growing up with college on my mind, to even consider how my leaving would affect him. Vy was one year behind me, but she never mentioned Patrick over the years. This was probably because, the year I graduated, had been the last year Patrick was a part of the boarding school lore. It seems the good nuns asked his grandmother to find another place for him to be after school and on the weekends. He was getting too close to the age of the incoming freshman girls and could pose problems for them in some way. I listened intently to what Patrick said about that first year after I left, realizing that my leaving had traumatized him. I just hadn't known. I felt terrible considering how difficult it must have been for him. I had promised I would write to him, but I didn't. My warm memories of him were set aside somewhere deep inside of me, only to be resurrected unpredictably on that street corner in Rapid City, South Dakota a few days ago. When that thought came to mind, again I heard the words of the Native American in the Rapid City bus station. I shook my head trying to make sense of the uncanny nature of the situation. But I could only consider there was something Divine afoot, and I smiled.

It was more than a notion for me to consider so much from the past and all that was taking place now. Vy's sign-off words shook me from my reverie, jogging me back to the here and now. This allowed me the delight of including Patrick, the handsome, gracious man of the present, in saying a sweet so long to Vy, who was forecasting all sorts of glorious things. In fact, she definitely noted that she would be giving our situation to God that night during her stint of perpetual prayer, which she fervently did every night (occasionally her assigned time for prayer would be scheduled at one or two in the a.m., but Vy never complained). She was on the perpetual prayer team and had been for many years. She was adamant about her devotional time and was a stolid Catholic who took communion to the sick and shut-ins weekly. Vy was a complicated woman who was certain God understood her perfectly, and she was not concerned about how others viewed her. I thanked her for her promise of prayer and signed off, wondering when the next phone call would come and from whom.

Eva had been curiously quiet throughout all of this, although she shouted a great hello to Vy at some point during our conversation. Eva and Vy had connected on many occasions, usually during my road trips home to Key West. They were like old friends now with many things in common, including New York, Eva's home before Milwaukee and Vy's summer vacation spot throughout most of her childhood and adolescence. Whenever they connected, they usually had a lot to say.

I didn't have to wait long before my cell phone rang again. It was Jodi doing follow up, and she had another question: "Would Patrick be staying a few days in Milwaukee, and could Russell and I meet him, perhaps dinner at our home?" She presented her question all in one breath, it seemed. I laughed, almost giddy with the thought, realizing I had hoped for years to be able to take someone of importance to their home for dinner. I felt all warm inside as I thought about the possibility and then boldly conveyed

Jodi's question to Patrick. He in turn grinned and said loudly so that Jodi would be sure to hear, "I am not letting her get away from me again, so the answer is yes, indeed, I'll be in Milwaukee for a few days at least." I couldn't believe his answer. I wondered what he meant by that since I knew about his forthcoming surgery and all that it would entail, particularly the preparation and meetings with various practitioners he had talked about. I knew there was some type of timeline, but I wasn't sure exactly what it was. I had questions, but I didn't ask them. I was certain by the time we reached Milwaukee the plan would be in place. When Jodi heard Patrick's response, she squealed like a little kid. I could just about feel the wheels turning in her head. The planning would begin, and we were in for a gala time for sure. I loved the way she embraced life with such passion.

We stopped for a bathroom break and to gas up somewhere in Minnesota. I called all three of my children in Milwaukee but reached only their voicemail. I left an upbeat message for each of them, noting I was coming home by car rather than on the bus and should arrive home sometime the following day; I noted it was a little before midnight Central time. I thought about my oldest son, Aimen, and wished I could touch base with him. His hermit-like life in the Upper Florida Keys made it hard to reach him; he intentionally didn't have a phone. I pushed myself to feel good about contacting my Milwaukee clan, despite my concerns about not having a way to reach Aimen. I mused a bit more about having reached only the voicemail of the Milwaukeeans and the same for Thea. Thinking about the unnerving nightmare of the night before, I prayed all was well with my family. Then, assessing the situation, I told myself that all of my children could have reached me by phone if they had chosen to do so. They hadn't, so all must be well. My spirit searched for peace again as I mouthed another prayer and engagingly touched Patrick's arm. In response, he smiled and winked, saying he was exercising his eye again.

At this stop we didn't buy anything to eat or drink. We were not hungry, though we all took part in savoring Eva's famous dried fruit and nut concoction. Patrick had all kinds of bottled water in his truck, which we drank freely. He seemed to enjoy Eva's nut and fruit mix just as much as she and I did, leading us to conclude he was a good fit for our road-trip ventures. The ease with which things were going was absolutely wonderful, although every now and again my mind would go back to the nightmare I had the night before. Each time I let myself return to it, there was a hint of foreboding that I could not shake.

We were still in the state of Minnesota when my cell phone rang again. We had been traveling for hours, but the time didn't seem long at all. The phone calls and conversation made our trip thus far festive and very exciting. This call was from Gahti, who was jubilant. Her thick accent simply spiced up her words as she recapped what Cullen had told her about the miracle in Rapid City. She made a point of reiterating her prayer, "Rest in God's grace, and expect miracles." She seemed quite certain prayers were being answered. Of course she had spoken with Jodi before she called just to be certain she had the particulars straight. She had so many questions still and hoped we would consider stopping by their place on our way to Milwaukee. I smiled when she put her bid in. Surely she and Jodi talked about this, noting that the route we were on would take us near La Crosse.

With Gahti's hopefulness in mind, I posed that question to Patrick, and he laughingly said, "Sure. I am open to inspection by all of your friends." I conveyed that to Gahti, and she, like Jodi, let out a joyful squeal. We gave her an estimate of our arrival time, but the time didn't matter. Cullen would be there if Gahti had to go to the hospital for an emergency or something else. I marveled at the love of my good friends, hoping that my children would be as excited about the miracle in Rapid City as my friends were. For a moment, my mind lingered on my children again, and I felt something. I didn't know what to call it, and I tried to dismiss it.

Pulling myself from thoughts, I entreated Eva's consideration of stopping by Cullen and Gahti's place in La Crosse for breakfast, and she was fine with the plan. I thought it was a great plan and felt excited about my friends' opportunity to meet Patrick. I found myself reflecting on the tasty breakfasts of my most recent visit to Cullen and Gahti's house, eager for Patrick to have the chance to enjoy the scrumptious food and kinship I was sure we would experience there.

It was clear Gahti was delighted about the prospect of our visit. She seemed to sing her sign-off as if she could barely contain her joy. Once again, I was grateful for good friends and felt so very blessed by them, but still a little apprehensive about how this windfall would play itself out with my children. In the midst of this thought Patrick began to share more of his thoughts about all that was unfolding. He seemed delighted to know he was becoming such a hit with my friends, as I certainly appeared to have been with his family and friends in Rapid City. I guess if it had been any man other than Patrick, I would have been embarrassed about the reactions of my friends to the miracle in Rapid City because in some ways it seemed as if people were just overjoyed I found someone. Upon a surface glance, one could conclude I had been a desperate woman before Patrick made his way into my life. That thought troubled me. But I knew I had not been desperate and believed Patrick knew this as well; at least I hoped he did.

Once again, I mused that perhaps Cullen was right on target with his assessment of the Kojo situation. That encounter cleared the way for this miracle, I thought. I looked at Patrick as he took my hand and pressed it to his lips. Again he said my name over and over just as he had done two nights before. As he did this, I remembered what it felt like when he gently slid three of my fingers between his lips into his mouth. The thought of his doing that excited and embarrassed me all at once because Eva was awake in the backseat. He released my hand gently, commenting that my fingers smelled good. I allowed a smile to overtake me while listening to the melodious sounds of George Benson. Without fanfare, Patrick had slid a great George Benson CD in the player again, and the brilliance of Benson's words and guitar uplifted me. The mood was set, and we were quiet for a while.

Almost fifteen minutes passed in silence. It was great. We just cruised along, breathing steadily, listening to the music and apparently lost in our thoughts — even Eva was quiet. Every now and then Patrick pecked me on the cheek, and I simply smiled and purred like a content kitty cuddled on the lap of a nurturing deity. When I looked back at Eva, she was asleep. As I focused on her, I heard the nearly inaudible sounds of snoring I had often chided her about. While she claimed no embarrassment about snoring, she still would challenge me each time I brought it up, suggesting she was not convinced she actually snored at all. Patrick noticed, too, that Eva was asleep and immediately took that opportunity to open a rather serious conversation with a compelling question.

"Do you think you could learn to love me, Jewelle?" he asked, seeming concerned about how I would answer. Yet, exigently, he rushed beyond his own question, not waiting for an answer. The bravado he had displayed over the past two days gave way to a seriousness that was strikingly engaging. He chose his words carefully as he expressed how he felt about connecting with me again. I thought I heard his voice crack a bit as if he were holding back tears when he explained he had begged God for a good woman with whom he could spend the rest of his life, a life to be spent in gratitude.

In an almost-whisper, he said, "I have spent most of my life feeling a kinship with you, Jewelle. I can't explain it. I feel we have some kind of bond from the first time we connected back in Virginia. I know it was a long time ago and you probably didn't feel it back then, but I felt it, and the yearning for it never left me. When we met again on that corner in Rapid City, in the land of my mother's birth, I knew my yearning over the years had led me back to you. I feel you are the other part of me that has been missing. I think you are feeling the connection at this time, too. I believe you can love me, Jewelle. You may already love me but have not yet given yourself permission to feel it." There was such tenderness and yearning in his voice I could hardly contain myself as I listened. I acknowledged to myself that he was on point with his assessment of the extent to which I was actually feeling connected to him. I was, and it felt wonderful.

Patrick went on: "I asked God to bless me with the missing piece I have been searching for all of my life." I wasn't sure what he meant by the missing piece, so I asked him to explain, and he lapsed into an engaging story. It was so touching. Patrick reminded me that at the age of five he had been in the car with his parents when they were killed in the accident. For years, that experience was not addressed, but in his therapy sessions after the fire and during his confinement in an alcohol and drug treatment center, memories surfaced. They were mostly feeling memories at first that were so intense he would shake and pace for hours at night. Later, his nightmares about the fire and the toddler he was unable to save were confounded by flashes of headlights and screams, glass breaking, and emptiness. The psychiatrists and counselors talked at length with him about the first trauma in his life, the one which rendered him parentless and alone. This was the trauma in which he was thought to have lost a part of himself, which seemingly led to his feeling there was a piece missing within him.

Through Patrick's sharing at length about his sessions and his healing, amazingly, I remembered the look on the face of the eight-year-old boy I encountered during my first year in boarding school. It was odd how that memory popped before me as if it were being unlocked from somewhere in my unconscious by some unknown trigger. I remembered he had seemed so sad and distant, particularly during that first year, but became more like a normal kid as time went on. As I thought about it more, another memory popped before me of my high school graduation day. I had never really thought about this particular scene before, but now it loomed before me like a news bulletin on television. Twelve-year-old plump Patrick stood near the entrance to the auditorium where the graduation had taken place. He was sobbing openly and looking in my direction; his grandmother, who seemed annoyed, was yelling at him about something. It was odd how clear that memory was at that moment.

Shaken back to the present as if I had traveled through time, I must have made some kind of sound because Patrick stopped talking and touched me tenderly. "What is it, Jewelle?" he asked with soberness. I hesitated before I told him about the memories I was reliving. Again, as we had experienced so many times over the past two days, we were locked in a moment that defied time and space. Reality seemed to blend the past and present together in some type of extrasensory transcendent glimpse of what the Sufis explain as the oneness of all things, including time and space. My heart raced, and I felt slightly dizzy. I felt a heightened self-awareness as if I were discovering something that had been put away, hidden from my own view. I was lost in my thoughts when Patrick went back to his story as if he were compelled to do so.

"I have done so many things in my life, Jewelle, that I am not proud of," he began, his voice taking on a remorseful quality that touched me deeply. "I have done my best to make amends," he went on soberly, giving the details of who he had been over the years. In his account of his life, he noted he had been angry for years, always feeling misunderstood and empty inside. He excelled in sports in high school and in the military, often sublimating his dark emotions through aggressive contact and bravado that made him a formidable foe to many men and a hit with women. He was not sure how he stayed out of the criminal justice system because his temper often incited volatile situations. He believed that perhaps the prayers of many people had shaped his destiny. He married young, not because he loved his high school sweetheart — the daughter of his grandmother's church pastor — but because she got pregnant with their first child, a daughter. That pregnancy increased his anger and to some extent his distrust of women because he felt trapped by his sweetheart's lie and his grandmother's ironclad rule.

His ex-wife, Myrna, told him she was on birth control pills when he had pulled out a condom. She was adamant that they were safe. "Nothing to worry about," she said. In turn, he gave up his responsibility in protecting them from an unwanted pregnancy. His grandmother had been furious about it. According to her thinking, her grandson had impregnated her pastor's daughter, and it was all his fault. Nothing short of marriage would satisfy his grandmother. His ex-wife's parents, though seemingly more understanding than his grandmother, were equally invested in the marriage. As such, he was married but never really committed to what it truly meant. He learned in therapy that his anger had been like a firewall that kept him from making a genuine connection with his bride. His anger was deep, reflecting so many underlying issues.

He shared that he seethed for years about the lie he had been told but initially tried to make the marriage work. His wife's cheerleader-type personality became more and more difficult for him to deal with. He felt her church responsibilities and image-driven ventures required more from him than he had to give. He found a job right out of high school working at the train station in Richmond. Ultimately he joined the navy to increase his income, but more importantly to get away. He realized in retrospect that his years in the military were what kept him married: he was away more than he was at home. He had not been faithful to his wife after making the move to join the navy. It was as if he gave himself permission to be distant from his wife, family, and vows on many levels.

He was stationed in Alaska and Japan during his tours of duty and had not taken his family with him. His wife seemed quietly complicit in keeping their distance as she kept having babies but would not consider relocating with him. She was attached to her parents and believed it would not be healthy to have the kids moving from place to place. In reality, he had championed her belief because he wanted to be away. Distance and anger were his armor for years. He went on to attest to his deep sadness about the years of dishonesty, clearly noting that he had come to believe the fire — though a tragedy — reshaped him figuratively as well as physically. The fire and its aftermath gave him new life and gave his wife the courage to leave him, something she should have done years before.

"I am basically a good man who has done some terrible things," he said. "I regret so many things, but my gratitude for life and the opportunity to be a better man outweigh my regrets," he went on, his voice conveying a genuine sense of certainty. As I listened to him, it was clear to me that he spent a great deal of time thinking about his life and working on himself. Spontaneously, a voice from deep inside of me asked, "Why didn't you just leave, Patrick?" I couldn't believe I asked that question. I realized I was hoping he would make sense out of the antics of so many men who just cheat throughout their marriages and yet continue to create children, promising to be good husbands and fathers. The question and its forthcoming answer could possibly apply to many of the batterers I worked with over the years and to my first husband, my children's father, as well. Perhaps in that moment I wanted Patrick to make sense of all the havoc my children's father wreaked in our lives with his unbridled philandering, abuse, and drinking. I waited, wondering whether he thought my question was unfair.

Patrick's response surprised me. He explained he knew he was capable of being a better person — and wanted to be better — but never invested in trying to do things differently. He pointed out that during his treatment after the fire, his doctors forced him to relive many of his transgressions to discover his thinking at the time of each one. In his therapy, he realized his sexual exploits had mostly become a habit at some point early in his life, one that required little intentionality. In order to cope with his life, he behaved in a nearly automatic way that kept him from dealing with a host of troublesome feelings.

Patrick used an example from his past to make a point. He explained that while in the navy he would look forward to being away from home, but he knew his wife missed him and his children needed him. He believed his wife never loved him but stayed with him out of duty because of her religious beliefs. He knew this and was angered by it. He knew that alcohol often set the stage for his extramarital affairs, but he would drink anyway and would actually expect to be sexual with women without fail. There were times it just didn't matter that he was a married man. He knew women found him attractive, and he enjoyed engaging them in seductive conversations and ultimately having sex with them. He was often immersed in his own misery and mostly unaware of its source.

He shared he sometimes felt unfulfilled after the sexual encounters, recognizing an emptiness inside of him that seemed to perpetuate the habit of acting out sexually. He said that after leaving the navy, there were times in his marriage when he had not touched his wife sexually for nearly a year. He would be hurt that she would not pursue him, but he understands now. After six children and all he had put her through, she did not have the energy or inclination to reach for him in that way. The births of his last two children, both sons, puzzled him, considering he and his wife were virtually in a sexless marriage by that time. But they were his children, both spitting images of him. He never doubted his wife's veracity in that regard. It was clear to him now that during those years he would convince himself it was his "just due" to have other women sexually.

Although he was a good provider, he had been absent from his other duties as a husband and father. He went on to say he was happy his ex-wife found someone to truly love her, and he hopes one day she will forgive him. He works daily on forgiving himself. He is working on building better relationships with his adult children, understanding they must have the latitude they need to forgive him or not forgive him for his past transgressions. While he remains in contact with them, he does not pressure them. His daughters, in particular, have issues with him, but they are working things out, he believes. With that said, he leaned over, pecked me on the cheek, and asked, "Have I frightened you away, Jewelle? I hope not. I just feel I can be open with you about all things I have been and what I am trying to do in my life now. I am a very different man now and have been different for a few years. I am on my way to being whole."

As he said all of this, I noticed a tear running down his right cheek. Automatically I squeezed his hand and said, "Je m'appelle Eagle Feather," and we both smiled. That statement alone was enough. It was a sign of deep friendship from our past and just spilled out of me with ease. It said, "No matter what, we are connected." Oddly, it was as if I were talking to both the pubescent Patrick and the seasoned Patrick at once and they both were my friend. I felt so close to him, so connected. I squeezed his hand tightly as we drove on in silence for a while, listening to George Benson. I still marveled at how well he handled driving the truck with his infirmed hand. I appreciated this because it felt so good to be touched with tenderness.

Somewhere in the melodious mix of soothing George Benson renditions, Patrick asked the question again, "Can you learn to love me, Jewelle?" He asked this again with such sincerity that I could feel the deep yearning in his words. "You are my bashert. We are in love's bond," he said confidently. I didn't know what he meant and said so, which spurred him into a most engaging explanation. He told me he had talked in his therapy sessions about me, and the psychiatrists and other therapists rendered various speculations about his yearning for the teenage girl from his past. But the only person who made sense to him was a Jewish doctor at the burn center, one of the doctors who performed many of the initial surgeries after the fire. They had become great friends. The surgeon, Dr. Pacht, spent hours telling him about a number of rather esoteric Jewish concepts like bashert, which he remembered to mean one's other half, similar to one's soulmate. As Dr. Pacht noted, it was a spiritual level of intimacy that people experienced when they connected with their bashert, and Patrick felt certain that I was his. It had been Dr. Pacht who agreed with him that he should not try to find me on the internet, because if it was to be, it would be. Patrick went on to say he had been so afraid to search for me on the internet anyway, because he didn't want to find out that I had passed away. I was stunned by what he shared. I opened my mouth to say something — perhaps to say yes, I am your bashert and/or I already do love you — but my cell phone jolted me, and the words seemed to evaporate into space. The moment was lost.

It seemed there was urgency to the ring of the phone, and I looked down and saw it was my daughter Lorri's number and it was nearly 1:30 a.m. Central time. I quickly clicked the incoming call button on the phone and heard Lorri's screams. My heart raced, and all of a sudden it felt as if a bucket of ice had been poured over me. I couldn't breathe. I heard myself saying in an almost shrill voice, "Lorri, Lorri, what's wrong?" All I could decipher from her disjointed words were, "Ajoy's gone and Squire Black is dead, shot to death. It's all on the news." In response to her screaming words, I heard myself say "Jesus!" with such fervor that Eva and Patrick in unison began to question me about what I was being told. I couldn't make out all that Lorri was saying because she was virtually incoherent, screaming at the top of her lungs. Soon I found myself going into triage mode, similar to how things work when I am on a domestic violence case and I have to get the data correct before I can intervene in some way. It just happens for me like that. Many of my colleagues over the years have called it a gift. Perhaps it is, but it can be a prison of sorts as well.

I could feel the rational Jewelle easing over me: my stoic, stolid, analytical, encamped persona showing up for duty just as she had done fastidiously over the years. For a moment, my mind went back to Patrick and then flittered away. There was no room for him right now in this cool, insensate place and I knew it. I took my hand from his and began asking question after question, but all Lorri would say was, "My baby. Where's my baby?" In my mind, I was calling out to God for clarity and help. From what I was hearing, my granddaughter Ajoy's father, Squire Black, the former drug lord, was dead, and Lorri didn't know where their daughter was. I remembered Kaimen told me two days before that Ajoy was going to spend time with her father. As my mind raced over that memory, I realized that if Squire Black had been shot, it was likely Ajoy had been with him. That speculation made me shiver. "LORD," I heard myself saying out loud, "please let my grandchild be safe."

Immediately, both Eva and Patrick queried me about the situation. All I could say was that something terrible had happened to Ajoy's father and Lorri didn't know where Ajoy was at the moment. As I tried to cajole Lorri into calming down and giving me more information, Eva and Patrick talked back and forth. Eva filled him in on the details about Ajoy's father and other pertinent pieces of information. I, on the other hand, was wrapped in a battle with myself about whether or not to get off the line and to call Kaimen for a clearer picture. Just as I made the decision to tell Lorri I would call her back, there was an abrupt silence. My heart stopped, and frantically I called out to Lorri, wondering if something had happened to her. I looked at my phone and realized it was dead on my end because I hadn't charged it before we left Rapid City.

I cussed and called out to God almost at the same time and then asked Eva for her cell phone, which she proceeded to tell me she hadn't brought into the car. It was packed among her things in the back of the truck. I knew Eva was not a cell phone person, and it was likely her phone needed to be charged as well. But neither of us had a car charger with us. With that thought, I turned to Patrick to see if his car charger would work on my phone. We tried it and it didn't work. For a moment I felt helpless, but Patrick put his cell phone into my hand and pushed me to use it. "Go on, Jewelle, use this," he said with an air of concern. I had turned to ice right before his eyes. I had become the mechanical lady my children talk about in those times they would be either mimicking me for fun or lambasting me for some missed opportunity of mothering during their childhood.

I prayed fervently as I punched in Kaimen's number, hoping she would be her true adventurous self and answer a call at this hour from someone in Virginia, because that was the area code on Patrick's phone. "Lord, have mercy" was all I could utter before I heard Kaimen's voice on the other end. In her own way, she could be rather crass when she wanted to be, and this was one of those times. She was very curt in how she answered the phone, demanding to be told immediately who was on my end. Once I identified myself, she softened and raised questions about my cell phone and the number of the phone I was using. Her opening was pure Kaimen. She, too, could operate like a block of ice in times of trouble, but most often the drama queen showed up. While I knew she had a right to ask the questions about the phone and other details, such minutiae were not in any way on my agenda for that call.

Deliberately, I bypassed her query, forging forward to the matter at hand. Yes, she said dispassionately: Squire Black had been shot to death in the apartment of one of his women. The woman had also been killed. No, she said emphatically: the police had not been able to locate Ajoy. She was not at the apartment where the bodies had been found but had been with her father earlier that evening. I asked question after question, trying to make sense of the awful situation, but Kaimen didn't know much more beyond what she had already reported. She was clear in stating she was on her way to Lorri's house right at that moment. But she wasn't sure Lorri would be there because Lorri had been hysterical and planning to go out to try to find Ajoy. I asked about Anthony, Lorri's soon to be 11 year-old son. "I don't know," Kaimen answered sadly. "Mom, you gotta come home right away. Lorri's freaking out, and I don't know what she is going to do if something has happened to Ajoy."

"Where's Korri?" I asked, thinking that Lorri's twin brother always had a way with his sister. They seemed to have a special connection and were in tune with each other's emotions at times. *Certainly,* I thought, *if anyone could calm Lorri down until I got there it would be Korri.* Kaimen just sighed as she said that Korri was with his girlfriend and they were not answering the phone. "Okay," I said with frustration. "Call Lorri now and tell her my phone died. Tell her to call Squire Black's sister to see if Ajoy is there. Tell Lorri I am on my way home and I will call her from a Virginia number real soon. Call me back after you have reached her." I took a deep breath realizing I needed to get to a restroom.

CHAPTER 14

Shifting to Crisis Mode

We pulled into the first gas station we saw and I ran into the bathroom. My stomach was expressing the intensity of the crisis for me. I could appear cool as a cucumber outwardly, but my stomach never lied. As I sat on the commode, I thought about Kaimen's calm demeanor and concluded she was probably handling this situation by returning to one of her loves, marijuana. I believed this was why she was not in the world of the dramatic when we talked. Once I had relieved myself, I told Patrick and Eva I needed to walk a bit. They looked at each other but said nothing as I walked back and forth in the gas station. There was an eating area near by, but no one was there but us. A Lady Gaga song played on the sound system, but I couldn't remember the name of it. I just recognized it from having recently seen her on Good Morning America.

Absentmindedly, I set my purse on one of the tables and continued to walk back and forth. I paced frenetically until I became winded. Patrick took the opportunity to get gas and to grab a cup of coffee as he and Eva talked. He seemed to recognize the importance of leaving me to myself, though I noticed a number of times he was staring in my direction. Eva, of course, had been in crises with me before and knew the drill. When Patrick's phone rang, he looked at the number and handed it to me. I mumbled something to him, but I am not sure what I said. Kaimen spoke deliberately as she explained that Lorri was drinking again and was beside herself with fear and grief. Some woman from the apartment building where the shooting had taken place told the police she saw a foreign-looking woman with exceptionally long black hair carrying a little Black girl out to her car sometime after the shooting. While this wasn't the best news, Lorri felt hopeful that Ajoy had not been hurt in the shooting. But she didn't have any idea who the woman could be. The police were calling her a person of interest.

Listening to Kaimen, I began to pace again, feeling a burning need for more information. I thought about my friend Flora, the meticulous homicide detective. I remembered she worked second shift, and I knew that once she got off, she was unlikely to answer her phone unless it was an emergency of some kind. Calling her from Patrick's phone would not work. She would look at her caller ID and assume it was a wrong number. I thought for a moment and told Kaimen to call Flora and have Flora look into this for me. When I hung up from Kaimen, Eva took the lead and asked a few questions, which I answered. Patrick handed me a cup of coffee and asked if he could help in some way. I thanked him for the coffee and just shook my head.

In times like these, there were always tears behind my eyes that I would not allow to fall. I don't know how that works for me. For some reason I can just sit on my tears at certain times, and that is exactly what I was doing. I was feeling so many things, but my overwhelming desire was to get home to my children and grandchildren. I found myself feeling guilty for not being there, and I felt so out of control with not having my own cell phone. I was about to pick up my purse off the table when Patrick's cell phone rang again. I still had it in my hand, and I made some weird gesture that knocked my purse off the table, with its contents spilling all over the floor.

Change of all sorts rolled everywhere. My makeup kit flew open, allowing lipsticks to roll here and there, and other items of various sizes spewed out onto the floor. It was a mess. And of course there were my panty liners. In a flash, it occurred to me that if it hadn't been such a crisis time, my tumbling purse and the attendant aftermath would have been funny. But it wasn't funny as I watched Patrick and Eva chase after my things. In the face of this frenzied moment, all I could do was speak a prayer into the phone. I hoped Eva would get to the panty liners first, but that was not the case. Out of the corner of my eye, I saw Patrick pick the packs of panty liners up and drop them in my purse. *Okay,* I thought. *What a time! This is truly too much for the blood pressure.*

I gave my full attention to the person on Patrick's phone. It was Kaimen again. In her report, she explained she hadn't been able to reach Flora, and she was having trouble keeping Lorri at home. Anthony was asleep now but had been up at the time of his mother's meltdown. Lorri was downing vodka and orange juice by the glass and was insisting on going over to Squire Black's sister's home because she wasn't able to reach her or his mother by phone. Hearing all of this, I shook inside. Once again, I barked out orders to Kaimen, "You take your sister wherever she wants to go, but you have to take Anthony with you or take him to wherever your kids are." I wondered where Kaimen had left her children since her husband worked third shift, but I knew it would be a safe place so I didn't ask. "Do not let Lorri drive," I continued, barking out orders like a MASH unit commander in the midst of an attack. "Be sure to charge your cell phone so I can stay in touch with you. I am going to try to reach someone else who has a connection with the police department, and I will try to get some more information." I seemed to say all of that without breathing because I gasped for breath once I hung up from Kaimen.

By the time I hung up the phone, Eva and Patrick had put my purse back together and were waiting for an update. I gave them a cursory report, remembering for a moment the scene with the panty liners, but shifted immediately and began to push my brain to come up with the best person to call at this hour to get more police-related information. Because of my work in domestic violence, I knew a lot of people, but I didn't want to open my family's business up before I had a better sense of the particulars. I began pacing again, and it came to me that Kojo had a cousin pretty high up in the police department. He could probably get inside information without letting on that it was for me. As the thought manifested into action, I hurriedly dialed Kojo's number and in doing so realized I was using Patrick's phone. It was very late, and I didn't know if Kojo would answer the phone for a number he didn't recognize. Again I thought about the sheer irony of the situation.

In my mind, I heard myself say, *God, you are more than a notion. I am calling Kojo on another man's cell phone at nearly 2:00 a.m. This couldn't have been scripted any better by a prize-winning playwright.* I dialed the number and waited. The phone rang and rang and rang. It did not go to voicemail: it just rang incessantly. I was about to hang up when a sleepy Kojo answered. I identified myself and quickly put the situation forth, asking for his help via his cousin. Before I could complete my request, Kojo said, "Jewelle, whose phone is this, and where are you?" It is in moments like this that I love my rational self because she could uncompromisingly approach a matter with clarity and most often with a sense of grace. "This phone belongs to a friend of mine," I said. "My cell phone died and we are on the highway heading home." And without further explanation, I went on to say, "I need your help, Kojo. Please check with your cousin and get back to me with any information about this situation, particularly any news about my grandbaby, as soon as you can. You can use this number. I would greatly appreciate it." With that said, I hung up.

I had to make another bathroom run before we piled back into the truck. It had begun to snow. Patrick was working with his GPS to come up with a more direct route to Milwaukee now that he heard me say we would not stop in La Crosse. I looked at him, and though he was sitting next to me in the car he seemed miles away. I said a few words to Eva about the situation at hand and then called Cullen and Gahti. I told them we would not be stopping by and of course let them know what was going on. I knew that a call at this hour would not be a bother to them because they both were accustomed to being called and/or paged at all hours of the day and night. Interestingly, when Cullen answered the phone, I almost found myself giving in to shedding a tear. But the rational Jewelle held firm. I got through my story efficiently, just as if I were relaying the details of a case to a police crisis unit, which I had done many times over the years.

Cullen sighed deeply, and his words seemed to encircle me. He appeared to be holding me in his arms over the phone. "Jewelle," he sighed into the phone, "I know this is rough for you right now, but don't go back into your shell. Remember we are *all* here for you. Let me know how Gahti and I can help." It was the emphasis he put on the word *all* that spoke to me loudly. I knew Cullen, in his own clinically efficient way, was telling me not to close Patrick out of my life. Through sheer determination, the best I could muster in response to my friend was, "I'll call you." In truth, I was not at all certain I knew how to do what Cullen was asking. I didn't know how to be rational, triage, stoic Jewelle and the lost love of Patrick's life at the same time. The two images of me seemed so disparate that I could not at that point reconcile them. Besides that, I thought, my children and grandchildren needed me and that came first.

During my call to Cullen, Patrick changed the tenor of music by putting in an instrumental comprised of melodious violins, cellos, and seemingly a harp. It was beautiful, so tender and sooth-ing. I was grateful but said nothing. Eva broke the silence by saying she knew someone she could call for information if my person did not get back to me soon. It came to me that she heard me call Kojo's name in the last phone call and knew how untenable that situation was. I was surprised at her offer because I knew how she felt about calling people late at night, and I had no idea to whom she was referring. My brow must have furrowed as I turned to face her because she answered my questions without my having to ask them.

"The old guy that volunteers at the reading center where I do sto-rytelling from time to time is a good friend of mine," she quipped. "He's retired FBI with all kinds of connections, and he never seems to sleep," she spat out staccato fashion. "He'll answer his phone just for the adventure of it," she continued with a great degree of certainty. I looked at my 73-year-old friend and thought how crafty she could be. She knew people throughout the world in all professions and of all ethnic groups. Eva was an ace in the hole for sure, and I was pleased to be her friend. "Okay," I said with urgency. "Call him." I gave Patrick's phone to Eva and waited. Patrick put his hand on my shoulder, but I didn't respond. He removed his hand and seemed to focus on the road.

Eva's friend answered immediately. She shared the story and what we needed in a very cool, professional way. I was grateful for her clarity and hoped her efforts would pay off. When she hung up, she reported that her friend, Myran, jumped at the job and would call us back very soon. Patrick connected his cell phone to the car charger, and out of anxiety I asked him if the phone would still ring while on the charger. Of course I knew the answer but needed reassurance. In turn, he was patient with me and simply replied, "Sure, Jewelle." He had barely spoken those words when the cell phone rang and Patrick passed it to me again. It was Jodi. Gahti had called her about the situation, and in turn she had called a friend who is a reporter at a major newspaper in Milwaukee County. Jodi had secured a bit of pertinent information. According to her, the police were pretty certain that the shooting was not a professional hit. Nor did it appear to be drug related.

While there was not a clear motive at the time, it seemed to have something to do with a love triangle. Neighbors reported that before the shooting there had been an argument about a failed relationship. There was name calling and cussing with women screaming at each other and a man trying to break up the argument. Jodi's source revealed that one neighbor was quite certain the man was shot first because the screams appeared to be coming from one of the women. All of the reporting witnesses, people in the apartment building and a guy at the 24-hour convenience store across the street, specifically noted that a light-skinned Black or Hispanic woman ran out of the building carrying a little Black girl who was crying. The woman, as had been observed earlier, had very long black hair that hung loosely below her waist. A police artist was working on a composite.

I thanked Jodi and immediately turned my attention to another incoming call. I didn't recognize the Milwaukee number, so I guessed it was Eva's friend on the line. I passed the phone to her, listening with a sense of urgency. As Eva received the information, she reported what she was hearing distinctively, making a point of reiterating specific things of interest. I just about jumped into the back seat with Eva when I heard her say a little Black girl was taken to the hospital on Lake Drive for issues of hypothermia. The police were flagged down on East North Avenue by a homeless woman known as The Can Lady. She insisted someone had put the little girl in the cart with her cans. She didn't know who, but she had heard horses running behind her.

Following that report, Eva said "Wow" quite emphatically, and I understood why. The report gave me a chill, too, but I didn't comment on the sheer unusual nature of it. I just grabbed my chest, hoping my heart would not jump out of my body with all this nerve-racking stuff. Eva went on to disclose that the old woman, The Can Lady, was still in police custody and would be taken out to the mental health complex to be interviewed by psychiatrists regarding her story. The police knew her as pretty delusional but not violent in any way. As I listened to Eva's report, I rubbed my chest because for a moment I couldn't breathe. I knew The Can Lady. She was well known in the Milwaukee community as a homeless mentally ill person who hung out most often either on the Eastside or in the downtown area. She and her decorated shopping cart were nearly iconic in Milwaukee.

The Can Lady searched for cans on an ongoing basis, but she was known to beg for food and money as well. I often gave her a dollar or two when I would see her panhandling on the street. When she was not searching for cans or begging for change, she could be found drinking a bottomless cup of Pepsi at the Grand Avenue Mall in downtown Milwaukee. She loved Pepsi Cola. Delusional, but harmless, is how people described her. She often talked about encounters with people from outer space. In fact, she was pretty certain that both God and Jesus were from outer space and were in contact with her on a regular basis. She interspersed her out-of-space ventures with tales about little people who lived in the sewer system under the city.

When Eva hung up from her friend, she immediately reminded me of the time she argued with me about giving The Can Lady money. Eva was a generous person, but she had a thing about panhandlers. Perhaps it was her New York background that dampened her view of beggars — she simply dismissed them as unworthy of her attention in any way. Eva and I had had some fairly heated arguments about my willingness to reinforce "bad behavior" as she called it. As she recapped the memory, it was clear she had some new thoughts about The Can Lady this morning, especially in light of her own belief in Karma. In this case, she would certainly make a connection between my kindness to The Can Lady and what her friend had reported about her role in finding my granddaughter.

I pushed Eva for every bit of her friend's report again, and Patrick had a few questions as well. He seemed to recognize my need for distance and directed all of his questions to Eva. As he and Eva conversed, I reached for the phone to call Kaimen to update Lorri on what we learned on the highway home. Kaimen's phone rang only once, and her voice chirped out a greeting that was upbeat. "I was just going to call you, Mom," she said. "We are on our way to St. Mary's Hospital on Lake Drive. They have Ajoy there. Some old crazy homeless woman had her in her shopping cart."

As if by instinct, I corrected Kaimen's use of the word crazy, encouraging her to realize The Can Lady was mentally ill and should be referred to with respect. In turn, Kaimen took issue with The Can Lady's story — which I relayed — that someone put Ajoy in the old woman's basket on the North Avenue bridge over on the Eastside. And, the old woman said she heard horses running behind her. *There it was again,* I thought. *The mysterious someone and the horses running behind the can lady.* I knew Eva would have an interesting take on this once we moved beyond this crisis, but until that point, I would just breathe myself through all of the strange coincidences. Interestingly, not only was Ajoy placed in the old woman's basket, but the police found a nine-millimeter gun in there as well. They were thinking it was the gun used to kill Squire Black and the woman thought to be pregnant with his child.

In the midst of processing what Kaimen was sharing with me, a call was coming in on her phone which turned out to be from Korri. He had finally learned what was going on. Korri and his girlfriend had been at her apartment. It seems that her younger brother had just arrived there, filling the couple in on what was happening in the outside world. Now Korri was heading to St. Mary's Hospital to be a support to his sisters. I breathed a sigh of something akin to relief, but I was still unsure of what was really going on with my grandbaby. I prayed in my heart and mind, *God, please let Ajoy be alright.* It was odd how the information bearers seemed to come forth in an orderly fashion.

Just as I hung up from Kaimen, after demanding she call me as soon as she reached the hospital, the phone rang again. This time it was Kojo. "Jewelle," he opened almost forcefully. "Yes," I responded with eagerness lacing the word. "I've got some good news and some bad news," he pushed on. "So here we go. The good news is that your granddaughter is in the emergency room at St. Mary's Hospital. She's safe. The police took her there after a homeless woman called The Can Lady flagged a squad car down on the North Avenue bridge."

Kojo gave me other details that I already knew through the other information bearers, but I didn't say a word, and then he went on to the bad news. "It seems Ajoy has some issues with hypothermia but is expected to be okay physically. However, there is no way to know the extent of the emotional trauma she has experienced, because they have found the woman of interest. They found this woman — the one with the long black hair — dead, apparently of a drug overdose. She was discovered in her flat on Bartlett Street on the Eastside. She apparently shot her dog and two cats before she ultimately overdosed on a combination of substances. Obviously toxicology has to figure that out, but she's dead, and not by a gunshot, either." He said all of this quickly.

After a brief pause, he went on to explain neighbors called the police because of the gunshots and loud music. "Curiously, a Phoebe Snow CD blasted for an extended period of time, waking up virtually all of the nearby households and alerting police to the havoc-like situation in her flat. No one saw her come in or was aware of a five-year-old Black girl in her presence." Kojo completed his report with a heavy sigh, indicating there were many unanswered questions but at least my granddaughter was safe.

I thanked him for his efforts, assuring him I appreciated his friendship and support. Oddly, the word friendship spilled from my lips with ease. Somewhere within me I now accepted that Kojo was just my friend. I had made the transition, for sure. He was just my friend now, no more than that. I didn't know what that meant in relation to Patrick, but deep within me I knew I was at a different place with Kojo and it was all okay. As we talked on, I promised I would keep him in the loop as my family and I waded through this awful situation. With this said, there was a long, pregnant silence on the phone. I waited for a while for him to say something else, but he didn't. Breaking through the silence, I thanked him once again and signed off. I took a long, deep breath, ultimately sharing the information I garnered from Kojo with Eva and Patrick. It amazed me how we had learned so much while still on the highway. I was grateful to God for good friends.

There were many other incoming and outgoing phone calls as we navigated our way to Milwaukee through heavy snow showers. About 60 miles outside of Milwaukee, we knew for sure that Ajoy was safe and had been taken from St. Mary's to Children's Hospital. She would stay there for at least a few days. Lorri and Korri were there with her. Kaimen was back at the house with all of the children, expecting her husband to join them there when he got off work. Deep inside, I knew I needed to see my grandbaby Ajoy and put my arms around Lorri. A sense of urgency pushed me to ask Eva and Patrick if it would be okay if I stopped by Children's Hospital on our way into Milwaukee. It was on the way home, and I just needed to put my hands on my grandchild and to hug both Lorri and Korri. Of course Eva and Patrick assented to my request. Patrick touched my hand warmly for the first time in hours, but my only response was a half-smile which seemed to say, *I am only half here right now.* Without a word, he removed his hand. He seemed to know his place; he didn't push for more than I could give. I was grateful.

When we pulled into the parking structure at Children's Hospital, I almost leaped from the car to race up to the information desk for directions. Korri had given me Ajoy's room number, but Children's Hospital is so huge that it is very easy to get confused with the various wings. I was pretty sure I was supposed to be heading to the 5th floor east, but I wasn't certain how to get there. The woman at the front desk asked my relationship to Ajoy and then gave me a visitor's badge that said "Grandmother" as she directed me to the correct set of elevators. Before I left the car, we had decided Eva and Patrick would go to the cafeteria to have breakfast while I went to be with my family. I would join them in about a half hour, and we would go from there.

On the ride up to the 5th floor, so many things went through my mind. I worried about what I would find, particularly Lorri's state of mind. When I made it to Ajoy's room, I was shocked to see how disheveled Lorri was. Her hair was all over her head. She wore a dingy-looking sweater over a pair of jeans, on which it appeared she had spilled something that looked like grease. And it was pretty clear she was downing coffee to try to sober up. On the other hand, Korri was impeccably dressed, as usual, in a pair of jeans and navy blue sweater with his shoulder-length locks held back neatly by a rubber band. Ajoy appeared to be asleep and Lorri was immersed in talking to a police officer, almost missing my entrance into the room.

Korri was the first to see me, and his face lit up. All of my children have marvelous smiles, but Korri's seems contagious and can penetrate any dark mood. "Mom!" he said with relief in his voice as he threw his arms around me. He was my most forgiving child; he always seemed to give people the benefit of the doubt, no matter what. He was different from his older brother, Aimen, the hermit down in Florida and from his fiery, judgmental sisters. I hugged my son and then reached for Lorri, who immediately began to cry. Out of habit, I think, I began to pat her hair down to try to make it more presentable.

With his notepad in hand, the cop watched us for a moment before asking my name. In truth, I wanted to slap him because he seemed not to recognize how tender the moment was and seemed too invested in doing his job. So rather than slapping him, I identified myself and asked him to leave the room for a moment to let us get grounded as a family. The cop hesitated but left the room, assuring us he would be right outside and we could get him when we were ready. I thanked him as Lorri fell apart in my arms. As I held her, I noticed she reeked of alcohol. Kaimen had said Lorri had been drinking vodka and orange juice, and I wondered what else she had been drinking. Her sobbing seemed to affect Korri, who also began to weep. Somehow the tears that had stayed behind my eyes for hours began to fall liberally, and the three of us held on to each other for dear life and wept quietly.

A nurse interrupted our family moment by asking if we needed a cot for Lorri to rest in. The plan was for Ajoy to stay a few days for observation. In addition to issues of hypothermia, there was concern about shock from the trauma of the horrible events to which she had been privy. She was given something to help her rest and would likely sleep most of the day. Anyone from the family would be allowed to stay in the room with her and to rest as she rested.

I knew Lorri would stay with Ajoy, but I was actually embarrassed by how unkempt she looked. With that thought, I immediately inquired about the hospital gift shop and learned it would open soon. I excused myself from the room, telling Lorri I would bring a different outfit for her to wear. I also explained she would probably feel a lot better once she got all cleaned up. She didn't respond as I left the room. I didn't know what happened inside of me when I saw my children out of sorts or unkempt. But whatever it was, I pushed myself to make things better, to put things in order. And that is what I planned to do.

I was resolute as I passed the police officer standing near the door of Ajoy's room. I whispered to him that I would return soon and hoped he would wait a bit longer before resuming his task of questioning Lorri. He turned out to be more gracious than I had previously thought. He acquiesced, deciding to go down on the elevator with me to get some breakfast. He made note that he would return to Ajoy's room in about 30 minutes. I thanked him again and immediately became engrossed in my thoughts.

By the time I made it to the gift shop, with directions given to me by a number of people, I was pretty exhausted. The old woman behind the glass counter was friendly enough but smirked just a bit when I hissed about the prices. There weren't many items of clothing there, but I did find a markedly overpriced gray jogging suit in Lorri's size. Along with that, I bought a pair of small silver hoop earrings. I noticed Lorri didn't have on any earrings, and I always felt my girls looked better with at least a small pair on. I laughed at my own foolishness when I put the earrings and jogging suit on the counter along with deodorant and a white headband to temper Lorri's unruly hair. While her natural look was usually very becoming, today her hair seemed dry and out of order.

I searched for black hair products but could not find any and finally resigned myself to buying a small bottle of baby oil. *She could use this*, I thought, *to put a bit of moisture in her hair.* As I turned to pay for my items, my eye caught a beautiful stuffed butterfly, and I thought about Ajoy. I hissed again about the price but pulled out my credit card and handled the bill. I hoped Lorri would feel okay about what I bought for her. I hoped my efforts would help her feel better as she freshened up and made herself presentable. The stuffed butterfly was too big to fit in the bag, so I carried it in my arms, feeling pretty pleased about how Ajoy would squeal when she saw it. At least I hoped she would still have that little-girl vigor despite all she had been through.

When I arrived back at Ajoy's room, Lorri was on the phone talking with Kaimen and handed the phone to me as she took the bag and headed into the bathroom. I gave the butterfly to Korri, who was sitting next to Ajoy's bed watching the news on television. The sound was very low, but I caught a few words about the killings, Ajoy's rescue, and The Can Lady's account of the situation. A picture of The Can Lady came across the screen, seemingly taken earlier in the year outside the courthouse where she was interviewed about some city-wide cleanup effort.

I remembered seeing the picture before. It was interesting how The Can Lady seemed so lucid at times and then would turn on a dime and become delusional and agitated. Kaimen pulled my attention to the telephone by questioning me about Lorri's state of mind. I told her about the change of clothes I bought and said I thought Lorri was on her way to getting herself under control. I pointed out there was a policeman waiting to question her further about her relationship with Ajoy's father. Kaimen went on to say that Flora had called, stating she had tried to reach me on my cell phone but kept getting some weird message. I didn't know what message Flora was talking about.

Flora had given Kaimen more inside information on the shootings and death of the woman thought to be the suspect in the case. According to what Flora learned, Squire Black was involved for years with the woman. Witnesses from among her neighbors put Squire Black at her home early on the day of the shooting, and he had Ajoy with him then. Two witnesses saw the three of them having breakfast at a nearby George Webb restaurant. As I listened to Kaimen's report from Flora, I wondered where Ajoy was during all of the shootings. I wondered how much she witnessed, how she got away from the suspected shooter, and how she ended up in The Can Lady's basket.

Once again Kaimen's words jerked me back to the present. "Mama, your house phone has been ringing off the hook," she said. "All kinds of people have been calling to speak with you about this situation, even folks from the church, including two priests, Father Cannon and Father Gramling. I turned off your voicemail because you don't need to be dealing with all of that when you get home." I thanked Kaimen and told her I would leave the hospital shortly and be home before long. I hung up the phone and tapped on the bathroom door. I noticed Lorri was putting herself together. She was spraying herself with some delightful body spray which she probably had in her purse. She had put the headband on, tempering her unruly hair, and was pulling on the pants of her jogging suit. "You smell great," I said, giving her a thumbs-up sign of approval. She looked me straight in the eyes and asked, "You had to buy *earrings*, Mom. *Really?*" I nodded in response to her question, realizing I do have a number of quirks, of which this thing with earrings was just one. In my mind, I smiled and decided that when we made it through this crisis, we would laugh about the earring thing for sure. In that moment, my mind returned to a question that had popped in my head when I was on the road. I had pushed it aside, but I really wanted to put the question to Lorri now. I opened my mouth to ask her this troubling thing, but the words wouldn't come out. I suppose it was the rational Jewelle that kept me quiet. To ask Lorri if she had a life insurance policy on Ajoy's father right at that moment could be an explosive thing to do, even though I hoped with all my heart she had followed my counsel and taken care of that.

Squire Black didn't ever pay child support for Ajoy. Although he would buy clothes and toys, he would not give Lorri any real money. I was furious with her about that, and we argued often about how she allowed him free reign in Ajoy's life without what I believed to be any real responsibility. But yes, it was the rational Jewelle who stole the words from my mouth about the life insurance policy, and I just hugged my daughter as I left the bathroom. I blew a kiss in Korri's direction, kissed Ajoy on the cheek, and left the room heading for the cafeteria to join Eva and Patrick. I hadn't thought much about what would happen with Patrick once he dropped me home, and my brain was too taxed to even try to think that through now. I felt in that moment that while we seemed to be moving toward the end of a crisis, we were really in the eye of the storm. The most turbulent winds were still to blow.

I shook that thought off as I spotted a women's restroom right in front of the cafeteria. I went in thinking it was a miracle my stomach had quieted down on its own. When I saw my reflection in the mirror, I didn't feel good about it. I had dark circles under my eyes, and my usually neatly-cropped thick afro seemed unattractively frizzy. I didn't have eyebrows or any other makeup on at that point. After relieving my bladder I made an effort to spruce myself up a bit by patting my hair down with a bit of lotion, replacing my eyebrows, and dabbing my lips with a little lipstick. With all of my repairs done, I put a breath mint in my mouth and headed for the cafeteria.

Moving among the tables in the cafeteria, I saw the cop from Ajoy's room. He nodded in my direction, and I responded in kind just as my eyes found Eva and Patrick. They appeared to be deeply engrossed in conversation. Patrick stood up when he saw me and immediately passed half a grapefruit and two boiled eggs in my direction, moving quickly to the counter to get some coffee for me. I was pleased at how efficient Eva was in securing the things I often chose for breakfast, certain she had schooled Patrick well about my likes and dislikes because he brought my coffee with two creamers but no sweeteners. "They don't have stevia here, Jewelle," he said as he passed my cup to me. Again I was amazed at how much Eva had passed on to Patrick about my likes and dislikes. I tried to smile in response to Patrick's chivalry but was certain it was another one of those half-smiles: I was not completely there.

With a sigh of exhaustion, I updated them about Ajoy's situation, revealing as well how Lorri appeared to be doing. Patrick didn't waste any time in reporting his plans. It was clear he and Eva had been very busy setting things in place in my absence. Eva nodded in agreement as Patrick explained he would be staying for a couple of days in one of Eva's efficiency units; they had worked that out. In addition to the condominium Eva owned and lived in at the Knickerbocker Hotel near the downtown area, she owned three efficiency units in the building, active rentals during the spring and summer months but less so in the winter. As such, Patrick didn't have any trouble finding a place to be for a few days. Again I thought about how resourceful Eva could be. I realized how blessed I was to have her as a friend.

I wondered for a moment what Patrick meant about a few days, but I didn't ask. I just assumed he needed to rest and get his bearings before he headed back to Virginia. Eva shared details about her arrangement with Patrick, characteristically noting in a rather nonchalant way that she was pleased to have a unit available on the 4th floor near the east side of the building. She pointed that out to underscore that Patrick would have a great view of the rising sun if he chose to be a sun watcher, and he would be able to see a small part of Lake Michigan. As she talked, although preoccupied with many disparate thoughts, I managed to sip my coffee and wolf down the two boiled eggs and grapefruit before I felt a bout of fatigue engulf me. It just seemed to drop over me in one great swoop.

Virtually overcome by the weightiness of a host of feelings and fatigue, I didn't say much as we readied ourselves to face the frigid outdoors again. But I did manage to smile and look in Patrick and Eva's direction from time to time. For some reason I couldn't shake the feeling that something else was about to happen, and I knew my reserves were taxed at that point. I wondered if I could hold up under another shock. The thought of Lorri and the life insurance policy kept popping in my mind, and I worried about Ajoy, musing about the residuals of all the trauma she had experienced. My thoughts even went to The Can Lady again, and I wondered how she was managing in her interview with the psychiatrists. I was certain she had a great deal of contact with the mental health complex throughout the years, having to be evaluated for one issue or the other in her homeless status. These thoughts were buzzing through my head when Patrick asked if I was okay, pulling me back to the moment. In response, all I could mutter was a weak yes.

Walking through the massive parking structure, we were all surprised at how the snow had accumulated while we were in the hospital. Despite the barriers to the weather presented by the parking structure, snow and ice still managed to find their way to Patrick's truck, making it necessary for him to brush the windshield vigorously before we could depart. Once we were on the highway, Patrick put in a CD by Andre Crouch, and I found the song about faith quite engaging. It was speaking to my soul in a way I could not explain, so much so that I asked Patrick to make the song repeat a number of times. He seemed gratified to be included in my world again, and the song about faith filled the car.

I was amazed that while I savored the promising words of the song, I was vividly visualizing my home, the old two-story dwelling. Memories of its history were juxtaposed with the promising words in the song, seemingly reifying the power of faith. I was reminded that I had overcome so many obstacles through faith. We rode along in silence except for the songs from the CD player. There were no words from us on this part of our journey. I was on my way home, and that thought comforted me as I reminded myself of how faith had carried me so far. I smiled to myself, reflecting upon how my home had come to be. It was an interesting story because my first husband, my children's father, and I had moved to a house very similar to my current home in 1970 when he was still in the navy stationed in Illinois. We were renters back then, and that house — like my current one — was originally a two-family dwelling with a mother-in-law cottage in the back. A unique old black woman who spoke German fluently, Miss Schroeder, was our landlady. We lived downstairs and her quarters were upstairs, but we became like a family. That house held many memories, one that peeked over my shoulders and permeated my dreams from time to time. But in this moment I pushed that memory aside and rested in the faith that had brought me this far. As one song after the other spilled from the CD player, I prayed silently, holding fast to faith, believing my family would get beyond this situation.

It seemed that just as I was about to drift away into a nap we pulled up to my home on 60th Street near Mill Road. Eva had navigated well. I was drawn back to the present by Patrick's remark about the number of cars in the driveway and on the street near my home. Climbing out of my reverie, I took stock of all the vehicles around my place, recognizing Flora's Jeep, Jodi's Lexus, and Tina's Cadillac right away. There were many other cars, but aside from Kaimen's Honda, I didn't recognize any of them. With great effort I stepped out of the truck and headed up my walkway, feeling as if I were in some kind of time warp. There was so much going on inside of me.

As I made my way to my front door, I invited both Patrick and Eva to come in with me. Both of them declined. Carrying my luggage, Patrick indicated he would get on to the Knickerbocker to get some rest. I realized he must be pretty tired and probably not up to being quizzed by so many people. I was fine with their decision because I had so much on my mind and didn't want to get into any questions about the miracle in Rapid City at that time. Without fanfare, I thanked Patrick as he put my bag on the porch. Hesitantly, he leaned over and pecked me on the cheek, promising to call me as he turned quickly towards his truck. The confident warmth he had shown over the past few days seemed far away. That observation flitted through my mind as I thanked him again and waved to Eva. I rang the doorbell; I didn't even feel like searching for my key.

CHAPTER 15

Family, Friends, Rumors, and a March Snowstorm

The chimes barely rang before Kaimen opened the door and grabbed me into her arms. "Mom, so many people are here to see you. I hope that is okay," she whispered in my ear while looking around eagerly for Eva and the Virginia man with the phone. I explained that Eva and Patrick were going over to Eva's place. "We are all very tired," I said with a great sigh, but the words were hardly out of my mouth when Jodi came to me almost running. She stood out as the one White woman in a sea of Black people, but it didn't appear to bother her at all. She knew many in the room and seemed comfortable with everyone. In jeans and a royal-blue sweater, Flora was on Jodi's heels, followed by high-fashion Tina, who had a chicken leg in her mouth. The three women made a visually novel triumvirate, disparate in so many ways and yet all demonstrating genuine anticipatory excitement. Jodi's petite, feminine elegance stood out in contrast to Flora's rather androgynous demeanor, which was bland in the face of Tina's high-end statuesque personage.

There were a couple of people in the dining room I didn't recognize, and upon query they turned out to be Kaimen's friends. One had come by to bring a whole home-cooked meal for us, although

I was certain that in the mix she was hoping to take away a bit of inside information. I was pleased with my expansive office/sitting room space that had been converted from a living room, dining room, and bedroom together. It was a lovely, spacious room with many plants, a surround bookcase filled with an array of books, a group of colorful chaise lounges, lamps, artwork depicting Chief Crazy Horse and Harriett Tubman, many African and Native American artifacts, and beautiful cushy throw rugs with matching throw cushions on the chairs and lounges. Smiling and waving to the group, I ushered my friends up the circular stairway to my personal quarters. Though the entire house is my dwelling space, I had recently renovated the upstairs to make it my dream place. This was Jodi's first time upstairs in my house since the new stairway had been installed. She marveled at the beauty of the staircase and the wonderful deal I got on it as I shared a few details about the luck I encountered in renovating my place.

Hand-tailored buff-colored shades adorned each of the many windows and were a unique addition to the room. They were specially made by an old family friend who was open to my idea of putting together unique window treatments for an unusual room. Tina was with me when I secured the throw rugs and cushions at a fabulous estate sale, but she had not seen the room in its completion. She marveled at the ultimate layout and the vibrant colors. This pleased me. The room was filled with many hues of brown, burgundy, rust, and off-white, with a hint of red and aqua at strategic points. Of course, the green from the many plants highlighted the space. As I took in the room with pride, I was so grateful to Korri and Kaimen for keeping my plants watered.

"This is you, for sure," Jodi offered as she walked around and picked up the various butterflies that adorned the shelves and corner tables. I had a number of beautiful mounted butterflies from a shop down in Key West that really stood out. Flora played an integral part in helping me position the artwork in the room because that was an area she thrived in, and she had a great eye for quality. Of the three women with me, she had been in my respite space in the most-recent past. She beamed as we gathered, satisfied with her artful contribution to the room. As we all took off our shoes and got comfortable, the questions began. Kaimen brought up some wine for Tina and Jodi while Flora and I had peppermint tea without sugar. The tea was great, and my fatigue seemed to lift for a while. I hoped Jodi would not harp on anything related to Patrick because I was not really in that space, but she started to do just that. I deflected her question by turning it to something about Ajoy and the hospital, which set Flora off on her theory about what actually happened to Squire Black and why. In Flora's view, the shooter had caught Squire Black with one of his outside women. Police now identified the shooter as Christina Laveau — a mulatto woman with roots in New Orleans — and it was too much for her. Witnesses put Squire Black, Christina, and Ajoy together that morning: a real family scene. Seemingly, Christina, a massage therapist, had been in Squire Black's life for many years and accepted the situation with Ajoy and that he had flings with other women occasionally. But this new woman, the one she allegedly killed, had become like a wife to Squire Black, taking up a lot of his time and spending too much of his money.

"Rumor has it that the new woman was pregnant by Squire Black and was talking about it all over town," Flora said, hunching her shoulders, a mannerism she exhibited often. She was seemingly unaware of the confusing effect it had on the people with whom she was communicating. "We are waiting to hear from the medical examiner's office about that," she added about the rumored pregnancy. She went on with confidence, clearly using her authoritative homicide detective voice. As she pontificated about what was known and what she speculated about, it became clear Ajoy was lucky to be alive. Christina, the shooter, seemed to have snapped, and people did not know how Ajoy escaped her wrath. According to Flora, the police were still trying to figure out how Ajoy ended in The Can Lady's basket a number of blocks away from Christina's flat. Neighbors did not see a little girl at the scene of the suicide, and there were no reports of Ajoy's walking on the bridge. It was all still a mystery.

With bravado Tina took center stage. She pranced around as she talked about her connections to the lore of the projects. According to her she has many friends in the projects, along with members of her foster-care family, who live near Squire Black's mother and sisters. They had heard something "on the street," as she put it, that troubled her, and she wanted to tell me what they heard. As Tina spoke, she looked around the room, saying that what she was about to say had to stay in the room. Flora quickly cautioned her that she should not be talking about anything illegal in her presence, to which Tina let out a cuss word and winked in Flora's direction.

Tina's street information mirrored some of what Flora had passed along. Then she went on to say, "There is this rumor about a lockbox that Squire Black's mother is trying to track down." She gave her news with an air of authority, looking directly at Flora as she delivered it. Flora seemed to flinch and then turned her back on Tina. Tina reported Squire Black's mother seemed to believe the lockbox was at Lorri's house and was planning to talk to Lorri about it. When I heard Tina's account, the breath caught in my throat. I couldn't believe what I was hearing. I hoped Lorri would not have a safe or lockbox in her house belonging to Squire Black, and I hoped his mother would not try to confront Lorri about a lockbox while they were both in such a state of grief.

I could hear myself thinking that the events of the past day and a half had traumatized both Lorri and Squire Black's mother, and we still didn't know how Ajoy was affected by all of this. *This is not the time to broach uncomfortable questions,* I thought. I questioned Tina about the information she had and was told it came from someone close to Squire Black's mother. The lockbox was important because the contents would be needed to provide Squire Black with an honorable burial, Tina mused. This statement, of course, made my head nearly spin off and explode because I hoped Lorri had gotten a life insurance policy on him (not for his burial, but for her and Ajoy). Flora covered her ears and just glared at Tina. I stopped Tina in midsentence and told her I had to call Lorri at the hospital and let her know about this. Tina did not appear bothered by Flora's piercing glare or my statement as I picked up the house phone and made the call. When Lorri picked up, she was curt in her responses, noting she was still with the police officer who was trying to track down her actual connection to Squire Black. He was asking about some kind of lockbox that was supposed to be at her house.

Lorri's statement took my breath away again, and I asked if Korri was still in the room with her. She said yes, and I hung up from her and called Korri on his cell phone. He answered immediately, telling me they really didn't want people to use cell phones in the hospital. I just about yelled at him to go to the men's room so that we could talk. Korri was always so rule-conscious. Even as a little boy, he was the one to follow rules while his twin sister insisted on breaking them just for the fun of it.

When Korri came back on the line, I couldn't believe his next statement. It seemed that he, too, was in awe of what he was witnessing. He said, "Mom, you aren't going to believe who just walked into Ajoy's room." I was about to guess when he told me that Squire Black's mother and two sisters arrived just as he was leaving. At that point, I got out of my chair and began to pace. Jodi immediately began to question me, and I waved her questions away. My mind went back to the day Ajoy was born and Squire Black's mother and sisters brazenly came to Lorri's room with a camera. Squire Black was in prison at the time. He was serving a short stint on a drug charge which was ultimately reversed. It was an odd set of circumstances, which I guessed cost someone a lot of favors and a barrel of money.

When his mother, Ruby, and sisters, Tamika and Shamila, entered Lorri's room back then, they were not personable or polite. They mumbled something to Lorri but did not acknowledge me at all. I always regretted my passiveness in that instance, but I hadn't considered creating a scene in the hospital on my granddaughter's birthday. I still feel sad inside when I think of that day. Lorri hasn't forgiven me for that, either, though I am not sure what she expected me to do when in fact Ajoy is Squire Black's child and his mother's grandchild. All of this pushed through my mind as I just about yelled at Korri again to go back in Ajoy's room and to keep an eye on things.

"Where's the police officer?" I asked Korri, almost out of breath, and he told me to calm down, that the cop had left the room. I hung up the phone realizing that I had to keep myself from running out to the garage. I could envision jumping in my car and driving to the hospital to be with Lorri. I told myself no and hoped she could hold it together if Ruby questioned her about a lockbox being at her house. I knew that through the years Lorri and Ruby bumped heads on a number of occasions. In one instance, I had to keep Kaimen, my warrior child, from going to her sister's aid. I explained to Kaimen that Squire Black's people were street fighters and we were of a different ilk.

Reflecting upon this, I remembered Tina was helpful with difficult situations involving Squire Black's family and intervened in one circumstance which could have led to violence. Tina had a way of stepping up to the plate and hitting a home run without breaking a sweat when you needed her to do that. That possibility made me come back to the present by directing a question to Tina. I questioned her about Ruby's motives for going to Ajoy's room to speak with Lorri at such a time. I wanted to know if Tina thought Ruby would get into a conversation with Lorri about the lockbox in the midst of all that was going on with our granddaughter. As Tina began to answer my question, Flora got up and began to move around, showing her annoyance with the situation. Flora was with me at the hospital the day Ajoy was born and was really upset with what happened. For years, she expressed her disdain for Squire Black's mother and sisters while she chided me for taking such a passive posture. Now she was irritated a similar thing could happen again.

Tina's take on the situation was different. She pointed out that Ruby was probably as concerned about Ajoy as I was and would want to see firsthand that her grandchild was being cared for properly. If she mentioned something to Lorri about Squire Black's lockbox, it would be more about trying to put in place a sure plan for Squire Black's funeral than to be in any way disrespectful to Lorri. Tina said I needed to remember that Ruby's son had been murdered and her granddaughter had experienced things we could not even guess about at this point. Tina was very pointed in stating her disapproval of any judgment being leveled upon Ruby and her daughters. She made it clear that while they were probably unso-phisticated in their approach to things, they were not bad people.

I watched Tina and Flora glare at each other. This was just one of many issues that set my two friends apart from each other. At times, it was difficult to be with both of them in the same room because they almost always had dissimilar views, particularly about the plight of Black people. Both were rather Afrocentric in that they celebrated Kwanzaa, often were adorned in African garb, and patronized most Black events, including various festivals and church-governed festivities. But Tina operated from a position of what is owed Black people while Flora was more conservative in her thinking, constantly harping on issues of accountability, letting it be known she believed in pulling yourself up by your bootstraps.

Jodi, of course, stayed on the periphery of any discourse relating to Black progress, but saw herself as committed to the eradication of racism and poverty. Both Flora and Tina knew of her activist work in the community and the money she and Russell donated to various social programs. Jodi would not say anything when Flora and Tina battled, and that was best. At any point, the tide could shift and both women could readily displace their anger and resentment about racism and its residuals upon Jodi. While that hadn't happened yet, I was never comfortable with their battles in Jodi's presence. I would often get weary with Tina and Flora but understood the source of their perspectives. Today, however, I didn't want to entertain their social/political angst. I just wanted to understand better what we could be up against if Ruby's main purpose for visiting Ajoy were to talk about a phantom lockbox. In that moment I began to pray silently, calling upon God to keep Lorri in check.

Kaimen came into the room with a rather strange look on her face, and my heart sank. She called me aside, sharing that Korri had called her. He said Lorri and Ruby were talking about a lockbox and while Lorri was calm, he wasn't sure how things would go if Ruby kept pushing her. I heard myself say the word bitch before I could edit myself, and I turned to look directly at Tina. "She's questioning Lorri about the lockbox," I said dryly. Tina shrugged her shoulders nonchalantly, encouraging me to relax, again saying it would be fine. Flora jumped up, saying she had to leave to go to work. I looked at the clock to learn that it was early in the day, and I knew Flora didn't have to be at work until 2:00 p.m. I was certain she was leaving because she had had enough of Tina. She had heard enough and didn't want to hear any more "street smart" talk. I gave Flora a hug, asking her to stay in touch. She waved to the others in the room and ran down the stairs and out into the winter weather. We soon heard her Jeep take off.

Before long Kaimen announced that Korri had called again, indicating Ruby and her daughters left the hospital abruptly after Ruby received a phone call. It seemed the call came from Squire Black's baby brother, Malcolm, an army chaplain who was doing a tour of duty in Germany. I was pleased, feeling certain I would be present for the next conversation with Ruby. I mentioned to Tina that I thought Ruby left the hospital after taking a call from her youngest son. She immediately smiled, noting that if there were any lockbox or money to be found from Squire Black, Malcolm would know how to put his hands on it. Again, Tina spoke with authority, and I was intrigued with all she had to say about Squire Black and his younger brother. The mood shifted, and I breathed a sigh of relief.

I had heard about the deep connection Squire Black had with his younger brother, but I was not aware of the years he spent paying for his brother's education. According to Tina, Squire Black subsidized his brother's high school years at a military academy out East somewhere and made a major contribution to his brother's college education, although Malcolm received a number of academic scholarships. In Tina's view, when Malcolm was born he seemed to bring some kind of hope to Squire Black's life. The brothers became more like father and son, with Squire Black looking after his brother, who was 16 years his junior.

Squire Black was good to his sisters, too, but he doted on Malcolm to the extent that "everyone" knew Malcolm held Squire Black's heart in the palm of his hand. There were all sorts of rumors about Squire Black and his mother's relationship. Tina noted that while he looked after his mother in crises, he was never pleased with the men she had in and out of her life and demonstrated that by being rather distant towards her most of the time. Listening to Tina talk at length about Ajoy's father, I realized there was so much I never knew about Squire Black and his family. I knew very little about his younger brother, who was really his half-brother because they had different fathers. Without a doubt, Malcolm appeared to be different from the other sons in Squire Black's family. Not only was he a clergy person, but he had graduated from top schools and spent several years in the Peace Corps. I guessed his love for his older brother/father figure would make him blind to much of what Squire Black was all about.

Tina continued, pointing out that Squire Black's two older brothers were both locked up for serious violent crimes, one of which made the national news for the sheer horror involved. In this particular crime, it was revealed that Squire Black's brother Max cut off the fingers and toes of a guy who raped one of his cousins. He did all of this before he shot the guy in the penis and the head. Max's trial had been spectacular and controversial, with many people claiming him a hero despite the gruesome act to which he ultimately confessed. I remembered the case. Interestingly, many people gave money to his defense fund, which seemed to effect the ultimate long-term sentence Max received.

The other brother, Duke, the oldest in the family, was doing time for murder too; he killed the batterer of one of his sisters. In a rather odd way, many in the community viewed both of Squire Black's older brothers as heroes, protectors of the boundaries. For about another hour, Tina, Jodi, and I talked about Malcolm, Max, Duke, Squire Black, and a number of other things, but we didn't get in depth about Patrick and the miracle in Rapid City. Of course, Tina was on pins and needles to hear about Patrick, but I wasn't in that place. I allowed Jodi to share a bit of what she knew. I sat quietly, sipping on my third and fourth cups of peppermint tea.

Listening to my friends' chatter, an overwhelming sense of fatigue engulfed me again, seeming to weigh me down from the top of my head to the tips of my toes. I stretched my eyes wide trying to stay awake but was losing the battle. It was Jodi who noticed my silence and drowsiness. She boldly cut Tina off in mid-sentence and announced they should let me get some rest. Surprisingly, Tina didn't offer a struggle, and the two women agreed to give me time to unwind. I was grateful to see my friends head for the stairway, soon to be out the door and into the cold winter weather.

As they left, I imagined myself in a hot tub of foaming bubbles, scented by mint and soothing to my senses. I could not make myself get up and put this glorious scene into place. I thought about my morning and night spiritual rituals and chastised myself for not reaching for my travel bag that contained my Bible and prayer books. I tried to move, but sleep was overtaking me. I was on the brink of deep slumber when my house phone rang. I heard it, but it sounded very far away. Nothing seemed real to me in that moment. Even my hands didn't feel attached to my arms. Kaimen must have picked up the downstairs phone because she called out to me. "It's the Virginia man, Mama," she said quite comfortably as if she had known him for a lifetime. It occurred to me that Eva must have given him the house number. She was certainly being resourceful, I thought.

Exhausted, my body didn't want to move, although in my mind I raced to the phone on my desk. Kaimen must have read the situation because she bounded up the stairs with the downstairs phone in her hand. "Here, Mama," she said emphatically as she handed me the phone. She kissed me on the cheek and whispered in my ear, "He sounds great." Shakily I breathed a hello into the phone, and Patrick's response made my heart skip a beat. For a moment, the magic was there again but fleetingly so as Patrick asked how I was and then went on to share that he found Eva's unit quite comfortable. He explained he would be resting for a while but would be available to me for anything I needed. He emphasized the word anything. I could hear fatigue in his voice, but even in this state he was so comforting. I couldn't remember the last time a man other than Cullen had said something like that to me. Kojo was always friendly, implying his friendship was solid. But to have a man say he had my back — and convince me of it — had not happened since before my beloved Emory died.

For a moment as I listened to Patrick, I wanted to run over to Eva's place, curl up beside him, and ask him to make things better for me. I wanted to crawl inside of him. That thought felt good, and then I felt afraid of it; the very thought that I wanted to depend on another human being (a man) to make things better for me just rocked me at my core, and tears rolled down my face. I thought about the fantasy I shared with him back in Rapid City and marveled at my willingness to share such a thing. I felt so vulnerable. Soon more tears fell. I wiped them away and then heard Patrick say, "Jewelle, I will not let you get away from me again, but I know this is not the time for more talk about that. I'll just wait. I am here for you." He sighed into the phone, and my breath caught in my throat. I covered my mouth to protect myself from what I might say. In response to his words, another flood of tears spilled down my face. My eyes seemed to have a will of their own, and I wept quietly as I mumbled "Okay" and hung up. I set the phone aside, muttered a prayer, and cried myself to sleep.

Curiously, I had another strange-yet-revealing dream. I was watching two of me eyeing each other. I identified with both of them, seemingly able to feel the feelings of both almost at once. Oddly, my feelings vacillated between weariness and exaltation. From moment to moment, I waded through a sense of encumbering captivity to an exceedingly jubilant state of freedom. In the dream, I was here and there and up and down and in and out, all of these states of being juxtaposed amidst fire and water.

The two Jewelles focused on each other intently, as if to figure something out. One had on a dark brown coat with matching earmuffs, and the other was wearing a peach-colored frilly dress with thin straps. The two Jewelles stared at each other and walked in a circle in sync with flute music that seemed out of place. The music reminded me of the call of the Ecuadorian flute players that perform at the annual Indian fest at the lakefront in Milwaukee. The sound had a hint of mountain ecstasy. This circle dance seemed to go on for a while. Then a blast of cold mountain air showered the two Jewelles, and they froze. They became ice sculptures connected by their gaze. And before me, encased in ice, was the bud of a lotus flower.

The cold in my dream was prescient. There was record snowfall for the month of March and even a below-zero wind-chill factor on one evening. In all of the winter frenzy, I took time off from the Center and Ajoy was released from the hospital. She, Anthony, and Lorri took shelter in the warmth of my house along with Kaimen and her crew, minus her husband. He elected to take advantage of some unusual overtime hours and worked days of double shifts with great overtime pay. With that schedule, he stayed at home near his job on the south side of Milwaukee. And of course Kaimen's oldest son, Orion, was with his father's people, working in their bakery when not in school, which he seemed to prefer.

Korri was nearby in the mother-in-law cottage out back, which in a way put most of my children and grandchildren under my proverbial wing. While we hadn't heard from Aimen down in Florida, Thea contacted us from Burkina Faso, Africa a number of times. She emailed her sisters, who passed messages on to me. She, Norbert, and their son were not scheduled to be home until April, but she would cut her contracted assignment short if we needed her to do so. I made sure she understood we would keep her informed but did not need her to disrupt this major assignment, a boon to her career, by coming home ahead of schedule.

In the snow-filled days, I learned that Squire Black's brother Malcolm had arrived from Germany and revealed financial means to handle Squire Black's funeral. His brother's body was released by the police, and funeral arrangements were in full force. A noted wedding planner from Chicago — a former friend who was the wife of one of Squire Black's "boys" — drove the planning process with great vigor. Tina called with the lowdown on what was going on. According to her sources, Squire Black had instructed Malcolm years before as to how to handle his burial and had given his brother the means to do so. Apparently the money was in a safe deposit box in a bank in Evanston, Illinois near where Malcolm attended his first leg of divinity school. Tina's report both relieved and annoyed me. I couldn't shake my concerns about what help would there be for Ajoy.

According to Tina's sources, Malcolm would officiate at the services, and the entire event was now scheduled to occur on this coming Saturday, in just a few days. The funeral would be at the Garden Orbs an elaborate greenhouse-like multiunit facility on the near east side of Milwaukee. When Tina passed that information on, I couldn't believe what I was hearing. I had never heard of such a thing, a funeral at the Garden Orbs. All I could say was, "What a time!" My comment seemed to encourage Tina to go into more detail about the forthcoming services. There would not be an open casket, reportedly because of the way he had been killed, but a huge banner displaying his picture would hang over the casket, which Tina had been told would be magnificent. Tina was certain Squire Black was shot in the face a number of times, making it pretty clear that the shooting had been personal.

While there would not be a wake the night before, the funeral services were slated to just about fill the entire afternoon. With confidence, Tina predicted the services would be a gala event, and she wondered if I planned to attend. Speechless, I couldn't answer her at first, but I knew I would go if Lorri attended. I felt I needed to be there to bring a hint of reason to what could turn out to be an unusual set of circumstances. After weighing this in my mind, and after a number of labored sighs, I told Tina I would probably be there with Lorri. I knew Tina would pass that bit of information on. That was just her way.

"Great" was all that she said, promising me she would be right there beside me. And without missing a beat, she went on to explain that after the repast, Squire Black's body would be flown to Mississippi. A more traditional funeral service would occur in Belzoni, Mississippi at his grandfather's church, which was rumored to be renovated by Squire Black a few years before. Squire Black would be buried in Mississippi near his grandfather, his mother's father. His mother and sisters, along with others from Milwaukee, would attend the funeral in Mississippi as well. Malcolm would not. He would return to Germany right after the Milwaukee services. Finally, she mentioned that folks were still talking about some kind of safe or lockbox that was missing, but no one really knew if that was a myth or something the police had planted.

Listening to Tina, I became more certain I would talk with Lorri about the life insurance policy I had for years been urging her to secure on Squire Black. At that point, I dismissed the whole idea of a lockbox being at my daughter's home. I began to feel a bit more relieved, thinking the lockbox had just been a rumor. At that point, there was no way for me to even prepare myself for how the lockbox would surface again.

Despite my interest in raising the insurance policy issue with Lorri, I didn't do it. Actually, in the snow-filled days before the funeral, I was very careful not to raise any issues with Lorri that could be upsetting to her. We all were concerned with the care Ajoy needed. She was having nightmares and was very clingy, making Lorri struggle with her emotions even more than just dealing with grief over the loss of Squire Black. I recognized Lorri's struggles and saw the way she was downing alcohol. She hadn't mentioned anything about an insurance policy, which made me feel she probably hadn't taken my advice. That, too, had to disturb her, as she realized she was now left to raise Ajoy without any financial help.

Patrick and I talked a few times during the days affected by our winter blast, his calling me each time to get an update on my wellbeing and the state of family affairs. He laughed about the winter wonderland, noting he had not been outside in days and had taken most of his meals in the restaurants housed in Eva's building. I was surprised to learn Eva had even made dinner for him one night. Again I thought of the resourcefulness of my friend and smiled inside. She had to be up to something with this cooking thing, I thought, because Eva did not enjoy being in the kitchen at all. She and I had talked a few times during the snow-filled days, but she had not told me about her cooking adventure. We spent quite a bit of time reviewing her doctor's reports, discussing at length the recommendation that she schedule the surgery for her ankle in the very near future — a state of affairs that irked Eva. She was fretting about having to experience general anesthesia.

Overriding her concern about her forthcoming surgery, Eva encouraged me to remember Patrick was looking to hear from me. She even seemed annoyed one day when I admitted I was too immersed in my family's issues to consider spending time with Patrick. I knew when I heard myself say that to Eva that something was very wrong with the picture I was portraying, but I didn't feel like fixing it. I had too much on my plate. Cullen, too, seemed annoyed with me when he called to check on us. He was gracious but pointedly gave caution about losing myself in Lorri's stuff. My cousin Vy had been calling daily from Key West to get updates, and she, too, asked a number of times when I planned to see Patrick and how long he would be staying in Milwaukee. I didn't have any answers for her, but each time she asked I got a strange feeling in my chest.

Flora called to let me know the woman who was killed along with Squire Black had been pregnant, and everyone was waiting for DNA results to confirm that the now-deceased baby had been Squire Black's. Flora gave me other bits of information about the case, making special note that The Can Lady was now in the county hospital psych ward. Flora underscored the point that The Can Lady continued to replay her story about how Ajoy was placed in her shopping cart by someone and she heard horses running behind her. Flora wondered what I thought about that. I gently dismissed her question, knowing how squeamish she could be about anything that had a hint of what she called "fringe" spirituality or her take on the "occult." In her mind, it was all unreasonable and not to be taken seriously. Kojo called a few times during the snow-filled days. He was interested in what was going on and made a point of giving me information he had garnered from his cousin on the police force. I was appropriately civil with him, but again I was immersed in what was going on with my family. Frequently my thoughts did run to The Can Lady's story. I wondered if somehow my spirit guide, the spirit of the warrior chief, had played a role in saving Ajoy's life, but I didn't say that out loud to anyone, not even Eva. I just thanked the Creator for all blessings, promising myself that I would certainly look at this mystical experience in great detail at some point in the future.

CHAPTER 16

Secrets, Mysteries, Records, and Warnings

O n the Thursday before the heralded funeral, the temperature moved above freezing. Lorri would attend the funeral, and I would join her. Tina would join us as well. Still feeling as if we were in crisis, we huddled together as a family at my house. People were everywhere in my house, which was more than I wanted to deal with. I was just about to water my plants, thinking I would sneak away and have a long hot bath, when my grandson Anthony asked that I come down to the basement to see one of his science projects. At first I thought it was an odd request. Then I reminded myself Anthony often found a way to keep himself immersed in one project or another regardless of where he was. So it wasn't strange for him to have a project in my basement. I thought maybe this was his way to get a bit of attention; he was so often put on the back burner.

As Anthony and I headed for the basement, Kaimen made a point of noting Anthony brought a lot of science stuff from home. She wondered what he was creating. I noticed my grandson seemed a bit nervous, and he appeared concerned that Kaimen would join us in the basement. But it turned out that Kaimen was just giving her usual commentary, chronicling events with dramatic flair, and was not interested in following us downstairs. Thinking about it a bit more, I realized Kaimen probably wanted a little quiet time herself. Her 15-year-old son, Orion, was still at the home of his paternal grandparents, and her two younger children were with Ajoy, mainly watching some kids' movies or something. I wasn't sure what Lorri was doing. With Anthony and me out of the way in the basement, Kaimen would probably engage in some form of self-soothing behavior.

I was surprised when we reached the basement that Anthony walked straight to the laundry room, where I kept two chest freezers in addition to my washer and dryer. He put his finger to his mouth as if to quiet me as he opened one of the freezers and removed many articles of meat and other frozen items, finally lifting out a square item covered in a blue towel. His pre-pubescent arms struggled with his treasure. I watched my soon-to-be eleven-year-old grandson methodically unveil a white fireproof lockbox and set it on the washing machine. He looked me straight in the eyes and said, "Granny, I saw him put this down inside some tires in my mom's garage a long time ago, and I never told anyone about it. I got it out and hid it in my room the night he died." The name was not mentioned, but I knew he was talking about Squire Black. He went on to say, "My mom and Aunt Kaimen saw it but didn't really see it for what it is. I guess everybody thinks I am weird, you know, Granny." His eyes filled with tears. I couldn't believe what I was hearing and seeing. My grandson was telling me he had the infamous lockbox, and it was right here in my house. I wanted to scream.

Anthony explained the lockbox was in his possession all the while people, including the police, were looking for it. For a moment I thought I would laugh, but Anthony unnerved me with a question. "Did I do something wrong, Granny?" I didn't know what to say. I just went to him, put my arms around him, and kissed him on the top of his head while wiping his tears. I had so many questions, but I knew I needed time and prayer to deal with this. With soothing assurance in my voice, I hugged my grandson, telling him he and I would figure out what needed to be done. My thoughts and feelings were all over the place. In the midst of a deep sigh, I asked that he continue to keep the box a secret between us for a few more days, and he seemed to melt in my arms in relief. I kissed the top of his head again and quickly wrapped the lockbox in the towel and returned it to the freezer, thinking my nerdy little grandson had found a unique place to hide his treasure. And together he and I replaced all of the frozen items atop the special treasure, gingerly closing the freezer. I hugged Anthony again and told him we would talk about it later. He seemed so relieved. We hugged each other tightly. I knew I didn't have to reiterate my request for him to keep his secret just between us for now. My grandson, the budding scientist, knew exactly what to do. "Lord, have mercy" was about all I could muster as we went back upstairs to join the rest of my family. I knew I needed to pray for guidance on this. My entire body was shaking.

Kaimen was waiting for us at the top of the stairs, and I knew I needed to steer the conversation in the direction of Anthony's project. So I talked about the many items he brought over to the house, many of which I noticed as I moved through the basement to the laundry room. I focused on the upper part of an ice cream churner which Anthony had long ago expressed an interest in. I talked at length about his interest in using it to make some type of weather-monitoring machine. I am not sure where that story came from, but it just jumped out of me as I winked at Anthony. I felt a twinge of guilt about lying in front of Anthony, but it needed to be done, so I made myself shake it off. In my heart, I asked for forgiveness and proceeded to my bedroom for a bit of peace. Before closing my door, I encouraged Anthony to join the other kids in the room where Lorri and Ajoy had taken up residence. He followed my instructions without saying anything.

As I looked around my spacious bedroom, I realized I didn't know where to sit or lie in order to be comfortable. There was so much on my mind that I felt small under the weight of it all. Normally my bed was an inviting respite spot, but for some reason I was drawn to the big brass rocking chair with the puffy rust-colored cushions near the window. I seldom sat in the chair, but tonight I sat and rocked and rocked, perhaps engaging in some kind of self-soothing behavior myself because things seemed so weighty at the moment. As I rocked I prayed, and as I prayed my thoughts were all over the place. I tried to calm my mind, but it took a while to find the space within me where I was quiet in my spirit. I grabbed my night ritual writing material and began to write my prayers. "Help me, God," I wrote repeatedly, and finally I found myself saying out loud what I knew I needed to say: "I surrender it to you, God; I give it to you." I wrote those words over and over and soon found a place of peace. Once I got there, I stayed in the stillness for a while.

The door chimes followed by Kaimen's animated voice shook me from my quiet place. Kaimen answered the door, and I strained to hear the voice of the person she let in. I couldn't identify it. It was a man's voice but not one I readily knew. Soon Kaimen knocked on my door and quickly handed me a manila envelope. "Mom, Ms. Spencer's son dropped off the CD you wanted," Kaimen said, pointing to the envelope. She went on, "He said his mom's surgery on her knees went well, and she wants you to call her when you are up to it. She's praying for the family." For a moment I had to strain to recall what Kaimen was talking about, but in a flash I remembered my friend MiMi Spencer was one of the few people in my circle I had not heard from since my return from Rapid City. I felt ashamed of myself for a moment because I had totally forgotten about her surgery.

With my mind racing, I forced myself to come up with MiMi's cell phone number. I knew she wouldn't be at home after recently having two knee replacements. I was pretty sure she would be in a rehabilitation center for a period of time. I felt so bad about not being there for her in her time of need. MiMi's voice on the other end of the line seemed very tired, but she perked up as soon as she recognized my voice. True to form, MiMi jumped right in, "I heard about your troubles, Jewelle," she said directly. "Everybody is talking about this thing nonstop." She went on, making a point of listing the groups of people who seemed invested in the gossip, including nurses and doctors, physical therapists, and other staff at the rehabilitation center. Her own family kept her updated on what was being said in the community. It turned out that the son who dropped off the CD was a recovering drug addict and was very informed about the world in which Squire Black operated. MiMi was glad I called because she wanted to warn me about the funeral on Saturday.

There was some talk that a couple of the women who also had children with Squire Black thought he treated Ajoy better than he treated their children, and they had some crazy idea that he may have kept a stash of money at Lorri's house. Some people thought they might confront Lorri about that at the funeral, wanting to split whatever there was, if there was any money to be shared. She wondered if Tina had said anything about any of this. I explained a number of people were talking about a lockbox, but she was the only one warning me about a potential confrontation at the funeral.

While I talked with MiMi, my head began to ache. I appreciated her talking with me well before the funeral on Saturday, but on top of Anthony's secret, MiMi's concerns were disquieting. I felt dizzy and lightheaded. I sighed deeply, realizing that with this new information, I would have to find a way to inform Lorri about the women without alarming her. She was already on edge, and I didn't want to make things more tense for her. I knew there was no way to keep her from the funeral — I really wished she wouldn't go, but that was not going to happen. MiMi told me about her surgeries and how things were going with her recovery. I apologized for not getting to the rehab center to see her and promised I would be there sometime after the funeral on Saturday if all went well. In turn, MiMi told me she would have one of her sons sit near Lorri and me to be certain we were safe. I was grateful for her insight and offer to look after us via her son.

I didn't open the manila envelope from MiMi. I set it on my desk, thinking I would be sure to take it to the car with me one day soon to hear the CD. I enjoyed listening to music while driving. That thought made me think of Patrick, and I smiled as I returned to my brass rocking chair. The matter of the lockbox loomed before me. I knew I had to figure out what I needed to say to Anthony that would be healthy for him, and yet I wasn't sure of the right thing to do. Again I found myself in prayer. I must have dozed off because the ringing of my house phone seemed far away — almost as if it were coming from the other side of the room — though the phone was on the night stand near me. Kaimen answered the phone downstairs. "It's Patrick, Mom," she called up to me, and for a moment I wondered whom she was talking about. Everything about him seemed far away, and yet there was something in the way he said my name when I picked up the phone that brought a smile to my face and tears to my eyes. "Are you there, Jewelle?" he asked with urgency in his voice. Not waiting for me to answer, he whispered into the phone, "I miss you, Jewelle. I don't want to bother you right now, but I just need to hear from you." There was such sincerity in his voice. It was so welcoming, uncomplicated, and warm.

He was still in Milwaukee and thinking of me. Considering all of that, my face became wet with tears. When I was finally able to speak, I heard myself say, "I miss you, too, Patrick," which surprised me. Patrick laughed, and his cheeky side immediately showed up, reminding me of the night we spent in the casino in Rapid City. For just a moment my heart raced. He asked for an update on the situation with my family, and I gave him a synopsis of things as they were, leaving out, of course, anything about Anthony and the lockbox. I didn't say anything about MiMi's concerns, either. But I did tell him I would attend the funeral with Lorri on Saturday and would make an effort to connect with him sometime that weekend, perhaps even after the funeral. I could hear the joy in his voice when I told him about connecting with him soon. He ended the phone call by simply reiterating a promise: "I am not leaving, Jewelle. I am here if you need me." His words warmed my heart but unnerved me as well.

When I hung up the phone, I noticed Lorri had come into my room. She must have veered away from her favorite drink of vodka and orange juice because I could smell the alcohol on her. She had been drinking something else. She looked disheveled, and I could see she had been crying. She threw herself on my bed and just sobbed. "I wish I could hate him, Mom, but I love him," she said. I knew she was speaking about Squire Black, and my heart dropped. On one hand, I understood her grief. I, too, had lost my love, Emory, to death. But on the other hand, I had so much anger towards Squire Black for so many things that I wanted to shake her out of her grief. I wanted to scream about his infidelities and how he flaunted his "street" lifestyle before her. I wanted to point out the danger he continued to bring into her life and into the lives of her children, especially Ajoy. In truth, I wanted to slap her out of her hysterical place. But I sat quietly and let her sob and talk about her love for Squire Black and how hard it was going to be bringing up Ajoy without him. When she said that, I thought I would scream. I shook my head in disbelief. It was beyond me that she clung to the idea of his being a good father. In the midst of these thoughts I remembered my own plight with my children's father, my first husband, Claude, his violent antics and emotional abuse. I remembered and I told myself to stop judging my daughter.

Thoughtfully engaged, I sat, listened to my daughter weep for her love, and grudgingly remembered there was a time in my life that I also held on to a man who disrespected me and hurt me in many ways. With that memory, I got up out of my brass chair and wrapped my arms around my daughter. In a flash, I remembered the evening my children's father had come home drunk and had thrown up in his plate at the dinner table. In his near stupor-like state, he yelled at me, "Clean this shit up, bitch." In response, I hurried the kids from the room, but Lorri had been the one sitting on her dad's lap and had his vomit on her face and in her hair. Korri, Thea, and the older twins, quietly left the dining room, but I had to pry Lorri from her dad's lap. That horrid memory brought up so much pain, and in my shame I wrapped my arms around my daughter even tighter, praying quietly as we cried together. There are no words sometimes to describe the places you go within yourself; there are just no words. Immersed in our feelings, Lorri and I said nothing. After a while, holding on to each other, we fell asleep.

I don't know what roused me from sleep, but I looked at the clock to find it was just before three in the morning. Lorri was in a deep sleep in my bed. I covered her and headed to the kitchen for some tea. As I walked through the house, I took note of who was where. Kaimen was in bed with her daughter, Cherish, and her son Junior on one side of her and Ajoy on the other side. They slept comfortably in the queen-sized bed. I went to the next room, where Lorri had camped most of the days, and there Anthony rested in the center of the king-sized bed. I smiled thinking he looked so much like his father, the hard working barber whom Lorri in her fickleness refused to marry after she met Squire Black. *I wish she had chosen differently,* I thought as I stood over my grandson. He was propped up on a number of pillows in a way that made him seem almost regal. Watching him sleep, his specialness reverberated in my mind. There was something about him that stood out. He just didn't seem to be a kid. He had seemed old from birth. He never asked regular questions that other children would ask. He always had the hard questions, such as, "Why does God allow tornadoes to kill people and destroy people's homes?"

Over the years we had talked often about his desire to make the world a better place. He was on a mission and always interested in justice and fairness issues. It was clear his thoughts about the lockbox in my freezer had to do with justice. I needed to be careful how I handled the situation. The weight of it all came over me again, and I sighed deeply, tired of life's challenges. I continued to wander aimlessly throughout the house, finally deciding to have a cup of tea. I sat in the dark kitchen, allowing the silence and darkness to lull me into deep thought. I don't know why my mind went to my childhood, but it did, and I experienced an engulfing mixture of emotions. Whenever I thought about my siblings, I hovered between sadness and anger. Most people didn't know that I had six siblings — three brothers and three sisters — because I rarely talked about them. I had told Cullen about my siblings, and I think Eva had over the years come to know a bit about them. But not another soul outside of my children and my two husbands were ever briefed about all of my brothers and sisters, most of whom never seemed to accept me.

Most people know I have an older brother, Leo, in Key West. That's all. I was considered the black sheep of the family. My siblings, especially my sisters, often called me Blackie, telling me I was adopted because our mother and father felt sorry for me. I have felt closer to my cousin Vy and even my friend Eva than I do to most of my siblings, who are now dispersed throughout the United States. Only my oldest brother is still at home in Key West, living in the family house with his wife of over fifty years along with all of their dogs. He and I stay in contact, through which he brings me up to date about the others, even the two who pass for White or Hispanic who live somewhere in New York City. As the youngest of seven, there is so much about the family I hadn't experienced firsthand. I still don't know all of why my father's people didn't particularly like my mother or why our mother didn't allow me to visit my dad's people. I heard it had something to do with my mom's color consciousness. This would render my dad's people of less value, because most of them were very dark-skinned and my mom and her people were either very red or nearly white in complexion and with straight hair.

I was told my siblings, minus my oldest brother, didn't want to be around our dad's people. I, on the other hand, yearned to be with them, but they did not embrace me. I never understood why our dad allowed that, but I know our mom was a forceful woman who probably directed most of what transpired. Actually, all of my siblings, with the exception of my oldest brother Leo who is a light honey-brown, were light-skinned like our mother. Our mother was often taken for Hispanic or a suntanned White woman. She seemed to enjoy that whenever it happened. I was, of course, the darkest child, our mother's disappointment, the one our mother rubbed lime juice over to lighten my face up. My mom always said we should marry light to lighten up the race.

I guess I was quite a challenge for my parents because in addition to being an ebony disgrace for my mom, I was considered a change-of-life baby, almost nine years younger than my next sibling, a brother. I guess my parents were tired by the time I came along. My precociousness, coupled with the many issues I had about color, led my mom to find a way to keep me at a distance from her. I am told I spent days on end with my mother's mother, Mamacita, who died when I was very young. I don't remember much about that, but I was told she had been good to me. She died many years before my mother sent me away to boarding school to be with the nuns in Virginia. I remember my dad argued against it. But my mom could be resolute, and she won the argument. In the heaviness of the moment, I found myself smiling because the thought of the boarding school in Virginia set me to thinking about Patrick again. A picture of him as a boy popped in my head. It occurred to me his grandmother must have had an issue with his hair because he always had a close-cropped haircut so very different from the luscious braid he brandished today. I smiled as I thought about how free he must feel at this stage in his life.

In the darkness, my mind flittered from one memory to another. I even thought about my father's twin brother, who had been a character. He and my father were great softball players, I was told, something I missed out on by being born too late. But my eldest brother, Leo, played softball, too, playing in the catcher's position, the same as our father. For some reason, my mind went to a game when my father and his twin were cheering for my brother, who had done something quite spectacular on the field. I was pretty young, but I remember it was one of the few times I saw my father so happy. He and his twin yelled and jumped up and down while slapping each other on the back.

My father's twin was a drinker and could be difficult to be around at times. He never came to our home; my mother would not allow it. But my dad loved his brother, and they would often connect at softball games. I would be with them soaking up all of the attention and laughter. My dad's twin, Uncle Biddy — named for some prank he pulled with baby chickens when he was a boy — never held back on his love for me. He always told me I was special and would buy me potato chips and a Coke at the softball games. Those moments at the games would forever be with me. My dad and his twin brother died 8 days apart. His twin was killed in a car accident, a victim of his own habits, and my dad died of a massive heart attack. One was buried the Saturday before Father's Day, and the other was buried within two weeks of then. Their funerals had been very sad occasions. They both made their transition before the age of sixty.

Recalling one memory after another, ultimately my mind rested on the last months of my mother's life. Two months before she died, she asked that I come down to Key West for a visit, and I did just that because she had never called for me like that before. I took a plane to Key West, a feat that was out of the ordinary for me, given my irritation with airplanes. I spent four days in the Keys over a long weekend and truly enjoyed my mother's wit. I learned things about her I had not known, such as her penchant for jumping rope as a child and where she learned to make coconut candy. She had so many stories I had never heard before, and I was engaged by the intimacy of our conversations.

She didn't ask much about my life, but one comment she made the morning I left for home let me know she had some thoughts about my future. "Jewelle," she said with laughter in her voice, "you must look ahead and straighten up for a good man. There's one for you out there." I couldn't believe what I was hearing, but I didn't challenge her in any way and just hugged her tightly and kissed her on the forehead. But my entire flight home was steeped in deep thought about the trip, especially my mom's statement about my straightening up for a good man. She had lived to be 96 years old and remained lucid up to the end. My brother Leo and his wife looked after her for years, though she handled herself well nearly until the fatal stroke. Her death was a life-challenging experience for many people, including a number of my siblings who had virtually disconnected themselves from the family. Oddly, she left the family homestead in Key West to only two of her seven children, Leo and me, the two darkest of her children. Her will raised eyebrows and the blood pressure of many. Given that Key West property is of prime value, there were threats of all kinds of legal recourse leveled by the five who were left other things, but not the house and land.

Our mother's will spoke volumes to the entire family. There were those who swore she was apologizing to me for her disenfranchising behavior throughout the years and at the same time thanking Leo for remaining steady in his fervent commitment to family. Leo, despite many challenges, tried to keep the family intact. He and his wife, Myra, were childless and seemed to thrive on connecting with others in the family. They sent Christmas and birthday cards to all in the family they knew how to contact. They kept up with baptisms, marriages, graduations, and other developmental milestones expressed in the family. Leo was the family's glue. That thought kind of jolted me because I had not gotten back to Leo about the situation with Ajoy. We had spoken a couple of times during the winter surge, but I owed him a call and made a mental note to do just that later in the day.

For some reason my mind fell on my mother's funeral procession. It had been classic in true Black Key West style with the island's band leading a great line of funeral cars to the church and then to the cemetery, mournful dirges setting a tenor of grief. Streets were lined with onlookers, some bowing respectfully, others waiting for after the internment routine, the New Orleans style jazz jam session when folks would dance in the street to the rousing tunes offered from the island's band. I thought about the beautiful pall I had someone make for my mother's funeral. It was a spectacular addition to the sweet requiem Mass done in full Catholic tradition. Jodi had been a true friend in finding a person to make the pall so quickly. The Polish seamstress was a Catholic and understood the importance of a burial pall. Her intricate work using vivid African print was fabulous, leading many people to rave at the sheer beauty of the pall. In my mind, it was my act of forgiveness for my mother. I could still see her coffin draped in the luscious pall before the altar in the center aisle of St. Mary Star of the Sea Catholic Church in Key West.. Even the Cuban priest, a friend of Vy's who officiated at the service, made mention of the beautiful pall. I was proud of the product of my decision to have our own pall rather than use the traditional one from the church. I knew what it meant to me, and my heart smiled that day.

Other than Leo, not one of my siblings mentioned the pall, though I am certain they noticed the singular quality of that particular item. As I thought of this, I found myself heading to the basement and directly to a large storage bin. It had been years since I looked in this particular bin, where so many memories rested. I removed the blue top easily and saw the flag from Emory's funeral and the flag from my father's funeral that had been given to my mother so many years ago. Under the flags was the special pall made for my mother's casket folded neatly. Something seemed to come over me. I pulled the pall out and, along with the two flags, wrapped myself in them while sitting in an old wingback chair. Notably, the African print in the pall was in stark contrast to the stars and stripes of the flags, reflecting divergence in color, fabric, and cultural meaning. After reminiscing for a moment, I looked down in the bin again, and there was a large plastic freezer bag filled with various types of papers. Draped in my coverings from the past, I positioned myself to reach for the freezer bag and found birth certificates of my children and grandchildren. I smiled as I remembered when I had decided to hold fast to the birth documents for the entire family. I didn't remember putting them in the bin. But I certainly must have done so, probably sometime after Ajoy was born since hers was the last birth in the family.

Puzzled, as I opened the freezer bag, I wondered why I chose to store documents of the living in the bin with remnants of the dead. I thought it was odd, but concluded I was probably trying to put things from my loved ones in a special place that was out of the way and safe. As I examined the papers, it was clear that I had been painstaking in positioning the birth certificates because they were set up in chronological order by birthdate and time with even the order of the twins defined by which twin came into the world first. I smiled as I remembered how I had come to name all of my children, gracing them with middle names of Black historical icons and I had fought to do the same for each of my grandchildren as well.

Warmth spilled through me as I moved from one birth certif-icate to another, mouthing the name on each with reverence. The journey was satisfying, but particularly so when I came to the final birth certificate in the stack; that of my little chocolate grandbaby, Ajoy. As I held her birth certificate, all of the troubles surrounding her short life seemed to melt away in the gratitude I felt for having her come back to us safe and sound. As I thought about that, my mind went to The Can Lady again and then to her story about someone placing Ajoy in her shopping cart and horses galloping behind her. Considering that possibility, I felt a presence around me but saw nothing. Gratefully I whispered a prayer. I didn't know how my granddaughter got into The Can Lady's shopping cart, but I thought it was possible a miracle happened and I thanked God for the miracle!

With a smile I read out loud the name on the birth certificate, Ajoy Tobias Truth Pinder. Squire Tobias Pinder, a.k.a Squire Black had insisted on his baby girl carrying his surname and pushed to have Tobias as a part of her middle name. After a battle, he allowed me to give her a middle name as well. Lorri created the name Ajoy, which everyone appreciated. I chose the name Truth, taken from Sojourner Truth, the abolitionist and feminist. Her story was a testament to gumption and grit. At her birth I gave Lorri, Ajoy's mother, the middle name Tubman, taken from Harriett Tubman, the noted conductor of the underground railroad and it pleased me immensely to have the mother daughter dyad represent these particular powerful black women in history.

Once I looked over Ajoy's birth certificate, I set the freezer bag aside and nestled deeper into the wingback chair. When I came down to the basement, I did not intend to take such a journey into the past, but the past seeped over me and awakened something in me that fed my spirit. *I love my family,* I thought. Each of those birth certificates spoke to me of the investment we make in the lives of those close to us. I smiled as I thought about the lockbox and Anthony. I said a prayer believing that somehow it would all work out. With that thought, I snuggled amidst the remnants of my transitioned loved ones, acknowledging the pain in losing them but basking in the deep love they left behind. I held the flags and pall close to me, and for some reason I looked down at my feet, realizing for the first time that I had come down to the basement in my pink house slippers, something I never do anymore. It was something I vowed never to do again because of what happened many years ago. I looked at my feet soberly and decided not to worry. There was so much to think about, and I didn't want to touch upon raw places, namely the untoward birth and death of a child not accounted for among the other birth certificates; those things chronicling his coming and leaving were in my safe deposit box at the bank along with many documents bearing my wishes upon my death. Shaking my head to clear it of troublesome memories, I let the pall encircle my feet and finally, after consoling myself in prayer, fell into a deep sleep.

Before long, the recurrent dream that had plagued me over the years surfaced, but this time I didn't shy away from the baby with the light eyes. I lovingly rocked him, not concerned at all about the incongruity of the sailor cap and the army-green jacket he was wearing. I held the baby, focusing only on his eyes, which seemed to be speaking to me. This time the dream was not troublesome. There was no confusion, guilt or shame, only a mother's love.

CHAPTER 17

The Funeral of Squire Black

I must have been crying in my sleep because the front of my robe along with sections of the flags and pall were damp in places. I awoke with a start when Kaimen called my name. She was standing over me noting it was morning as she looked directly at me seemingly with many questions in her eyes. I know I must have been quite a sight to behold all shrouded in the flags and the colorful pall, but I didn't venture an explanation. Quickly I folded the items from my past and returned them to the storage bin, hoping I could make sense out of my behavior for my own good later in the day. *It is Friday*, I thought, *the day before the big funeral, and there is so much to do.*

Once solidly awake, I realized my entire household was buzzing with activity. Kaimen and Lorri were preparing the children for school, and to my surprise Lorri moved with conviction, though her eyes were bloodshot and her hair stood all over her head. Ajoy would still be at home today while the other children, including Anthony, would be taken to school by Kaimen. I was informed that Korri stopped by for a ginger smoothie, a specialty of Kaimen, before he went to work, and he, too, had seen me wrapped in splendor in a deep sleep in the basement. I was certain my children had been talking among themselves about my odd behavior. But they would not push me today to get too far into the reasons behind my apparent journey into the past. *I will certainly hear about it at some point in the future,* I thought. But for now they left me alone on that issue.

Before Kaimen left with the children, she mentioned she had taken turkey wings out of the freezer. I almost tripped over my own feet trying to remember in which of the two freezers I kept the turkey wings. Anthony heard his aunt's statement about the freezer, and he looked at me wide-eyed. In return, I smiled at him as I headed back down to the basement to check things out in the freezers. Realizing where I had kept the turkey wings gave me a bit of relief because I was sure they had been in the other freezer. Apparently Kaimen magically went into the right freezer because she certainly did not say a word about a lockbox wrapped in a blue towel. Deep inside, I knew I had to do something really soon about the lockbox, but I hadn't come up with a real plan of action yet. I shook my head trying to make sense out of my life. Nothing had been disturbed in the freezer bearing the notorious lockbox. I breathed a sigh of relief, realizing just how deep in the frozen secret place Anthony and I had put the lockbox. I was gratified to find it was still buried under a horde of meat and frozen vegetables. With this awareness under my belt, I said another quiet prayer and headed upstairs to discuss the details of the forthcoming funeral with Lorri.

Friday flew by, and as evening arrived we planned our moves for the day of the funeral carefully. Lorri and I talked at length about how she would conduct herself, making special note that she would not give an expression during the time allotted for remembrances. I had spoken with both MiMi and Tina, through which we essentially learned the entire order of service for the funeral and repast. It was going to be a gala event. Lorri insisted she would wear black because she was in mourning, and I didn't have much to say about that. I, on the other hand, felt like wearing red — something my southern roots would say was an insult — yet I knew I would never do such a thing. I would wear a navy blue suit with an off-white short-sleeved sweater. Both Lorri and I would wear our dark-brown cashmere coats. We were both pleased we had something appropriately stylish and perhaps even classy to wear to this event. We were sure there would be many minks and high-end outfits flaunted throughout the funeral festivities. Various people would be making fashion statements, and both men and women would likely go into debt in order to be famously clad for this event.

Tina was clear she would wear her mink. She loved style and jumped at any opportunity to display the gems in her wardrobe. She would sit with Lorri and me along with one of MiMi's sons, who probably would be in true "hip-hop" mode with heavy gold jewelry and expensive shoes I call gym wear. I would feel safe with both Tina and MiMi's son to protect us, but still there was a gnawing in my chest with the thought of what could happen. Flora had called to talk about the security plans for the funeral. Apparently there would be a lot of security at the Orbs for the entire afternoon. Many people had arrived from around the country for this event, some infamous individuals the police were hoping to take hold of after the main events of the day. Flora hoped all would be well, but she was pleased that Tina and MiMi's son would be with us.

When Patrick called that evening, I was in the midst of laying out my clothes for the funeral and thinking apprehensively about all of what could possibly happen there. I had so many feelings brewing within me, but hearing Patrick's voice the most reachable was a sense of comfort that was so welcoming. I let that feeling engulf me and promised I would come to him sometime after the funeral on Saturday. I didn't know what that would mean, but I intended to find out. When I signed off from him that night, I was in a very special place. I slept well and dreamed of the first time I saw Patrick. It was an odd dream because eight-year-old Patrick was talking to the adult Patrick, who had a huge eagle on his shoulder and a feather in his mouth. I was standing near both of them, but for some reason they did not know I was there. The adult Patrick had the use of both of his hands. He was not burned. There was no patch on his left eye. Soon the young Patrick began to move into the distance, and the adult Patrick began to change. His hair took on gray threads, there was a patch over his left eye, and his left hand became disabled, the way it was in the present. The eagle took the feather into its mouth and stood majestically upon Patrick's head. I could hear the sound of flute music. I had heard it before but could not place it. That sound blended into the stirring sound of my alarm clock, which pulled me from my dream and to the matters of the present. When I opened my eyes to meet the day, I told myself this was the morning of the funeral and I had so much to do to get things ready. I jumped out of bed with great anticipation. *I will process my dream later,* I thought as I raced to put things in place for the day.

Just as I stepped out of the shower, a call came in from Thea. She reminded me that they were in Burkina Faso, Africa. Speaking excitedly, she made it clear that she had been in constant contact with both Korri and Kaimen throughout the ordeal of Squire Black's murder and ultimate recovery of Ajoy. Now she had concerns about the funeral. She was advising us to stay to ourselves and to reach out for help if a crisis were to come up. She would be praying for us, she said, and I knew she would. I thanked my prayer-driven daughter and sent my love to Francis and Norbert. Assured that things were going well in Burkina Faso, I signed off from her as soon as I could. My mind was taken up with all I needed to do to prepare to be with Lorri, my much-wounded daughter.

The funeral was scheduled for 2:00 p.m., but Lorri and I were dressed and ready to leave the house by 1:00 p.m. Our drive there would be about 30 minutes. We would pick up MiMi's son on the way and meet Tina there. The weather was cooperating. It had stopped snowing, and the temperature was above freezing, nothing too formidable for seasoned Wisconsinites. Lorri and I looked each other over carefully, giving a thumbs-up sign of approval for the outfits we had chosen. Even Kaimen, the diva of our family, sanctioned our choices and offered her approval. I took one last look at myself in the mirror before we headed for the garage, thinking I would be pleased to let Patrick see me in my classy coat, lovely leather tam, and matching gloves. *My daughter and I will make a good showing at this funeral,* I thought as we put our seatbelts on. For some reason, Kaimen had used my car the day before and left her Andre Crouch CD in the player. When we pulled out of the garage, the song lifting faith filled the car. I thought to myself, *God really shows up on time.* I smiled, remembering how we listened to that same song in Patrick's truck a few days before.

While driving to MiMi's condo to pick up her son, I replayed the song extolling faith for the third time. Lorri looked at me as if she'd had enough of that song but didn't say anything. I was driving, but I was deep in prayer. Interestingly, an uneasiness came over me once we picked up MiMi's son. Maybe it was his attire that brought home to me what we were about to encounter. He was dressed in full hip-hop regalia with his hat turned backwards and all, seemingly foreshadowing what was to come. He was very polite, graciously offering condolences to Lorri, in my view his demeanor belying his attire.

I eyed him carefully in the rearview mirror and it was clear to me we were on our way to the funeral of a person on the margins of society, who some claim had many underworld connections. He, Squire Black, "former" drug lord and owner of B-Black Towing Service, now deceased, was the father of my granddaughter Ajoy. I needed to keep that in mind. Additionally, he was the man my daughter still loved. I was certain we were about to encounter individuals from all walks of life, including criminal elements, federal agents, and a host of police persons — most undercover. There would be all sorts of spectators, many of whom would be among us just for the celebrity of the event. We would be among people who had ideas about Lorri, the mother of one of Squire Black's children, and we would be watched and talked about no matter what we would do. The more I eyed MiMi's son, the more uncomfortable I became. The God-exalting songs coming from the CD player did not quiet the churning in my stomach. I looked over at Lorri and saw her flask, which she had pulled to her lips in a gesture of urgency. She was drinking, perhaps, to quell the same kind of feelings I was having in my gut. I opened my mouth to say something but thought better of it. I mumbled a quiet prayer and began to sweat.

Amazingly, the Garden Orbs, known fondly as the Orbs, are four glass- and steel-encased half spheres that appear to be four glowing egg halves. Each, I guess, is close to 90 feet high and more than a couple of hundred feet in diameter at its illuminated base. Together, the Orbs appear to offer thousands of square feet of lush and diverse climate-determined plants and flowers aesthetically presented among rock mounds, waterfalls, vines, and theme-determined decorative statues. The four Orbs are linked by spacious halls, meeting rooms, colorful nooks, including a number of restrooms, a tea room, and two gift shops.

The Orbs are normally beautiful year-round, but this winter day they were exquisite, colorfully showing flowers and plants of all kinds. The white orchids that lined the entranceway were breathtaking. Aside from the orchids, I could not discern the other attractions added just for the day's spectacular funeral; everything was so beautiful. When we arrived in the parking lot, it was amazing to see it was already nearly full and people were coming from all directions. Matching the people were sounds of all kinds, including horns blaring and even loud music spilling from cars boldly showing spectacular rims. But once we entered the actual Orbs, a hush came over everyone. The beauty of nature coupled with a huge banner of Squire Black — certainly over sixty feet tall, hovering in one of the center Orbs above a coffin that seemed to be made of mahogany — gave me and others pause. I actually gasped, and one woman standing near me uttered, "You a bad brother, Squire Black, even though ya dead."

Tina must have been watching for us because she waved her arms vigorously above the crowd, beckoning us to join her. Her six-foot frame was an advantage, and her full-length white mink with the matching hat made her stand out. She was striking, clearly projecting the high-fashion diva air she wanted to convey — people were noticing her and offering their approval. Lorri, MiMi's son, and I walked quickly in her direction, taking note that she had saved enough chairs for all of us. *Tina certainly knows how to handle herself,* I thought as we took our seats.

Lorri whimpered when she took in the banner, and I understood her reaction. I had never seen anything like it. Squire Black was an unbelievably handsome man in life; his coal-black skin against his near-perfect white teeth turned many heads. Now his image on the banner hovering over his expensive coffin boldly attested to his suave, deep-ebony handsomeness. Beauty was everywhere. White orchards rested majestically upon the coffin, and a huge red, black, and green candle stood a few feet in front of it. It was a stunning sight. Chairs were set in a semi-circular format so that a small circular platform stood a few feet from the candle and could be seen from three sides of the room in the largest Orb. The layout made a perfect three-quarter circle set against the backdrop of the banner and coffin. It was tastefully structured, and I immediately thought about the wedding planner from Chicago Tina had spoken about. In my mind, the wedding planner had taste and a flair for theatrics. All of the ushers, both male and female, wore black T-shirts with Squire Black's name on the front and the phrase "Black was here!" on the back written in white letters. The ushers wore black pants and white gloves and were gracious in their demeanor as people were seated and given programs. The grace of it all did not match my expectations. I was in awe.

The program of the day's events was something to see. It was beautifully done. The detail and elegance of the layout floored me, particularly the journalistic flair evident in the presentation of the obituary, which was titled "Squire Black Was Here!" The program was a 12" x 17" sheet of elegant off-white paper folded twice, yielding three distinct sections. The center section showed the actual program, and the front section showed a picture of the deceased with his birth name, "Squire Tobias Pinder III," with the addition "a.k.a Squire Black." His birthdate and the date of his demise were noted beneath his name. He was 49 years old.

The picture in the huge banner was replicated on the front page of the program, and there was another picture in the center on the back. It was of a young man, probably 19 or 20, holding the hand of a male toddler. The writing beneath the picture identified them as Squire Black and his little brother at the age of 3. Aside the picture in bold letters was written, "My brother reflects the best of me!" Under the picture was a brief bio of Squire Black's younger brother, the army chaplain who would be rendering the eulogy. Beneath the bio and picture was a note of gratitude from the family coupled with the date and time of the second funeral service and ultimate interment. They were scheduled for the following week down in Belzoni, Mississippi. Tina shared this is the birthplace of his mother and the home of her father, Pastor Squire Tobias Pinder II, for whom Squire Black had been named.

I must have muttered to myself in amazement because Tina chimed in with her glowing approval of the program. She squeezed my hand as she watched me read the obituary. I was sure she knew I remembered all of the things she had told me about Squire Black's history, things that were clearly omitted from the document before me. As I read on, I filled in the gaps with what Tina had told me. According to her, Squire Black was the result of a gang rape. His mother's father, the Belzoni pastor, had given the baby his name in sympathy for his daughter and as an honor to her for not having an abortion.

Tina remembered when Squire Black had been born, nearly fifty years before, and all of the drama around the rape case. It seemed for years his mother had felt a lot of shame because the rape occurred during a relapse when she had returned to using cocaine. She tried to keep the unseemly nature of his origin from him. He found out the truth when he was about seven years old and was sent to Belzoni to live with his grandfather for a while. He lived there until he was about thirteen, when the first of his older brothers went to prison.

Some said he started selling drugs soon after he came back to Milwaukee from Belzoni. But he was certainly involved in the drug business by the time his second brother went to prison two years later. He was fifteen then, and his baby brother was born the following year. According to Tina, drama was common in the family. With both of her elder sons sent to prison following very public and even sensational trials, Squire Black's mother relied heavily upon him for all kinds of support. Of course the obituary said nothing of these things. It did say Squire Black had been in prison and turned his life around by developing his own towing business which prospered in the years before his tragic death. In the obituary were a number of things I was not aware of and found to be intriguing. I had not known that Squire Black was an avid capoeira practitioner — a Brazilian dancer — and had started a competitive dance group which traveled to New York annually. The obituary noted that capoeira dancing was thought to have originated with Brazilian slaves as a way to mask their adeptness in the martial arts. Squire Black and his group embraced the dance for its historic value and for the skill of self-defense.

It also surprised me that Squire Black had been a major force behind the annual Stomp the Yard event on the last day of Kwanzaa, New Year's Day, in Milwaukee's inner city. While I had never attended the event, I heard from many people throughout the years, including Flora and Tina, that young people — particularly young African-American men — benefitted from the festivities and attendant connections that followed the event. As I read all of this, I glanced at Lorri and wondered why she had never shared that part of Ajoy's father's life with me. As that question raced through my thoughts, I knew the answer immediately: I had not been open to hearing any of it. That recognition saddened me as I touched my daughter on her shoulder. Her response was one of surprise, but I didn't let on that I saw the look she gave me.

At exactly 2:00 p.m., a fabulously dressed young African-American woman stepped to the microphone, and a hush went over the entire place. Striking burgundy leather boots accentuated her cream-colored, exquisitely-tailored suit. Her shag haircut did not interfere with the diamond studs in her ears, which twinkled like boldly lit stars winking at the huge star on her left hand and the equally present blinking star on the left lapel of her stylish suit. She looked polished, sophisticated, and chic as she moved with ease, her voice hugging the mike with confident clarity. She welcomed everyone then identified herself as Mercedes, director of the Chicago House of Mercury, a renowned event-planning firm.

She then said that Squire Black had given bone marrow to her husband and had been a major support to her family as her husband battled the aftermath of a rare form of cancer more than 12 years before. She pointed to a well-dressed man in a wheel chair, acknowledging him as her husband. He lifted his hand in assent.

She wiped a tear from her right cheek as she said, "I am honored. My husband and I are honored that our firm will officiate over this tribute today. It is expected that we consider moving beyond the tragedy of Squire Black's death and recognize the man. Those of us who truly knew him at his core will always remember that Squire Black was here, and he made a difference!"

As she moved away from the microphone, a roar of applause swept the place, and then there was another hush. I was dumbfounded by the way things were going. It wasn't what I expected. Tina leaned over to me and whispered, "Ain't the girl bad?" Her eyes twinkled as if she knew something I didn't and wasn't about to share it. Again, I looked at my daughter. I wondered how much of this she knew. I felt ashamed for having judged this man, and yet I knew his dark side. I struggled within myself and then thought about Ajoy. What would I want her to know about her father?

I pulled myself out of thought to look at the program, then saw an elderly White man wearing a tight-fitting black suit stepping to the lectern with a Bible in hand. On the program he was listed as Rev. Cabott Kiley, director of the Faith, Food, and Rest Rescue Mission. The program deemed his task to be the presentation of the first scriptural reading, taken from the Book of Luke. The pastor cleared his throat, raised himself to his full height, and began by stating, "We must never judge people." In a booming voice, seemingly too large to spill from his physical frame, he read the scripture then said he had known Squire Black as a little boy. With a warm smile, he said he was present when Squire Black's mother bought him a secondhand bike from one of the mission's resale shops many years ago. He, the reverend, personally fixed one of the pedals on that bike in the young boy's presence. This enabled the young Squire Black to ride the bike immediately upon getting the refurbished gift home. Apparently, this was a lasting memory for him because through the years he often came by the mission to check in, and there was always a sizable donation in the gift pot when he left.

The reverend spoke with fervor, setting an engaging tone for those who followed him to the lectern. A noted jazz singer rendered a compelling rendition of *The Lord's Prayer* by Duke Ellington. She scatted beautifully, reaching towards the skill of Ella Fitzgerald, grandly enthralling the crowd. I had to look at the program twice to be sure I had not read it wrong. I was not aware Duke Ellington had made such a contribution, but, yes, there it was in all of its grandeur. *The Lord's Prayer* by Duke Ellington and the jazz singer was remarkable.

The second scriptural reading was presented by Mother Bailey, an African-American woman who said she was ninety-two years old. In a slightly quivering voice, she told of the times Squire Black had seen to it that her snow was shoveled properly and her lawn cut neatly. She read from the Book of John haltingly, and her investment in her task was emotionally moving. She rested on the lectern as she read and had to be helped back to her seat when she was done, but she did her deed and did it well.

Mother Bailey was followed by two young men who sang a rousing gospel favorite. They were listed on the program as cousins of Squire Black from the Pinders on the East coast, family members on his grandfather's side. They were fantastic vocalists, rendering a moving presentation. The program rolled on with songs and scriptural readings and a spectacular presentation from the prison chaplain of one of the state's largest maximum security prisons. Squire Black's oldest brother had been incarcerated there for more than 30 years; he was currently in the "hole," the jail within the prison, and was not allowed to attend the funeral. The prison chaplain read a heart-stirring statement from the confined brother in which he said, "I am sorry that I failed you, Squire, my brother. I am weak with sadness and shame." And by the time the handsomely adorned mass choir came forth and belted out an exceptionally moving rendition of an old-time gospel song about the excellence of God, the entire place was filled with emotion, with tears flowing freely.

I looked around and saw men weeping and Squire Black's entire family — mother, sisters, and others — on their feet with hands raised in the air. There were shouts of praise and just shouts of all kinds. The sound system was fabulous, making each note from the

musicians seem nearly palpable, reverberating effortlessly, melodiously transporting us to some place beyond the reality of the
moment. I kept thinking there was no way I could have predicted
anything as Spirit-filled as this. As the old people would say in
times like these, "This is too much for the blood pressure." The
moment was rich, fertile, and touching, and Lorri sobbed openly.
Tina had her arms raised in praise; MiMi's son was quiet with his
head down; and I stood, arms raised in praise, too, affected by all
that was going on around me. I was amazing myself by getting
caught up in the fertile tidal wave of praise.

Once again Mercedes took the lectern, this time to announce
the moment had come for remembrances, pointing out clearly that
the two-minute time frame would be followed explicitly. And to
make her point even more clear, two rather large men from a private
security firm (Tina said it was a Chicago firm) stood on each side
of the circular platform, giving an unmistakable picture of what
could occur if a person traversed the boundaries set by the time
frame allotted. One of the men held a stopwatch, which punctuated
Mercedes' warning that the timing would be precise.

Many people of all hues, shapes, and sizes — some in hip-hop
garb with their hats turned backwards and expensive sneakers,
others in furs and business suits — stepped up to share stories.
Some stories were rather sobering, but many were humorous. A few
were adolescent-like in that it appeared the individuals were simply
grandstanding, but you always have that sort of thing at funerals. A
number of Squire Black's "baby mamas" spoke, all without venom
and most with professions of deep love for him. As they came one
after the other, I took Lorri's hand because I knew this part of the
service was difficult for her. She had promised me she would not
go to the lectern, and I was grateful she kept her word.

The news coverage of the murders and Ajoy's miraculous recovery put our private lives in shambles. It left us all open to far too
much speculation and venomous gossip, which in some cases might
be dangerous for Lorri. I was too afraid that anything she'd say
would be misconstrued. It might spark some form of retaliation
from any of the people who were already upset with her because

Ajoy was seen as Squire Black's favorite child. In addition to all of the other aggrandizement, Ajoy's name was in the obituary as one of his children, along with two other names I didn't recognize. Apparently there were many children who were not mentioned.

On top of all of the fanfare, the memory of the lockbox in my freezer gave me a shiver. I pushed that thought away, telling myself I would deal with it when Lorri was in a better place. With that bit of mental management, I came back to the present. Amidst the remembrances were a few heart-wrenching ones that jarred me to my core. One of Squire Black's nephews, a son of his eldest brother and devoted worker in the B-Black towing business, strolled to the microphone with a confident air. He spoke of how his uncle forced him away from a "street" life and put him to work in his business. His moving statement was amplified by Tupac's poem listed in the program and identified as a favorite of his uncle. As he spoke and read, he sobbed openly, something that I had not expected to see.

Equally moving was the presentation by Squire Black's other brother, the one allowed to come from prison, the older brother closer to him in age. His statement was striking. He walked to the lectern in a prison-orange uniform flanked by two guards, both White men; he was cuffed and wore leg chains. That image in and of itself carried a heavy message, but his words poignantly gave the moment clarity. He said, "Like my older brother who could not be with us today, I, too, have failed you, Squire Black. As did your father fail you, and my father failed me, and our older brother's father failed him. And yes, America has failed us all in many ways. You, Squire Black, did not fail our younger brother, and for that I lift you up. I ask every Black man in this room today to look at me and these two White guards who are my keepers. Look and know that you do not want your sons to present such an image. We have work to do." With that said, flanked by the two guards, he walked back to his seat.

Interestingly, Black men around the Orbs stood and applauded. In an impromptu move, the two Pinder cousins from out East began singing a beautiful but mournful song, the lyrics pierced my heart. Soon the musicians joined in, and the entire place stood, me included. It was something to behold. I had the feeling for the second time that this funeral was not really about Squire Black the man. It was about a much larger set of issues that needed to be addressed on all levels of our community. I wondered if other people were getting that. I also wondered about the thoughts running through the mind of Squire Black's mother. Here were the images of her sons and grandsons. One son was dead, another was shackled, and one was in the jail within the prison. And she had grandsons, I was told, in juvenile detention. *Lord,* I thought, *this has to be painful for her.* The mother in me reached in spirit for the mother in her, and I wept. Again I was surprised.

The fervor in the Orbs was enthralling as the singing continued. People stood with arms raised and eyes closed. Old and young called out for a new day. Then out of nowhere a booming voice over a microphone from the back of the Orbs could be heard singing a powerfully uplifting praise song. The man's voice was strong and clear, and he sang boldly. Soon the other singing stopped, and the musicians chimed in with the bold voice. And then there he was: the other son, the son not incarcerated or dead. Squire Black's words on the back of the program that said, "My brother reflects the best of me" jumped out at me as he, the youngest brother, moved to the lectern and the room exploded in applause. Here was that brother in his army uniform, including the hat and clergy collar.

Singing jubilantly, he strutted to the lectern and removed his hat. Two men brought out a striking mud-cloth robe trimmed in red stitching around the sleeves. He adorned the robe with a regal move as his tall, slender frame towered over the candle near the coffin. *His father must have been a tall man*, I thought because he was tall; I guessed at least 6'5". In his Afrocentric mud-cloth robe — standing near the huge red, black, and green candle near the lavish mahogany coffin beneath the massive banner of Squire Black — he made quite a sight to behold. It was almost mythic in its capacity to convey many messages all at once. I wished I knew how to use the camera in my phone. Then I saw Tina was using her phone's camera to capture the moment, and I was relieved it would not be lost.

I had actually forgotten about the candle for a while, but it was lit now as Squire Black's youngest brother continued to belt out bold songful praises. Once again the entire place was caught up in song and expectation. It was clear to me this young preacher was on a mission and was on fire with it. He asked us to let him sing as we read the obituary silently, and that is what we did. He sang and moved back and forth on the platform as if he owned it. As he sang the musicians played. After a while he called out, "Raise your programs in the air when you are done reading. Raise it high! Raise it high!" Again the entire place was caught up in the spiritual energy of the moment. People were singing and crying and praying, and some were smiling. It must have been difficult for the prison guards and other officials to stay in their roles because the place was electric. Even cool, sophisticated Mercedes of the Chicago House of Mercury was on her feet waving her program in the air. Her husband, though seated in his wheelchair, waved his arms in the air as well. What I was experiencing amazed me. It was truly a memorable experience. Out of the corner of my eye I saw a television camera, and I became concerned. I hoped they would not denigrate this service in any way with the images they chose to convey. I couldn't believe I was thinking that, but I was.

When the time came for the young preacher to eulogize his brother, he deftly slid out of song into a magnificent spiritual place of oratory eloquence. His scholarly command of scripture was impressive, making it clear he was a learned man infused with a genuine love of God and on a mission. He did not bypass the foibles of his brother. In fact, using a scriptural quote he eloquently journeyed through many of the images Squire Black projected in his lifetime, including that of a felon, an absentee father, and a womanizing gangster drug lord who existed on the outside of the law for years. And with clarity he listed as well the ex-felon who had become an adept businessman revered by many for his phil-anthropic passions and who ultimately became a murder victim.

He set forth the images in a rhythmic, lyrical manner, punctu-ating each with a brief story from Squire Black's life. Then he went to the final two images, which he presented gracefully with great care. These were portrayed with reverence and were breathtaking. He spoke at length about the image he had of Squire Black as his brother, noting the love they shared allowed him to see beyond all of the other images to embrace a father figure and nurturer in his older brother. And as if propelled by a force outside of himself, he dove into a sea of scriptures that revealed the all-knowing power of God, through which he proposed the final image of his brother as a wounded child of God. Over and over again he repeated that only God knows what is in our hearts. He said, "Saint and sinner alike, we are all children of God. All are God's sheep, hungering in the wilderness for the breath of life, searching for the hand of the Master." His message was bold and preached to the middle. Some of his ideas were certainly esoteric in their underlying meaning, while others were simple, concrete, and easily grasped by all. No one, regardless of their sophistication, could leave this place without having been firmly steeped in the proverbial word. He was absolutely magnificent in his authentic intimacy with scripture. Spirit filled the place. I couldn't believe I was having such a deep, Spirit-filled experience at the funeral of Squire Black, the infamous father of my grandchild.

No one could have told me where the young preacher planned to take us in his mission of eulogizing his brother, but the four bare-chested Black male drummers in multicolored pants moving towards the circular platform were a visible clue to a journey on its way. The young preacher lifted his arms in a welcome to the drummers, who were followed by seven bare-chested men in stark white balloon-like pants with red, black, and green bandanas tied on their heads. They moved gracefully in unison towards the platform as if they were one. The young preacher said quietly, "Masked inside Squire Black was a wounded child of God." Then the seven bare-chested men repeated in unison, "Masked inside Squire Black was a wounded child of God." The seven formed a circle around the young preacher as the drummers sent forth a mystical cadence. They drummed quietly but with pregnant anticipation, as a jet-black young man who was the spitting image of Squire Black moved to the microphone. There was murmuring throughout the place.

Certainly people were in awe of this young replica of Squire Black that no one seemed to know. I turned to Tina with a questioning look, and she hunched her shoulders in an I-don't-know response, making it clear this was something she had not been made aware of. Even MiMi's son shrugged his shoulders and had a questioning look on his face.

As the drummers poured forth their rhythmic majesty and the seven men encircled the young preacher, he seemed to be making some kind of change in his attire. The young replica of Squire Black, who appeared to be in his early to mid-twenties, spoke with a pronounced southern twang. He confirmed what everyone was probably thinking, sending lightning-bolt-like energy throughout the crowd. "Squire Black was my father," he said, stating a name listed in the obituary as one of Squire Black's children. With that said and without further explanation, he lifted a sheet of paper and began to read the Laurence Dunbar poem in the program about masks. He read slowly, punctuating each word with a brief pause. His resonant voice commanded attention and was striking in how it blended with the drumming. The theatrics of it all were stunning. The drummers drummed softly again, but by the time he was finished with the poem, an engaging crescendo had seemed to lift the entire place.

Then, in one fluid motion, the seven men stepped away from the young preacher, who was now bare-chested and wearing a bandana like the others. They all began to dance. The eight, including the young preacher, danced with vigor as they chanted, "Masked inside of Squire Black was a wounded child of God." Their movements were reminiscent of fluid martial-arts stances, which hovered between elegance and aggressive fervor. Charmingly, they chanted and hummed, creating an other-worldly quality that made the hair stand up on the back of my neck and caused chills to move all over me. The young replica of Squire Black went on to say, "My father was a capoeira dancer. It is thought that the capoeira dancers of Brazil and other places where slavery flourished masked their warrior abilities to protect themselves by putting their fighting skills to dance movements. They were masters at masking. This tribute

261

to the life of my father by his fellow capoeira brothers serves to remind us that some masks are for the purpose of survival." With confidence, he stepped away from the microphone, removed his shirt, pulled a bandana from his pocket, tied it on his head, and joined the dancers. It was a theatrical, breathless moment. There was a hush in the room, a form of unspoken reverence.

The entire afternoon was not what I had expected. Words couldn't describe its messages. When the dancers stopped and the young preacher offered benediction, I believed the general state of almost everyone in the room was that of amazement. For a moment, I could not move my lips to join in the closing song, which was led by the jazz singer. She belted out the historic Black Conclusion Anthem that proclaims a hopeful future despite perilous times. If this had been a concert, I am sure people would have been clamoring for an encore. But because it was a funeral, people just stood waving their hands in the air and singing. It was an uncommon experience.

CHAPTER 18

Falling from A High Spiritual Place

As eloquently as Mercedes opened the service, she closed it by inviting all to partake of the repast in one of the other Orbs off to the side. And finally, she spoke of the funeral that would take place down in Belzoni, Mississippi the following week, noting that Squire Black would be laid to rest there. People by now were milling around. There was some applause, but mostly people just seemed overwhelmed by the sheer intensity of the service. Many people surrounded the young preacher, who was embracing the young replica of Squire Black. They were standing near the other family members. It was interesting to see Squire Black's mother beaming as she stood near her preacher son. She looked at him with pride. She didn't touch him; she just stared at him with awe in her eyes. In that moment, I forgave her for many things. As a mother, I understood her gratification with this son, the one son yet unsullied. I felt compassion for her in that moment.

I was taking that in when I realized Lorri had gotten up and was heading towards the preacher and the crowd that surrounded the family of Squire Black. I felt anxiety rise in my throat as I called to her, but she was invested in reaching Squire Black's mother and brother. I quickly looked to Tina, but she was closing in on Lorri. I saw that MiMi's son was heading after her as well. Lorri had promised me she would not speak during the time of remembrances, but she hadn't said anything about commiserating with the family. As

I watched my daughter reach her destination, I got a strange feeling in the pit of my stomach. It was exacerbated by what I caught out of the corner of my eye when the young preacher grabbed Lorri in his arms in a big bear hug. One of Squire Black's baby mamas who spoke during the remembrance portion of the service was standing close to them with hands on her hips. She whispered something in the ear of the woman standing next to her, and they both shot hostile glances in Lorri's direction.

It was strange that I caught all of that, but I suppose it was a matter of prescience, foreshadowing what was to come. I became really anxious and without being aware of it began to pace back and forth. I could hear myself saying, "Lord, have mercy," but I couldn't get Lorri's attention, although I waved at her and called to Tina. For a moment, I thought about going over to where Lorri was, but I knew she could get very annoyed with me for seeming to limit her mourning with Squire Black's family. I watched and waited and I heard from person after person passing by me about the lavish spread in the other Orbs. Apparently there were foods of all kinds, including a pasta bar and soul food galore. One woman was taken with the ice sculptures and the huge sheet cake with Squire Black's picture on it. Nervously listening to the talk all around me, I wished I could blink my eyes and Lorri and I would be out of the place and back home. The same uneasiness that enveloped me on my way to the funeral returned, though I tried desperately to recapture the Spirit-filled moments of the funeral service.

Over the years I often heard old black women say that negative experiences often come on the heels of a spiritual high; it was as if the devil would try to steal your joy, they would say. My mind went to the wisdom of these old women because what followed the wonderfully Spirit-filled service was a nightmare, full of darkness. As Lorri connected with the young preacher in a warm embrace, she was soon caught in another embrace by Squire Black's son. Then she stopped by his mother and sisters, sharing words and embraces with all of them. Tina stayed close to her, and MiMi's son was not far away. They, too, were engaging in conversation with various members of the family. I watched Lorri and the two women watching her: the baby mama and her cohort. Something about the way they eyed her made me nervous. Both women had huge black purses with white flowers on them. I wondered what they were thinking about my daughter and was unnerved by the number of "what-if" questions going on in my head.

I couldn't put my finger on it, but something seemed threatening about how they followed Lorri with their eyes. When she was beside me again and Tina and MiMi's son were walking side by side, I felt a bit of relief for a moment. But I was still unsettled as we headed towards the door leading to the parking lot. I could see it was now dark outside. The winter evening was upon us, and I wanted to get out of the Orbs and head home. Then without warning Lorri broke rank and headed for one of the women's restrooms. In a flash the baby mama and her cohort, who had been lurking behind us, slipped into the bathroom right behind her. Tina seemed to be oblivious of their move because she was in deep conversation with a guy who was asking about her coat. I called to her, but she was so deep in conversation she didn't hear me. Of course MiMi's son saw Lorri head to the restroom, but I don't think he made the connection with the two women, and he wouldn't go into the ladies' room anyway.

With a sense of urgency, I walked toward the women's restroom along with a few other women who were headed there. Opening the outer door, I heard the ruckus, immediately identifying my daughter's scream. In the center of the room were two women, one with her phone/camera held high, standing and watching the baby mama and her cohort beat my daughter. Lorri was on the floor. One of the women was banging her in the face with what appeared to be a jar of pickles while the other was holding her down, pulling at her clothes, and ultimately kicking her. My mind went blank. I don't know how I got across the room so fast, but there I was in the brawl with the two young women, fighting for dear life. My greatest weapon was my rage. Adrenalin pumped within me with such force that I felt ready to tear the two women apart to save my daughter. Lorri was fighting, too, but she was bleeding profusely and seemed stunned.

I had never thought of myself as a brawler, but in that moment I found myself trying my best to tear these women apart, allowing fury to help me get them away from my daughter. That was all I wanted to do at first: get them away from her. But when I saw all of the blood on Lorri's s face, I lost it. I began fighting as if death were before me, using everything in me to take these women down. There was screaming and cussing and blood everywhere. The blood was coming mostly from Lorri's face and mouth, a number of her teeth now missing. When I saw the gaping wound on my daughter's face, I intentionally and with all the force I could muster began jabbing one of the women on her hand with the point of my car key. I beat against her with everything in me, calling her a bitch with each jab to her hand. The pickle jar had broken, and my daughter's face was covered in blood and pickle juice. There was glass around us, making things dangerous. It was horrible. I didn't recognize myself when I bit into the baby mama's arm, intending to draw blood but only jarring my own dentures out of place. In that moment I wished I had invested in dental implants. Rage filled me. As I fought, I wished I'd had a gun.

Someone got security, and then there were police officers in the ladies' room. Finally, Tina was standing there. She was amazed to see me disheveled, wet in pickle juice and blood, holding my daughter's face, and screaming for someone to get a doctor. I moved Lorri around the broken glass, pickles, pickle juice, and blood that were all over. The police were holding the baby mama and her cohort back. It was an awful scene, but I was not ready for what was to come next. People had cell phones out capturing the moment, and one woman who was in the restroom all along — but had not helped in any way — was bragging to her friends that she had it all in her phone and was putting the entire fight on line. I was mortified. I am a very private person and could not imagine having pictures of my daughter and me embroiled in such a primitive melee being sent via the internet all around the country. If the police had not been present, I believe I would have jumped that woman and taken her phone. I was just that angry. I thought all of this as I held Lorri close to me and applied pressure to the gaping wound in her face directly under her right eye. She tried to speak to me, and I realized she was missing at least two teeth in the front right side of her mouth. "Lord, have mercy," was all I could get out. It was awful.

To make things even worse, as we left the restroom, reporters and the TV camera person I saw earlier were standing waiting for anything they could get. Of course Lorri's bloody face and mouth were the immediate topic of the moment. One of the women who had been in the restroom but not directly involved in the melee was in true star mode. She stepped up to the microphones the reporters thrust in her face and began talking as the camera rolled. She gave minute details of what transpired, making a special point to note that Lorri, whom she called the beaten woman, hadn't done anything to the two women who beat her. They jumped her as soon as they entered the bathroom, called her an uppity bitch, and hit her in the face with some kind of jar. The woman grinned broadly as she pointed to her phone, clearly letting everyone know that she recorded it all. She went on to talk about my involvement, commenting, "That grandma sure can fight." She pointed to me, and I wanted to slap her right there.

The way she was grandstanding you would think she was at the Academy Awards or something like that, but she was certain to be popular for all that she knew. A reporter for a major newspaper began throwing questions our way as did the TV reporter. It was surreal. I couldn't believe this was happening, and I pushed Lorri towards the ambulance that was pulling up. "We have to get her to a hospital," I said with authority as I looked at the young police woman who was positioning her notepad to take more statements. I wondered if the female cop was blind. Surely she could see my daughter was bleeding and in need of medical care. By now there was actually a crowd around us. People were coming from everywhere, and the young preacher found his way to us. He went into military mode and deftly managed the crowd as we maneuvered our way to the ambulance. The paramedics went to work immediately, and I was surprised to hear I had a cut on the back of my left hand. I hadn't felt it and didn't know when it had occurred. The female paramedic just smiled at my surprise, gently pointing out it was quite common for people not to know they had been injured, even from gunshots sometimes. As we were ushered inside the ambulance, Tina promised to follow us to the hospital, and MiMi's son said he would get a ride home. He was on his cell phone, and I thought he was probably calling his mom about the fiasco. She would have some choice words for Tina and her failure to keep us safe. I called to him and handed him my car keys, gesturing to him that he could drive my car to the house and someone would give him a ride home from there. He hesitated for a moment but then took the keys. When the ambulance pulled out of the parking lot, I prayed that MiMi's son had a driver's license.

Tina was not the only one to follow us to the hospital. Two reporters — one from a major Milwaukee newspaper and the other from one of the Black newspapers — along with the female cop and her male partner came as well. As Lorri was being attended to, they had questions for me. From deep inside of me, the cool, stoic Jewelle showed up for a moment to handle the questions, and I was grateful for her. In talking with the reporters, I made a point of staying away from why I thought the attack occurred in the first place. It was interesting when I gave my name that the female cop said, "I thought that was you," making it clear she was aware of my work in domestic violence in the community. She had been in court with me previously and seemed to sympathize with my current circumstances. I was pleased she was familiar with my work, but I did not feel good about the situation I was in. I wanted to shrink out of sight.

It turned out I needed two stitches in my hand, while Lorri ended up having 18 stitches beneath her right eye. She had two black eyes and would have to have extensive dental work; she lost three teeth, and her gums were damaged. I couldn't believe what had happened to us. The two assailants — the baby mama and her cohort — were taken into custody, the female cop told me. The witnesses, with their cell phones and their statements, had given enough to the police to show their guilt in the assault. With authority, the young female cop gave me that report as I wondered whether my car key had done any damage to either of the women.

I had jabbed one of them pretty good with the key, but there was no report of her needing any medical attention. I was not proud of this, but I wished my car key had done some damage.

In the middle of the young cop's report about the two women, Tina broke in with an apology that went on and on. She was so very sorry she was not there to offset what happened to Lorri and me, she whined. Listening to my friend, I realized I was not sure what she could have done or what she would have been willing to do in her full-length white mink coat anyhow. She was there for moral support, I told her, and I appreciated this. She was in tears by this time and made a point of saying the people who hurt us would not get away with it. Calls had been made, and folks would take care of it. I didn't want to hear any more of that, certainly not while we were standing so close to the police. For a moment I just looked at Tina, thinking she must have had something to drink on the way to the hospital because she was talking crazy. I didn't say a word. I told myself to just breathe and pray.

I was in the midst of a deep breath when a nurse came in to tell us Lorri's blood pressure was dangerously high and they wanted to watch her for a while. They would take her pressure again in a half an hour and then every half hour — until it was in a reasonable range for one full hour — before they felt it was safe for her to leave the hospital. By that time, we had already been at the hospital nearly two hours. We left the Orbs about 5:45 p.m.; I had looked at my watch as we left the parking lot. Just as I was thanking the nurse for taking such good care of Lorri, I looked up and saw Kaimen running into the room. She was all excited and had one question after another. In all that was going on, I did not think to call home. Seeing her there, I wasn't sure who alerted Kaimen about our situation. I looked at Tina thinking maybe she called, but she was so immersed in her feelings that I couldn't get her attention. Kaimen answered the question herself, noting that MiMi's son called while he was driving my car to the house. I had forgotten about that. Following his report, she went to the wrong hospital as she tried to reach me on my cell phone. She chided me about not keeping my cell phone on. I smiled to myself thinking I wasn't in the mood for Kaimen's antics. In fact, I didn't much feel like being bothered at all. I felt sick to my stomach all of a sudden and ended up running to a restroom. There I found myself falling victim to the perilous throes of an upset stomach that often announced my clouded response to stress. In truth, when I returned to the waiting room, my stomach began to bubble audibly, seemingly leading the nurse who was keeping an eye on Lorri's blood pressure to bring me a powerful antacid. She directed me to drink it down slowly and then to just sit quietly, which I did without any hesitation. I felt weird in my chest area and for a moment remembered Oprah's show on women and heart attacks. I wondered if that was happening to me.

We were heading out of the emergency room around 10:15 p.m. when Tina, Lorri, and Kaimen's phones rang together as if on cue. I supposed mine would have been ringing as well, but I still hadn't turned it on. All three women yelled out in shock, and I believe my heart really did stop for a moment. All I could discern from the babbling going on around me was that we were on the news. Kaimen looked at me and said, "Mom, you are really going to lose it. They have you and Lorri on TV, and some woman is talking about Lorri being attacked in the restroom." I was angry, but I was also disappointed in the reporters because it seemed they chose to report only the dark side of the funeral. I had hoped that would not happen, never imagining I would be a part of the dark side. As I listened to Tina report to us what she was being told about the news segment, all I could do was breathe and pray. They talked about Ajoy's being Squire Black's daughter, offering speculation that perhaps the two mothers of Squire Black's children were in some kind of conflict.

There was even speculation about the jar of pickles used in the attack; the woman who saw it all speculated that one of the women in the melee must be pregnant. I was outraged about the public way they were talking about Lorri, Ajoy, and me. And they didn't miss a beat pointing out that Lorri's mother was a respected domestic violence interventionist in the city who stepped up to the plate to protect her daughter in the violent altercation. While the way my involvement was slanted was not actually negative, it was all so very public. This was, of course, what I hoped to avoid, but there it was on television for all to see. Lorri looked at me through tears; both eyes were puffy, with her right eye now almost swollen shut. I wasn't sure what I was feeling at that moment, but I did just want to run away. Kaimen was engrossed in searching the internet on her phone and soon let out a horrible scream. I was not sure how she accessed it, but she had in fact found the assault online, and all she kept saying was "Jesus!" "Stop it," I yelled, admonishing her about calling Jesus's name in vain. And then I thought about it; maybe that was her way of praying because God knew we needed prayer right at that moment.

When we reached the hospital parking lot, I told Tina to go home and rest, promising her I would give her a call when I got settled. I thanked her for being with us at the funeral again and tried to help her move away from feeling bad about the attack. In truth, I needed her to just leave us alone now. As a family, we had a lot to handle. Once seated in Kaimen's car, I decided to take a look at my phone. There were 13 voicemail messages. Without delay, I began listening to the messages and was stunned to learn the number of people who already saw the news story about the attack. The first call was from Jodi, who had a number of medical questions about Lorri's wounds. I could hear the urgency in her voice and knew I would have to get back to her soon. The next message was from Kojo. He, too, had urgency in his voice but didn't have any questions. He simply stated emphatically that he was there for me if I needed anything and asked that I call him.

The next message was from Flora, whose voice was laced with anger. She was clear about her disdain for the job Tina had done in protecting us and was equally dissatisfied with the news media for their "racist" slant on the coverage of the funeral. She heard about the deeply spiritual tone of the funeral and found the media's choice of coverage upsetting. She would write letters leveling her concerns. She, too, asked that I call her when I could. The next call surprised me. It was from Cullen, whom Jodi had alerted of the brawl. I guessed I shouldn't have been surprised by Jodi's vigor because she could be tireless in her efforts to find answers and secure justice. Cullen's warm words evoked tears. I struggled to keep them back because I was too worried about Lorri's emotional state to allow myself to acknowledge my own feelings.

Cullen's words were soothing, and I intended to call him as soon as I waded through the rest of the messages. I thought there was no way for me to even speculate about what I would find when I reached my house. The next call was from MiMi, who saw the news and had spoken to her son. She had a number of choice things to say about Tina, clearly venting years of contentiousness between the two of them. She went on and on about my being naïve. She made a special point about how sorry her son was for not being able to handle the situation, but she was certain things would be taken care of. I actually got a chill when I listened to her call because I had had enough violence in my life and did not want anyone else to be hurt. The chill I felt informed me that I would not call MiMi until much later.

The next call was from my cousin Vy down in Key West. Jodi had been busy. She had informed Vy about the news clip. Of course Vy had some choice things to say about the media but made a point of noting she would be in deep prayer for my family and me. As I listened to my cousin's words, I marveled at how she always seemed to draw upon her faith to get through crises. No matter what challenge was set before her, she turned to prayer. God was her warrior. Something about her fervent faith made me feel better. I uttered a prayer myself as I turned to the next message, in which Jodi was again asking the same medically related questions.

Nearing the end of my messages as we pulled into my driveway, I heard Eva's voice and was shocked. Eva, who almost never left voicemail messages, was saying she had seen the news and was concerned about me. She said she had called the house and spoken with Korri, who was pretty upset. She went on to say that Patrick was with her and she was going to put him on the phone. Engulfed in fatigue I walked into my house listening to Patrick's voice, his tone conveying concern. Instantly, I remembered I was supposed to meet him after the funeral. I had promised I would set aside time to see him. He didn't bring that up, but I remembered and felt sad. His concern sent a warm feeling through me, and I was pushing myself to figure out how I could muster the energy to still connect with him that evening. That was my thought as I was walking through my dining room to my kitchen flanked by Kaimen and Lorri. It was then that Anthony ran to us crying, and my world turned upside down. He began sobbing as he ran to me and then to his mother. My soon-to-be eleven-year-old grandson was near hysterics. He was babbling about something I couldn't make out at first. Then I saw the lockbox on the kitchen table, the blue towel placed under it as if it had been a gift unwrapped.

I am sure I staggered forward to the table, looking first at Anthony and then at Korri. Korri was now hunching his shoulders, indicating he was unsure of what was going on. I felt lightheaded and weak in my knees as I grabbed one of the kitchen chairs to balance myself. Lorri raced past me and picked up the lockbox. I forgot about the cell phone. I was sure an observer would see the volatility in the dynamics of the room. The energy was revving up. Many things happened at once. Anthony was now hysterical, screaming about the lockbox and how sorry he was about taking it and hiding it in the freezer. He didn't mean to get his mother hurt. Apparently he had overheard Kaimen's conversation with MiMi's son when he called about the fiasco at the Orbs. Kaimen was grabbing her head and heart dramatically, showing her dismay over the situation as Anthony blurted out his confession.

Lorri was breathing hard and pacing as if she were an animal in the wild revving up for a choice kill. I sat down in one of the kitchen chairs, too weak to do anything else. Korri stood near the window watching all of us unravel. The pending explosion came when Anthony said, "Grandma said we would work it out. She said I didn't do anything wrong." When his words hit my ears, I knew a volcano would erupt. Both Lorri and Kaimen screamed, "You knew about this, Mom!" I couldn't discern if it was an exclamation or a question, but the knot in my throat made it impossible for me to say a word. This was just too much for me. As I struggled to find words, my cell phone fell on the floor. Korri stooped to pick it up and checked to see that it was turned off. Somehow in the midst of all that was going on, I had managed to turn it off. I had shut Patrick out again.

Korri handed the phone to me, but I still couldn't say a word. I felt helpless. Certainly I had meant well, but now in the unraveling of this shocking truth, I knew my intentions would not be seen as pure. I was not prepared for the venom that came from Lorri. She screamed at me, "You controlling bitch. You had the nerve to keep this from me." As she screamed, Anthony screamed, too, and I thought my head would explode. I laid my head on the table, thinking I was much too weary for this, but I couldn't muster the energy to leave the room. I rubbed my chest, feeling an uneasiness under my left breast. Tonight I felt the full force of my 63 years. Out of the corner of my eye, I saw Korri grab Anthony by the hand. Anthony struggled to get free from his uncle. But Korri wrapped his arms around him in a most tender gesture, and Anthony followed him. Quickly, Korri called Ajoy and the other kids from the bedroom, and they disappeared out of my back door, heading to Korri's place. I knew he was being protective; he was taking them to his place because he had no idea of what would happen next between his mother and his sisters. I could feel tonight would be the slaughter of Grandma Jewelle, and it was good that he and the children would not be privy to that.

Just as the back door closed behind them, Lorri picked up the lockbox and threw it across my kitchen. It hit the wall and fell to the floor but did not open. She screamed and screamed, calling me one foul name after the other, again making her point that I was a controlling bitch. My heart hurt, but I could not speak. The cool, triage-operating Jewelle that people raved about was nowhere to be found. Certainly any hint of my cool persona was being incinerated in the venomous guile being spewed from Lorri's rage. She paced back and forth with her arms flailing, and I wondered where she found the energy to be so angry. I concluded that this fury was as much a form of displaced anger couched in grief — emanating from Squire Black's death and all of the attendant matters of the past few days — as it was about the rage triggered in response to her evaluation of my actions. All of this was being showered upon me, and it felt assaultive. She spewed her anger and grief at me, and I wondered why Kaimen just sat there and did not venture even one word of caution to her sister about disrespecting their mother. I thought about Thea and wished she were there.

When I was able to muster the energy to look up, I peered directly into Lorri's swollen, marred face. Instantly I was filled with empathy for all she was going through. I guess it was the mother in me that made me reach for her, but I quickly retreated, recoiling at her words. "You think you know every damn thing, and you don't know how you just keep destroying your children year in and year out. You are one self-centered bitch," she screamed as she pushed my hand away from her. She spat words at me, "You and your Jesus-calling daughter Thea are both full of shit. She is so much like your old ass with her pontificating about how life should be. Both of you need Jesus, and he ain't hearing your asses anyway." When she began to be blasphemous, I leaned in her direction and reached for her. I wanted to shake some sense into her, but Kaimen raced between us. Lorri, in turn, forcefully shoved her sister out of the way. She stood directly over me, pointing her finger at me in an accusatory way as she went on about all that I had done wrong in raising them.

I didn't know what she was talking about. I had no inkling of what she meant. Vengefully she went on, spewing a stream of expletives. At one point, I tried to stand up but found no strength in my legs to move away from her. So haltingly, I sat down again at the table and rested my head in my hands. I listened to an onslaught of condemning refrains couched in story after story, heralding a reign of hellish selfishness that belied everything I ever believed about myself as a mother. She punctuated the fact that I had been studying all the time, trying to get one degree or the other, and I constantly put one babysitter or the other over them when they needed me. For some reason she didn't seem to recognize that I had to work to make life better for all of us, and school was to attain the same goal. I struggled to better myself for the sake of lifting up my family, I thought. She didn't seem to understand that the irritability she accused me of was grounded in the rage I felt so often for their father's alcoholism and abuse in their early years.

She swore I ruined my sons, rendering one a weird hermit who lived in the woods in the upper Florida Keys and the other a timid mama's boy too afraid to venture far from home. She spat her disdain out with such venom that I cringed each time she said her brothers' names, nearly holding my breath in preparation for the attendant allegations of dysfunction in my role as mother. Pacing like a caged animal, she immersed herself in a vociferous and hostile diatribe that made my head spin. When she shifted from her brothers to what I had done to injure her and Kaimen, I thought Kaimen would speak. But she said nothing as her sister cited instance after instance of her take on my domineering character and how it forced Kaimen to act out in high school. She blamed me for Kaimen's out-of-wedlock pregnancy with her first child. She said I hadn't taught them enough about birth control or been open to discussing their various sexual exploits with them. I didn't know what she was talking about! But I said nothing. She said I was more sensitive and patient with the people I counseled at the domestic violence centers than I was in dealing with my own children. "You put everyone before us," she screamed, "always on call being paged about some violent situation or another or leaving home to handle some situation. We had problems in our house, too." Listening to my daughter lambast me for doing my job, I felt helpless, particularly for all the things I hadn't realized she resented. I felt vulnerable to her wrath as she spewed out pent-up disdain at that moment. She continued her verbal assault, the wound within my heart seemed to fester, infected with abject sadness. But this hurt couldn't compare to what was about to come.

Lorri seemed to be working up to something even more injurious, and soon her rage took her to a place I did not allow people to visit. In fact, I was riveted by her words, wondering where she had gotten the information that she aggressively dumped on me. Her face was close to mine, her missing teeth making way for tiny droplets of spit to fly in my direction. After a deep breath, she began almost as if she were giving a world-altering oratory. "You pushed

Daddy to drink," she said with authority. "You killed his first son, and that made Daddy a drunk. It was your stubborn, arrogant, controlling, bitchy ass that fucked this entire family up," she spat out. The baby from the recurrent dream flashed before me.

To say my head was spinning would be an understatement because my head and body churned with emotions I couldn't readily describe. I was livid, but I felt impaled as well, broken in half. She went to a place that had always been so raw for me that I almost never spoke about it. I never even told Cullen about the awful thing that happened to my first son. And, yes, one of the things I was feeling, along with pure rage, was deep guilt that seemed to never go away. She certainly struck a major nerve. I guess that is why I came up out of my chair when she began to enumerate the details of what happened the day she said I killed my first son. I didn't catch all of her accusations because I went into something akin to a flashback, but I did hear the words basement and laundry basket just as my hand landed across her face.

I don't know where I found the energy, but I hit my daughter with everything I had in me. As I hit her I heard a scream come from my mouth that sounded primal, almost animal-like. I saw blood on my hand, and then I ran. I ran from my daughters. I ran to get away from the awful feeling inside my chest. I was trying to run from my own thoughts. I ran from my kitchen, up the stairs to my bedroom and I heard the house phone ringing. But I ran past it in the large sitting room, and I locked myself in my bedroom. As I was running, I had mumbled something, but it was virtually incomprehensible, almost gibberish. I was out of breath. Somehow I found myself lying face down on the floor in my bedroom with my Bible clutched to my breasts and my mother's pearl-like rosary around my neck. I didn't remember putting the rosary there or grabbing the Bible. I was sobbing in a way that seemed almost infantile. I heard Kaimen banging on the door, asking me to please let her in. She seemed to be crying, but I didn't care. I was somewhere in between, a place on the brink of hell and totally without volition. It seemed that time stopped. I felt strange, as if I were out of my body watching and listening to all that was going on around me. I blocked out the banging on my door and curled up in a fetal position. All of a sudden I was back to the day I had fallen down the basement stairs and lost my first son. The day I almost bled to death. The day a part of me went somewhere else.

I still don't know where I went that day, but it was a dark place without sound. It was a place I never wanted to revisit, and here I was heading for that place again. All I could do was cry out to God: "Help me, Jesus! Help me, Jesus! Help me, Jesus!" Curled up on the floor in my bedroom, I gave in to the memories. They engulfed me, transporting me back to many years ago, during my second year of marriage to Claude. I was near the bottom of the steep, rustic basement stairs writhing in pain, soaked in my own blood. The fluids from the ruptured amniotic sac and an injured (soon to be dead) baby hung out of me. I remembered the smell of blood. I could hear my own screams and remembered thinking I was going to die. I couldn't move because my right leg was broken. I was on the stairs for what seemed a long time, and I remembered knowing my baby was dead. Somehow I knew that.

I didn't know then that it was a son who lost his life in that awful fall. I remembered thinking I could have saved my baby, if I had been wearing underpants: such a foolish thought at such an awful moment. All I was sure of was that death was everywhere around me, and I might as well welcome it to take me away from my shame and pain. I was told many times I was lucky to be alive because I lost so much blood. In truth, there was a gaping wound in my right tibia where my bone protruded. It had made its own way, creating another place for my blood to run free. I can remember hearing one of the paramedics cuss under his breath when he saw me. I must have been a sight. If it hadn't been for the old woman, Miss Schroeder, I guess I wouldn't have made it. Although in her nineties, she came downstairs when she heard my screams. She was the one who found me.

The memory of that day brought back all of the warnings I had been given about wearing those ragged pink house slippers I loved so much. And my children's father had begged me to stop taking the wash down to the basement. He said he would do it, but I felt capable of handling the chores, though I was almost nine months' pregnant. Miss Schroeder warned me a number of times that the basement stairs were much too steep for me to be climbing up and down with a laundry basket in my hands at that stage of my pregnancy. I didn't listen. Memory of all of the warnings fed my guilt. Though I thought I had forgiven myself years before, a true sense of guilt and shame engulfed me in that moment as I lay on the floor in my locked room. *Jesus,* I thought, *did I really kill my son?*

PART IV

"...angels, ancestors, and spirit guides sitting at the feet of the Great I AM will lift you.... Your secrets will hold you captive till you speak your story /and yet/ You have a healing kindness. You will heal many.... Late in life from the mire you will bloom like the mud flower...."

CHAPTER 19

Out of the Depths I Cry Out for a Healing

I don't know how long I revisited my past that night before I fell into a promising deep sleep. All I know for sure is that I cried out to God for a healing. Facedown on my floor I humbled myself. Serendipitously, in the midst of lamenting before I closed my eyes, I put my hands on an old bottle of pain pills I had put away in the bottom drawer of my nightstand. I had put them there, months before, following a bout with an inflamed hip. Two of them relieved me of consciousness, casting me into the arms of nethermost slumber, justifiably far away from all peevishness and pain. Fortuitously, it turned out to be a slumber that led to the dream which addressed many of my lifelong concerns, ultimately priming me to encounter a forthcoming healing. In the dream, I found myself encased in the confessional of my childhood church, St. Mary Star of the Sea Catholic Church in Key West, Florida, where I was christened, received my first communion, and was confirmed all by the time I turned 13 years old.

Vividly, the dream brought back the odd smells of the confessional, which seemed to engulf me. The confessional reeked of furniture polish, leather, and tobacco smoke. The tobacco smoke was probably from the breath of the priest on the other side of the confessional wall waiting to hear my sins, which spilled from my lips as if they had a will of their own. Oddly, the priest seemed to hear my sins, but I could not. Though I felt the words rush from my mouth, I could not hear them. Out of habit, I bowed in fervent supplication, bent under the weight of my transgressions. Graciously, the soft leather under my knees made my posture of contrition seem less punitive as I waited to receive the penance that would set me straight with God.

I heard the priest clear his throat and move about on the other side of the confessional. His voice laced with a heavy Spanish accent gave me absolution, but not before I was given the entire rosary as my penance. The mandated rosary was to be uttered as I walked the replica beads cemented into the earth at the grotto directly next to the church. Then for some reason — I don't know why — I peeked out of the confessional stall into the church and saw a baptism going on. The baptism was taking place near the rear of the church, off to the side. I saw a Black baby about six or seven weeks old being dowsed on the forehead with water. I strained to identify the baptismal party, but I couldn't at first and then I realized I was the baby.

In a flash, I became a child, probably around eight or nine years old. Along with a few cousins, including Vy, I was playing in the garden near the grotto of the church. Everything was vivid and vibrant. The grass was invitingly green, and the statue of the Virgin Mary was luminescent, shimmering in the sun. I knew my task was to walk the rosary as my penance. The replica of the rosary was beautifully etched in the ground in front of the grotto, which was famous worldwide because of the special promises made there. There was always someone praying there. Diligently, I walked the rosary as my cousins skipped and played. I walked the rosary and grew from a child to a teenager. I felt light and strong, very much alive.

Then, near the gate on Truman Avenue in front of the grotto, I spotted the Warrior Chief. He was sitting majestically on his horse. Soon, he beckoned to me with a feather and I left the grotto to follow him. In the blink of an eye, he and I were on the corner of Truman Avenue and Whitehead Street, highway US #1. It was a very familiar place. I was all grown up, a seasoned woman, wearing combat boots and a stunningly elegant off white dress that hung slightly off my shoulders, the same dress from the cornucopia nightmare.

We entered a walled garden where there were Poinciana trees, plants and shrubs of all types. The place was mystical, exceptional, aesthetically pleasing and very familiar. In a flash, the garden was filled with old ladies of all races, shapes, sizes, and medical conditions. Some carried oxygen tanks, while others moved about with walking canes. Yet, they were all nursing babies at their left breasts. Even the old ladies with walkers and those in wheelchairs had a baby at their breast. Their white hair glistened in the sun, but their chiseled and wrinkled faces held a blank look. The aroma of eucalyptus filled the air suddenly and a little chubby Black baby boy came from behind some trees while ringing a large golden bell. The sharp clanging of the bell sent shivers through me. There was something familiar about the Black baby boy, but I couldn't put my finger on it at first. And then, in a flash, he was wearing the army-green jacket and the sailor cap. He was the baby from the recurrent dream.

Mysteriously, upon the first few clangs of the bell, all the other babies jumped down from the breasts they had been sucking and began to grow into adults. In another flash, the baby from the recurrent dream, in a dramatic move, tossed the sailor's cap into a nearby pond. He clasped the army-green jacket around himself, all while looking knowingly into my eyes. Something in me sighed a conclusive *YES!* After a while the Warrior Chief stood beside me in the garden. He touched me with the feather and immediately I was pulled upon the back of his horse just as I had been in the dream at Cullen's place weeks earlier. I held on to him with everything in me as we hovered there on the corner for a moment across the street from the lighthouse and up the street from Hemingway's house. We breezed by Poinciana trees. Memories flooded me, and I cried. Soon we headed up highway U.S. #1. We crossed Duval St., passed the grotto and magically galloped over bridges and then mountains in a flash. Something major had happened! I could feel

285

it in the center of my being. There had been closure, an answered question I couldn't yet say out loud.

The Warrior Chief and I, of course, were heading north; he was bringing me home to Milwaukee, back to face my life. Upon that recognition, I woke up with a start. My bladder had jarred me out of my healing dream, and I raced to relieve myself. As I crossed the mirror in my bathroom, I saw myself and was put off by the bags under my eyes. In response, I grabbed my face cloth and held it to the coldest water I could draw from the faucet. I hoped the cold rag would erase the strain under my eyes. I reflected on the dream, experiencing both uneasiness and a sense of promise. There was a hint of finality in the ride home with the Warrior Chief, and yet there was this oozing feeling of something awakening within me. I closed my eyes, trying to savor all of the dream's messages.

Upon returning to my room, I realized someone had been there during the night. Someone had covered me with a blanket from the closet in my room. *The blanket had to have come from the closet,* I thought, *because my bed is still made.* It was then I realized I had spent the entire night on the floor. For a moment, I sat on the bed and tried again to make sense of the dream, also trying to figure out who was in my room. I knew I locked my door, but that was of no real consequence because all my children knew I kept the master key to all the rooms in a bowl on top of the refrigerator. Of course that key was to be used only in an emergency.

Thinking the situation through, I guessed anyone in the house that night could have deemed it an emergency and used the key. *It could be anyone but Lorri,* I thought. As I mused a bit more about the key, I caught a glimpse of the clock at the head of my bed and was startled. The digital clock read 1:00 p.m. I looked out the window, and the winter sun was high in the sky. *It is early afternoon,* I thought. I had slept a long time. I was confused and felt jittery inside. My mind raced, trying to identify the day, and then it came to me that it was Sunday, the day after the funeral. That realization stirred details of the painful night before. It all rushed back to me vividly. My heart began to race. I eased into my brass rocking chair, taking slow, deep breaths as I did my daily meditation, hoping to calm myself and open up to what the day would bring. The juxtaposition of uneasiness and promise had a paradoxical impact upon me. I wanted to pace, but I didn't. I just rocked and prayed, telling myself to surrender.

While working on my eyes, flashes of the dream came back to me again, and I was particularly moved by the ride home. Ominously, there seemed to be a climate of finality to the ride. I felt sadness wash over me, which eerily seemed to coagulate in the center of my body, yielding a rather odd burning-like sensation. I felt as if I needed to cough up something. It seemed something was stuck in my throat. Instantly, I thought about a probable heart attack but dismissed that, believing this feeling was spiritually based. The feeling in my center churned. As I prayed, many thoughts rushed through my mind. But one mundane thought in particular stopped me abruptly. It was the recognition of the silence in my house. *Where is everyone?* I wondered. The silence troubled me.

Gazing tentatively around my room, another thought was driven by the bright yellow envelope on my pillow which I noticed for the first time. When I reached for the envelope, I recognized Kaimen's handwriting immediately. Inside the envelope was a single-page note that said,

> "*Mom I am sorry!!! I hope you don't hold last night against us. I am sure Lorri will apologize for her behavior when she comes back to herself.*
>
> *It was all just too much for me. All I can say is that I am sorry!!!!!*
>
> *You have many telephone calls. I left a list for you near the kitchen phone. Your Patrick called twice. You need to call him, mom!!*
>
> *The kids are with Korri, and I am going to be with my husband most of the day.*
>
> *Lorri is in the room knocked out. She's been drinking quite a bit.*
>
> *I think you should leave her alone. I love you !!!*"

She signed the note with a number of hearts drawn around her name. Tears fell as I noticed the hearts because it was something she would do when she was a little girl. It had been years since I saw those little-girl-like hearts, and it was a very tender moment for me. The note answered the question of who had been in my room and I smiled.

On impulse and with the note in hand, I walked to the room where Lorri had been sleeping over the past week, and sure enough she was sprawled across the bed. Kaimen's account was pretty accurate. Lorri truly appeared to be knocked out atop all the bed covers. I wondered why Kaimen hadn't covered her. I reached into the closet and pulled out a quilt. I threw it over her, hoping I didn't disturb her because I didn't want to deal with her just yet. It would take a while for me to get past all that had happened the night before. Upon leaving the room, my eyes found their way to the infamous lockbox, placed formidably near the door. For all the hell it brought the night before, I couldn't believe it hadn't been the first thing on my mind when I ventured back from my dream state. But it wasn't, and I marveled about that within myself. I picked up the lockbox and examined it carefully. It wasn't even scarred by having been hurled against the wall as an expression of Lorri's fury. *This is an impervious foe, shrouded in mystery,* I thought as I returned it to its resting place. I had no idea of its contents or its destiny. "I am surrendering this," I said emphatically as I moved away from the lockbox.

I walked by the telephone in the kitchen and quickly glanced at the long list of people who had called. Kaimen was meticulous in keeping the message roster. I saw Patrick's name listed twice and thought about giving him a call. But then I saw the call from Leslie Wilson, the volunteer coordinator of one of the nursing homes where I volunteered on a monthly basis. "Jesus," I said out loud as I read her message, reminding me of my time at the facility that day. I had totally forgotten about my volunteer commitment for the afternoon. I needed to be at the Forevermore Assisted Living and Care Center by 3:00 p.m., the note said. I don't know why it didn't occur to me to cancel, to simply call and say I was not feeling well. But I didn't do that. I put Kaimen's list of calls down and pulled energy from a place deep within me. I raced full force to do what I had done at least once each month since Emory's death. My volunteer work had helped me throughout the years and I would draw upon it today. I had to race in order to be on time. The stoic Jewelle stepped up and I believed she would carry me through the day.

It didn't take me long to get cleaned up, but I noticed I still had that churning sensation in my chest. It was odd, like something was brewing inside of me. On my way out of the house, I grabbed the manila envelope MiMi's son had brought a few days before. I knew there was a CD inside that she had been talking about for a while. I hoped MiMi's promise of the CD would be on target; for months she had gushed about its truly "jamming" tunes. "Jamming" was a MiMi word. She had a way of describing things that always made me laugh. I smiled as I thought about her and her antics. *I need to call her,* I thought. As I pulled from the garage, I heard a news reporter on the radio talking about Haiti. I shook my head, chastising myself for not making the promised donation to the Haiti Restoration Fund that was being handled by a number of churches and an organization championed by Flora. I told myself I would give a donation to Flora soon.

Once I slid the "jamming" CD into the player, it immediately brought a huge smile to my face. The beat was something else. It was Stevie Wonder, and the tune was purely funky. MiMi said the CD titled, *A Time to Love,* had been around for quite a while. She had just discovered it and knew I would love it. As I listened to the bold beats rolling from the CD, my smile broadened. I thought of Patrick, instantly recalling our special moments in Rapid City. I reached for my cell phone to call him, but curiously just as I put my hand on the phone, it rang.

I set the phone to my left ear, deftly negotiating the wet road while listening intently for the voice on the other end. I considered it might be Patrick, but it turned out to be my cousin Vy down in Key West. I was a little disappointed, but still it was good to hear Vy's voice. She quickly asked about ten questions all at once, seemingly desperate to make sense out of the reports she received about the funeral and the unseemly aftermath of that event. Of course, she didn't know anything about the horrid scene at my house after I got home from the funeral. But she was concerned about all she had gleaned from Jodi and Kaimen about the attack, and someone sent her images of the melee on Facebook. Patiently, I approached each of her questions the best I could, hoping she would not push for minute details. I was not yet ready to delve into the minutia of such a troublesome set of circumstances. I did give her a fairly graphic picture of the funeral services, though. I made special note of the uncommon quality of the entire event with the exception of the behavior of the people who attacked us afterward.

As always, Vy repeated her willingness to keep me and the family in prayer and asked something she had never raised before. At least I didn't remember her ever asking me if I wanted her to come up. I was taken aback by her offer and acknowledged that I knew she loved me and could feel her concern through the phone. I then changed the subject by bringing up my dream of the night before. She was candid in her assessment of the part of the dream involving the garden and the old women. She called me a "weird heifer," making a number of wisecracks about my needing to have an orgasm so I could release a lot of garbage and clear my mind.

With laughter, she dovetailed into asking about Patrick and seemed pretty disappointed I hadn't connected with him in the physical yet. Without fail in her true Vy way, which she attributed to her Key West candor, she directly stated she thought I was avoiding Patrick. She followed that statement with a couple of questions that made the churning inside of me "rev" up. She asked, "What are you afraid of, Jewelle? You are scared about something. And you are messing with God's work. Don't you trust your own prayers?" Of course, I told her to stop worrying about my orgasms and to stop calling me weird. We laughed and talked until I pulled into the parking lot of the Forevermore Assisted Living and Care Center, mostly referred to as just Forevermore.

Moving towards the place of the volunteer assignment, I tried to hold on to the levity from my conversation with Vy, but that churning feeling in my chest kept revving up. I made a mental note to call Patrick as soon as I had a free moment. I dismissed Vy's questions and threw myself into thinking about my tasks for the afternoon. I knew people at Forevermore would be aware of my troubles. The residents and workers were all TV junkies, so I knew they would have many questions. I could hear myself bemoaning the fact that my private family life had probably become the topic of the day for many people. *Damn,* I thought as I crossed the parking lot. I actually ran into the facility, trying to beat the clock.

Even though this was a volunteer placement for me, I valued my commitment and did not want tardiness to be an issue. I made it on time, and Leslie, the volunteer coordinator was waiting for me with a somber look on her face. She said some of the residents were aware of my troubles and looking forward to seeing that I was okay. I looked the rather homely Caucasian woman straight in the eye as I asked her, "And what are you thinking?" I knew she had questions and perhaps some concerns about how my well-publicized untoward experiences could ultimately affect some of the residents and what their families might have to say about that. She responded with her eyes averted, "we all appreciate your service here and we are praying for you and your family." I responded with direct clarity that I appreciated their prayers and well wishes, but was most interested in getting on with the business of the day. Without further comment, she went over my assignments for the day.

Moving away from Leslie, I made my usual rounds and received warm wishes from those residents who were lucid and concerned. In other cases, I just stopped in and offered words of support. A couple of the African-American staff members, whom I knew well, came to me and gave me a hug, whispering warm wishes of encouragement. I was deeply moved; the churning in my chest kept humming along. At 4:00 p.m., I officiated at the Sunday bingo game, passing out bingo cards as I chatted with each resident. It took a while for many of the infirmed residents to amble in; some were on walkers while others were on canes and in wheelchairs. Watching them enter the recreation room, my mind went back to my dream of the night before. Along with the churning in my chest, I felt a chill run through my entire body. With effort, I shook off the chill, throwing myself into the moment.

Before long I was lost in the festive atmosphere of the bingo game, calling numbers, helping people mark their cards, and replenishing popcorn trays. There was a lot of laughter, particularly in light of the delightful basket of prizes donated by a local college. Normally the prizes were rather insignificant items such as bookmarks and pencils. Today there were lovely gifts, including hand lotion, socks, and a few $5.00 gift certificates. The grand prize was a $10.00 gift certificate. The Effective Citizenship group from the college put together gift baskets like this one for the next six weeks. The residents were all excited about that. It was a festive time!

CHAPTER 20

It is All Good

My involvement in the bingo game did not keep me from noticing there were quite a few visitors milling around out in the
hall. A number of times I noticed people coming to the door of
the recreation center and pointing inside, and it seemed they were
pointing at me. One young fellow in particular came to the door
twice and just stood there. He seemed familiar to me, but I dismissed it, thinking I probably had seen him around Forevermore
sometime in the past. In truth, I let my newfound notoriety roll off
me far better than I thought I would, believing it would blow over
before too long. At 5:00 p.m., the bingo game ended with a roar.
We all laughed because an unlikely person won the grand prize.
Mr. Brunner, who never had come to bingo before — though he
had been in the nursing home part of the center for quite some
time — won the grand prize, and we all cheered for him. He smiled
and waved his gift card in the air for all to see. It was great fun. By
the time I completed my assignments and was rolling one of the
residents to her room, the young Caucasian man, perhaps in his
mid-thirties, who stood in the doorway a couple of times during
the bingo game, came to me and asked if he could speak with me.
Again I thought, *he looks familiar,* but I could not place him and
certainly had no idea of the gift he was leading me to.

With hesitancy, I said yes, joining him in the hall as soon as I
pushed Miss Billie, one of my longtime favorite residents, to her

room. The young man gave me his hand and introduced himself as Dylan, the manager of a restaurant that I had visited on occasion. I took a good look at him again, finally putting together where I had seen him before. His manner was warm and friendly, and he asked that I join him in the chapel. I wasn't sure what he wanted but followed him to the chapel, which was down the hall near the west entrance to Forevermore. I routinely went to the chapel after I had signed out from my volunteer duties. The chapel in this facility is very fine. The wood carvings alone are magnificent, showing a distinct Catholic hue with the Stations of the Cross encasing the entire room. I found it interesting that many remnants of Catholicism could be found in a place that is now multi-denominational and no longer owned or operated by the religious order that managed it for more than 60 years.

As Dylan and I entered the chapel, I noticed an elderly Caucasian woman in a wheelchair. She seemed deep in prayer as we approached her. He said with a huge smile, "This is my grandmother." The old woman, who had warm, welcoming eyes, put her thin hand out to greet me. She was very thin and wore a deep-rose-colored sweater that made her gray hair stand out. I guessed her to be in her early eighties, though she had a very youthful hair style. A pink barrette held locks of hair away from her face. Shaking her hand, I made note that I had not seen her before. She seemed to read my mind. She immediately stated in a soft voice that revealed a hint of a southern drawl that she was new to the center and actually resided in the assisted-living section but had come over to the nursing home today to meet me.

Her words surprised me. I looked to Dylan and then to his grandmother for an explanation. The old woman motioned for me to sit in a pew near her wheel chair. I did as I was told, almost as if beguiled with intrigue. The churning in my chest returned, and for a moment I thought I could hear my insides churning away, sort of like the whizzing of a cake mixer or something like that. I couldn't shake the feeling that something out of the ordinary was about to happen. Once I sat down, Dylan took the initiative and began to tell me why we were all there together. "I will never forget you, Miss Jewelle," he began, shaking his head to emphasize his statement. "I tried to locate you before now, but I didn't have a full name for you. I am relatively new to managing the restaurant, and when you were there last fall you didn't use a credit card. From what I gathered, there is no record of you ever having used a credit card there. You and all of the people with you paid cash, and you didn't have a reservation. Therefore, we did not have a name or number for you. Some of the other help who have been around for a while know you only as Jewelle, no last name. So I couldn't find you until I saw you on the news last night and on Facebook.

"I was visiting my grandmother this morning, and one of the workers here was talking with a group of residents about your situation. She told us you were supposed to volunteer here today. So here we are." He said all of this quickly, taking short breaths in between sentences as if he were racing to get to some urgent point, which I was still waiting to hear. "Why were you looking for me?" I asked as the churning in my chest escalated. My mind was racing, and I was getting warm all over. I didn't know what this was about, but I knew I didn't need any more drama. *I've had enough drama to last me a lifetime,* I thought. Before he could answer, his grandmother, now identified as Addie McAdoo, reached over and put her hand on my shoulder. "He wants to tell you thank you, dear," she said warmly. "He wants to tell you what you did for one of the employees of the restaurant. He has a surprise for you. And I believe God is behind all of this right now. You need to hear this now, today. It is your blessing." She spoke with confidence, her face seeming almost angelic.

I held my breath as I waited with all sorts of thoughts racing through my mind. Dylan shifted in his seat. Now he was sitting in the pew on the other side of his grandmother's wheelchair. He asked gingerly, "You remember when you were last at the restaurant?" I nodded almost mechanically, wary of what was going to come next. He went on, "Well, you and your friends — I think it was four of you sitting together — you were being served by a new fellow, a young guy who was very nervous." As he spoke, I recalled the very thin, young African-American man with the exceptionally long fingers. I remembered that his hands shook nervously and his voice cracked when he took our order. Then I remembered that awful couple sitting at the table next to us and their cruelty towards the young the man.

For a moment, I struggled to remember who was with me that day, and then it came to me. Eva and I had gone to a yoga class which was located near the restaurant, the last class in a series of six. We decided to celebrate having made it through six weeks of challenging maneuvers. We took the yoga instructor, Irma, a physically-fit, health-conscious African-American sister probably in her early fifties, out for a bite to eat. Joining us was Colleen, one of the other ladies from class, someone Eva and I got to know and like through the class. Colleen and I were both new to yoga and Eva is a seasoned yoga practitioner. While many people in the class were being challenged by the expectations of our yoga instructor, Eva just sailed through, actually keeping pace with Irma, to the chagrin of many.

I snapped back to the present and to the conversation with Dylan. "Yes, I remember him," I said, squinting my eyes trying to figure out his point. "Well, the young man's name is Kelton," Dylan said with a huge smile, looking directly in my eyes. He went on, "Kelton says you saved his life that day. For months he's been telling people what you did for him. He says your kind voice and what you did that day by speaking up for him gave him a reason to go on. If you remember, you asked for the manager, and I came over to your table. You praised Kelton for how he served you and your friends, and you did that with an intentional high volume to your voice. You focused on the surly couple seated next to your table who had leveled a number of complaints against him and demanded to have a free meal because he made so many mistakes. You asked each one of the people at your table to speak about Kelton's service, and they all praised him. And when he brought the change from your bill to the table, you all gave him a huge tip. It was interesting because it seemed each of you had to search through your things to pull out as much cash as you could for him, including lots of coins. Certainly your monetary graciousness to him was not planned."

Dylan said all of that with such fervor and precision that it was as though he had been rehearsing for the occasion.

I remembered he was right. That whole venture was a spur-of-the-moment thing. None of us had our credit cards. We didn't bring purses to yoga class, but Eva and I both would keep cash along with our driver's licenses in our pouches that we wore around our neck. It turned out that among the four of us we managed to come up with a large tip for the beleaguered waiter, whom I now know as Kelton. Actually, our tip had been almost what we paid for our bite to eat, seeing that we had mostly soup and tea. The substantial tip was to give him our vote of confidence, shown monetarily. At least that was my idea, and the others agreed. I remembered glaring at the Caucasian couple that was abusive to Kelton. The woman in particular had been most disparaging in her comments to him, leading me to think she was either just a bitch or she had an agenda, such as lobbying for a free meal based on underscoring Kelton's mistakes. That infuriated me, and I wished I could have slapped her and called her a host of names in addition to praising Kelton.

Dylan brought me back to the present again. "No one at work knew Kelton was suicidal and had been for a while. Later, he told me he had attempted once in his past, when he was in high school, but survived it. This time, at age 23, so many things had been going wrong for him, including the brutal murder of his best friend with whom he shared an apartment. His friend was mugged and died from blows to his head only a few weeks before, leaving Kelton to handle the rent and other bills alone. He has no family to speak of. At least he believes he has no one to rely on." As Dylan told Kelton's story, I could feel compassion come forth within me. It was right there alongside the churning that still bubbled up inside me. I could feel a tear roll down my right cheek, and I tried to make it stop. I spoke to my eyes about the tears, but they wouldn't listen; the tears kept rolling. It felt so good to be appreciated — particularly in light of the fiasco from the evening before — that I guessed my tears were as much for me as they were for Kelton.

Before long, Dylan pulled out an envelope and handed it to me. He said with misty eyes himself, "After I found out this morning you would be here volunteering today, I went to the restaurant to see Kelton. He's working today, and he needs the tips. Otherwise he would have come with me to see you. He wrote this letter to you." My hand shook as I took the letter from Dylan. I didn't know what to do; the situation was all so moving. I looked from the grandmother to the grandson. Both had tears trickling down their faces, and I knew I needed to share the contents of the letter with them. So I took a deep breath and opened it.

The sprawling adolescent-like handwriting was difficult to make out at first, but I took my time and began to read the three-page letter out loud.

> "Dear Miss Jewel, Dylan told me he would see you today. I wish I could come too, but I have to work, but maybe you will have lunch with me one day (my treat). I am sorry you and your daughter got attacked. They should not treat you like that on TV I thank God for you!! There are not many people like you in the world today who are kind to other people. You saved my life! You stood up for me when I was alone and no one cared. That $22.00 you and your friends gave me REALLY! REALLY! HELPED me make it. I will never forget that. That is the biggest tip I ever got so far. Tell your friends thank you too! I want to live now. I am in therapy now at a clinic that lets me pay what I can. Dylan told me about it. I don't have health insurance yet. I want to go to school one day to be a chef. I like to cook. I was going to let you see the suicide note I wrote the day before I met you. I changed my mind for now about that. I carry it in my wallet all the time. I look at it to know where I was in the past. I will let you see it one day, if we ever meet again. I will keep that note forever. Thank you for being a kind lady. I wish I had a mother like you. If you have children and grandchildren, I bet they think you are the best. I think you are great. Thank you! I pray for you because I know God sent you to show me a different side of people and life. My phone number is written on the envelope. God be with you, Kelton"

I couldn't stop the tears. I sobbed out loud when I got to the part about my children and grandchildren thinking I am the best. The memories of the night before rushed through my mind again, and the pain of those memories lingered for a moment, snuffed out by the authenticity of Kelton's abiding gratitude. But more than that, I was awestruck by the unfailing power of God. I was amazed how all of this was playing itself out. My being on the news and Facebook made it possible for Dylan to connect with me via a caregiver at the facility who happened to be talking about my situation in his presence while he was visiting his grandmother. *This is more than synchronicity*, I thought. *This has to be the handiwork of the Divine.*

That thought had barely materialized when Dylan's grand-mother whispered, "Isn't God good, Jewelle? He's right on time as usual." She spoke with such confidence that I wondered how this old lady seemed to key into me so accurately and so deeply. I felt I wanted to respond to Kelton, but I was not ready to call him. *Anyway, he is working*, I thought. Again Miss Addie seemed to read my mind, and she sent Dylan to her unit to retrieve a box of cards and a pen. "Send him a note," she said, smiling. "I bet he will keep that note forever, too." When Dylan left the room, Miss Addie said, "I know visiting hours will be over in this part of Forevermore soon, but you can come up to my unit for as long as you want. I would like that because I believe we have more business to attend to," she whispered. Oddly, I didn't question her or hesitate. I was still caught up in the awesomeness of the Creator. It all amazed me. I said okay to Miss Addie's invitation and allowed her to show me the way to her unit in the other part of the Forevermore complex, realizing she intentionally sent her grandson for the cards to have a private moment with me.

In all the years I'd come to Forevermore, I had never considered the vastness of the complex. It turned out to be much larger than I thought. We went down hallways I hadn't seen before. The place was well kept and beautifully decorated. We met Dylan on the way and explained to him that I would be spending more time with his grandmother. He smiled knowingly almost as if he expected something like that to happen. He handed the box of cards to his grandmother, who passed them on to me. I sat down in one of the chairs along the hallway and wrote a brief note to Kelton. I wrote:

"Kelton, thank you for taking time to bless me with such a beautiful letter. I am truly grateful for your decision to embrace life! I pray that you will continue to learn about all of the glorious gifts that God has for you. I will pass your kind words on to the ladies who sat at the table with me a number of months ago. I am sure they will be pleased to know you are well and moving forward in your life. Yes, I will call you for lunch. You can count on that! May God continue to bless you real good. Jewelle"

As I signed my name to the note, the churning within me reached a fever pitch, and I felt as if I could shout.

I've had people tell me about what it is like to be so filled with the Holy Spirit that you just have to shout. While in my life I have often been filled with the Spirit, the feeling inside of me right then set me to my feet. I stood up with uplifted hands and shouted "Praise God!" Neither Dylan nor Miss Addie seemed surprised by my actions. They both said, "Amen," smiled at me, and waited for my next move. I gave the note to Dylan without saying a word. He then kissed his grandmother on the forehead and shook my hand, which turned into a hug, and made his way towards the exit. As he was leaving, he called out, letting me know I could have a lunch on him at the restaurant anytime. In turn, I thanked him for his graciousness and promised I would visit the restaurant soon. He then disappeared through the door, leaving Miss Addie and me to experience special time together. If it was to be anything like what had transpired in the previous hour, it would be a Spirit-filled, mystical time. I could feel it coming. There was something so familiar about Miss Addie. She reminded of Miss Ella for sure, but there was something else about her that I just couldn't put my finger on.

CHAPTER 21

You Must Tell Your Story to Be Free

Miss Addie's unit was surprisingly plush. I wasn't sure what I expected, but I was taken aback by its lavishness and timeless elegance. Upon first glance, one would think a young wealthy diva lived there. Yet, who was I to decide that Miss Addie was not a wealthy diva, though no longer young? In the living room, various shades of mauve and deep rose spilled forth from ceiling to floor. There was a soft quality to everything. The silk flowers atop the round table were elegant. The only things that indicated this could be the home of an elderly woman were the three beautiful mahogany rocking chairs interspersed among an array of other elegant pieces of furniture, including a lovely mauve sofa baring rose and off-white throw cushions.

My facial expressions must have given me away because Miss Addie chuckled as she explained that her daughter Jinny, Dylan's mother, had insisted on having her personal decorator prepare the place for her as a gift. She made a point of noting that Dylan's mother was her youngest child and only daughter, who had been hopelessly spoiled by her father and as a result saw the world as her oyster. It was her way or no way! Miss Addie went on to say that Jinny had married a wealthy man and believed she should do what she pleased with their money. "And, I just let her have her way" Miss Addie quipped. I nodded as she spoke, resonating with her opinion about not fighting needlessly with adult offspring.

Surprisingly, Miss Addie pulled herself up from her wheelchair and pushed it against the wall out of our way. She explained she didn't always need it. The chair was of great use when she had to travel long distances, such as from her place to the chapel at the other end of Forevermore. At first, she moved with a bit of effort to one of the rocking chairs, motioning to me to take one of the others. "I love rocking chairs," she mused. "So Jinny found these lovely chairs at an estate sale and decided I should have all three of them. They are all in the living room because I have my old one, the one from my home, in my bedroom. It's a hand-me-down from my grandmother — the one thing I was able to retrieve from our family home after my mother's death," she laughed.

I eagerly chose the rocking chair directly across from her, thinking we could look each other in the eye as we talked. Maybe then I could figure out what this gathering was really about. Not knowing what to expect or why I was so comfortable with this woman, I took my seat and waited for her to direct the course of our time together. I barely got settled in my chair when Miss Addie popped out of hers as if she just remembered something. Moving rather spryly, she invited me to follow her into the kitchen for a bite to eat. For just a moment, I found myself wondering if Miss Addie were having some type of dementia episode, but I followed her in quizzical anticipation, again thinking she reminded me of someone.

Her kitchen was small but equipped with every appliance you could think of. As she pulled things from the refrigerator to warm up, I learned that she, too, was diabetic. She had been for more than 30 years but had not progressed to needing insulin yet. She said all of that with clear pride. Without prompting, she rattled off the various parts of her self-care regimen that she believed had kept her healthy. With her chest puffed out and a big smile, she told me she was 86 years old but felt a lot younger.

"I still walk at least a mile each day on the treadmill," she quipped, looking directly at me seemingly to gauge my reaction. "I have to do it in more than one effort now, whereas I used to be able to do it all at once, but I still get it done." I was amazed at her vigor and spunk, silently hoping I could be as zest-filled when I reached her age. The longer we were together, the more vibrant she seemed to become. Her laughter was enchanting! The meal she put together was delightful and very healthy by her estimation. As we enjoyed our food she talked on and on. I learned about her dietary habits at length, but I had no idea what else she planned to share with me. I was caught up in her reports about the various ways to combat Type II diabetes, when she touched me on the arm and whispered, "I killed a man many years ago, Jewelle." I almost fell off my chair! I immediately thought maybe I had heard her incorrectly or that this was some kind of weird senior moment or something like that.

I didn't have to wonder long because Miss Addie soon filled me in on what she meant and why she was telling me about something that had happened so far back in her past. Through a deep sigh, she explained she wanted to share some things with me from her life that she believed could help me with self-forgiveness. She looked me directly in the eyes when she said that as if she could see inside of me. She had detected in my countenance that I was holding something inside that I needed to let go of. She said confidently. Her words pierced me, leaving me mystified about how she seemed to know so much about me, but I didn't question her. I just struggled to figure out who she reminded me of. I steeled myself, listening with anticipation and apprehension. And with another deep sigh, she began her story.

"Yes, I killed a man on a bicycle. It was an accident, but I killed him! I wasn't supposed to be driving that day," she said as she rubbed her forehead. Her words really rattled me. She explained she had been preparing to go to college. The day of the fatal accident, her parents told her to get all of her packing done and to take care of some other chores around the house. Defiantly she decided to go shopping instead and her defiance was her downfall. She had a plan, but as she turned to get onto the major road to town, a man on his bicycle rode in front of her, and she hit him head on with the family's old pickup truck. It was an awful day, she reflected. The bicycle rider was not wearing a helmet — people didn't bother too much with helmets back then — which led to his fatal head injuries. He died at the scene of the accident. "I saw him die," Miss Addie said in a whisper. I listened and heard my story within her story. It was eerie!

Miss Addie's voice quivered, and her hands shook. I waited, thinking she must be reliving the hell she went through on that day. And the churning in my chest began again as her hell triggered memories of my hell on the stairs to the basement the day my son died. Uncanny as it may seem, I heard myself say in my head, *I killed my son*! Miss Addie confirmed my thoughts of hell as she pointedly stated it was still difficult for her to talk about, even to this day. But she went on with her story, letting me know she had been taken from the scene of the accident to the hospital and then to a psychiatric unit a few days later where she spent many months. As I listened, I began to wonder if this woman had been sent to me. I shook my head to gain some semblance of order within myself. The churning in my chest kept going.

She went on with her story. It seemed important to her to share that she was originally from North Carolina where her father was a Presbyterian pastor. And, while he paid all of her medical and legal bills, he never spoke with her again after the fatal accident, dismissing her from the family. Her mother, on the other hand, essentially took to her bed. She died of a massive coronary about five years after the accident, and Miss Addie's siblings blamed her for their mother's death. Haltingly Miss Addie explained that by the time of her mother's demise, she was a married woman of three years living in Wisconsin with one child, and another on the way. She had become the mistress and then the wife of the neurologist (a much older man) who was called in specially to attend to her medical and legal needs. Lawyers, constructing a defense for Miss Addie, postulated that a seizure was the culprit in the fatal accident, creating a medical infirmity for Miss Addie. Through that defense Miss Addie had not served time for her part in the fatal accident. But, the illicit relationship with the neurologist became an eyebrow-raising scandal in their community, with the neurologist's wife leveling venom upon his reputation and bank accounts, pushing unsuccessfully for his license to be revoked.

"That part of my life is still a blur," she said. "At the time, I didn't think of the unethical nature of all that was going on with me and my first husband. All I knew was that I wanted to stop hurting inside, and he knew how to look after me and ease my pain. So, I became his mistress and then his wife," she continued pensively as if she were actually seeing her life unfold on a screen before her. With her head bowed, Miss Addie shared she had been about to turn 19 years old at the time of the accident, far too young for the weighty consequences that came with marrying a man more than twice her age who was very controlling. She was totally dependent upon him. In her estimation, for years she became a shell of a woman defined by the whims of her husband.

Shaking her head as if clearing away dark remnants from the past, she smiled as she shared that it was in mid-life that things began to shift for her. She explained that in the year she turned 55 all of her prayers and hard work came together. Within a nine month period she divorced the neurologist and attained a Master's degree in education — longtime dreams of hers. It was around that time she finally began to forgive herself for the death of the man on the bicycle and for so many other things. "I always felt guilty and I knew I could not be free until I gained the courage to get my first husband out of my life," she said, making it clear that it had been a real struggle to even feel worthy of joy. Squaring her shoulders and looking at me directly she pushed forward, "My second husband, brought great joy to my life. He was a kind man; my good friend. He died just a year ago, and I miss him terribly," she sighed, allowing grief to lace the tenor of her report. I listened in amazement. *She has navigated through guilt, shame and great suffering to find joy,* I thought, wondering if that could happen for me.

I was intrigued by Miss Addie's report about her second husband. Her entire countenance changed when she talked about him. She lit up, her eyes sparkled. Throughout her story, I was quiet but asked my first question after she began talking about her second husband, Morris Chase, whom she referred to as Chase. I wanted to know what it was like to experience romantic love late in life. I was not prepared for her answer. "For me, it was better than anything I could have expected," she said. "Even the sex was magnificent! We were two people seasoned in life who were starved for tenderness and hope. Touch was so important to us," she said while smiling broadly. She pointed out that everything they did was driven by gratitude and a yearning for the best for the other. "I don't think a day went by that we didn't say out loud how we felt about the gift of connection that had been given to us. We learned to savor each moment, and nothing came between us, not even his illness or death. I still feel him with me," she said, her eyes tearing up. I sat enthralled in her story. I thought of my deceased husband, and I thought of Patrick too.

Curiously, as I absorbed each word, another question popped into my mind, one that seemed peripheral to the essence of Miss Addie's story. But, I wanted to know why she still carried the surname McAdoo rather than the name of her second husband. Her explanation was simple. She had taken her maiden name back when she divorced her first husband and decided she would never give up her birth name again. Although she loved Chase deeply, she felt no need to carry his name, and it was not an issue for him. When Miss Addie explained her decision, I marveled at her sense of clarity of what she wanted and what really mattered to her and what didn't!

I must have been pondering this with great depth because her touch on my hand startled me. Immediately I realized I had been caught up in listening to and analyzing the inspirational features of her story all while attending to the churning feeling that had returned in full force at the center of my chest. "What's holding you hostage, Jewelle?" she asked boldly with her hand placed on mine. I couldn't believe her directness. She was pushing me to talk about things I didn't unearth freely, and the rawness of the night before with all of my daughter Lorri's belligerence made it even more difficult to consider delving into the piercing nature of what she was asking of me. *There has to be a reason for this,* I thought.

I turned it over in my mind, playing and replaying her words in my head, feeling a pull to share that which was holding me captive. While she seemed presumptuous, I knew deep inside that she discerned something was there. She had been keying into me from the moment we met. She sensed something; maybe it was all Spirit-driven, I told myself. Many disparate feelings raced through me, in addition to the churning in my chest. At first, I was surprised that I felt annoyed with the old woman for digging into my life. Then another, sobering thought came to me that I was at liberty to just shut the conversation down and to leave. Yes, I knew I could do this, but I was certain I was not supposed to leave. I had a very strong feeling I was supposed to answer her questions and to just talk this thing out with her; to tell my story. I felt compelled to do so! With this thought came a curious hint of relief rushing through me as if the promise of joy and peace were being whispered in my ear. Abiding with the promise, I took a couple of deep breaths. I struggled to figure out how to begin my story or, more importantly, where to begin it. I thought I couldn't just say to her, "I think I killed my infant son."

Wringing my hands, I began my story with my eyes averted from hers. "I must give you a bit of history," I began, speaking barely above a whisper. "I have had two husbands. The first I divorced after 20 years of marriage, and the second died after eight years of marriage." I explained that with the second, there was a very long period of many illnesses, almost the entire marriage. I stopped for a breath and took a glance in Miss Addie's direction. She was looking at me intensely, seemingly weighing each word as if there were something very specific she was waiting to hear. Again, I wondered why I was about to bare my soul to this woman I had just met. Then I decided I would only go so far, not realizing at that time once the flood gates were opened, I would be swept up.

With hesitancy, I returned to my story. "I came to Milwaukee from Florida with my first husband. He was in the navy and was stationed at Great Lakes base for a short period of time. He became a plumber after he left the service and decided to stay here to build a business that never prospered. He was controlling and a very violent man who drank heavily. I was most often the object of his violent temper. We have five children, two sets of fraternal twins and a daughter born as the middle child. And, of course, there would have been the sixth child, a son, who would be the eldest of the children had he survived. He died tragically. I believe I caused his death through my irresponsible behavior." As the words tumbled from my mouth, tears began to fall, and my breathing became labored. I gasped as the churning in my chest revved up. The thought of the recurrent dream popped into my mind, but I pushed it aside. I was not ready to put it into words yet.

"What do you mean by irresponsible behavior?" Miss Addie asked pointedly. I stumbled over my words. In a flash I could see my daughter Lorri's face from the night before and hear her scathing accusations about the death of my first son. Again, glimpses of the recurrent dream raced through my mind, and I willed the dream to depart from me. I pushed myself to go on, hoping the promise of peace I glimpsed a short while earlier would be the ultimate result of this weary walk through pain. "People had been telling me to throw my raggedy pink house slippers away and to stop carrying baskets of laundry up and down the steep basement stairs," I said. I was almost certain the churning in my chest must be audible because it was writhing within me in a powerful way. I forced myself to go on with the story. "Even Miss Schroeder, our kind landlady who lived upstairs, scolded me about the basement stairs and the ragged slippers. I am still not sure why I didn't listen." Just then, remnants of the recurrent dream rushed through my mind. I could hardly breathe. I stammered, but haltingly returned to my story.

"I decided on a whim to do the wash and didn't give any thought to the admonishments I had been given about the stairs or my tattered slippers. When I was falling my mind went to the gravity of my disobedience. I tried to break the fall, but ultimately tumbled over headfirst down the stairs. I was told my body ended up in a precariously strange position of brokenness. The entire stairway was bathed in blood,other bodily fluids, and my dead infant son." Miss Addie whimpered as she touched me warmly on the hand. I shivered and my mind raced as I rocked back and forth. I could hear Lorri's voice indicting me and I felt like running! Miss Addie encircled me in a warm embrace. She uttered soothing words urging me to forgive myself. I held on to her, remembering that Miss Schroeder had saved my life. The old woman on her aged legs had come down from her flat. She heard my screams. It was her call that brought the paramedics who saved me, but my son could not be saved. Standing, encircled in Miss Addie's arms I wept. I wept until I was emotionally spent.

For quite a while Miss Addie held me, but when she released me from her soothing embrace, it was clear she still had questions. She pushed on like a healer on a mission. When she spoke, I heard a quiver in her voice. And when I looked at her, I could see tears on her face. "Have you forgiven yourself, Jewelle?" she asked while blowing her nose on a frilly white handkerchief. I answered the best I could, "I don't know. I would like to believe I have, but sometimes I hurt so inside that I feel as if it all just happened yesterday." I almost said something about the recurrent dream, but the churning in my chest surged piercingly, forcing me to shut down. I put my hands over my mouth and began to rock back and forth again. Immediately, Miss Addie launched into a teaching/ preaching mode that I believe would have made her pastor father proud. "You know, Jewelle," she said, "forgiving yourself doesn't necessarily mean you won't hurt anymore. Forgiveness just offers you the opportunity to stop hating yourself and others. In doing that you open yourself up for joy. You know joy must have a place to be!" I listened intently to her words. There was something about the word forgive that evoked a host of feelings and memories that I couldn't quite place. I was deep in thought when Miss Addie shook me back to the present again by asking another question that felt like a blow to the jaw. "And your second husband?" she asked, clearly still mining for more deep places in my life. For a moment I thought I couldn't take much more pain, but I was pulled to her question like a wandering bug to light. Thoroughly engaged by the call to purge, I prepared myself to stumble through the story of my beloved Emory.

CHAPTER 22

There's More to Your Story

Settling into my chair, I began, "As you shared about your second husband, Miss Addie, my Emory was the love of my life. He was charming and handsome. He was a very dark-skinned man with beautiful white teeth. He was six feet two and solidly built. By the time we met, I had been single for nearly four years and was not really seeing anyone seriously. I found I wasn't very good with playing the dating game." I stopped my story for moment and smiled as I remembered how magnetic my first meeting with Emory was and how quickly things moved for us. He had been so easy to get to know! In almost a whisper I went on with my story, "It was my oldest brother who introduced us. I was visiting my family in Key West when my brother surprised me with his eagerness to connect me with a childhood friend Who had left Key West before I was born. Someone who had retired home after living in New York for many years. At the first handshake the energy passing between us was enthralling. His smile was engulfing and the New York accent he had acquired over the years coupled with the slight Bahamian lilt, which is common to Black Key West Conches made his words magical. Plus, he was kind, optimistic, and very affectionate. I was smitten and the four days I spent in Key West were fabulous. Emory and I were together as often as we could make it happen. My children seemed to enjoy his upbeat demeanor too. The four days flew by. We all whished we could stay longer, but the kids were on spring break and I had to get them back home; I had to hit the road."

Miss Addie poured two glasses of wine and passed one to me. I could feel my mood lifting as I remembered the sensual courting phase with Emory. I eased back to my story, "On my drive back to Milwaukee, it was when my children and I stopped in Macon, Georgia for the night that I knew I wanted Emory in my life and needed to tell him that. I told him how I felt and the things Emory suggested on the phone made me blush, but my body said yes to all of the torrid future possibilities." I smiled remembering that my first night back in Milwaukee, Emory and I had phone sex. It was a first for me and it was amazing! I stopped to look at Miss Addie. I had actually said that out loud. I couldn't believe how graphic I was being with this woman. Unruffled, Miss Addie chuckled and motioned for me to go on with my story and I did. "Emory visited during the Memorial Day weekend and it became clear he would be moving to Wisconsin. Many of his friends and most of his family thought he had lost his mind. We were married seven months later, on December 30th in Key West.

"The wedding took place in my mother's garden. The weather was a perfect 72 degrees, which for the Milwaukee group was bordering on being too warm. I wore red, as did my mother and my daughters. On the other hand, Emory and my sons wore white linen Cuban shirts, black pants, and red boutonnieres on the left upper pocket of their exquisite shirts. We all looked spectacular. It was a wonderful event with mounds of indigenous foods, island music, and lots of laughter. Relatives and friends from both of our families celebrated with us.

"For many years, I would return in my mind to that glorious afternoon and on occasion would take out the video of the wedding just to rekindle the joy I felt that day. Certainly the memories were substantive for both Emory and me because we would reminisce often as we struggled with his various illnesses over the years. It was about six weeks after the wedding that Emory had his first stroke. That scheming thief stole the light from my beloved husband's eyes and left us with many struggles. The days following the stroke were difficult because it seemed our bubble of joy had burst. While we continued to love each other and to carry on the day-to-day functions of living — with my going to work and Emory assuming the role of homemaker, although he continued to work on a plan to start a business — there was a tentativeness that hovered over us.

Stepping away from my story, I could feel myself shift again, sliding towards a somber place. I knew the story and I knew what was coming; more pain. Miss Addie saw the shift in my mood again and she asked a number of questions that let me know how intent she was on unearthing other residuals from my past that could be holding me hostage. "Go on with your story dear," she urged and I followed her directions, realizing I had never come to terms with so many things about Emory's death. Tentatively I resumed my story, "The following year the results of Emory's annual physical sent us into a frenzy. His PSA was high, and there was a nodule upon examination. His doctor suspected prostate cancer."

Miss Addie watched me intently as I became more and more solemn in relaying my story. I actually shivered as I recalled, "It was the Saturday after the doctor told us his concerns that my beloved husband asked I help him find a Black Presbyterian church. I was jarred by his request, not certain what to make of his sudden interest in going to church, but made calls to a few friends and came up with a Presbyterian church. Emory asked that I attend the church with him. When it came time to join the church, I shut my eyes and said all of the things I needed to say and signed the documents I needed to sign. But deep inside I don't think I ever really became a Presbyterian." Again Miss Addie had questions, but urged me to go on with my story.

"The day Emory made his decision to use an alternative approach to address his cancer, I cried all day because I was afraid he had made the wrong decision. Emory's doctors, of course, were not pleased with his decision, but what could they do other than monitor him and voice their concerns? We all voiced our concerns! For the next four years, our lives were filled with colonic appointments, wheat-grass regimens, expensive body adjustments, and a host of other supplements and potions. During this time, Emory began to have bouts of dizziness, which defied the doctors. Despite the dizzy spells he went to the Million Man March in Washington D.C. in the Fall of 1995 and had a life changing experience. It was three days following the march that sent me into near hysterics when Emory opted to take a road trip alone to Savannah, Georgia, seeking the help of a healer, the grandmother of two men he had met at the march."

I stepped away from my story for a moment, remembering that this was the time the Warrior Chief had come into my life. I considered how to summarize that story, but in doing so, my mind went to Patrick. Curiously, I didn't know what to feel; it was a confusing moment, so much going on inside of me. Shaking my head vigorously I managed to push forward. I told Miss Addie about the dream that introduced me to Chief Crazy Horse and many of the attendant facts surrounding Emory's trek to the healer. Miss Addie had many questions and I answered them as best I could, but I promised to come by another time and to bring books and artifacts from my trip to South Dakota for her to learn more about the Warrior Chief. She was grateful and urged me to go on with my story.

Wondering again about the hold Miss Addie seemed to have on me, I resumed my story. "It was near Christmas in 1995 that Emory had a seriously challenging bout of light headedness and dizziness which led to a fall in the shower and a two day stay in the hospital from which another dreaded diagnosis was rendered. Two neurologists explained that Emory was presenting with something called dysautonomia, which is viewed as a disorder of the autonomic nervous system. They needed more time to pin down the exact type of dysautonomia Emory was evidencing. I think I blocked out anything else they had to say. It was too much to digest. I think both Emory and I went on automatic pilot; we just went through the motions of living life and time flew by."

I could hear the solemnity in my voice as I pushed on. I knew I was coming upon another point in my story that I was not proud of and had not completely worked through. I knew I was heading to another place of pain and self-imprisonment, but I pressed on, "We had been married nearly eight years when the doctors told Emory that the prostate cancer seemed to be progressing. It was then that Emory went into a deep depression. All he wanted to do was read his Bible or listen to it on tape. He stopped his colonics and all of the other alternative procedures but would not even consider surgery, proton therapy, or any of the other procedures suggested by his doctors. He would not discuss it with me. We seldom talked and almost never had intimate moments." My heart ached as I went on.

"We had been to church that Sunday morning. Emory was unusually teary during the services, particularly when the choir sang his favorite song. He just sobbed, repeating again and again, ' I won't complain'. He held me tightly and whispered in my ear, 'I am so sorry, Jewelle.' I didn't know what he was talking about, but I held him close, telling him things would be alright. Later that day when he reached across the table during dinner to put his hand on top of mine, I smiled, welcoming the tenderness and intimacy. I was thinking my upbeat words in church had made a difference. Then I saw the grimace on his face and heard a deep groan coming from him as he closed his eyes and slumped forward with unseemly-looking stuff running out of his mouth. I'll never forget the sound that came from him. It was so telling; it was a sound of finality."

I stopped my story, remembering that I did not even try to do CPR. I looked at Miss Addie and just about screamed, "I didn't even try to do CPR. Why didn't I try to do CPR? For years I have wondered why I did not try to do CPR." In my mind I questioned if the unseemly substance oozing from his mouth had been too offensive to me. I just didn't know why I hadn't tried to save my beloved Emory. Miss Addie patted my hand warmly and in a soothing voice encouraged me to let it go. Once again crying in her arms I continued to think about that awful day. I remembered that I did call 911, but I didn't even try to do CPR. Holding on to Miss Addie I questioned myself about where the stoic Jewelle had gone that day. Why hadn't she shown up to do CPR on Emory? I have never been able to answer that question to my own satisfaction, even though I have been told Emory died instantly; even with CPR it was unlikely he would have made it. I was told that he had a massive stroke.

I wept for the second time in the old lady's arms as she soothed and challenged me all at once. Again she raised the question of self-forgiveness. "You can forgive yourself and let it go Jewelle," she encouraged as she wiped her own tears. Seeing her emotional investment, I was touched by her warmth and deep connection to my healing process. She seemed to know my pain firsthand and I wondered if she knew intuitively about the recurrent dream. Holding on to her I was certain I was supposed to be there with her and I was grateful. When I said that out loud, Miss Addie raised her arms and shouted, "Praise God." Her fervor caught me by surprise, but I knew she understood what I meant and was moved by the consideration that God does work in mysterious ways.

After a while Miss Addie released me from her embrace and without prodding I went directly back to my story. "Well, Emory made his transition in 1998. For a while I existed only through work, volunteering and my family. But, in the summer of 1999 a light came on in my life. It happened the day I discovered that two of my daughters were pregnant. I couldn't believe my ears when they stood before me proclaiming they were with child. For Kaimen, this would be her second child but her first with her husband. For Lorri, it would be her first, and this child would be born out of wedlock. I can remember looking to my daughter Thea asking about her status at that time. She was adamant that she was not pregnant. I went into a near frenzy buying things and planning for the new additions to our family. It was as if someone had flipped a switch and there was light in my life again." I smiled remembering how close my girls and I were at that time.

Recalling the sense of renewal I felt back then I went on with my story, "Lorri was the first to give birth. She went into labor on March 13th, ten days after my birthday. After a long labor she delivered a healthy baby boy. She named him Anthony. I was disappointed that Kaimen didn't go into labor until March 30th, appreciably beyond the scope of the sign of Pisces. My new granddaughter, Cherish, came into being under the sign of Aries, the ram. I was with both of my daughters through their labor and delivery processes, standing with them through their pain and ultimately basking with them in the joy of the births of my grandchildren. It was a time of deep closeness for us and I began to move beyond my grief."

Miss Addie's eyes sparkled as I talked about the births. When she made a point of stressing the great connection I must have with my daughters, I felt that churning in my chest return and a deep sadness rushed over me again. I found myself thinking about the awful scene with Lorri from the night before. But, I was jarred from that memory by Miss Addie's next statement and subsequent rather presumptuous question. She said with candor, "I know about your professional life because my grandson and I looked you up on the computer this morning, but what about the men in your life after Emory?" I couldn't believe her cheekiness. She seemed to be probing with a specific point of interest in mind. I wondered again if she knew intuitively about the recurrent dream and all of the attendant troublesome factors. I breathed deeply and considered how I would answer her question. I was clearly drawn to share with this woman who appeared to be on some kind of mission. The more time I spent with her the more certain I was that she had been sent to help me purge and was connected to me in ways I did not yet understand. Then, she shifted from drinking wine to tea again. When she poured milk in her tea memories from long ago welled up within me. They were familiar, but unclear.

CHAPTER 23

Purging and Owning My Story

Instantly, I was pulled again from my thoughts by Miss Addie. This time she underscored her question by tapping on the table in a rather urgent way, making sure to shake me from my reverie. "Jewelle, what about the men in your life after Emory?" she queried as if compelled to have the answer seed some conclusion she must ultimately reach. *She's still searching for something,* I thought, reminding myself that she and I were on some kind of spiritual journey that seemed to involve my healing process. Then, without provocation she announced in a rather authoritative way that she would not interrupt me as I shared this part of my story. "Talk, tell your story. I will sit back and listen to you. Please know it is important for you to hear yourself tell your story. That is how it must be", she said as she repositioned her glasses and crossed her legs. I was stunned for a moment by the way she gave the directive. I played and replayed her words, sifting through them trying to identify the nugget she was searching for. Finally, I told myself, *trust the process.* I obliged her and leapt into the story of the men in my life since Emory, wondering what needed to be purged from this part of my life.

In reflecting, the face that appeared immediately in my mind was that of Merlin, the first man I went out with after Emory's death. I began my story, "It had taken nearly three years before I even considered going to lunch with a man other than for business or professional purposes. In the year of our national tragedy, the awful 9-11 incident that shook the world. Somehow the awfulness of the massive losses made me feel very vulnerable, assessing where my life was going and I began to think about making an effort to live life more fully. With resolve, I pushed myself to be more open to a life beyond my children and grandchildren. I think I will always remember Merlin's odd way of relating to the world. He seemed uncommonly self-contained. I met him while browsing in a resale shop looking for crystal glasses that I had been curiously lucky to find over the years. Though I am not really a shopper, I would go to the resale shop near my home just to browse and put my hands on a treasure or two. Merlin eventually told me he came to that particular shop often. But while he said he had seen me there a number of times before we actually met, I couldn't say the same.

"For some reason that particular day, I was looking at an array of picture frames. Merlin and I both reached for the same frame, and the awkwardness of the incident made us draw back in the midst of a host of apologies. I immediately noticed Merlin would not make direct eye contact with me, although he was gracious about not meaning to bump into me. I ended up buying the frame and apologized to him on our way out of the store. He laughed and I noticed a gentleness about him. I observed he was a nice-looking man of medium height with the lean body of a swimmer. His horn-rimmed glasses, balding head, and thick gray moustache led me to believe he was probably a senior citizen by the standard of 55 and above. I also noticed the absence of a wedding band on his finger when we were reaching for the frame. And he was a lefty with well-manicured fingernails. I noticed also that his jeans were sharply creased and he smelled great. For a moment I thought he might be a gay man, but that thought was dispersed when Merlin asked if I would like to have an ice cream sundae with him. I was taken aback by his approach, particularly in light of the fact that he still was not giving me eye contact and the ice cream invitation was right on the mark for me because I love Ice cream.

"Over ice cream sundaes, I learned so much about Merlin. He was originally from Arizona and was the eldest of six children. He was single, never married, and had no children that he knew of. He retired from the military and had worked as a merchant seaman. For the past 12 years he had been working as a steamfitter for an area furnace company. He expected to retire the next year upon turning 66. I was shocked to learn his age. He looked well. He was considering that upon retirement, he would move south somewhere close to his youngest sister, a widow, so that he could help her with her nine children. As I listened to him, I began to think again that perhaps he was a gay man.

"I never really found out firsthand about Merlin's sexuality. But over a three-month period we had great fun. In fact, he gave me two of the most heart-warming experiences I'd ever had up to that point in my life, including the delightful times I had with Emory. After learning how much I loved rain, one fall night he called me and asked if I'd like to go for a ride with him. As I climbed into his pearl-colored Volvo, the rain began to beat down, and he laughed, pointing out he knew I would enjoy my ride. I must say that the evening was magical. He drove me all over the city of Milwaukee and surrounding areas while Billie Holiday, Esther Phillips, Sarah Vaughn, and a host of other jazz greats melodiously filled the Volvo. He didn't say a word; not one word was uttered by either of us as we rode and rode, and for some reason I understood it was important for me not to speak. I savored the majesty of the ride. After hours of splendor, he dropped me back home and said only a good night. He didn't even touch my hand. 'Wow' was all I could say to that.

"The other truly memorable experience with him was equally magical and again orchestrated totally by him. Out of the blue one evening when we were walking in the mall (he was an ardent walker and swimmer, believing it was important to make exercise a priority), he asked if I had ever witnessed the sunrise over Lake Michigan. I had to say no because that had never occurred to me. With urgency that night, he asked to set a time we could share a sunrise together, and for a moment I wasn't sure what he was really asking. But it turned out he really meant just sharing a sunrise together near Lake Michigan. Actually, I found it to be a very unusual experience in that we spent the entire night together but were never alone until it was time for the actual sunrise. In a park on the south side of Milwaukee that was bordered by Lake Michigan we watched the sunrise while he prayed..That day he held my hand. It was quite a moment.

"It was on Christmas Eve that Merlin kissed me on the cheek and told me how grateful he was to have had the opportunity to spend such a wonderful three months with me. He said with staccato clarity and eyes trained towards the floor, 'You are special, Jewelle, and I wish things could go further with us. But I am going to move south soon, and I feel I need to do that without being connected to anyone here.' His kiss was rather mechanical, and he stepped back immediately as if to be sure to put distance between us. It was an awkward moment for me.

I think it would have been hurtful, if I had been truly into him, but I wasn't. So, I thanked him for the wonderful ride in the rain and the beautiful sunrise. Before he left that evening, we exchanged gifts and promised to stay in touch. He would be leaving the following day to spend Christmas down South with his sister. He gave me a beautiful butterfly on a silver bracelet, showing that he had listened attentively. I never heard from him again. After much thought, I concluded that my time with Merlin had been a gift. What I took away from that experience was that I could enjoy the company of a man again. I was grateful to know that."

Stepping away from my story again I smiled in Miss Addie's direction and she waved her hand smiling in return. I was actually surprised that she had followed her own dictum and remained attentive but quiet. Again I found myself wondering about what was happening at this point in our time together, but I told myself, *trust the process*. I eased back into my story acknowledging to myself that there were many things with the next fellow that warranted purging. I found myself wondering if Miss Addie could remain quiet as I told this part of my story.

"As was my habit after Merlin, I threw myself into my work and socialized just a bit with colleagues and friends. Then I sort of stumbled upon Buddy, the man who brought me face to face with my vulnerability as a single woman and eventually sent me into a self-imposed prison/fortress. It was quite interesting how we met. It was about one year and one month after I had experienced the gracious goodbye from Merlin when another adventure came my way. It was a cold January evening. I was waiting in the takeout line of an area restaurant to pick up a batch of chicken wings I had ordered by phone well over an hour before. They were behind with their orders, and people were muttering and complaining about the long wait and the cold weather. But no one left the line, showing how impressive the food was at this particular place.

"One of the customers who had finally grabbed his bag of food and rushed outside came back into the restaurant cussing under his breath about needing jumper cables. The young man went from person to person in the line asking to borrow jumper cables, but no one seemed to have what he needed or they just didn't want to get involved. I knew I had a set, but I really didn't want to be bothered with the process of having them hooked up to my car. For a long time I was quiet. Then it came to me that I was not behaving in a kind way. With that thought, I asked the young man if he had someone to give him a jump if he found jumper cables, and he said yes. I then proceeded to have the person behind me in line take note of my number if it would be called while I went out to the car to hand over my jumper cables. It was freezing outside, a state of affairs that made me hand over the cables quickly as I instructed the young man to bring them to me inside the restaurant when he was done. Once back inside, I realized I might not see the cables again, but that thought couldn't compete with the freezing temperature.

"The warmth inside the restaurant was so inviting, I realized the line hadn't moved much. Another twenty minutes or so passed. My number was next to be called when a tall, rather large man dressed almost Eskimo style came into the restaurant with my jumper cables in hand. I hadn't seen him before, so I was surprised when he walked directly up to me and handed me the cables. 'The young man thanks you,' he said. He then leaned close to me and whispered, 'I am going to give you a call the next time I need a jump. Okay?' Then he walked away. Even with all of his heavy clothing he smelled wonderful, and what I could see of his face that wasn't shadowed by a heavy cap and earmuffs seemed fairly attractive. I just laughed in response to his comment because I knew he didn't know me and certainly didn't know my phone number.

"Interestingly, while he was whispering to me, the number for my order was called. I moved to the pick-up window with confidence, thinking again that the big, good-smelling man in the Eskimo garb was just joking. Well, two days later I found out he was not joking at all. His phone call unsettled me at first because once he identified himself as the man who returned my jumper cables, I wasn't sure how to handle him. But his jovial manner and quick wit put me at ease for a while, particularly when he noted he was one of the owners of the restaurant. He had gone over the call-in and pick-up list to find the phone number associated with order 33, which had been my number that night.

"He told me his name was Langston Bates, but his friends call him Buddy and he was a retired postman, a divorced Vietnam vet, the father of four children, and the proud grandfather of 15 youngsters whose names he could never remember. He was originally from Mississippi, where he was building a home to move to in the near future. He said all of that quickly, seeming to make sure that he got as much out before I decided to stop the phone call. As we talked for a while, I couldn't shake the thought of how easy it was for him to get my cell phone number. It was unnerving that people could gain information about you without your knowledge. Although I was uncomfortable with the situation, Buddy intrigued me. When he called again three days later asking that we have coffee, I thought about it only for a moment and said yes. I told a number of people about the entire situation, and there were mixed reviews. I remember Flora told me not to engage in anything with buddy while Jodi and MiMi were excited about him, pointing out the positives. 'Give yourself the chance to meet someone new,' MiMi had advised in her best Chicago-girl way. Meanwhile Jodi was making dinner plans, hoping she would be able to include him at a forthcoming social event. Eva was out of the country and didn't have a say.

"My first two dates with Buddy were pure fun. We went for coffee once and to a movie with a stop for coffee for the second date. Each time I met him at the mall. It was clear there was chemistry between us, and he made a point of sharing rather risqué but harmless jokes about his interest in snuggling with me. It was the third date that ultimately set me running for the hills and back into hiding. It was early in February, and the weather was still typical Wisconsin cold. Buddy called about a birthday party for one of his retired post office buddies. He thought we should ride together since the party was to be in Franklin, Wisconsin, which is a suburb of Milwaukee on the south side of the city. With hesitation, I agreed to allow him to pick me up from my home. By this time my girls and I had done the usual computer checks on him and not found anything of significance using the name given to me, which ultimately turned out not to be his real name. I had no idea of the unseemly things about to transpire.

"Our ride to the party was full of fun. He made jokes and kept the conversation light. When we arrived at his friend's home, which was sort of out in the country, people seemed surprised to see me with Buddy but were very friendly. For a moment, I began to wonder if he had lied about his marital status because more than one person asked how long I had known him. They made a point of saying he hadn't mentioned me. But finally Buddy made the announcement that I had been his best-kept secret for the past few weeks and went on to tell the entire room how we met. To say I was uncomfortable with that would be an understatement. But his theatrics seemed to break the ice, and things began to flow at a more comfortable pace. That was the case until I noticed how much Buddy was drinking. And the more he drank, the louder he became and the more risqué his comments became.

"By midnight I was ready to go home and bemoaning the fact that I didn't have the latitude to say goodnight, jump in my car, and drive away freely. I mentioned to Buddy that I would like to leave soon, and he snapped at me about being a party pooper. 'You are messing with my high, Jewelle,' he said as he pushed his way past me to get to the bar. There was so much liquor at the bar; every kind of spirit you could imagine was there waiting for your indulgence. And indulge Buddy did. He had a penchant for Crown Royal and boldly guzzled it down by the tumbler full. As I watched him, I began to get nervous realizing he was driving and I was riding with him. I began to problem-solve worst-case scenarios. If necessary, I thought, I could drive his truck back to the city and then have one of my kids pick me up, or I could have someone come to get me. That, of course, would be the last resort, but I would pull that one out if I needed. I was deep in thought when one of Buddy's friends came to me and, in slurred speech, told me Buddy was waiting for me in the truck. I knew he had left the room, but I hadn't noticed he'd left the house. I was fed up with the situation and rushed to get my coat and hat while saying all of the proper goodbyes to the party hosts, who were clearly three sheets to the wind themselves. By now, I was certain this was a group of people that embraced alcohol with a passion.

"Once outside, the cold wind slapped clarity into the situation as I noticed Buddy leaning over the steering wheel as if he were asleep. I banged on the locked door, and he immediately cussed at me, pointing out he saw me and didn't need me to be banging on his truck. He said all of this amidst a host of expletives. I began to feel afraid of him. Nonetheless and against my better judgment, I got into the truck, and we took off towards a side road to ultimately pick up the expressway north to the city. I kept thinking I should offer to drive, but — to tell the truth — I was afraid of sparking his wrath. I didn't know how he would handle the situation. So I said nothing, but I was praying we would at least get back to the city safely. We were on the road about ten minutes when all of a sudden Buddy began to vomit.

"The liquor-laden fluid flew from his mouth with such fervor that it went all over the dashboard, windshield, and on me. The first batch was awful enough but was immediately followed by another round of unseemly mush that smelled not only of alcohol but of the raw beef he had consumed as well. I never eat raw beef, but Buddy and his friends had gorged on it while making jokes about his friends' German heritage and tradition of having raw beef as a delicacy. Now I had raw beef and alcohol all over me; they spilled out of Buddy. The stench was more than I could take.

I rolled down the window as I begged him to pull over, which he did without a fuss. But just as we made it to the side of the road, he began vomiting again and became flatulent. He passed gas that sounded as if he were actually messing on himself, and he began to moan in pain.

"That was it for me. Although I was on the south side of Milwaukee in the wee hours of the morning, I was not about to stay in the truck with the disgusting situation he was in. Quickly assessing my surroundings, I got out of the truck and realized I knew the area. It was not too far from the House of Corrections a jail-like facility, where I had done interviews with batterers throughout the years. I knew there was a 24-hour service station not far away. I thought about just leaving him there and walking to the service station, but it was very dark, and I wasn't sure how safe I would be. As I stood outside in the cold, I could still hear Buddy groaning and vomiting from time to time. It didn't take me long to decide to call 911. I would stay close to the truck trying to hide myself. I had no intention of getting back into the truck with Buddy. Curiously, that was taken care of because he fell limp over the steering wheel. I didn't know if he passed out or if something more serious had happened to him, but looking at the vomit around his mouth I dismissed any thoughts of CPR. For a moment I thought I would have regrets about not doing my Christian duty, but I shook that off quickly. Whatever his condition was, I knew it was unnecessary for me to have to explain that I had called 911. I learned later that was not what Buddy would have wanted me to do. He had a warrant against him and a long history of DUI encounters with the police. I learned all of that later when the highway patrolman arrived. It was a nightmare !

"I was shaking through and through when the highway patrolman arrived. I don't know how long it had taken, but when he arrived I was praising God out loud. It turned out I was lucky because the patrolman was an efficient professional who treated me with respect. He gave me a blanket to cover myself and allowed me to sit in his patrol car while I waited for my son to come and get me. The ambulance was called for Buddy because the patrolman was unable to rouse him; he didn't do CPR, either. I learned Buddy had lied about so many things. In reality, Langston was his middle name, and the surname he gave me was indeed incorrect. His driver's license, which was in the glove compartment of his truck along with the registration, listed him as Walter Langston Baily, and there was a warrant out for his arrest. I could barely believe what I was hearing. I was shaken and felt utterly dumb when the patrolman noticed I was not aware of with whom I had been riding.

"I guess the look on my face gave me away, particularly when he'd said, 'Ma'am, do you know there is a warrant out for Walter's arrest?' I then asked who Walter was, not realizing he was really talking about Buddy. Out of panic, I rattled off the fact that we had looked him up and he had come back clean. The officer laughed and noted, 'That works only if you have the right demographics, ma'am.' I felt stupid and duped. I wondered what the young red-haired officer thought about this. Clearly I wasn't a teenager, and there I was in the kind of predicament unthinking young women find themselves. So many things ran through my mind that night, not the least of which was what my brazen daughters would have to say about the situation. When my son picked me up I could see the concern on his face, but he waited until we were far away from the scene of my foolishness before he asked for any details. Amazingly, Korri and the ambulance had arrived almost at the same time. I was certain my son had broken speed limits getting to me. Silently that night I thanked God for so many things, including my son, who saw me in a very compromising situation and didn't appear to judge me. I was so grateful. The aftermath of Walter Langston Baily a.k.a. Buddy was dramatic. I was fearful and ashamed. I went into near-hermit mode and blocked out with a vengeance anyone who even appeared to be a suitor. My family, my work, and volunteer efforts engulfed me for the next four years until Miss Ella broke through the barrier with her sharp wisdom and wit."

When I completed my story about Buddy, Miss Addie threw her arms around me again and whispered "What an awful experience, Jewelle. Let that go! Let that go! Shame takes up space too." Holding on to her, I felt I was shedding layers of encumbrances in preparation for something, but I didn't know what. Before long, without prodding, I told her about Miss Ella and how she directed me to come out of hiding and consider a another male companion, perhaps even another husband. I told her about how Miss Ella taught me to call for my next male companion, the whole story behind the creation of Ell Joi Di Crazy Horse. I described how I began calling for Ell Joi Di Crazy Horse. As I went back into myself, the richness of these experiences gushed through me. I was on fire with memories, the churning in my center drowned out from time to time by whiffs of hope or expectancy of what was possible. The memory of Miss Ella lifted me. I gave Miss Addie an overview of how I thought Kojo was the response to my call for Ell Joi Di Crazy Horse. I told her about my disappointment. She advised, "Let that go Jewelle."

As I told that story, I realized how difficult it had been for me to become vulnerable and when Kojo opted for the younger, light-skinned woman, I had to meet myself on unseemly turf. I had to own my rage, bigotries, and fears. I told Miss Addie about Cullen and Gahti and my last trip to La Crosse, where I had the dream that led me to Rapid City, South Dakota. Laying out the details of that trip, including the unusual encounter with the Native American in the bus station, I could feel my heart race, seemingly in anticipation of what took place on the corner after Eva slipped on the ice and the Good Samaritan rolled up and into my life. My recapping of the story about Patrick, the miracle in Rapid City, made Miss Addie smile and she just about hollered "Hot damn!" as she gave me a thumbs up sign. She resumed a questioning posture and I answered her queries about Patrick, explaining that I argue with myself about my next move with him. Without hesitation Miss Addie advised somewhat wearily at this point, "fear takes up room too Jewelle. Joy needs room to grow."

Holding me close, Miss Addie began to pray over me. It was clear at this point that she was weary. Our time together had stretched well beyond our expectations. I looked at my watch and was amazed to find that it was nearly two in the morning. I apologized to her for keeping her up so late, but she waved my apology off and continued to pray. She called out to God to heal me, to restore me. I could feel her tears on my face. I heard the trembling in her voice, and I knew why I had spent an entire evening with her. She was on a mission. I was certain she had been sent. I realized this was a healing time for both of us. Her empathic journey with me bore fruits for her and for me. Miss Addie rocked me in her arms for a while and I let her. She whispered with conviction, "God grants us grace and mercy, but we must give ourselves permission. We must let go and make room for joy in our lives. What you haven't told me tonight Jewelle, tell God and make room for joy." She spoke with confidence and a sense of deep knowing. I was certain she knew intuitively about the recurrent dream. I absorbed her words and let them saturate my spirit. I knew deep inside there was more to be released, I could feel it coming. I was grateful it was a permission-giving day!

Releasing myself from Miss Addie's embrace, I realized that after the awful experience with my daughter Lorri the night before, I had swum in a sea of serious doubt, questioning my basic nature, wondering if I could nurture properly those who had come from me. This day, I was given the opportunity to be purged of that which had sullied my spirit for so long. Forgiveness and hope were calling my name. The churning in my chest had spoken to me of what must be done. I thought again about Miss Addie's words, "What you haven't told me tonight Jewelle, tell God and make room for joy."

It was odd that as I readied myself to leave Miss Addie's place, she spoke to me in words very similar to Miss Ella's of many years before. She said, "Take little sister off the shelf, girl. Go to your firefighter and let him love you." Miss Ella, at age 93, had talked about little sister, too. It had taken me days to figure out what she meant. Now, hearing that same phrase from an 86-year-old Southern-born White woman really made me smile. Both women, in their own way, were talking about the joy of making love, being sexual again with someone you really care about. I laughed to myself as I hugged Miss Addie and promised I would be in touch soon. I meant it. I would stay in touch with her for as long as she would allow me to do so. Though weary, she laughed heartily and reminded me what I should do: "Go and be with your firefighter, girlie, and accept your blessings."

CHAPTER 24

Forgiveness, Blessings, and Beyond

With Miss Addie's words ringing in my ears, I looked at my watch. It was nearly 2:00 a.m. I took another look to be sure. The time had flown by. We had spent hours walking through our lives. As I strolled through the lobby and out into the parking lot, my mind went over my entire day, and I smiled to myself about the awesomeness of God. Never in my wildest dreams would I have believed when I woke up after that awful night with Lorri that I would be standing in this particular parking lot feeling like a million dollars. I opened my mouth to catch a few of the snowflakes showering the earth. Though it was the middle of March, close to the date spring was to arrive, we were still immersed in the wonders of winter. I opened my mouth, and the churning in my chest rushed to my throat. Words spilled forth that I'd never said out loud, words that had plagued me for years, words I now knew I would only utter in God's presence.

Standing in the parking lot of the Forevermore Center, I began to speak that which I had never said out loud, that which permeated the recurrent dream. I screamed out to God that I was never sure of the father of my first son, the son who died on the basement stairs. As each word fell from my mouth, I felt lighter. "God, you know I have struggled with this quandary most of my life, trying to discern if my son was fathered by my husband Claude or by Kenneth Rayburn, my former lover from FAMU with whom I had

331

an affair. Only you know for sure, God," I screamed into the night as the snow fell upon me. For so long I had battled within myself about this thing, wondering if my stubbornness about the slippers and the basement had been my silent way of making my guilt-ridden quandary go away. Had I out of fear and guilt unconsciously contrived to take a cowardice way out by ending things that way? Had I intentionally killed my son? *Lord, I hope not*, I thought! But finally I was willing to surrender that question and believe that the dream of the night before with the old women and the fat baby had finally given me a reprieve. It allowed me to be satisfied in accepting that the baby was fathered by Ken. In the dream, the baby ringing the bell was, as always, adorned in an army-green jacket and a sailor's cap. And he had definitively removed the cap, tossing it away while smiling at me. He had closed the jacket around himself as he walked away from me. His actions mattered; they spoke to me beyond words. From the dream, I accepted that Claude was not his father, and the jacket pulled close around him represented Ken, his father. And I needed to let go of all of this. "God, that is how I will interpret this dream, but you know the ultimate truth. I believe You have forgiven me. Now I am forgiving myself." I said all of this with arms lifted in the snowy night. "Within your grace, tonight I give myself permission to move forward," I cried, and I paced in the snowy night, each morsel of snow sending a message of hope.

With a sense of gratitude, I jumped in my car and turned the key in the ignition. At the sound of the engine turning over, I jumped out to do the ritual of brushing snow from the windshield. It was a heavy, wet snow which required a bit of force to really get it off the car. As I worked steadily, my mind shifted to the reality that I had turned my phone off many hours before, and I knew people must be looking for me. I thought about Patrick and felt all warm inside. I promised myself he would be the first one I called. When I slid into the car, the CD that MiMi had given me was playing. One song had just ended, and the next one grabbed me by surprise. Stevie Wonder was promising God's protection through storms and hard times. All I could do was breathe deeply. It was as if God were speaking to me. I smiled as I looked through my phone for

Patrick's number and dialed it. I didn't care that it was well after 2:00 a.m. I wanted to do exactly what I had promised Miss Addie I would do. I planned to go to my firefighter. I didn't know why I was so certain he would still be waiting for me, but I just knew he would be. When Patrick heard my voice, he laughed and said my name over and over again. "Jewelle, where have you been? Come here, Jewelle, and let me hold you," he said emphatically, and all I could do was laugh. Through my laughter I asked, "In which of Eva's efficiencies are you?" He responded, "I am in 413, the one farthest away from the elevator." We both laughed, and I told him I was on my way. I hung up thinking, *Wow! This is really happening!* As I drove out of the parking lot, my cell phone rang. I looked at the number, and it was Korri. For a moment my heart began to race and I felt cold all over. I remembered having seen all of the missed calls from him. Korri seldom called me without a good reason. I took a deep breath, pulled over to the side of the road, and answered his call. I hoped with all my heart this was just a check-on-Mom call.

It was unlike Korri to be excitable, but his voice had a clear, anxious overtone. "Where are you, Mom? Are you okay?" he asked hurriedly. He went on to say people had been trying to reach me all day, including Thea. "She just wants to hear your voice, Mom." Korri insisted, showing emotion beyond his customary persona. "Everyone is worried," he sighed into the phone. With great care, I assured him I was fine and would look to him to let people know I was okay. I would be home later and would connect with everyone, including Thea. When I said the part about coming home later, there was a long silence on the other end of the phone, but he finally said okay as if he were throwing up his hands in surrender. I wasn't sure how to tell my son I was heading to a man's apartment that late at night. I finally told him I was just leaving a senior center, one of my volunteer sites, and was heading over to spend time with Patrick at Eva's place. "Oh, he's called here a lot looking for you," Korri said with relief now in his voice. I smiled to myself hoping my son would really move past worrying about me.

I was about to hang up when Korri eased into the surprise. I held my breath as he said, "You'll be pleased to know that your oldest son is home, Mom. Aimen is standing right here, Mom. He's here, and he has a wife." I thought I would choke on my own breath. All I could say was "What?" Immediately Aimen got on the line. My son, the hermit, was certainly full of surprises, but this one gave me a whirl. Laughingly, he told me that he and his wife of two months essentially hitchhiked to Wisconsin to see about the family. They were briefed by my brother in Key West about Ajoy's abduction and her father's murder and were worried about us. It took them nearly a week to complete their trip. It had been "a life-enhancing adventure," he said with laughter still in his voice.

His wife was part Asian and part African-Jamaican. He met her in Jamaica more than a year before when he was there with his fishing buddies. They were married in Key Largo, Florida two months previous, and she loved their hermit-like lifestyle. He called her Ling. She, like Aimen, was a marine biologist, on leave. They would decide within the next year where life would take them. Once I found out that they would be staying in Milwaukee for a while, I settled into feeling fine about not rushing home to see them. I knew Aimen had a way of taking charge of things. He would keep everyone in check, including Lorri. She would not dare mess with her eccentric older brother. He was definitely her match in many ways. I thought of her words about Aimen and Korri in the heat of our awful encounter, and I wondered what he would say about them if he knew. I doubt Korri would say anything to him about that night, but Kaimen might. In her dramatic way, she would find a reason to share that, but I hoped not before I got home. It was then that Aimen talked about the lockbox and its contents. In the presence of his sister Lorri he managed to open the box, and together they explored Squire Black's legacy to his daughter. The box held $5,500.00 in large bills and a letter containing details about accounts in Ajoy's name in the Bahamas along with a key to a safe deposit box in Lorri's name in a bank in Illinois.

Aimen was matter-of-fact as he shared the information, but I heard myself shout. From deep inside of me, I felt relief and a new sense of hope for Lorri. In all of her pain, she could finally experience a true sense of Squire Black's willingness to provide for her and their daughter. For me, it was an answered prayer. I breathed deeply and asked about my grandson Anthony. Aimen chuckled at Anthony's precociousness, assuring me Anthony was fine and fittingly engrossed in some new weather project. As we both laughed, my heart seemed to sing. With so many loose ends coming together, I was about to sign off from Aimen when he said, "You know I love you, Mom!" Immediately my eyes watered and I said through my tears, "And I love you back, son. See you later." This left it to Korri to tell his brother I would probably not be home until the morning. In truth, I knew I needed this time away from all of them. As I hung up the phone, I decided I would shut it off. I would not even call Eva to let her know I would be in her building. I didn't want any more distractions. My mind was on Patrick. Stevie Wonder's CD melodiously continued to set the tone for all things possible.

This CD titled, *A Time to Love*, set forth one track after the other filled with words of genuine intimacy and fulfilling love. I smiled as I listened, allowing the pleasant mood set by the CD to govern my driving. I was enjoying the space I was in. As I approached the Knickerbocker Hotel, the place where Patrick was waiting for me, I became a bit concerned about how I looked. I hadn't thought about it before that moment and decided before I went up to unit 413 to stop in the ladies' room off the dining area. I had run there many times during my visits to Eva. Walking into the hotel lobby, a thought of Haiti flittered through my mind. I prayed that she, too, would be healed.

The woman at the front desk was someone I had met before. According to Eva, this particular woman was very gracious but was a consummate rule keeper. I wondered if I was breaking any rules with my after-hours visit. After a brief chat with her, I went immediately to the ladies' room. I refreshed my makeup, gargled with handfuls of warm water, and sprayed a bit of Biotene throughout my mouth after I rinsed and re-rinsed it a number of times. I made a point of relieving myself, too, recognizing that I had taken in more ounces of tea than I ever had before in one night. I was sure my kidneys were dancing for joy due to the generous hydration, but my bladder was less approving of my venture and was pushing for relief.

With a host of refreshing things done, I checked myself one more time in the mirror, rubbed a few drops of scented oil on my neck, and headed up to the fourth floor. I knew the woman at the desk would see that I wasn't stopping by Eva's place if she watched the numbers on the elevator; Eva was on the third floor, and I would be going to the fourth floor. For just a moment, I was cognizant of that and wondered what she would do with that information, but then I decided I didn't care. As the elevator did its job, I began to get a little nervous, and by the time I reached the fourth floor I was breathing heavily. I was both excited and afraid. Walking down the long hallway to unit 413, many thoughts raced through my mind. I wondered if I would stay the night, how I would get out of staying the night, or whether he wanted me to stay the night. This mental chatter kept me occupied right up to the time I stood in front of 413. I knocked softly on the door, and it opened on its own. It wasn't closed completely. As I walked into the dimly-lit room, I heard Stevie Wonder singing a song from the CD *A Time to Love*. For a moment, I felt as if I were in some kind of time warp. And then I saw him. Patrick was standing across the room, smiling. In the soft light I saw he was barefoot. He had on a pair of jeans and a white shirt of which he was undoing the buttons. His hair was pulled back, and — God — he looked so good. The room smelled of him. Moving slowly toward him, I savored every breath of him.

The picture of him standing there loosening his shirt sent my entire being into a tailspin because I knew he was showing me that he remembered. He remembered our conversation in his truck in Rapid City when we left the casino that early morning. He was making himself ready for me. My legs were weak as I moved towards him, and I could feel the smile on my face broadening as he opened his arms for me. He called my name repeatedly. I thought I might pass out from the intense energy between us. He smelled so good, like vanilla and hickory. Stevie was singing and Lord, my heart was pounding so loudly. I found myself wondering how he could have known I had that CD and it had been playing in the car as I drove to be with him. I wondered if there were something mystical about Patrick, and in my mind I answered the question with a resounding *Yes.*

When I reached him, he felt warm; he smelled wonderfully inviting. He called my name as he wrapped his arms around me tightly, and I thought I would not be able to breathe. As he held me like that, we danced, our bodies gliding rhythmically to Stevie's invitations. Everything in me came alive. I was sure I would sing opera in that moment if I could sing at all because my very soul wanted to sing. He felt so good, and what was so thoroughly satisfying was that he seemed to be enjoying me in every way, too. He kept saying my name. I allowed my hands to wander over him. As I caressed his left side under his shirt, I could feel the scars from the fire and many surgeries. I opened his shirt to take a look at his scars, and in turn he took his shirt completely off. He was wonderful to see that way. There were many scars, but his body was firm and well-developed. It was clear he continued to work out. He was strong and fit.

I looked at him for a while to savor his luscious maleness. Then I nestled into him again, allowing my face to be buried in his chest. And he said in a raspy voice, "Crawl inside me, Jewelle. Crawl near my heart and stay forever. I want you here. Stay with me." His words made me cry because he was replaying our conversation on the road from the casino, my fantasy. I looked up and saw a tear falling from his right eye. I reached up to wipe it away and he smiled. At that moment, I felt so safe. It was a moment in which I totally believed everything would be alright. Everything about our embrace felt so right. It was as if every cell in my body knew the answer, and the answer was right there with me, holding me and, yes, loving me. "I love you, Jewelle. I prayed for this moment, and it is here. Love me back, Jewelle, please," he whispered. The yearning in his voice was endearing, and I clung to him for dear life.

There was nothing between us in that moment. It was all very clear to me. Breathing deeply, I said, "I do love you, Patrick," and I meant every word. In response, he smiled as he kissed me on my forehead. We danced slowly, holding on to each other with passion and joy, clearly conveying the willingness to be one in every way. We allowed Stevie Wonder to transport us. It was as if we had left our physical selves and were soaring to a place somewhere out in the cosmos, far beyond all mundane trappings. We were in the midst of flow as we savored every moment of the pleasure we gave and received. After a while and without hesitation, I reached up and gently took the band away from his hair. The beautiful silken-like strands fell loose beyond his shoulders; a few threads of gray shimmered in the light. I ran my fingers through his hair, taking the time to gently caress his face and neck. He moaned in pleasure at my touch. I remembered what touch meant to him and smiled knowingly, bent on showering him with purpose-driven delight.

His joy fed my joy. As I caressed his chest again, I noticed for the first time he didn't have a nipple on his left breast. He saw my surprise and said with a smile, "Lost it in the fire." We both laughed. Then he leaned down and kissed me fully on the lips. It was a deep kiss, engagingly sensuous. It was a kiss that spoke of love, hunger, and unbridled joy. With purposefulness, he reached up and took the patch from his left eye. He looked directly at me and kissed both of my eyes while saying, "Je m'appelle Eagle Feather, we are in love's bond, Jewelle." I responded by kissing him in a way that I had never kissed anyone before. It was a kiss that spoke volumes about forgiveness, worthiness, and permission. It was a kiss that took me beyond the logistics of how we would make this work. It was a kiss of gratitude and of praise. It was a kiss that said *I am not afraid to love you*. It was a kiss born of rising above all of the muck of life. In that moment, the image of a magnificent lotus flower, a radiant mud flower, flashed through my mind, and I knew for sure I intended to crawl inside of him, to nestle near his heart and to stay there forever!

CHAPTER 25

Joy Amidst Boulders

Enthralled by the intensity of the moment, I was not prepared for the forthcoming shift in the tenor of our connection. Being in Patrick's arms was so comforting. We held on to each other fervently, sharing a level of intimacy that surpassed any fantasy I could imagine, but we didn't have sex. Curiously, it was Patrick who redirected my wandering hands as he pulled me close to him, squeezing me vigorously as if he actually wanted me to crawl inside of him. I was stunned at first by what appeared to be an abrupt halt to our escalating passion. But his honest words carried me to a place of raw vulnerability that spoke of pure intimacy, fostering an even deeper connection. "Jewelle," he began haltingly, "since my treatment after the fire I have been taking medicine for nightmares associated with post-traumatic stress disorder, and that medication causes problems with erections. I am sorry, Jewelle! But because I am going to have surgery on my hand and arm soon, my doctors advised me not to use any erection-enhancing meds for at least thirty days before the surgery. I think that has something to do with preventing problems with excessive bleeding during and after the surgery. I can't remember now what they said, but I haven't been taking them and I need you to...." He stopped for a breath, and I stood very still, hoping my heart would not burst from the intense pounding it was doing ; he was holding me so tightly. I wondered if he thought I would run away. My mind flipped from one question to another, but I said nothing.

Before long he returned to his halting explanation, "I want you, Jewelle, in all ways possible and can feel that you want me, too, but I ask that you indulge me now by allowing intimacy to override sex. Let me just hold you, Jewelle." He said all of that with fervor, his voice trembling just a bit. I cried quietly as I squeezed him with a force that belied my paltry feminine strength. And in response to his precious words all I could say was "Hold me, Patrick." What happened next was truly amazing. We crawled under the covers together, he naked from the waist up and I fully clothed, our bare feet exploring and finding warmth as they touched. As the hours ticked by we held each other and whispered reassuring words that gave promise for a future together. I listened to his heartbeat. I touched his scarred chest again, making note of the pain he must have endured after the fire. He kissed my eyes and massaged my shoulders, vowing to always encircle me with love and protection. Falling asleep in his arms was easy. Everything about our connection felt right. I didn't think I had ever felt so safe in my life. As we slept I rested completely.

When the noonday sun pushed its way upon us, we met it head-on like a seasoned couple, sliding past the proverbial "morning breath" phase with ease, each of us making our way to relieve ourselves and to gargle; I dealt adeptly with my dentures. We laughed about our mutual graciousness, preparing ourselves for the first kiss of the day. And then we talked for hours, stopping only to partake of sandwiches and tea secured by Patrick from the restaurant on the first floor of the Knickerbocker. In our talking I learned that Patrick was doing research on Black Indians in the Americas and belonged to a national group of Black Indians which meets annually to share books and other materials collected through their research efforts. I learned as well that he had been dedicated for a number of years to putting together an annual trip to Sapelo Island for adolescent boys who were burn victims. One of his sons — the budding psychologist — assisted him in this annual summer venture.

Patrick talked at length about the time he had spent with the Seminoles in Florida, expounding on their history. He was pleased to know I was aware that it is believed that Chief Osceola of the Seminole nation had at least one Black wife. Excitedly Patrick proclaimed his identity as a Black Indian, noting, "My grandmother tried to keep me from my true identity, but I am who I am, and I am sharing all of that with my children and grandchildren." As he talked about his grandmother, Mrs. Johnson, I remembered bits and pieces of our time together in Virginia years before. I smiled considering how life was unfolding for us today. I was amazed when Patrick told me that he had been studying the history of Blacks in Key West. "Yes Jewelle, you come from a place with a rich Black history and a strong Yoruba influence." He offered confidently. "I read a book about Key West, by Sawyer and Wells-Bowie. Are you aware that many years ago there was a part of your hometown known as La Africana?", he went on with a smile, seemingly proud of himself to be quizzing me about my place of origin. In turn, I kissed him deeply and began an in depth discussion about the book, which Vy had sent me. It felt so good to be able to connect with him on so many levels.

Our time together led us to many places and after a while I candidly recapped for Patrick the awful night with my daughter Lorri. He listened as he held me close but challenged me to connect with her and to do it soon. "Reach for her, Jewelle," he said with feeling. "You must be the source of reconciliation for your family, and you can get help with that if you need it." I listened to him give me counsel and smiled, thinking that I could appreciate his wisdom; he seemed so certain about what I needed to do. And, as with his advice for how to deal with my family issues, he ventured a guess that I might not be as financially prepared for retirement as I could be. He said he wanted to provide me with support so that I could relax and enjoy life. He was clear in stating that I would be receiving a major credit card via the mail in a few days (he had gotten my address from Eva) and there would be no limits on its use. It would be handled by his financial people.

"This is to make you comfortable, Jewelle, until we decide where life and love will take us. Hopefully you will fly out to see me often. Once again, there are no limits on this card," he offered in that cheeky way he had shown in Rapid City. I listened to him and couldn't believe my ears, but I smiled knowing that he was serious and meant for me to be happy.

One other matter of business was very important to Patrick. He couldn't understand why I had not learned to text and was completely invested in teaching me to do so before he made his way back to Virginia. He turned out to be a great teacher, and I willingly tempered my Luddite-like position on technology as he coached me to become efficient in texting. We laughed a lot and ended up dancing once I could proclaim my texting proficiency.

When evening came, it was clear that I needed to go home to my family. Patrick would be leaving the next day, heading home for the surgery that would take place in a few days. We decided to have breakfast together before he left. We would meet at a café equidistant from my home and the Knickerbocker. With our plan set in place for the morning, we kissed and hugged seemingly a million times before I made my way to my car. I did so without stopping by Eva's, though I did call her on my way out, and she chuckled often in our brief conversation. I was certain my friend was happy for me.

Once I was in the car, my mind went from one thing to another, but I thought mostly about the Native American in the Rapid City bus station. I played and replayed his words the best I could remember them. He had said I would be claimed by a third husband, one with whom I had been earlier in life. And he said that men bring me boulders to carry as they come to me. I shook my head in amazement as I thought about Patrick and all that was unfolding between us. I thought about his problems with PTSD and erectile dysfunction and wondered how that would work out for us. Each time I thought about the level of intimacy we shared I would become teary, remembering how wonderful it was to be held by him. Each time I thought of it I knew I wanted more times like that. I smiled as I thought about the promise of a future with

Patrick, and I turned up the CD player. Stevie Wonder filled the car with words that solidified my belief that this is a time to love. Before turning onto the expressway, I thought I caught a glimpse of the Warrior Chief riding down an alley away from me. A chill went through me as I remembered that my spiritual father had said many years before, "Your spirit guides will be with you as long as you need them, but you give them permission to leave." I smiled at that memory, allowing myself the luxury of speculating on a new and different life.

By the time I reached home I was emotionally spent, but I made a point of calling Lorri and setting up a time to talk. She seemed surprised to hear from me but quickly agreed to meet two days later. She said sheepishly, "I love you, Mom," and I forced myself to respond in kind, though I knew I needed to do a bit more praying before we connected. With that done, I shifted my attention to Aimen and his Asian Jamaican bride, who turned out to be quite a character. She appeared to be as eccentric as her husband. She prepared a meal for the family. We enjoyed her delightful spicy dishes. We laughed and talked about their adventures hitchhiking to Wisconsin. It was really beautiful to see Aimen and Korri together, too, both brandishing long dreadlocks and both demonstrating a laidback countenance with quick smiles and gracious manners. I watched my sons and was proud of them. By the time I got home Kaimen like Lorri had left, but not before she had shared with Aimen the horrors of the situation with Lorri. Aimen was concerned, wondering if I needed him to intervene. But I assured him that Lorri and I would talk it out and would be alright. While I spoke confidently, I was hopeful but not at all certain of how things would go. Forgiveness was something we needed to address. That evening, in the presence of Ling, my sons and I spent a jovial time together. I learned that Aimen had spoken with Thea, who had many adventures to share with her brother, and she had spoken with his wife as well. Things were falling into place.

That night my prayer ritual was rich with praise. I fell asleep bowing before God, and the dream that came reflected my gratitude and revealed the healing in my spirit. In the dream I was in Key West at the intersection of Whitehead Street and Truman Avenue on U.S. 1. At first I was both my senior-self and a little girl. Then it was just my senior-self kneeling in a beautiful garden. Through my clothes I could see my bones. It was odd that my bones were radiating light. I could hear myself thanking God for my bones and for what was in my bones. As I was praying, butterflies surrounded me. They were singing! And on a table in the garden were sugar cookies and chocolates. I recognized the sustaining value in all of the memories surrounding me and smiled. The air was warm and refreshing. I knew all would be well with my soul.

Early the following morning the dream was freshly with me when Patrick called to say that we would have to forego breakfast because he had to get a new tire for the road. To his surprise, upon loading his gear onto his truck he discovered that he had a flat tire, which he would not trust to patch. He needed a new tire and would come to my office to give me a so-long kiss once the tire matter had been addressed. Though I was disappointed about breakfast, I gave him the address to the Center, the ebullient power of my dream kept me lifted, and I remained excited about seeing him before he set out on the road for home. As I sipped my morning tea I mused about the puzzles, and paradoxes that punctuate the ebb and flow of life's journey. I marveled at the juxtaposition of joy and suffering, old and young, the coupling of the transcendent and the mundane. I smiled thinking about how love beams spiritually and carnally, creating a wondrous tapestry of healing light. *I am blessed! I accept life's journey,* I thought as I made my way to the shower.

I put on my red sweater and took special pains with my hair, hoping to look my best as I prepared for work, knowing that Patrick would stop in. Just as I had been in Rapid City the night we went out for the first time, I was filled with expectation, feeling almost girlish as I made my way to the office. The traffic didn't bother me. Although there was talk of Haiti on National Public Radio, I was in such a good place that I actually smiled when I heard that support was coming from as far away as Australia and Japan. "That's a good thing," I said to the radio, realizing it was a blessing to be able to bless others through giving. *It all comes full circle*, I thought.

I had completed my first anger-management group when an excited administrative assistant told me I had a visitor by the name of Patrick Grovnor Rawlston. I had to laugh at her excitement because I knew she had trouble containing herself in the presence of such an absolutely striking brother. I knew there would be all kinds of inquiries after he left. As he strolled down the hall to my office I could barely contain myself. He looked so very fine, wearing a pair of jeans, a navy blue turtleneck sweater, and of course his snake skin boots, navy blue knit cap, and a black leather jacket. As usual he smelled wonderful; his scent permeated my office. Before I could say anything I was swept up in his arms and held there in a big bear-like hug. We both laughed about the tire, but we spent most of our time holding each other and promising to call and text often. Our last kiss took my breath away, and my tears flowed freely as he prepared to leave my office. But before he shut my office door he handed me an envelope, telling me to open it later.

I had to lean against my desk to remain steady as he walked away. I didn't follow him to the lobby because I didn't know if I could keep it together. So I sat at my desk holding the envelope in my hand, breathing deeply, trying to force back more tears. When I finally opened the envelope, I wasn't prepared for what was there. Its contents warmed my heart. Enclosed was a note stating,

> "Jewelle, while I was waiting for you to resolve your family business, I wrote this poem for you.
>   Love, Patrick"

I cried as I read his poem:

· · · · · ·

In Love's Bond

To touch so sweetly, so effortlessly
To be wholly engrossed
In all that makes the two of us be
Is beauty beyond that which bodies hold
It is more than laughter
More than song
It is life stretching its wings
Soaring
Smiling in commitment's face
It is hope placed above ominous clouds
Showering soft cries with meaning
Giving birth to vibrant flowers
This thing we promise to be
Is far more than mist above shallow ponds
It is the earth's core
Strong and pregnant with sounds of
Immortal truth
It is yesterday clothed in
Today's habit
Resting upon tomorrow's
Far reaching energy
Piercing time and space
With its awesome ring!

My hands shook as I took out my phone and sent this text to Patrick: "B blessed. C U soon. Luv U!!!!" And then I smiled.

THE END

For now!

Book Club Questions

1. In this book there is quite a bit of intentional symbolism. One example is the use of the lotus flower. Reflect upon the symbolism therein and give other examples.

2. There are many instances of suffering throughout the story. Choose three and reflect on what they appear to reveal.

3. How does the title of the book help you understand the author's purpose in writing the book?

4. Diverse spiritual/religious beliefs and practices are portrayed in the book. In some instances a single character expresses traditional and nontraditional views of the Divine almost simultaneously. What are your thoughts on that?

5. There are a number of dreams revealed throughout the story. Do any of them seem particularly rich in portraying the underlying themes in the life of the female protagonist? Explain.

6. Are there situations in the book that evoke strong emotions within you? Name them and explain.

7. Are there characters in the book that reflect who you are and how you handle relationships? Name them and explain.

8. Does the book resonate with your perspective on later-life romance?

9. What aspects of the story give insight into the value of intergenerational relationships? Reflect upon your own family and friends with an emphasis on the intergenerational relationships in your life.

10. Identify and discuss the ethical dilemmas and issues of civility revealed in the story.

Dear Reader,

Thank you for the purchase of my book, *Mud Flower Blooming — A Tale of Transcendent Love,* and for taking the time to read it. I hope you enjoyed it, and I look forward to bringing you more stories in the near future.

Blessings to you!

J. MARTIN-THOMAS

www.mudflowerblooming.com